PENGUIN ENGLISH LIBRARY

NIGHTMARE ABBEY
CROTCHET CASTLE

D1011796

Thomas Love Peacock

NIGHTMARE ABBEY
CROTCHET CASTLE

EDITED
WITH AN INTRODUCTION BY
RAYMOND WRIGHT

PENGUIN BOOKS

Penguin Books Ltd, Harmondsworth, Middlesex, England
Penguin Books, 625 Madison Avenue, New York, New York 10022, U.S.A.
Penguin Books Australia Ltd, Ringwood, Victoria, Australia
Penguin Books Canada Ltd, 2801 John Street, Markham, Ontario, Canada L3R 1B4
Penguin Books (N.Z.) Ltd, 182–190 Wairau Road, Auckland 10, New Zealand

—

Published in Penguin English Library 1969
Reprinted 1974, 1976, 1979, 1981

—

Introduction copyright © Raymond Wright, 1969
All rights reserved

—

Made and printed in Great Britain
by Richard Clay (The Chaucer Press) Ltd,
Bungay, Suffolk
Set in Monotype Modern

CONTENTS

*

BIOGRAPHICAL NOTE

*

PEACOCK was a man who specially valued his privacy, and as he attracted little notice among his contemporaries and had an antipathy to writing letters, it is not surprising that biographical materials should be scanty. He was born in 1785, the son of Samuel Peacock, a London merchant, and of Sarah Love, who came of a naval family. After the death of his father, which occurred while Thomas was still a small boy, mother and son lived at Chertsey, in the district where he was to spend much of his life. His schooling ended before he was thirteen and for a brief period he and his mother moved to London, where he was a clerk in a City office and in his spare time began the sustained private study that laid the foundation for his excellent classical scholarship and his wide knowledge of French, Italian and English literatures. His next regular employment was as a secretary on board H.M.S. *Venerable*, stationed in the Downs, in the winter of 1808–9, but he found life in that 'floating Inferno', as he called it, impossible. Back in Chertsey, he resumed the literary career on which he had already made a start when he published *Palmyra and Other Poems* in 1806. For his next long poem, *The Genius of the Thames*, he followed the course of the river for most of its length and then, as if to gratify to the full his taste for landscape, long walks, and quiet study, went off to North Wales for more than a year, until the spring of 1811.

Apart from one or two elegiac pieces and the songs included in the novels, Peacock's verse is unremarkable. It had, however, the merit of bringing him to the notice of Shelley, and their friendship, which began in 1812, continued till the latter's death. They were a good deal together at Bracknell, at Marlow, and in London, as well as on excursions such as the boating holiday on the Thames that Peacock made use of in *Crotchet Castle*. Among the enthusiasts and oddities who gathered round Shelley he must have seemed, as one of them called him, 'a cold scholar', and he for his part laughed, as he said in his *Memoirs of Shelley*, at the fervour with which they debated their impracticable schemes for the betterment of mankind. Nevertheless, his basic views on politics and religion were probably similar to Shelley's at that time, though tempered by good sense and less ardently held, and they had a common interest in the Greek classics as well as in contemporary literature and ideas. As a poet he was himself within the periphery of romanticism and through Shelley and in other ways he became acquainted with many of the newcomers to the literary scene, so that when he came to write *Nightmare Abbey*, his satire on 'black' romanticism, he was writing from an inside position. That was in 1818, the year in which he published *Rhododaphne*, his last and best long poem, and in which Shelley left England for good.

Peacock's second literary career, as a satirist, began with *Sir Proteus: A Satirical Ballad*, a clumsy attack on the Lake Poets, Scott, and the reviewers, that came out in 1814. His first novel, *Headlong Hall*, was published late in the following year. With it, he arrived at the first attempt at his own distinctive method and it was well enough received to run into a second edition within a few months. It was followed by *Melincourt* and *Nightmare Abbey* in 1817 and 1818 respectively and then Peacock's spell of high productivity unfortunately came to an end. Although he made a start on *Maid Marian* almost at once, its completion and publication were delayed until 1822. The delay was occasioned by his taking, at the close of the year 1818, a well-paid and responsible post at the India House, where he was to work for almost forty years. There is a tradition that he suffered a financial loss at the time and this may have been the reason for his seeking the appointment. It made great changes in his way of living in that he had to leave the country for London, where he worked among a new set of acquaintances very different from those among whom he had moved till then, and it made it possible for him to marry. He had leisure enough during his first year at the India House to read proofs for the absent Shelley, to try to get *The Cenci* produced, and to act for him in various business matters, but his own writing seems to have been confined to one essay, *The Four Ages of Poetry*.

Shortly after taking up his appointment, Peacock proposed, in a remarkably cool letter that happens to have survived, to Jane Gryffydh, whom he had met during his stay in Wales during 1810–11 and neither seen nor corresponded with since then. In 1807 he had been engaged to a Chertsey girl but the engagement had been broken off and she had been succeeded by Marianne de St Croix, to whom he was attached for several years. It was during this attachment that the extraordinary episode occurred of Peacock's going off to live with a supposed heiress who had fallen in love with him, finding she was penniless, and being arrested for debt. (See the introduction to *Nightmare Abbey*, below, for a further reference to the episode.) The attachment seems to have survived this interlude, which belongs to the winter of 1814–15, but there are grounds for believing that Marianne eventually rejected him and that his proposal to Jane Gryffydh quickly followed her rebuff. The marriage took place in 1820 and the couple seem to have been well-suited to one another. They were harassed by misfortunes that began when their second child, a daughter, died at the age of three in 1826 and Jane Peacock never recovered from this loss. Eventually she became an invalid and Peacock's mother took charge of the household.

In taking his post with the East India Company, Peacock became in effect a high-ranking civil servant and chose amateur status as a novelist. After *Maid Marian* appeared in 1822 there was an interval of seven years before his next novel, *The Misfortunes of Elphin*. The former is the slightest of his works and can have cost him little trouble, but for the latter he seems to have read fairly widely in Welsh

legend, perhaps with his wife's help when he needed translations. His only other publications between *Maid Marian*
and *Crotchet Castle* were reviews that he contributed to the
Westminster, the organ of the Philosophic Radicals. One of
them, a devastating attack on Tom Moore's novel, *The
Epicurean*, as a travesty of 'the noblest philosophy of
antiquity', affords a rare glimpse of his Epicureanism;
another, a review of Jefferson's *Memoirs*, is republican in
sympathy and expresses his admiration for Jefferson's contribution to the liberty and happiness of mankind in terms
so unqualified that they surprise the reader accustomed to
the ironies and reservations of the novels. To what extent
Peacock identified himself with the Philosophic Radicals is
debatable, though he was certainly regarded by some of his
contemporaries as being one of their number. He knew the
most prominent members of their circle, presumably
through James Mill, his superior at the India House, and
he was on very friendly terms with Bentham, but he
probably went no further than accepting some of their
basic principles and parted company with them as practical
reformers. *Crotchet Castle*, with its questioning of progress
and its mockery of political economy, came out in 1831 and
can be regarded as marking his divergence from them, just
as *Nightmare Abbey* defines his position with regard to
romanticism.

Peacock's mother, with whom he had been accustomed to
discuss whatever work he had in hand, died in 1833 and he
said that after her death he wrote with no interest. Twenty-
five years elapsed before he wrote another novel and his
whole literary output for the 1830s amounted to little more
than two linked articles, 'French Comic Romances' and
'The Epicier', that he wrote for the *London Review*, and a
number of opera notices. His *Paper Money Lyrics*, which
appeared in 1837, had been written in 1825-6 and withheld for fear of giving offence to Mill. When Mill died in
1836, Peacock succeeded him as Examiner and continued
in that appointment, at a salary of £2,000 a year, till his
retirement twenty years later. Besides his other duties at

the India House, he made himself an expert on communications with India and, remarkably in a man who disliked speed and machinery, not only advocated that the East India Company should have iron steamships but also helped to design some of them and took part in their trials in the Channel. By 1836 his family had been established for many years in a riverside house at Lower Halliford, near Chertsey, and he spent his weekends there until the extension of the railway made it possible for him to live at home and travel up to London daily. His wife lived on, a complete invalid, till 1851.

From 1838 to 1850 Peacock seems to have written nothing. We catch occasional references to him in those years as a first-class administrator who was greatly valued by the Company, a teller of good stories, an outstanding amateur of the classics, and a unique personality. One of the best of these glimpses is provided by Thackeray, who met him at Lord Broughton's country house in 1850, in a letter describing his fellow guests: 'A charming lyrical poet and Horatian satirist he was when a writer; now he is a whiteheaded jolly old worldling, and Secretary to the E. India House, full of information about India and everything else in the world.' Actually, he was about to take up writing again, at least intermittently. He collaborated with his eldest daughter, Mary Ellen, the wife of George Meredith, on an article on 'Gastronomy and Civilization' and began a series of essays on classical drama, *Horae Dramaticae*, that was interrupted in 1852 and resumed in 1857. None of these essays is of much interest; his important works in the 1850s were his *Memoirs of Shelley*, which appeared between 1858 and 1862, and his last novel, *Gryll Grange*, which was serialized in 1860. After his retirement in 1856 he seldom left home, saw very few visitors, and spent his time in his library, in his garden, or on the river. His closing years were saddened by the deaths of his daughter Rosa Jane in 1857 and of Mary Ellen, whose marriage had ended very unhappily, in 1861. His only other published work, a part-translation of *Gl'Ingannati*, which is interesting for its connexion with *Twelfth Night,* appeared in 1862, four years before his death. He wrote nothing more after that but occupied himself with Greek and, in the last year of his life, we are told, read the works of Dickens afresh with great enjoyment, 'as a rest from more serious study'.

INTRODUCTION

*

NOVELS that depend for their comic or satiric effect on the interplay of ideas and opinions are rare and the reader coming new to Peacock is disconcerted at finding that he cannot be fitted into any traditional pattern. The simple truth is that he is too individual to be classified, that there are not sufficient examples of his kind of writing to warrant the making of generalizations, and one has to fall back on naming particular works or genres to which his novels show some indebtedness or resemblance if one wants to provide him with a literary ancestry. Obviously he learned something from Swift, more from Rabelais, and perhaps still more from Voltaire and other French writers of philosophical tales who tried to give eighteenth-century fiction a stiffening of moral and social satire, but his difference from them in method and tone is more apparent than the similarity. Moreover, there are scenes that could be described as colloquy or imaginary conversation, a minor genre with a very long history of its own, and others that belong entirely to stage comedy. It is his tendency to dramatize rather than narrate that makes him unique among novelists of ideas and explains his preference for dialogue rather than incident, for a cast of more or less equal characters rather than, say, a single comic hero, and for very limited changes of scene. The end product, however, must be described as a novel, or at least as a 'conversation novel'. One does not hold it against Peacock that his fictions lack most of the usual properties of the novel, or have them only in short and perfunctory supply, but quickly learns to accept him on his own terms for the sake of enjoying a remarkable minor talent.

All Peacock's novels have a basic plot, however slight and predictable it may be, but, with the exception of *Maid*

Marian and *The Misfortunes of Elphin*, his historical or pseudo-historical romances, one reads them for the sake of the conversation. His method is to draw into a disputatious though friendly circle as many eloquent and well-informed individualists as he can conveniently handle, plus a few supernumeraries who are no more than embodied ideas. They talk with only so much interruption as is necessary to give variety to the whole, or to give the narrative a push, and Peacock is often so exclusively concerned with what is said that he can set out whole chapters as dramatic dialogue. The major interruptions are provided by farcical episodes or by the younger members of the party falling in love, the minor by the singing of choruses or the drinking of toasts. Nobody changes his mind or concedes a point to an opponent and at the end the conversation simply stops. In the concluding chapters the underlying romance is brought quickly into the foreground and the novels usually end with two or three weddings, which give a sufficient impression of finality. It would be a mistake, nevertheless, to conclude that the romance was no more than a vehicle or that the happy endings, touched with mockery though they are, were imposed *ab extra* just to meet the reader's expectations. Peacock laughed at the conventions of romance but there are many indications that he liked an opportunity for sentiment, and nowhere more than in the concluding chapters of *Crotchet Castle*.

All the novels begin with a gathering of guests at a country house on some slight pretext and men are invariably in the majority, with only sufficient young women to keep the love stories going and sufficient older ones to act as their chaperons. Incidentally, it is interesting to notice that Peacock, who was no anti-feminist, rarely included the women in the general conversations. The young ones lack neither wit nor articulacy when they talk, as they almost exclusively do, with their suitors, and one can only suppose that they are given no part in the discussions because they are too normal and too sensible. The suitors, who are amiable and ingenuous young men in their capacity

as such, take as full a part in the discussions as their atten-
tions to the ladies allow and they have their own distinctive notions and hobbyhorses, but the middle-aged are free
to talk from breakfast to bedtime. With the exception of
one or two titled ninnies like Lord Bossnowl in *Crotchet
Castle*, all the male characters are mouthpieces for topical
opinions and nostrums and Peacock covers almost all of
them in the list of *dramatis personœ* that he gives in the
preface to his first collected edition of 1837: 'Perfectibilians,
deteriorationists, statu-quo-ites, phrenologists, transcendentalists, political economists, theorists in all sciences,
projectors in all arts, morbid visionaries, romantic enthusiasts, lovers of music, lovers of the picturesque, and lovers
of good dinners'. The list is incomplete in so far as it passes
over some types or individuals who are invariably pursued
with satirical animus, among them renegade Lake Poets
and *Edinburgh* and *Quarterly* reviewers, and it can give no
indication that there are in the novels a few characters like
Dr Folliott of *Crotchet Castle* and Sir Oran Haut-Ton of
Melincourt who are quite unique.

The characters are either given type-names of the kind
traditional in stage comedy, such as Cranium for a phreno-
logist, or normal-sounding names like Escot or Jenkison
that also prove to be type-names when Peacock has explained their derivation in a footnote with a fantastic
etymology. The type-names might lead one to expect the
novels to proceed by schematic confrontations between
type characters but this is only true of parts of *Headlong
Hall*, the first of them. Peacock soon learned how to make
individual characters serve more than one purpose, so that
they can be vehicles for satire as well as its victims, and how
to conduct a dialogue for several voices that sometimes
advances by brisk exchanges and sometimes by involved
digressions. The characters have sufficient resources of wit,
learning, folly and self-assertiveness to give them at least
a two-dimensional existence and their conversation has so
many cross-references to real-life personalities, controversies and literary topics that there is no danger of their

seeming abstract. Moreover, many of the characters are caricatures, in a greater or less degree, of real-life individuals and it may be said that they gain added life and interest from that source. Though a few of the originals such as minor members of the Shelley circle are too obscure to be generally recognized and the caricatures of them are no more than private jokes, many are public figures and quite unmistakable.

By Regency standards, Peacock's satire on his contemporaries was by no means harsh. He handled Robert Southey more severely than any other victim, but to attack Southey, who was very capable of taking care of himself, as a renegade was almost *de rigueur* for any satirist of reaction. Peacock seems to have lacked the anger, the intense conviction of his own rightness and the didactic urge that go to make up a major satirist and there is only one chapter in the whole range of his novels that might make one qualify such a judgement: the chapter in *Headlong Hall* where Mr Cranium sets out his collection of human and animal skulls and lectures his fellow guests on comparative phrenology. Its unusualness consists in the indignation that is directed against the permanent moral shortcomings of humanity; it is as if what set out to be a skit on phrenology had been taken over by a lesser Swift. But this degree of forcefulness was rare with Peacock, perhaps because he was reluctant to have his peace of mind deeply disturbed or because he was more interested in the sheer comedy of conflicting opinions. He had, besides, a disabling tendency to look at both sides of a question. As J.-J. Mayoux said (*Un Epicurien Anglais*, p. 606), he had the type of mind that is incapable of holding a position without perceiving the force of the contrary position and that therefore takes naturally to dialogue.

There is a certain amount of evidence, biographical as well as internal, that Peacock took a pleasure in making it difficult for his readers to guess which, if any, of the opinions expressed by his characters were his own. It is not remarkable, granted this built-in difficulty and the added difficulty of knowing when he was being serious, that critics who have tried to describe his political and social views have had to resort to cautiously expressed paradoxes. One can get some indication of his antipathies from the narrators in the novels, in spite of the bantering tone, but very few hints about his more positive views. The satire is so often double-edged and characters who hold antithetical views are so often made to confound one another that one has to proceed by tenuous inferences when trying to define his position, and if one turns for help to his essays and reviews one seldom finds them more revealing than the novels. All that can be said with assurance is that Peacock was an independent radical, an enemy of reaction, and a critic of received opinions. To have committed himself to a political party or to have taken up without reservations any fashionable theory would have been constitutionally impossible for him, as well as imposing a limitation on his comic material, but he was neither perverse nor irresponsible. As readers will find, the mockery and high spirits do not entirely obscure a serious concern for the health of literature in *Nightmare Abbey* or for the health of society in *Crotchet Castle*.

*

NIGHTMARE ABBEY

THERE is a letter from Peacock to Shelley dated 30 May 1818 in which he says, 'I have almost finished *Nightmare Abbey*. I think it necessary to "make a stand" against the "encroachments" of black bile. The fourth canto of *Childe Harold* is really too bad. I cannot consent to be *auditor tantum* of this systematical "poisoning" of the "mind" of the "reading public".' And again, in a letter to Shelley written on the 15th September following, he says that his object in writing the novel has been 'merely to bring to a sort of philosophical focus a few of the morbidities of modern literature, and to let in a little daylight on its atrabilarious complexion'. These remarks of Peacock's probably offer between them an adequate account of the initial satirical impulse that prompted him to write the novel and in Chapter XI, where the conversation of Mr Cypress, the Byron figure, is largely made up of glum phrases borrowed from the recently published fourth canto of *Childe Harold*, we have an excellent local example of that impulse working itself out. But Mr Cypress appeared only in the episode that takes up Chapter XI and what Shelley, who had left England in March that year, was apparently not told was that the central figure in this satire on the more bizarre aspects of romanticism was to be a caricature of himself. Shelley does not, however, dominate the scene; others are almost as prominent, among them Coleridge, who represented areas of romanticism where neither Byron nor Shelley would serve and was useful besides as a poet of the older generation that had outlived its earlier millennial hopes.

The plot of *Nightmare Abbey* turns on the hesitation of Scythrop Glowry, its central character, between his two loves, Marionetta and Stella, and it has not been seriously questioned that Peacock had in mind in devising it Shelley's relations with Harriet Westbrook and Mary Godwin. Scythrop's dilemma seems like a parody of Shelley's situation when he realized he had outgrown his charming but inadequate first wife and fallen in love with a girl more nearly his intellectual equal. If this had been all, it might not have mattered that Peacock had seen in it a subject for comedy, but Harriet, whom Shelley had deserted in favour of Mary in 1814, had committed suicide in late 1816, not much more than a year before the novel was begun, and the reader inevitably wonders how the novelist could have ventured on to such ground. The likeliest explanation is that Peacock, who had been very close to Shelley in the years prior to the latter's departure for Italy, knew that his friend had protected himself with an unshakeable conviction of his own rectitude in his conduct towards Harriet and that he was unlikely to be disturbed unless that conviction was impugned. It is possible that Peacock delayed sending Shelley a copy of the novel for a few months after publication, as if doubtful of its effect, but in the event the latter's reaction to the novel was to praise it unreservedly. In the letter to Peacock of June 1819, in which he acknowledged receipt of his copy, he said, 'I am delighted with Nightmare Abbey. I think Scythrop a character admirably conceived & executed, & I know not how to praise sufficiently the lightness chastity & strength of the language of the whole. It perhaps exceeds all your works in this. The catastrophe is excellent' (*Letters*, ed. F. L. Jones, Vol. II, p. 98). There can be no doubt, of course, that he recognized a great deal of his younger self in Scythrop and occasional remarks of his, as when he referred to his roof-top study as 'Scythrop's tower', suggest that he had enjoyed the caricature.

No reader of Peacock's description of Harriet in his *Memoirs of Shelley* could fail to see that she had contributed something to Marionetta, but in describing Stella he seems to have taken some trouble to insist, and perhaps too obviously, that she had no physical resemblance to Mary, and this has led to suggestions that she was primarily drawn from Elizabeth Hitchener, who paid a prolonged visit to Shelley and Harriet in 1812, or from Claire Clairmont, who accompanied Shelley and Mary when they left England. Shelley's odd tendency to include in his household a woman friend of his own or a sister of his wife could have provided the idea for the Marionetta–Stella situation in *Nightmare Abbey* and Peacock had presumably observed with amusement that in both of Shelley's terror novels, *Zastrozzi* and *St Irvyne*, the hero is loved by two women at the same time. To complicate these not very serious issues still further, there is quite a possibility that Peacock, in setting Scythrop between his two loves, also had in mind a recent predicament of his own. Though he had been attached to Marianne de St Croix for several years and intended to marry her, he had gone to live, towards the end of the year 1814, with a supposed rich heiress who had fallen in love with him. An entry in Mary Shelley's journal, the only known source for this story, records under 3 January 1815, while the affair was still in progress, that the heiress was very miserable, that Peacock was miserable on her account and that of Marianne, and that Marianne was miserable on her own account. Eleanor L. Nicholes, who quotes this journal entry in *Shelley and his Circle* (ed. K. N. Cameron, Vol. I, p. 100), comments appropriately, 'It is a tale worthy of *Nightmare Abbey*', and adds that it evidently suggested one element in the name Marionetta.

There were, however, precedents in literature as well as in life for the plot of *Nightmare Abbey* and when Peacock made Celinda assume the name of Stella he was pointing a mocking finger at the most celebrated of them. In Goethe's *Stella* the hero is torn between his love for Cecilia, his wife, and Stella, his mistress, and shoots himself; Peacock's hero, trapped in the same sort of situation, also decides on suicide, and the author works in another Goethe reminiscence by making him call, like Werther in *his* similar impasse, for a bottle of wine as well as a pistol. One might have thought that, after a whole generation of parodies of German romantic melodrama, its possibilities for comedy would have been as exhausted as its capacity for being taken seriously, but Shelley, like other poets of the younger generation, had read these back numbers of romanticism and had to act out their heroics for himself. One remembers his saying in the letter that he wrote to T. J. Hogg on 3 January 1811 after hearing that his cousin Harriet Grove, with whom he was then in love, was to be married, 'I slept with a loaded pistol & some poison last night but did not die.' The Werther influence was obviously still active and a satirist could find rich material in a life that imitated literature.

The account of Scythrop planning the regeneration of the world in his tower that takes up Chapter II is a superb caricature of Shelley. He has read Godwin, has published a treatise full of matter 'deep and dangerous', and, above all, has read German tragedies and masses of Gothic romances and found in their secret tribunals and bands of illuminati his crazy machinery for reforming the world. His name, which might be translated Gloomy Face, has no appropriateness to Shelley. It is no more than a type-name, like the names of Flosky and Cypress, to mark him as a character in a comedy where the theme is the morbidity of contemporary literature. Scythrop is most like Shelley in his enthusiasm for regenerating mankind, in his formidable-ness in argument (his father, incidentally, dreads his logic), and in his love of mystery for its own sake. But he is no poet, and Peacockian invention takes over where carica-ture ends, so that the Scythrop who lives with his indulgent father, who has learnt to drink deep at the university while finishing his education 'to the high satisfaction of the master and fellows of his college', and who is regarded in London society as 'a very accomplished charming fellow', is a completely unShelleyan creation. When Peacock has him suggest to Marionetta that, like Rosalia and Don Carlos in *Horrid Mysteries*, they should open a vein in each other's arm, mix their blood in a bowl and drink it as a sacrament of love, he is operating at the extreme limit of caricature, whereas when he makes him order the butler to bring in the boiled fowl and Madeira instead of the port and the pistol, he is engaged in pure Peacockian invention.

Though Peacock's attack on the 'morbidities' is presented most fully and amusingly in Chapter XI in terms of Cypress–Byron, there are several earlier occasions when the topic is raised in a general way and without reference to Byron, as when Mr Asterias denounces the inexhaustible varieties of *ennui*, including blue devils, time-killing, discontent and misanthropy, that have infected both society and literature. Even Mr Listless, who is himself a personification of time-killing, has noticed that blue devils constitute 'the funda-mental feature of fashionable literature', and Mr Flosky underlines the truth of this with his accurate thumb-nail summary of Godwin's newly published novel, *Mandeville*, here referred to as *Devilman*: 'Hatred – revenge – mis-anthropy – and quotations from the Bible. Hm. This is the morbid anatomy of black bile.' The nub of Peacock's case was that discontent and misanthropy made virtue and energy seem futile and, for all the lightness of treatment, his charge was seriously preferred. It was, of course, deliberately overstated, for there were well-known current alternatives to *Mandeville* and *Childe Harold* such as the innocuous Waverley novels, which were to be described in *Crotchet Castle* as 'the pantomime of literature'. Among the less well-known there were Jane Austen's novels, where Peacock might have found virtue and energy undiminished, but there is no evidence that he had ever heard of them.

As well as the case against the 'morbidities', there is the related case against the Byronic hero and it too is taken up from time to time as occasion offers. The most extended statement of it is given to Mr Flosky, the Coleridge figure, and there are sufficient resemblances in phrasing to suggest that Peacock had in mind when writing it Coleridge's own objections to hero-villains in his critique of C. R. Maturin's *Bertram* (first produced at Drury Lane in 1816) in *Biographia Literaria*. Mr Flosky explains that as the depraved palate of the reading public had grown tired of Gothic ghosts and skeletons such as he himself had once provided, it had become necessary to excite it with a new sauce. It was to meet this demand that characters had been invented in whom a single virtue was not only supposed to redeem multiple vices but also made to seem capable of existing only in conjunction with the vices. For Mr Flosky, who speaks here with untypical lucidity, it is a method of administering a mass of vice under a thin coating of virtue, 'like a spider wrapt in a bit of gold leaf, and administered as a wholesome pill'. He was, strictly speaking, wrong about the novelty of morally ambiguous characters in so far as they had come in years before with German drama – as Hazlitt said in the last of his *Lectures on the English Poets*, the Germans had made heroes of robbers and honest women of cast-off mistresses – yet he was right in that Byron was currently giving them new force and new dimensions.

Mr Flosky is a much improved version of Mr Mystic of

Melincourt. The latter is little more than a foggy-minded transcendental philosopher, whereas Mr Flosky has other ideas and attributes besides his Kantian metaphysics. Several of those ideas and traits have at least a basis in Coleridge's works and Peacock knew them well enough to put them to mischievous use. (One recognizes the obvious clues, such as Mr Flosky's ability to compose verses in his sleep or his claim that the best parts of his friends' books were written by himself, easily enough, but the points of origin of his prudishness, insistent humility and irritation at being charged with talking in paradoxes are less readily discoverable in Coleridge's works.) This is not to say that Mr Flosky is a character from life or that Peacock recognized, or needed to recognize for the purposes he had in mind, the complexity of Coleridge and his central importance. Mr Flosky is just a character in a comedy, and quite as preposterous as Scythrop, as witness his splendid big scene with Marionetta in Chapter VIII or the passage of cumulative nonsense in Chapter VI that ends with the crowning *non sequitur*, 'and for these reasons I have christened my eldest son Emanuel Kant Flosky'. Where Peacock was serious was in querying Flosky's nostalgia for the good old times of feudal darkness, his love of mystery and his retreat into the opacity of metaphysics; that was an essential part of his case against the contemporary abandonment of sweetness and light, of which the political *volte-face* of the older poets, including Wordsworth, Coleridge and Southey, was an especially offensive aspect.

It is the function of Mr Toobad, with his repeated discoveries of new evidence that 'the Devil is come among us', to act as Chorus of the novel, though he might equally well be described as a farcical personification of the general retreat from sense or as the last and craziest term in a series that runs through Scythrop, Mr Cypress and Mr Flosky. Peacock, with a fine sense of the appropriate, made him the father of the joyless Stella and had him send her to Germany, the fountain-head of 'black' romanticism, to finish her education. Since he is the buffoon of the novel, as well as a particular object of the Evil One's malice, it is he who tumbles downstairs, whose carriage overturns, and who falls out of the window into the moat, to be netted by Mr Asterias in the belief that he is a mermaid. As for Mr Asterias, he is a left-over from the eighteenth century, a gentleman scientist who is unscientific enough to post off to Lincolnshire on the news of a mermaid's having been sighted there. Even so, he is not entirely a credulous figure of fun, as is evident from the scientist's *credo* that he pronounces in Chapter VII; high-flown and old-fashioned though it is, one cannot doubt that he is meant to be respected when he contrasts the virtues and pleasures of the scientist's life with the evils of *ennui*, despair and misanthropy.

Almost all the positives to be set against these contemporary evils, apart from those put forward by Mr Asterias, emerge in Chapter XI. They are not forthcoming from Mr Larynx, the clergyman of the party, whose only discernible belief is that 'a very good dinner is a very good thing', and it is left to Mr Hilary, who is out of his element as a guest at this party, to reply to the joint lamentations of Cypress, Flosky, Toobad and Scythrop with the arguments for a cheerful pragmatism. His name and the description of him on his first appearance as 'a very cheerful and elastic gentleman' indicate his role and though Peacock adds a touch of self-protective mockery to the description, we can be fairly confident that he is one of the rare characters in the novels whose opinions obviously merge with the author's. He may be sound enough when he says that it is a disease to expect too much and that misanthropy originates in the pursuit of impossible ideals, but one demurs at his wholehearted recommendation of cheerfulness, even as an antidote to romantic gloom, and actively dissents when he claims that 'the highest wisdom and the highest genius have been invariably accompanied with cheerfulness'. Whether Peacock has parted company with him when he gets to this point is not certain, but it looks like one of those cases where a satirist's positives would have been better left unformulated. It is, however, only a small point, a momentary failure in tact, and he does better elsewhere in the same chapter when he puts into the mouth of Mr Flosky an ironic summary of his charges against the whole company in a passage that is, in effect, the thematic centre of the novel. Addressing Mr Cypress, Mr Flosky says:

I must do you, myself, and our mutual friends, the justice to observe, that let society only give fair play at one and the same time, as I flatter myself it is inclined to do, to your system of morals, and my system of metaphysics, and Scythrop's system of politics, and Mr Listless's system of manners, and Mr Toobad's system of religion, and the result will be as fine a mental chaos as even the immortal Kant himself could ever have hoped to see; in the prospect of which I rejoice.

Nightmare Abbey is remarkable among Peacock's novels for its coherence. He keeps closely to his single 'morbidities of modern literature' theme and the conversationalists, with the major exception of Mr Cypress and the minor one of the Reverend Mr Larynx, are all actively engaged in the events. Where theme and plot most completely coalesce, the novel is at its very good best, as in the scene where Marionetta tries in vain to get a plain answer to a plain question from Mr Flosky, and where plot predominates we have a rare display of Peacock's resources of comic invention, above all in the hilarious episode where Scythrop tries to distract his father from his search for the hidden Stella with a lecture on the structure of the ear. There are, of course, passages of debate where the action stands still, but such passages are the staple of a Peacock novel and in this case they are unusually relevant to the theme. Penetrated as it is with contemporary allusions, it is not an easy novel to do justice to and something more than the common stock of knowledge of Regency personalities and trends is required if one is to get the best from it. On the other hand, modern readers who take the trouble can see more in it than its first readers could, unless they actually appeared in it, and *their* pleasure cannot have been entirely unqualified, even though its satire on individuals is good-humoured rather than destructive.

*

CROTCHET CASTLE

WITH *Crotchet Castle*, which was published in February 1831, thirteen years after *Nightmare Abbey*, Peacock reverted to the conversation novel. The intervening works, *Maid Marian* and *The Misfortunes of Elphin*, were historical romances of a curious satirical kind and they were named after leading characters, but as a reader familiar with the *hall, court,* and *abbey* of previous titles might expect, the new novel followed the old and easy plan of assembling in a country house a group of talkers and crotcheteers. As the author himself remarks in one of his very rare comments, they are engaged in 'discussing everything and settling nothing'. Like its predecessors in the same kind, *Crotchet Castle* was largely concerned with contemporary ideas and personalities and it was topical enough to include references to Henry Brougham's taking office and a peerage two months before it was published and to the 'Captain Swing' riots of the closing months of 1830. Though some of Peacock's most persistent antipathies reappear and we have, for instance, his stock objection to paper money and his usual quip that the universities can be regarded as seats of learning only on the principle of 'once a captain, always a captain', we get a distinct impression that time has moved on since the writing of *Nightmare Abbey* and that some of the ideas that are aired in the novel are those of a new era.

The underlying narrative of *Crotchet Castle* is less perfunctorily handled than that of *Headlong Hall* or *Melincourt*, the two previous novels with which it is comparable in this respect, even though the principal heroine, Susannah Touchandgo, is introduced in the first chapter and then left, with scarcely a mention, in the wilds of Merionethshire until she is required a dozen chapters later. In her absence, Peacock's usual romance interest is intermittently provided by Captain Fitzchrome's courtship of the second heroine, Lady Clarinda, who repeatedly refuses his offer of love in a cottage when she can have a handsome establishment elsewhere. The outcome is as predictable as it is indispensable. Susannah is clearly a heroine of romance for whom a happy issue is preparing and Lady Clarinda, the strongest-minded and most articulate of Peacock's heroines, must be saved from an over-rational marriage with Mr Crotchet Junior who, as a 'bubble-blowing' company promoter, is one of the novelist's commonest objects for contempt. The two heroines are eventually married off to worthy young men and all the intervals in their story are filled either with general debate, usually over the dining table, or with loosely attached but thematically relevant episodes like that in which Dr Folliott is called before the Charity Commissioners.

Peacock's intention in writing *Nightmare Abbey* was indicated in his letter to Shelley about that novel and it was fairly closely adhered to, but there is no comparable 'statement of intent' discoverable for *Crotchet Castle*. Perhaps the nearest we can get to an open acknowledgement of its themes is Mr Crotchet's list of certain great controversies that he would like to see settled in his lifetime: 'the sentimental against the rational, the intuitive against the inductive, the ornamental against the useful, the intense against the tranquil, the romantic against the classical'. Though these topics certainly recur in the novel and are discussed by characters who take up these antithetical positions, they are less prominent than the main debate, which is, to put it in its broadest terms, between common sense and rationality. On one side is the Reverend Dr Folliott, an amateur of the classics, traditionalist and spokesman for a pragmatic *via media*, on the other is Mr Mac Quedy, the political economist. Peacock is content that some of the minor debates should, in the nature of things, be incapable of ever being concluded, and it might almost be said that he has a vested interest in keeping them going, but he makes sure that the brusque and forthright Dr Folliott has the best of the argument in his skirmishes with Mac Quedy. Moreover, Chainmail the medievalist, Toogood the co-operationist, and Skionar the transcendentalist can make sensible contributions on Folliott's side, even if they are figures of fun in their own right, whereas Mac Quedy stands alone.

Mac Quedy was based on J. R. McCulloch, professor of political economy at the newly founded University College in London, though James Mill and Robert Mushet seem to have contributed a little to the caricature. He is one of the 'reasoning people' described by Lady Clarinda – 'people that talk nonsense logically' – and a product of Edinburgh, a 'modern Athenian'. As Clarinda goes on to say of him, he turns all the world's affairs into questions of buying and selling and romance and sentiment wither at his touch. These are, of course, the popular objections to the political economists. Peacock's more serious criticisms are voiced by Folliott with a characteristic blend of trenchancy and good humour and without the indignation that moved a later generation of idealists and humanitarians such as Ruskin to make their protest against political economy. Folliott, who is no idealist and not obviously a humanitarian, bases his criticism simply on the grounds of common sense. It is true that Peacock cannot be continuously identified with Folliott, but there seems to be no doubt that he is underwriting him here. If one asks why he took up this position, the answer may be that he was still too much of a humanitarian radical of Shelley's kind to be able to accept inequities in income that the political economists regarded as inevitable and there is some unobtrusive evidence for this view of him in the novel. On the other hand, it is possible that he was arguing from that characteristic independent position of his middle and later years when he was apt to regard most of the fashionable ideas that were taken up and parroted by his contemporaries as being either cant or nonsense.

It was from the latter position that Peacock, through
Folliott, made fun of the idea of 'schools for all' and of the
'march of mind' in general. This was a new theme in his
novels and one that was to be permanent with him, as is
evident from *Gryll Grange*, for instance, where 'schools for
all' is lumped with competitive examinations for appointment to public office, the temperance movement and deci-
mal coinage, as a contemporary folly. 'Schools for All' was
originally the title of a celebrated pamphlet by James Mill,
Peacock's superior at the India Office, which put the Radicals' case for universal non-sectarian education, but it was
Henry Brougham, their temporary ally among the Whigs
and the outstanding advocate of education over the whole
range from infant to adult, who had to bear the brunt of
Peacock's disapproval. Brougham, lightly disguised as 'the
learned friend', is something of a *bête noire* in *Crotchet
Castle*, though he does not actually appear, and it is impossible to distinguish between Peacock's antipathy to the
man as a demagogue, place hunter and would-be polymath
and his antipathy to him as a source of, and spokesman for,
contemporary cant. Mac Quedy, who also puts in a word for
schools for all, is allowed to be an honest if mistaken victim
of his own theories, whereas 'the learned friend' is represented as a humbug on any evidence that comes to hand,
from the errors in the pamphlet on hydrostatics that he
wrote for the Society for the Diffusion of Useful Knowledge
to the ineffective meddlesomeness of the Charity Commission that he originated.

Peacock includes among Folliott's occasional supporters
in his brushes with Mac Quedy both a deteriorationist and a
perfectibilian, to adopt the terms that he himself uses in
Headlong Hall. The deteriorationist is Mr Chainmail, who
sets up an idealized twelfth-century society, when there
was 'community of kind feelings between master and man',
against the political economists' conception of society as
bound together only by the cash nexus. He lives out his
dream in Chainmail Hall, his 'fortress of beef and ale', out
of reach of arguments such as Mac Quedy's to the effect that

his supposed golden age was an age of tyranny, fanaticism and ignorance. There is a touch of Peacock himself in Chainmail, if only in their shared dislike of the disadvantages attendant on coal-gas and steam, whereas Toogood, the perfectibilian of the novel, centres his whole conception of the good society on a steam-engine. As Lady Clarinda briskly puts it, he 'wants to parcel out the world into squares like a chess-board, with a community on each, raising everything for one another, with a great steam-engine to serve them in common'. (This is only a mild parody of Robert Owen's plan for co-operative communities which he originally conceived as a means of making the poor self-supporting and then developed into his panacea for the whole civilized world.) Although he is only lightly sketched, it is evident that Toogood is another critic of the injustices inherent in *laissez-faire* society. He and Chainmail are neatly opposed representatives of the two most important trends in romantic utopianism and Peacock deserves credit for the almost casual ease with which he embodies them and sets them on either side of Folliott, the mouthpiece of common sense, as his occasional allies against Mac Quedy.

Apart from Chainmail and Toogood, there are two more minor figures who have in common an antipathy to Mac Quedy's ideas. One of them is Mr Skionar, who is a slighter version of Mr Flosky, the 'transcendental poet' of *Nightmare Abbey*, and Peacock's last and mildest caricature of Coleridge. Like Chainmail and Toogood, he is a figure of fun who can nevertheless make a valid point against Mac Quedy. This disciple of 'the sublime Kant' has his moment in the scene at the Roman camp in Chapter III when he rejects Mac Quedy's reduction of the relative ages of the camp and a nearby beech tree to a matter of simple arithmetic. What he says is so wrapped up in his transcendental verbiage that the baffled Mac Quedy can only reply, 'Well, sir, if you understand that, I wish you joy', but it is at least apparent that he is speaking for intuition and imagination against the other's rationality and literal-mindedness. It is

an anti-rational attitude that the second of these minor
characters, Captain Fitzchrome, wholeheartedly approves,
though his approval is not disinterested since he is trying to
persuade Lady Clarinda to abandon her Mac Quedy-style
view of marriage. Incidentally, the captain has another role
besides that of a lover who puts forward the claims of heart
over head; he is a 'picturesque tourist', to use the phrase
current in the early years of the nineteenth century,
and when temporarily rebuffed by Lady Clarinda he re-
treats to North Wales, where, a stock figure in a stock
romantic landscape, he sketches waterfalls and mountain
pools.

The outermost circle of guests at Crotchet Castle is made
up of oddities and monomaniacs who, like Chainmail and
Toogood, represent contemporary types, personalities, or
theories, but they have neither a part in the plot nor anything of significance to contribute to the debates. Though
there is no discernible principle of selection and the immediate reasons for some of the inclusions baffle conjecture, one
can, in certain cases, guess at the circumstances that suggested their appearance. Thus Sir Simon Steeltrap, a caricature of the die-hard landowner who was a focus for the rural
disturbances of 1830, appears quite properly as a feature of
the social background, and Mr Philpot, the geographer, 'who
thinks of nothing but the heads and tails of rivers', perhaps
owes his inclusion to public interest in the Lander brothers'
expedition to identify the mouth of the Niger in the same
year. In the case of Mr Eavesdrop, the 'violator of the confidences of private life', we can be almost sure that among
those Peacock had in mind were Thomas Medwin and Leigh
Hunt, to whom he referred in very similar terms in connexion with their published reminiscences of Byron in a
review that he wrote in 1830. This was a review of Tom
Moore's *Letters and Journals of Lord Byron*, and Moore
himself appears in this outermost circle, with attributes
that put his identity beyond doubt, as Mr Trillo, the
pianist, cellist, versifier, improviser and welcome guest at
any party. The rest of the minor figures – Firedamp,

Henbane and Morbific – are shadowy representatives of current scientific and medical preoccupations, but there is no way of discovering why these particular examples should have been chosen.

The discussions at Crotchet Castle come to an end half-way through the novel and are resumed in peripatetic form when the whole company sets off for North Wales. The interval is taken up with brief comic scenes, all of them centring on Dr Folliott and all of them nearer to stage comedy than anything else in the novel. In one of them, where the doctor expostulates with Mr Crotchet for filling his house with statues of Venus, Peacock casts a satirical eye on yet another aspect of contemporary cant, the increasing prudishness of the times. (It had, in fact, been increasing for some years, if one can judge, for instance, from the publication of Bowdler's *Family Shakespeare* in 1818 and its having gone into a fourth edition by 1825.) In another excellent scene, Dr Folliott is set upon by footpads and Peacock improves the occasion by having him suppose that his assailants are members of the Steam Intellect Society or, in other words, of Brougham's Society for the Diffusion of Useful Knowledge, whose object is to burke him and so provide 'some flinty-hearted anatomist' with 'a subject for science'. It is all good fun and any stick will serve to beat Brougham with, both here and in the following scene where Dr Folliott is called before the Charity Commissioners who have come, at great expense, to inquire into the misappropriation of a bequest of one pound per annum. Peacock cannot have forgotten that the Charity Commissioners as originally conceived by Brougham were reduced to this kind of ineffectiveness by the government. He still preferred to regard them as being 'a job of the learned friend'.

The move to North Wales has to take place if the principal pair of lovers, Mr Chainmail and Miss Susannah Touchandgo, are to meet. She has all the intelligence, independence of mind and background reading in the Italian poets and Rousseau that the role of a heroine of romance, as conceived by Peacock, requires, as well as the more conventional attributes of beauty and the ability to accompany herself on the harp, but she is no exception to the rule that everybody in the novel can somehow be laid under tribute for grist to the satirical mill. Her retreat into obscurity in Merionethshire is explained by her being the daughter of a banker (i.e. a manufacturer of *paper money*) who has absconded to America owing half a million. By an extraordinary freak of fancy, Peacock took the circumstances attending on the flight of the real-life Lombard Street banker Rowland Stephenson and his clerk James Lloyd in December 1828, and gave them to Timothy Touchandgo and his factotum Roderick Robthetill. It was a notorious case with repercussions that went on for months and one can imagine the astonishment and amusement of the first readers of *Crotchet Castle* at this piece of opportunism. However, to be the daughter of an absconding banker is not a fatal disqualification for being a heroine; Susannah assimilates herself to the landscape and is said to be soothed and healed by it in near-Wordsworthian terms, and the novelist takes an evident pleasure in carrying the romance to its normal conclusion.

If, on considering the novel in retrospect, one asks where Peacock himself stood, from what basis of conviction he developed his satire, one finds, as usual, that no easy answers can be given, not only because he meant to be elusive but also because he set out to demonstrate that all the obvious convictions were open to ridicule. Progressives and conservatives, utopians and reactionaries, scientists and transcendentalists, all provided opportunities for comedy and Peacock was ingenious in arranging encounters where their representatives exposed their own follies in exposing each other's. The nearest approach to an author's mouthpiece is Dr Folliott, though the identification must be subject to reservations. In so far as he is a snugly beneficed gourmet with an antipathy to anything that disturbs his peace, he is himself a subject for satire and an unreliable witness against change of any kind. In his other aspect, however, that of the independent scholar, he is quite close to Peacock. One finds sufficient of his tastes and opinions elsewhere in Peacock's works, in essays and poems as well as novels (opinions about the *Edinburgh Review,* for instance, or on political economy as a pseudo-science) to be tempted to guess at the novelist's fundamental attitudes from the scattered evidence that Folliott incidentally provides. But in practice almost the only certainties that emerge are the truisms that Peacock was neither a reactionary nor an identifiable kind of radical. Whereas in *The Misfortunes of Elphin,* published two years before *Crotchet Castle,* it was reactionaries who were the principal victims, in the latter it was the theoreticians of progress and those who mistook the march of machinery for 'the march of mind'. He was irritated, or at best wryly amused, by their assumption that reason was all on their side and by their confidence that their logic, like the austere kind of progress they envisaged, was inescapable. We need not conclude from this, as some of his critics have done, that he was turning conservative, but merely that, as a reasonable man, he distrusted logicians and new orthodoxies as well as old ones.

*

EDITORIAL NOTE

FOUR of Peacock's novels, *Headlong Hall, Nightmare Abbey, Maid Marian* and *Crotchet Castle,* were lightly revised by the author for their appearance as Volume LVII in Bentley's Standard Novels in 1837. The text of both the novels in the present volume follows that revised edition. Peacock's distinctive custom, when setting out passages of debate as dramatic dialogue, of putting the name of a speaker above his speech rather than in the margin has been retained and his occasional idiosyncrasies of punctuation have been reproduced. His footnotes have been incorporated with my own notes at the end of the volume and distinguished with his initial.

The standard edition of Peacock's verse and prose is the 'Halliford', edited by H. F. B. Brett-Smith and C. E. Jones and published in ten volumes between 1924 and 1934. The notes to that edition are mainly confined to bibliographical and textual matters. By far the most useful edition of the novels is that of David Garnett, who published all seven novels in two volumes in 1948 (revised 1963). He supplies in his introductions and notes the information essential to a full reading of a novelist who was both learned and allusive. There is a critical biography by Carl Van Doren (1911) and a long biographical introduction in Volume I of the 'Halliford' edition that supplements Van Doren, but there is no recent biography. An indispensable bibliography is included in Bill Read's doctoral dissertation submitted at Boston University in 1959 under the title *The Critical Reputation of Thomas Love Peacock with an Annotated Enumerative Bibliography* and available in xerographic form.

I have also benefited from reference to Richard Garnett's edition of the works (1891), A. M. Freeman's *Thomas Love Peacock, a Critical Study* (1911), J. B. Priestley's *Thomas Love Peacock* (1927), J.-J. Mayoux's *Un Epicurien Anglais: Thomas Love Peacock* (Paris, 1933), and Eleanor L. Nicholes's chapter on Peacock in *Shelley and his Circle*, edited by K. N. Cameron (1961). There is really not much else on Peacock, apart from one or two articles, that the reader can be referred to for information of a factual nature and there is still a good deal to be done in the way of identifying the originals of certain characters in the novels who appear to be caricatures and explaining hitherto unexplained contemporary allusions. In the case of Peacock, who was nothing if not topical, this would not be to bury him still deeper under a mound of commentary but to help to keep his comedy alive.

I am indebted to many people who have helped me with their specialized knowledge and particularly to Mr Frank

Rutherford, of Durham University. I am also indebted to Mr Peter Rowley, my colleague at Liverpool University, not only for help with the Greek quotations but also for drawing my attention to relevant material.

R.W.

Superior figures in the text refer to the notes, pp. 261 ff.

Facsimile title page of the first edition of
Nightmare Abbey.

NIGHTMARE ABBEY:

BY

THE AUTHOR OF HEADLONG HALL.

There's a dark lantern of the spirit,
Which none see by but those who bear it,
That makes them in the dark see visions
And hag themselves with apparitions,
Find racks for their own minds; and vaunt
Of their own misery and want.   BUTLER.

LONDON:

PRINTED FOR T. HOOKHAM, JUN. OLD BOND-STREET;
AND BALDWIN, CRADOCK, AND JOY,
PATERNOSTER-ROW.

1818.

MATTHEW. Oh! it's your only fine humour, sir. Your true melancholy breeds your perfect fine wit, sir. I am melancholy myself, divers times, sir; and then do I no more but take pen and paper presently, and overflow you half a score or a dozen of sonnets at a sitting.

STEPHEN. Truly, sir, and I love such things out of measure.

MATTHEW. Why, I pray you, sir, make use of my study: it's at your service.

STEPHEN. I thank you, sir, I shall be bold, I warrant you. Have you a stool there, to be melancholy upon?

BEN JONSON, *Every Man in his Humour*,
Act 3, Sc. 1

NIGHTMARE ABBEY

Ay esleu gazouiller et siffler oye, comme dit le commun
proverbe, entre les cygnes, plutoust que d'estre entre
tant de gentils poëtes et faconds orateurs mut du tout
estimé.

RABELAIS, Prol. L. 5[1]

*

CHAPTER I

NIGHTMARE ABBEY, a venerable family-mansion, in a
highly picturesque state of semi-dilapidation, pleasantly
situated on a strip of dry land between the sea and the fens,
at the verge of the county of Lincoln, had the honour to be
the seat of Christopher Glowry, Esquire. This gentleman was
naturally of an atrabilarious temperament, and much
troubled with those phantoms of indigestion which are
commonly called *blue devils*.[2] He had been deceived in an
early friendship: he had been crossed in love; and had
offered his hand, from pique, to a lady, who accepted it from
interest, and who, in so doing, violently tore asunder the
bonds of a tried and youthful attachment. Her vanity was
gratified by being the mistress of a very extensive, if not
very lively, establishment; but all the springs of her sympathies were frozen. Riches she possessed, but that which
enriches them, the participation of affection, was wanting.
All that they could purchase for her became indifferent to
her, because that which they could not purchase, and which
was more valuable than themselves, she had, for their sake,
thrown away. She discovered, when it was too late, that she
had mistaken the means for the end – that riches, rightly
used, are instruments of happiness, but are not in themselves happiness. In this wilful blight of her affections, she
found them valueless as means: they had been the end to
which she had immolated all her affections, and were now

the only end that remained to her. She did not confess this to herself as a principle of action, but it operated through the medium of unconscious self-deception, and terminated in inveterate avarice. She laid on external things the blame of her mind's internal disorder, and thus became by degrees an accomplished scold. She often went her daily rounds through a series of deserted apartments, every creature in the house vanishing at the creak of her shoe, much more at the sound of her voice, to which the nature of things affords no simile; for, as far as the voice of woman, when attuned by gentleness and love, transcends all other sounds in harmony, so far does it surpass all others in discord, when stretched into unnatural shrillness by anger and impatience.

Mr Glowry used to say that his house was no better than a spacious kennel, for every one in it led the life of a dog. Disappointed both in love and in friendship, and looking upon human learning as vanity, he had come to a conclusion that there was but one good thing in the world, *videlicet*, a good dinner; and this his parsimonious lady seldom suffered him to enjoy: but, one morning, like Sir Leoline in Christabel, 'he woke and found his lady dead,'[3] and remained a very consolate widower, with one small child.

This only son and heir Mr Glowry had christened Scythrop,[4] from the name of a maternal ancestor, who had hanged himself one rainy day in a fit of *tædium vitæ*, and had been eulogised by a coroner's jury in the comprehensive phrase of *felo de se*; on which account, Mr Glowry held his memory in high honour, and made a punchbowl of his skull.

When Scythrop grew up, he was sent, as usual, to a public school, where a little learning was painfully beaten into him, and from thence to the university, where it was carefully taken out of him; and he was sent home like a well-threshed ear of corn, with nothing in his head: having finished his education to the high satisfaction of the master and fellows of his college, who had, in testimony of their approbation, presented him with a silver fish-slice, on which his name figured at the head of a laudatory inscription in some semi-barbarous dialect of Anglo-Saxonised Latin.

His fellow-students, however, who drove tandem and random [5] in great perfection, and were connoisseurs in good inns, had taught him to drink deep ere he departed. [6] He had passed much of his time with these choice spirits, and had seen the rays of the midnight lamp tremble on many a lengthening file of empty bottles. He passed his vacations sometimes at Nightmare Abbey, sometimes in London, at the house of his uncle, Mr Hilary, a very cheerful and elastic gentleman, who had married the sister of the melancholy Mr Glowry. The company that frequented his house was the gayest of the gay. Scythrop danced with the ladies and drank with the gentlemen, and was pronounced by both a very accomplished charming fellow, and an honour to the university.

At the house of Mr Hilary, Scythrop first saw the beautiful Miss Emily Girouette. [7] He fell in love; which is nothing new. He was favourably received; which is nothing strange. Mr Glowry and Mr Girouette had a meeting on the occasion, and quarrelled about the terms of the bargain; which is neither new nor strange. The lovers were torn asunder, weeping and vowing everlasting constancy; and, in three weeks after this tragical event, the lady was led a smiling bride to the altar, by the Honourable Mr Lackwit; which is neither strange nor new.

Scythrop received this intelligence at Nightmare Abbey, and was half distracted on the occasion. It was his first disappointment, and preyed deeply on his sensitive spirit. His father, to comfort him, read him a Commentary on Ecclesiastes, which he had himself composed, and which demonstrated incontrovertibly that all is vanity. He insisted particularly on the text, 'One man among a thousand have I found, but a woman amongst all those have I not found.'

'How could he expect it,' said Scythrop, 'when the whole thousand were locked up in his seraglio? [8] His experience is no precedent for a free state of society like that in which we live.'

'Locked up or at large,' said Mr Glowry, 'the result is the

same: their minds are always locked up, and vanity and interest keep the key. I speak feelingly, Scythrop.'

'I am sorry for it, sir,' said Scythrop. 'But how is it that their minds are locked up? The fault is in their artificial education, which studiously models them into mere musical dolls, to be set out for sale in the great toy-shop of society.'

'To be sure,' said Mr Glowry, 'their education is not so well finished as yours has been; and your idea of a musical doll is good. I bought one myself, but it was confoundedly out of tune; but, whatever be the cause, Scythrop, the effect is certainly this, that one is pretty nearly as good as another, as far as any judgment can be formed of them before marriage. It is only after marriage that they show their true qualities, as I know by bitter experience. Marriage is, therefore, a lottery, and the less choice and selection a man bestows on his ticket the better; for, if he has incurred considerable pains and expense to obtain a lucky number, and his lucky number proves a blank, he experiences not a simple, but a complicated disappointment; the loss of labour and money being superadded to the disappointment of drawing a blank, which, constituting simply and entirely the grievance of him who has chosen his ticket at random, is, from its simplicity, the more endurable.' This very excellent reasoning was thrown away upon Scythrop, who retired to his tower as dismal and disconsolate as before.

The tower which Scythrop inhabited stood at the south-eastern angle of the Abbey; and, on the southern side, the foot of the tower opened on a terrace, which was called the garden, though nothing grew on it but ivy, and a few amphibious weeds. The south-western tower, which was ruinous and full of owls, might, with equal propriety, have been called the aviary. This terrace or garden, or terrace-garden, or garden-terrace (the reader may name it *ad libitum*), took in an oblique view of the open sea, and fronted a long tract of level sea-coast, and a fine monotony of fens and windmills.

The reader will judge, from what we have said, that this building was a sort of castellated abbey; and it will, probably, occur to him to inquire if it had been one of the strong-holds of the ancient church militant. Whether this was the case, or how far it had been indebted to the taste of Mr Glowry's ancestors for any transmutations from its original state, are, unfortunately, circumstances not within the pale of our knowledge.

The north-western tower contained the apartments of Mr Glowry. The moat at its base, and the fens beyond, comprised the whole of his prospect. This moat surrounded the Abbey, and was in immediate contact with the walls on every side but the south.

The north-eastern tower was appropriated to the domestics, whom Mr Glowry always chose by one of two criterions, – a long face, or a dismal name. His butler was Raven; his steward was Crow; his valet was Skellet. Mr Glowry maintained that the valet was of French extraction, and that his name was Squelette. His grooms were Mattocks and Graves. On one occasion, being in want of a footman, he received a letter from a person signing himself Diggory Deathshead, and lost no time in securing this acquisition; but on Diggory's arrival, Mr Glowry was horror-struck by the sight of a round ruddy face, and a pair of laughing eyes. Deathshead was always grinning, – not a ghastly smile, but the grin of a comic mask; and disturbed the echoes of the hall with so much unhallowed laughter, that Mr Glowry gave him his discharge. Diggory, however, had staid long enough to make conquests of all the old gentleman's maids, and left him a flourishing colony of young Deathsheads to join chorus with the owls, that had before been the exclusive choristers of Nightmare Abbey.

The main body of the building was divided into rooms of state, spacious apartments for feasting, and numerous bed-rooms for visitors, who, however, were few and far between.

Family interests compelled Mr Glowry to receive occasional visits from Mr and Mrs Hilary, who paid them from the same motive; and, as the lively gentleman on these occasions found few conductors for his exuberant gaiety, he became like a double-charged electric jar, which often exploded in some burst of outrageous merriment to the signal discomposure of Mr Glowry's nerves.

Another occasional visitor, much more to Mr Glowry's taste, was Mr Flosky,[9] a very lachrymose and morbid gentleman, of some note in the literary world, but in his own estimation of much more merit than name. The part of his character which recommended him to Mr Glowry, was his very fine sense of the grim and the tearful. No one could relate a dismal story with so many minutiæ of supererogatory wretchedness. No one could call up a *raw-head and bloody-bones*[10] with so many adjuncts and circumstances of ghastliness. Mystery was his mental element. He lived in the midst of that visionary world in which nothing is but what is not.[11] He dreamed with his eyes open, and saw ghosts dancing round him at noontide. He had been in his youth an enthusiast for liberty, and had hailed the dawn of the French Revolution as the promise of a day that was to banish war and slavery, and every form of vice and misery, from the face of the earth. Because all this was not done, he deduced that nothing was done; and from this deduction, according to his system of logic, he drew a conclusion that worse than nothing was done; that the overthrow of the feudal fortresses of tyranny and superstition was the greatest calamity that had ever befallen mankind; and that their only hope now was to rake the rubbish together, and rebuild it without any of those loopholes by which the light had originally crept in. To qualify himself for a coadjutor in this laudable task, he plunged into the central opacity of Kantian metaphysics, and lay *perdu* several years in transcendental darkness, till the common daylight of common sense became intolerable to his eyes. He called the sun an *ignis fatuus*; and exhorted all who would listen to his friendly voice, which were about as many as called 'God save King Richard,'[12] to shelter themselves from its delusive radiance in the obscure haunt of Old Philosophy. This word Old had great charms for him. The good old times were always on his lips; meaning the days when polemic theology was in its prime, and rival prelates beat the drum ecclesiastic [13] with Herculean vigour, till the one wound up his series of syllogisms with the very orthodox conclusion of roasting the other.

But the dearest friend of Mr Glowry, and his most welcome guest, was Mr Toobad, the Manichæan Millenarian.[14] The twelfth verse of the twelfth chapter of Revelations was always in his mouth: 'Woe to the inhabiters of the earth and of the sea! for the devil is come among you, having great wrath, because he knoweth that he hath but a short time.' He maintained that the supreme dominion of the world was, for wise purposes, given over for a while to the Evil Principle; and that this precise period of time, commonly called the enlightened age, was the point of his plenitude of power. He used to add that by and by he would be cast down, and a high and happy order of things succeed; but he never omitted the saving clause, 'Not in our time'; which last words were always echoed in doleful response by the sympathetic Mr Glowry.

Another and very frequent visitor, was the Reverend Mr Larynx, the vicar of Claydyke, a village about ten miles distant; – a good-natured accommodating divine, who was always most obligingly ready to take a dinner and a bed at the house of any country gentleman in distress for a companion. Nothing came amiss to him, – a game at billiards, at chess, at draughts, at backgammon, at piquet, or at allfours [15] in a tête-à-tête, – or any game on the cards, round, square, or triangular, in a party of any number exceeding two. He would even dance among friends, rather than that a lady, even if she were on the wrong side of thirty, should sit still for want of a partner. For a ride, a walk, or a sail, in the morning, – a song after dinner, a ghost story after supper, – a bottle of port with the squire, or a cup of green tea with his lady, – for all or any of these, or for any thing else that was agreeable to any one else, consistently with the dye of his coat, the Reverend Mr Larynx was at all times equally ready. When at Nightmare Abbey, he would condole with Mr Glowry, – drink Madeira with Scythrop, –

crack jokes with Mr Hilary, – hand Mrs Hilary to the piano, take charge of her fan and gloves, and turn over her music with surprising dexterity, – quote Revelations with Mr Toobad, – and lament the good old times of feudal darkness with the transcendental Mr Flosky.

*

CHAPTER II

SHORTLY after the disastrous termination of Scythrop's passion for Miss Emily Girouette, Mr Glowry found himself, much against his will, involved in a lawsuit, which compelled him to dance attendance on the High Court of Chancery. Scythrop was left alone at Nightmare Abbey. He was a burnt child, and dreaded the fire of female eyes. He wandered about the ample pile, or along the garden-terrace, with 'his cogitative faculties immersed in cogibundity of cogitation.'[1] The terrace terminated at the south-western tower, which, as we have said, was ruinous and full of owls. Here would Scythrop take his evening seat, on a fallen fragment of mossy stone, with his back resting against the ruined wall, – a thick canopy of ivy, with an owl in it, over his head, – and the Sorrows of Werter in his hand. He had some taste for romance reading before he went to the university, where, we must confess, in justice to his college, he was cured of the love of reading in all its shapes; and the cure would have been radical, if disappointment in love, and total solitude, had not conspired to bring on a relapse. He began to devour romances and German tragedies, and, by the recommendation of Mr Flosky, to pore over ponderous tomes of transcendental philosophy, which reconciled him to the labour of studying them by their mystical jargon and necromantic imagery. In the congenial solitude of Nightmare Abbey, the distempered ideas of metaphysical romance and romantic metaphysics had ample time and space to germinate into a fertile crop of chimeras, which rapidly shot up into vigorous and abundant vegetation.

He now became troubled with the *passion for reforming the world*.[2] He built many castles in the air, and peopled them with secret tribunals, and bands of illuminati,[3] who were always the imaginary instruments of his projected regeneration of the human species. As he intended to institute a perfect republic, he invested himself with absolute sovereignty over these mystical dispensers of liberty. He slept with Horrid Mysteries[4] under his pillow, and dreamed of venerable eleutherarchs[5] and ghastly confederates holding midnight conventions in subterranean caves. He passed whole mornings in his study, immersed in gloomy reverie, stalking about the room in his nightcap, which he pulled over his eyes like a cowl, and folding his striped calico dressing-gown about him like the mantle of a conspirator.

'Action,' thus he soliloquised, 'is the result of opinion,[6] and to new-model opinion would be to new-model society. Knowledge is power; it is in the hands of a few, who employ it to mislead the many, for their own selfish purposes of aggrandisement and appropriation. What if it were in the hands of a few who should employ it to lead the many? What if it were universal, and the multitude were enlightened? No. The many must be always in leading-strings; but let them have wise and honest conductors. A few to think, and many to act; that is the only basis of perfect society. So thought the ancient philosophers: they had their esoterical and exoterical doctrines. So thinks the sublime Kant, who delivers his oracles in language which none but the initiated can comprehend. Such were the views of those secret associations of illuminati, which were the terror of superstition and tyranny, and which, carefully selecting wisdom and genius from the great wilderness of society, as the bee selects honey from the flowers of the thorn and the nettle, bound all human excellence in a chain, which, if it had not been prematurely broken, would have commanded opinion, and regenerated the world.'

Scythrop proceeded to meditate on the practicability of reviving a confederation of regenerators. To get a clear view of his own ideas, and to feel the pulse of the wisdom and genius of the age, he wrote and published a treatise,[7] in which his meanings were carefully wrapt up in the monk's hood of transcendental technology, but filled with hints of matter deep and dangerous, which he thought would set the whole nation in a ferment; and he awaited the result in awful expectation, as a miner who has fired a train awaits the explosion of a rock. However, he listened and heard nothing; for the explosion, if any ensued, was not sufficiently loud to shake a single leaf of the ivy on the towers of Nightmare Abbey; and some months afterwards he received a letter from his bookseller, informing him that only seven copies had been sold, and concluding with a polite request for the balance.

Scythrop did not despair. 'Seven copies,' he thought, 'have been sold. Seven is a mystical number, and the omen is good. Let me find the seven purchasers of my seven copies, and they shall be the seven golden candle-sticks with which I will illuminate the world.'

Scythrop had a certain portion of mechanical genius, which his romantic projects tended to develope. He constructed models of cells and recesses, sliding panels and secret passages, that would have baffled the skill of the Parisian police. He took the opportunity of his father's absence to smuggle a dumb carpenter into the Abbey, and between them they gave reality to one of these models in Scythrop's tower. Scythrop foresaw that a great leader of human regeneration would be involved in fearful dilemmas, and determined, for the benefit of mankind in general, to adopt all possible precautions for the preservation of himself.

The servants, even the women, had been tutored into silence. Profound stillness reigned throughout and around the Abbey, except when the occasional shutting of a door would peal in long reverberations through the galleries, or the heavy tread of the pensive butler would wake the hollow

echoes of the hall. Scythrop stalked about like the grand
inquisitor, and the servants flitted past him like familiars.
In his evening meditations on the terrace, under the ivy
of the ruined tower, the only sounds that came to his ear
were the rustling of the wind in the ivy, the plaintive voices
of the feathered choristers, the owls, the occasional striking
of the Abbey clock, and the monotonous dash of the sea on
its low and level shore. In the mean time, he drank Madeira,
and laid deep schemes for a thorough repair of the crazy
fabric of human nature.

*

CHAPTER III

MR GLOWRY returned from London with the loss of his
lawsuit. Justice was with him, but the law was against him.
He found Scythrop in a mood most sympathetically tragic;
and they vied with each other in enlivening their cups by la-
menting the depravity of this degenerate age, and occasionally interspersing divers grim jokes about graves, worms,
and epitaphs.[1] Mr Glowry's friends, whom we have mentioned in the first chapter, availed themselves of his return
to pay him a simultaneous visit. At the same time arrived
Scythrop's friend and fellow-collegian, the Honourable Mr
Listless.[2] Mr Glowry had discovered this fashionable young
gentleman in London, 'stretched on the rack of a too easy
chair,'[3] and devoured with a gloomy and misanthropical
nil curo, and had pressed him so earnestly to take the benefit of the pure country air, at Nightmare Abbey, that Mr
Listless, finding it would give him more trouble to refuse
than to comply, summoned his French valet, Fatout, and
told him he was going to Lincolnshire. On this simple hint,
Fatout went to work, and the imperials were packed, and
the post-chariot was at the door, without the Honourable
Mr Listless having said or thought another syllable on the
subject.

Mr and Mrs Hilary brought with them an orphan niece, a daughter of Mr Glowry's youngest sister, who had made a runaway love-match with an Irish officer. The lady's fortune disappeared in the first year: love, by a natural consequence, disappeared in the second: the Irishman himself, by a still more natural consequence, disappeared in the third. Mr Glowry had allowed his sister an annuity, and she had lived in retirement with her only daughter, whom, at her death, which had recently happened, she commended to the care of Mrs Hilary.

Miss Marionetta Celestina O'Carroll[4] was a very blooming and accomplished young lady. Being a compound of the *Allegro Vivace* of the O'Carrolls, and of the *Andante Doloroso* of the Glowries, she exhibited in her own character all the diversities of an April sky. Her hair was light-brown; her eyes hazel, and sparkling with a mild but fluctuating light; her features regular; her lips full, and of equal size; and her person surpassingly graceful. She was a proficient in music. Her conversation was sprightly, but always on subjects light in their nature and limited in their interest: for moral sympathies, in any general sense, had no place in her mind. She had some coquetry, and more caprice, liking and disliking almost in the same moment; pursuing an object with earnestness while it seemed unattainable, and rejecting it when in her power as not worth the trouble of possession.

Whether she was touched with a *penchant* for her cousin Scythrop, or was merely curious to see what effect the tender passion would have on so *outré* a person, she had not been three days in the Abbey before she threw out all the lures of her beauty and accomplishments to make a prize of his heart. Scythrop proved an easy conquest. The image of Miss Emily Girouette was already sufficiently dimmed by the power of philosophy and the exercise of reason: for to these influences, or to any influence but the true one, are usually ascribed the mental cures performed by the great physician Time. Scythrop's romantic dreams had indeed given him many *pure anticipated cognitions*[5] of combinations of beauty and intelligence, which, he had some mis-

givings, were not exactly realised in his cousin Marionetta;
but, in spite of these misgivings, he soon became dis-
tractedly in love; which, when the young lady clearly perceived, she altered her tactics, and assumed as much coldness and reserve as she had before shown ardent and ingenuous attachment. Scythrop was confounded at the
sudden change; but, instead of falling at her feet and re-
questing an explanation, he retreated to his tower, muffled
himself in his nightcap, seated himself in the president's
chair of his imaginary secret tribunal, summoned Marionetta with all terrible formalities, frightened her out of her
wits, disclosed himself, and clasped the beautiful penitent
to his bosom.

While he was acting this reverie – in the moment in which
the awful president of the secret tribunal was throwing
back his cowl and his mantle, and discovering himself to
the lovely culprit as her adoring and magnanimous lover,
the door of the study opened, and the real Marionetta
appeared.

The motives which had led her to the tower were a little
penitence, a little concern, a little affection, and a little fear
as to what the sudden secession of Scythrop, occasioned by
her sudden change of manner, might portend. She had
tapped several times unheard, and of course unanswered;
and at length, timidly and cautiously opening the door, she
discovered him standing up before a black velvet chair,
which was mounted on an old oak table, in the act of throwing open his striped calico dressing-gown, and flinging away
his nightcap – which is what the French call an imposing
attitude.

Each stood a few moments fixed in their respective places
– the lady in astonishment, and the gentleman in confusion.
Marionetta was the first to break silence. 'For heaven's
sake,' said she, 'my dear Scythrop, what is the matter?'

'For heaven's sake, indeed!' said Scythrop, springing
from the table; 'for your sake, Marionetta, and you are my
heaven, – distraction is the matter. I adore you, Marionetta,
and your cruelty drives me mad.' He threw himself at her

knees, devoured her hand with kisses, and breathed a thousand vows in the most passionate language of romance.

Marionetta listened a long time in silence, till her lover had exhausted his eloquence and paused for a reply. She then said, with a very arch look, 'I prithee deliver thyself like a man of this world.'[6] The levity of this quotation, and of the manner in which it was delivered, jarred so discordantly on the high-wrought enthusiasm of the romantic inamorato, that he sprang upon his feet, and beat his forehead with his clenched fist. The young lady was terrified; and, deeming it expedient to soothe him, took one of his hands in hers, placed the other hand on his shoulder, looked up in his face with a winning seriousness, and said, in the tenderest possible tone, 'What would you have, Scythrop?'

Scythrop was in heaven again. 'What would I have? What but you, Marionetta? You, for the companion of my studies, the partner of my thoughts, the auxiliary of my great designs for the emancipation of mankind.'

'I am afraid I should be but a poor auxiliary, Scythrop. What would you have me do?'

'Do as Rosalia does with Carlos,[7] divine Marionetta. Let us each open a vein in the other's arm, mix our blood in a bowl, and drink it as a sacrament of love. Then we shall see visions of transcendental illumination, and soar on the wings of ideas into the space of pure intelligence.'

Marionetta could not reply; she had not so strong a stomach as Rosalia, and turned sick at the proposition. She disengaged herself suddenly from Scythrop, sprang through the door of the tower, and fled with precipitation along the corridors. Scythrop pursued her, crying, 'Stop, stop, Marionetta – my life, my love!' and was gaining rapidly on her flight, when, at an ill-omened corner, where two corridors ended in an angle, at the head of a staircase, he came into sudden and violent contact with Mr Toobad, and they both plunged together to the foot of the stairs, like two billiard-balls into one pocket. This gave the young lady time to escape, and enclose herself in her chamber;

while Mr Toobad, rising slowly, and rubbing his knees and shoulders, said, 'You see, my dear Scythrop, in this little incident, one of the innumerable proofs of the temporary supremacy of the devil; for what but a systematic design and concurrent contrivance of evil could have made the angles of time and place coincide in our unfortunate persons at the head of this accursed staircase?'

'Nothing else, certainly,' said Scythrop: 'you are perfectly in the right, Mr Toobad. Evil, and mischief, and misery, and confusion, and vanity, and vexation of spirit,[8] and death, and disease, and assassination, and war, and poverty, and pestilence, and famine, and avarice, and selfishness, and rancour, and jealousy, and spleen, and malevolence, and the disappointments of philanthropy, and the faithlessness of friendship, and the crosses of love – all prove the accuracy of your views, and the truth of your system; and it is not impossible that the infernal interruption of this fall downstairs may throw a colour of evil on the whole of my future existence.'

'My dear boy,' said Mr Toobad, 'you have a fine eye for consequences.'

So saying, he embraced Scythrop, who retired, with a disconsolate step, to dress for dinner; while Mr Toobad stalked across the hall, repeating, 'Woe to the inhabiters of the earth, and of the sea, for the devil is come among you, having great wrath.'

*

CHAPTER IV

THE flight of Marionetta, and the pursuit of Scythrop, had been witnessed by Mr Glowry, who, in consequence, narrowly observed his son and his niece in the evening; and, concluding from their manner, that there was a better understanding between them than he wished to see, he determined on obtaining the next morning from Scythrop a full and satisfactory explanation. He, therefore, shortly after breakfast, entered Scythrop's tower, with a very grave face, and said, without ceremony or preface, 'So, sir, you are in love with your cousin.'

Scythrop, with as little hesitation, answered, 'Yes, sir.'

'That is candid, at least; and she is in love with you.'

'I wish she were, sir.'

'You know she is, sir.'

'Indeed, sir, I do not.'

'But you hope she is.'

'I do, from my soul.'

'Now that is very provoking, Scythrop, and very disappointing: I could not have supposed that you, Scythrop Glowry, of Nightmare Abbey, would have been infatuated with such a dancing, laughing, singing, thoughtless, careless, merry-hearted thing, as Marionetta – in all respects the reverse of you and me. It is very disappointing, Scythrop. And do you know, sir, that Marionetta has no fortune?'

'It is the more reason, sir, that her husband should have one.'

'The more reason for her; but not for you. My wife had no fortune, and I had no consolation in my calamity. And do you reflect, sir, what an enormous slice this lawsuit has cut out of our family estate? we who used to be the greatest landed proprietors in Lincolnshire.'

'To be sure, sir, we had more acres of fen than any man on this coast: but what are fens to love? What are dykes and windmills to Marionetta?'

'And what, sir, is love to a windmill? Not grist, I am certain: besides, sir, I have made a choice for you. I have made a choice for you, Scythrop. Beauty, genius, accomplishments, and a great fortune into the bargain. Such a lovely, serious creature, in a fine state of high dissatisfaction with the world, and every thing in it. Such a delightful surprise I had prepared for you. Sir, I have pledged my honour to the contract – the honour of the Glowries of Nightmare Abbey: and now, sir, what is to be done?'

'Indeed, sir, I cannot say. I claim, on this occasion, that liberty of action which is the co-natal prerogative of every rational being.'

'Liberty of action, sir? there is no such thing as liberty of action. We are all slaves and puppets of a blind and unpathetic necessity.'

'Very true, sir; but liberty of action, between individuals, consists in their being differently influenced, or modified, by the same universal necessity; so that the results are unconsentaneous, and their respective necessitated volitions clash and fly off in a tangent.'

'Your logic is good, sir: but you are aware, too, that one individual may be a medium of adhibiting to another a mode or form of necessity, which may have more or less influence in the production of consentaneity; and, therefore, sir, if you do not comply with my wishes in this instance (you have had your own way in every thing else), I shall be under the necessity of disinheriting you, though I shall do it with tears in my eyes.' Having said these words, he vanished suddenly, in the dread of Scythrop's logic.

Mr Glowry immediately sought Mrs Hilary, and communicated to her his views of the case in point. Mrs Hilary, as the phrase is, was as fond of Marionetta as if she had been her own child: but – there is always a *but* on these occasions – she could do nothing for her in the way of fortune, as she had two hopeful sons, who were finishing their education at Brazen-nose, and who would not like to encounter any diminution of their prospects, when they should be brought out of the house of mental bondage – i.e. the university – to the land flowing with milk and honey – i.e. the west end of London.

Mrs Hilary hinted to Marionetta, that propriety, and delicacy, and decorum, and dignity, &c. &c. &c.,[1] would require them to leave the Abbey immediately. Marionetta listened in silent submission, for she knew that her inheritance was passive obedience; but, when Scythrop, who had watched the opportunity of Mrs Hilary's departure, entered, and, without speaking a word, threw himself at her

feet in a paroxysm of grief, the young lady, in equal silence
and sorrow, threw her arms round his neck and burst into
tears. A very tender scene ensued, which the sympathetic
susceptibilities of the soft-hearted reader can more accurately imagine than we can delineate. But when Marionetta
hinted that she was to leave the Abbey immediately,
Scythrop snatched from its repository his ancestor's skull,
filled it with Madeira, and presenting himself before Mr
Glowry, threatened to drink off the contents if Mr Glowry
did not immediately promise that Marionetta should not be
taken from the Abbey without her own consent. Mr Glowry,
who took the Madeira to be some deadly brewage, gave the
required promise in dismal panic. Scythrop returned to
Marionetta with a joyful heart, and drank the Madeira by
the way.

Mr Glowry, during his residence in London, had come to
an agreement with his friend Mr Toobad, that a match between Scythrop and Mr Toobad's daughter would be a very
desirable occurrence. She was finishing her education in a
German convent, but Mr Toobad described her as being
fully impressed with the truth of his Ahrimanic philosophy,[2]
and being altogether as gloomy and antithalian[3] a young
lady as Mr Glowry himself could desire for the future mistress of Nightmare Abbey. She had a great fortune in her
own right, which was not, as we have seen, without its
weight in inducing Mr Glowry to set his heart upon her as his
daughter-in-law that was to be; he was therefore very much
disturbed by Scythrop's untoward attachment to Marionetta. He condoled on the occasion with Mr Toobad; who
said, that he had been too long accustomed to the inter-
meddling of the devil in all his affairs, to be astonished at
this new trace of his cloven claw; but that he hoped to out-
wit him yet, for he was sure there could be no comparison
between his daughter and Marionetta in the mind of any
one who had a proper perception of the fact, that, the world
being a great theatre of evil, seriousness and solemnity are
the characteristics of wisdom, and laughter and merriment
make a human being no better than a baboon. Mr Glowry

comforted himself with this view of the subject, and urged Mr Toobad to expedite his daughter's return from Germany. Mr Toobad said he was in daily expectation of her arrival in London, and would set off immediately to meet her, that he might lose no time in bringing her to Nightmare Abbey. 'Then,' he added, 'we shall see whether Thalia or Melpomene – whether the Allegra or the Penserosa – will carry off the symbol of victory.' – 'There can be no doubt,' said Mr Glowry, 'which way the scale will incline, or Scythrop is no true scion of the venerable stem of the Glowries.'

*

CHAPTER V

MARIONETTA felt secure of Scythrop's heart; and notwithstanding the difficulties that surrounded her, she could not debar herself from the pleasure of tormenting her lover, whom she kept in a perpetual fever. Sometimes she would meet him with the most unqualified affection; sometimes with the most chilling indifference; rousing him to anger by artificial coldness – softening him to love by eloquent tenderness – or inflaming him to jealousy by coquetting with the Honourable Mr Listless, who seemed, under her magical influence, to burst into sudden life, like the bud of the evening primrose. Sometimes she would sit by the piano, and listen with becoming attention to Scythrop's pathetic remonstrances; but, in the most impassioned part of his oratory, she would convert all his ideas into a chaos, by striking up some Rondo Allegro, and saying, 'Is it not pretty?' Scythrop would begin to storm; and she would answer him with,

> 'Zitti, zitti, piano, piano,
> Non facciamo confusione,'[1]

or some similar *facezia*, till he would start away from her, and enclose himself in his tower, in an agony of agitation, vowing to renounce her, and her whole sex, for ever; and returning to her presence at the summons of the billet, which she never failed to send with many expressions of penitence and promises of amendment. Scythrop's schemes for regenerating the world, and detecting his seven golden candlesticks, went on very slowly in this fever of his spirit.

Things proceeded in this train for several days; and Mr Glowry began to be uneasy at receiving no intelligence from Mr Toobad; when one evening the latter rushed into the library, where the family and the visitors were assembled, vociferating, 'The devil is come among you, having great wrath!' He then drew Mr Glowry aside into another apartment, and after remaining some time together, they re-entered the library with faces of great dismay, but did not condescend to explain to any one the cause of their discomfiture.

The next morning, early, Mr Toobad departed. Mr Glowry sighed and groaned all day, and said not a word to any one. Scythrop had quarrelled, as usual, with Marionetta, and was enclosed in his tower, in a fit of morbid sensibility. Marionetta was comforting herself at the piano, with singing the airs of *Nina pazza per amore*;[2] and the Honourable Mr Listless was listening to the harmony, as he lay supine on the sofa, with a book in his hand, into which he peeped at intervals. The Reverend Mr Larynx approached the sofa, and proposed a game at billiards.

THE HONOURABLE MR LISTLESS

Billiards! Really I should be very happy; but, in my present exhausted state, the exertion is too much for me. I do not know when I have been equal to such an effort. (*He rang the bell for his valet. Fatout entered.*) Fatout! when did I play at billiards last?

FATOUT

De fourteen December de last year, Monsieur. (*Fatout bowed and retired.*)

THE HONOURABLE MR LISTLESS

So it was. Seven months ago. You see, Mr Larynx; you see, sir. My nerves, Miss O'Carroll, my nerves are shattered. I have been advised to try Bath. Some of the faculty recommend Cheltenham. I think of trying both, as the seasons don't clash. The season, you know, Mr Larynx – the season, Miss O'Carroll – the season is every thing.

MARIONETTA

And health is something. *N'est-ce pas*, Mr Larynx?

THE REVEREND MR LARYNX

Most assuredly, Miss O'Carroll. For, however reasoners may dispute about the *summum bonum*, none of them will deny that a very good dinner is a very good thing: and what is a good dinner without a good appetite? and whence is a good appetite but from good health? Now, Cheltenham, Mr Listless, is famous for good appetites.

THE HONOURABLE MR LISTLESS

The best piece of logic I ever heard, Mr Larynx; the very best, I assure you. I have thought very seriously of Cheltenham: very seriously and profoundly. I thought of it – let me see – when did I think of it? (*He rang again, and Fatout reappeared.*) Fatout! when did I think of going to Cheltenham, and did not go?

FATOUT

De Juillet twenty-von, de last summer, Monsieur. (*Fatout retired.*)

THE HONOURABLE MR LISTLESS

So it was. An invaluable fellow that, Mr Larynx – invaluable, Miss O'Carroll.

MARIONETTA

So I should judge, indeed. He seems to serve you as a walking memory, and to be a living chronicle, not of your actions only, but of your thoughts.

THE HONOURABLE MR LISTLESS

An excellent definition of the fellow, Miss O'Carroll, – excellent, upon my honour. Ha! ha! he! Heigho! Laughter is pleasant, but the exertion is too much for me.

A parcel was brought in for Mr Listless; it had been sent express. Fatout was summoned to unpack it; and it proved to contain a new novel, and a new poem, both of which had long been anxiously expected by the whole host of fashionable readers; and the last number of a popular Review, of which the editor and his coadjutors were in high favour at court, and enjoyed ample pensions[3] for their services to church and state. As Fatout left the room, Mr Flosky entered, and curiously inspected the literary arrivals.

MR FLOSKY

(*Turning over the leaves.*) 'Devilman, a novel.'[4] Hm. Hatred – revenge – misanthropy – and quotations from the Bible. Hm. This is the morbid anatomy[5] of black bile. – 'Paul Jones,[6] a poem.' Hm. I see how it is. Paul Jones, an amiable enthusiast – disappointed in his affections – turns pirate from ennui and magnanimity – cuts various masculine throats, wins various feminine hearts – is hanged at the yard-arm! The catastrophe is very awkward, and very unpoetical. – 'The Downing Street Review.' Hm. First article – An Ode to the Red Book,[7] by Roderick Sackbut,[8] Esquire. Hm. His own poem reviewed by himself. Hm-m-m.

(*Mr Flosky proceeded in silence to look over the other articles of the review; Marionetta inspected the novel, and Mr Listless the poem.*)

THE REVEREND MR LARYNX

For a young man of fashion and family, Mr Listless, you seem to be of a very studious turn.

THE HONOURABLE MR LISTLESS

Studious! You are pleased to be facetious, Mr Larynx. I hope you do not suspect me of being studious. I have finished my education. But there are some fashionable books that one must read, because they are ingredients of the talk of the day; otherwise, I am no fonder of books than I dare say you yourself are, Mr Larynx.

THE REVEREND MR LARYNX

Why, sir, I cannot say that I am indeed particularly fond of books; yet neither can I say that I never do read. A tale or a poem, now and then, to a circle of ladies over their work, is no very heterodox employment of the vocal energy. And I must say, for myself, that few men have a more Job-like endurance of the eternally recurring questions and answers that interweave themselves, on these occasions, with the crisis of an adventure, and heighten the distress of a tragedy.

THE HONOURABLE MR LISTLESS

And very often make the distress when the author has omitted it.

MARIONETTA

I shall try your patience some rainy morning, Mr Larynx; and Mr Listless shall recommend us the very newest new book, that every body reads.

THE HONOURABLE MR LISTLESS

You shall receive it, Miss O'Carroll, with all the gloss of novelty; fresh as a ripe green-gage in all the downiness of its bloom. A mail-coach copy from Edinburgh, forwarded express from London.

MR FLOSKY

This rage for novelty is the bane of literature. Except my works and those of my particular friends, nothing is good that is not as old as Jeremy Taylor: and, *entre nous*, the best parts of my friends' books were either written or suggested by myself.[9]

THE HONOURABLE MR LISTLESS

Sir, I reverence you. But I must say, modern books are very consolatory and congenial to my feelings. There is, as it were, a delightful north-east wind, an intellectual blight breathing through them; a delicious misanthropy and discontent, that demonstrates the nullity of virtue and energy, and puts me in good humour with myself and my sofa.

MR FLOSKY

Very true, sir. Modern literature is a north-east wind – a blight of the human soul. I take credit to myself for having helped to make it so. The way to produce fine fruit is to blight the flower. You call this a paradox. Marry, so be it. Ponder thereon.

The conversation was interrupted by the re-appearance of Mr Toobad, covered with mud. He just showed himself at the door, muttered 'The devil is come among you!' and vanished. The road which connected Nightmare Abbey with the civilised world, was artificially raised above the level of the fens, and ran through them in a straight line as far as the eye could reach, with a ditch on each side, of which the water was rendered invisible by the aquatic vegetation that covered the surface. Into one of these ditches the sudden action of a shy horse, which took fright at a windmill, had precipitated the travelling chariot of Mr Toobad, who had been reduced to the necessity of scrambling in dismal plight through the window. One of the wheels was found to be broken; and Mr Toobad, leaving the postilion to get the chariot as well as he could to Claydyke for the purpose of cleaning and repairing, had walked back to Nightmare Abbey, followed by his servant with the imperial, and repeating all the way his favourite quotation from the Revelations.

*

CHAPTER VI

MR TOOBAD had found his daughter Celinda in London, and after the first joy of meeting was over, told her he had a husband ready for her. The young lady replied, very gravely, that she should take the liberty to choose for herself. Mr Toobad said he saw the devil was determined to interfere with all his projects, but he was resolved on his own part, not to have on his conscience the crime of passive obedience and non-resistance to Lucifer, and therefore she should marry the person he had chosen for her. Miss Toobad replied, *très posément*, she assuredly would not. 'Celinda, Celinda,' said Mr Toobad, 'you most assuredly shall.' – 'Have I not a fortune in my own right, sir?' said Celinda. 'The more is the pity,' said Mr Toobad: 'but I can find means, miss; I can find means. There are more ways than one of breaking in obstinate girls.' They parted for the night with the expression of opposite resolutions, and in the morning the young lady's chamber was found empty, and what was become of her Mr Toobad had no clue to conjecture. He continued to investigate town and country in search of her; visiting and revisiting Nightmare Abbey at intervals, to consult with his friend, Mr Glowry. Mr Glowry agreed with Mr Toobad that this was a very flagrant instance of filial disobedience and rebellion; and Mr Toobad declared, that when he discovered the fugitive, she should find that 'the devil was come unto her, having great wrath.'

In the evening, the whole party met, as usual, in the

library. Marionetta sat at the harp; the Honourable Mr Listless sat by her and turned over her music, though the exertion was almost too much for him. The Reverend Mr Larynx relieved him occasionally in this delightful labour. Scythrop, tormented by the demon Jealousy, sat in the corner biting his lips and fingers. Marionetta looked at him every now and then with a smile of most provoking good humour, which he pretended not to see, and which only the more exasperated his troubled spirit. He took down a volume of Dante, and pretended to be deeply interested in the Purgatorio, though he knew not a word he was reading, as Marionetta was well aware; who, tripping across the room, peeped into his book, and said to him, 'I see you are in the middle of Purgatory.' – 'I am in the middle of hell,' said Scythrop furiously. 'Are you?' said she; 'then come across the room, and I will sing you the finale of Don Giovanni.'[1]

'Let me alone,' said Scythrop. Marionetta looked at him with a deprecating smile, and said, 'You unjust, cross creature, you.' – 'Let me alone,' said Scythrop, but much less emphatically than at first, and by no means wishing to be taken at his word. Marionetta left him immediately, and returning to the harp, said, just loud enough for Scythrop to hear – 'Did you ever read Dante, Mr Listless? Scythrop is reading Dante, and is just now in Purgatory.' – 'And I,' said the Honourable Mr Listless, 'am not reading Dante, and am just now in Paradise,' bowing to Marionetta.

MARIONETTA

You are very gallant, Mr Listless; and I dare say you are very fond of reading Dante.

THE HONOURABLE MR LISTLESS

I don't know how it is, but Dante never came in my way till lately. I never had him in my collection, and if I had had him I should not have read him. But I find he is growing fashionable,[2] and I am afraid I must read him some wet morning.

MARIONETTA

No, read him some evening, by all means. Were you ever in love, Mr Listless?

THE HONOURABLE MR LISTLESS

I assure you, Miss O'Carroll, never – till I came to Nightmare Abbey. I dare say it is very pleasant; but it seems to give so much trouble that I fear the exertion would be too much for me.

MARIONETTA

Shall I teach you a compendious method of courtship, that will give you no trouble whatever?

THE HONOURABLE MR LISTLESS

You will confer on me an inexpressible obligation. I am all impatience to learn it.

MARIONETTA

Sit with your back to the lady and read Dante; only be sure to begin in the middle, and turn over three or four pages at once – backwards as well as forwards, and she will immediately perceive that you are desperately in love with her – desperately.

(*The Honourable Mr Listless sitting between Scythrop and Marionetta, and fixing all his attention on the beautiful speaker, did not observe Scythrop, who was doing as she described.*)

THE HONOURABLE MR LISTLESS

You are pleased to be facetious, Miss O'Carroll. The lady would infallibly conclude that I was the greatest brute in town.

MARIONETTA

Far from it. She would say, perhaps, some people have odd methods of showing their affection.

THE HONOURABLE MR LISTLESS

But I should think, with submission –

MR FLOSKY (*joining them from another part of the room*)

Did I not hear Mr Listless observe that Dante is becoming fashionable?

THE HONOURABLE MR LISTLESS

I did hazard a remark to that effect, Mr Flosky, though I speak on such subjects with a consciousness of my own nothingness, in the presence of so great a man as Mr Flosky. I know not what is the colour of Dante's devils, but as he is certainly becoming fashionable I conclude they are blue; for the blue devils, as it seems to me, Mr Flosky, constitute the fundamental feature of fashionable literature.

MR FLOSKY

The blue are, indeed, the staple commodity; but as they will not always be commanded, the black, red, and grey may be admitted as substitutes. Tea, late dinners,[3] and the French Revolution, have played the devil, Mr Listless, and brought the devil into play.

MR TOOBAD (*starting up*)

Having great wrath.

MR FLOSKY

This is no play upon words, but the sober sadness of veritable fact.

THE HONOURABLE MR LISTLESS

Tea, late dinners, and the French Revolution. I cannot exactly see the connection of ideas.

MR FLOSKY

I should be sorry if you could; I pity the man who can see the connection of his own ideas. Still more do I pity him, the connection of whose ideas any other person can see. Sir, the great evil is, that there is too much commonplace light in our moral and political literature; and light is a great enemy to mystery, and mystery is a great friend to enthusiasm. Now the enthusiasm for abstract truth is an exceedingly fine thing, as long as the truth, which is the object of the enthusiasm, is so completely abstract as to be altogether out of the reach of the human faculties; and, in that sense, I have myself an enthusiasm for truth, but in no other, for the pleasure of metaphysical investigation lies in the means, not in the end; and if the end could be found, the pleasure of the means would cease. The mind, to be kept in health, must be kept in exercise. The proper exercise of the mind is elaborate reasoning. Analytical reasoning is a base and mechanical process, which takes to pieces and examines, bit by bit, the rude material of knowledge, and extracts therefrom a few hard and obstinate things called facts, every thing in the shape of which I cordially hate. But synthetical reasoning, setting up as its goal some unattainable abstraction, like an imaginary quantity in algebra, and commencing its course with taking for granted some two assertions which cannot be proved, from the union of these two assumed truths produces a third assumption, and so on in infinite series, to the unspeakable benefit of the human intellect. The beauty of this process is, that at every step it strikes out into two branches, in a compound ratio of ramification; so that you are perfectly sure of losing your way, and keeping your mind in perfect health, by the perpetual exercise of an interminable quest; and for these reasons I have christened my eldest son Emanuel Kant Flosky.[4]

THE REVEREND MR LARYNX

Nothing can be more luminous.

THE HONOURABLE MR LISTLESS

And what has all that to do with Dante, and the blue devils?

MR HILARY

Not much, I should think, with Dante, but a great deal with the blue devils.

MR FLOSKY

It is very certain, and much to be rejoiced at, that our literature is hag-ridden. Tea has shattered our nerves; late dinners make us slaves of indigestion; the French Revolution has made us shrink from the name of philosophy, and has destroyed, in the more refined part of the community (of which number I am one), all enthusiasm for political liberty. That part of the *reading public* [5] which shuns the solid food of reason for the light diet of fiction, requires a perpetual adhibition of *sauce piquante* to the palate of its depraved imagination. It lived upon ghosts, goblins, and skeletons (I and my friend Mr Sackbut served up a few of the best), till even the devil himself, though magnified to the size of Mount Athos, became too base, common, and popular, [6] for its surfeited appetite. The ghosts have therefore been laid, and the devil has been cast into outer darkness, and now the delight of our spirits is to dwell on all the vices and blackest passions of our nature, tricked out in a masquerade dress of heroism and disappointed benevolence; the whole secret of which lies in forming combinations that contradict all our experience, and affixing the purple shred [7] of some particular virtue to that precise character, in which we should be most certain not to find it in the living world; and making this single virtue not only redeem all the real and manifest vices of the character, but make them actually pass for necessary adjuncts, and indispensable accompaniments and characteristics of the said virtue.

MR TOOBAD

That is, because the devil is come among us, and finds it for his interest to destroy all our perceptions of the distinctions of right and wrong.

MARIONETTA

I do not precisely enter into your meaning, Mr Flosky, and should be glad if you would make it a little more plain to me.

MR FLOSKY

One or two examples will do it, Miss O'Carroll. If I were to take all the mean and sordid qualities of a money-dealing Jew, and tack on to them, as with a nail, the quality of extreme benevolence, I should have a very decent hero for a modern novel; and should contribute my quota to the fashionable method of administering a mass of vice, under a thin and unnatural covering of virtue, like a spider wrapt in a bit of gold leaf, and administered as a wholesome pill. On the same principle, if a man knocks me down, and takes my purse and watch by main force, I turn him to account, and set him forth in a tragedy as a dashing young fellow, disinherited for his romantic generosity, and full of a most amiable hatred of the world in general, and his own country in particular, and of a most enlightened and chivalrous affection for himself: then, with the addition of a wild girl to fall in love with him, and a series of adventures in which they break all the Ten Commandments in succession (always, you will observe, for some sublime motive, which must be carefully analysed in its progress), I have as amiable a pair of tragic characters as ever issued from that new region of the belles lettres, which I have called the Morbid Anatomy of Black Bile, and which is greatly to be admired and rejoiced at, as affording a fine scope for the exhibition of mental power.

MR HILARY

Which is about as well employed as the power of a hot-house would be in forcing up a nettle to the size of an elm. If we go on in this way, we shall have a new art of poetry, of which one of the first rules will be: To remember to forget that there are any such things as sunshine and music in the world.

THE HONOURABLE MR LISTLESS

It seems to be the case with us at present, or we should not have interrupted Miss O'Carroll's music with this exceedingly dry conversation.

MR FLOSKY

I should be most happy if Miss O'Carroll would remind us that there are yet both music and sunshine –

THE HONOURABLE MR LISTLESS

In the voice and the smile of beauty. May I entreat the favour of – (*turning over the pages of music.*)

All were silent, and Marionetta sung:

> Why are thy looks so blank, grey friar?
>   Why are thy looks so blue?
> Thou seem'st more pale and lank, grey friar,
>   Than thou wast used to do: –
>   Say, what has made thee rue?
>
> Thy form was plump, and a light did shine
>   In thy round and ruby face,
> Which showed an outward visible sign
>   Of an inward spiritual grace: –
>   Say, what has changed thy case?
>
> Yet will I tell thee true, grey friar,
>   I very well can see,
> That, if thy looks are blue, grey friar,
>   'Tis all for love of me, –
>   'Tis all for love of me.
>
> But breathe not thy vows to me, grey friar,
>   Oh, breathe them not, I pray;
> For ill beseems in a reverend friar,
>   The love of a mortal may;[8]
>   And I needs must say thee nay.

But, could'st thou think my heart to move
　　With that pale and silent scowl?
Know, he who would win a maiden's love,
　　Whether clad in cap or cowl,
　　Must be more of a lark than an owl.

Scythrop immediately replaced Dante on the shelf, and
joined the circle round the beautiful singer. Marionetta
gave him a smile of approbation that fully restored his
complacency, and they continued on the best possible terms
during the remainder of the evening. The Honourable Mr
Listless turned over the leaves with double alacrity, saying,
'You are severe upon invalids, Miss O'Carroll: to escape
your satire, I must try to be sprightly, though the exertion
is too much for me.'

*

CHAPTER VII

A NEW visitor arrived at the Abbey, in the person of Mr
Asterias,[1] the ichthyologist. This gentleman had passed his
life in seeking the living wonders of the deep through the
four quarters of the world; he had a cabinet of stuffed and
dried fishes, of shells, sea-weeds, corals, and madrepores,
that was the admiration and envy of the Royal Society.
He had penetrated into the watery den of the Sepia Octopus,
disturbed the conjugal happiness of that turtle-dove of the
ocean, and come off victorious in a sanguinary conflict. He
had been becalmed in the tropical seas, and had watched, in
eager expectation, though unhappily always in vain, to see
the colossal polypus[2] rise from the water, and entwine its
enormous arms round the masts and the rigging. He maintained the origin of all things from water, and insisted that
the polypodes were the first of animated things, and that,
from their round bodies and many-shooting arms, the
Hindoos had taken their gods, the most ancient of deities.
But the chief object of his ambition, the end and aim of his

researches, was to discover a triton and a mermaid, the existence of which he most potently and implicitly believed, and was prepared to demonstrate, *à priori*, *à posteriori*, *à fortiori*, synthetically and analytically, syllogistically and inductively, by arguments deduced both from acknowledged facts and plausible hypotheses. A report that a mermaid had been seen 'sleeking her soft alluring locks'[3] on the sea-coast of Lincolnshire, had brought him in great haste from London, to pay a long-promised and often-postponed visit to his old acquaintance, Mr Glowry.

Mr Asterias was accompanied by his son, to whom he had given the name of Aquarius – flattering himself that he would, in the process of time, become a constellation among the stars of ichthyological science. What charitable female had lent him the mould in which this son was cast, no one pretended to know; and, as he never dropped the most distant allusion to Aquarius's mother, some of the wags of London maintained that he had received the favours of a mermaid, and that the scientific perquisitions which kept him always prowling about the sea-shore, were directed by the less philosophical motive of regaining his lost love.

Mr Asterias perlustrated the sea-coast for several days, and reaped disappointment, but not despair. One night, shortly after his arrival, he was sitting in one of the windows of the library, looking towards the sea, when his attention was attracted by a figure which was moving near the edge of the surf, and which was dimly visible through the moonless summer night. Its motions were irregular, like those of a person in a state of indecision. It had extremely long hair, which floated in the wind. Whatever else it might be, it certainly was not a fisherman. It might be a lady; but it was neither Mrs Hilary nor Miss O'Carroll, for they were both in the library. It might be one of the female servants; but it had too much grace, and too striking an air of habitual liberty, to render it probable. Besides, what should one of the female servants be doing there at this hour, moving to and fro, as it seemed, without any visible purpose? It could scarcely be a stranger; for Claydyke, the nearest village, was ten miles distant; and what female would come ten miles across the fens, for no purpose but to hover over the surf under the walls of Nightmare Abbey? Might it not be a mermaid? It was possibly a mermaid. It was probably a mermaid. It was very probably a mermaid. Nay, what else could it be but a mermaid? It certainly was a mermaid. Mr Asterias stole out of the library on tiptoe, with his finger on his lips, having beckoned Aquarius to follow him.

The rest of the party was in great surprise at Mr Asterias's movement, and some of them approached the window to see if the locality would tend to elucidate the mystery. Presently they saw him and Aquarius cautiously stealing along on the other side of the moat, but they saw nothing more; and Mr Asterias returning, told them, with accents of great disappointment, that he had had a glimpse of a mermaid, but she had eluded him in the darkness, and was gone, he presumed, to sup with some enamoured triton, in a submarine grotto.

'But, seriously, Mr Asterias,' said the Honourable Mr Listless, 'do you positively believe there are such things as mermaids?'

MR ASTERIAS

Most assuredly; and tritons too.

THE HONOURABLE MR LISTLESS

What! things that are half human and half fish?

MR ASTERIAS

Precisely. They are the oran-outangs of the sea. But I am persuaded that there are also complete sea men, differing in no respect from us, but that they are stupid, and covered with scales; for, though our organisation seems to exclude us essentially from the class of amphibious animals, yet anatomists well know that the *foramen ovale* may remain open in an adult, and that respiration is, in that case, not necessary to life: and how can it be otherwise explained that the Indian divers, employed in the pearl fishery, pass whole hours under the water; and that the famous Swedish gardener of Troningholm lived a day and a half under the ice without being drowned? A nereid, or mermaid, was taken in the year 1403 in a Dutch lake,[4] and was in every respect like a French woman, except that she did not speak. Towards the end of the seventeenth century, an English ship, a hundred and fifty leagues from land, in the Greenland seas, discovered a flotilla of sixty or seventy little skiffs, in each of which was a triton, or sea man: at the approach of the English vessel the whole of them, seized with simultaneous fear, disappeared, skiffs and all, under the water, as if they had been a human variety of the nautilus. The illustrious Don Feijoo[5] has preserved an authentic and well-attested story of a young Spaniard, named Francis de la Vega, who, bathing with some of his friends in June, 1674, suddenly dived under the sea and rose no more. His friends thought him drowned; they were plebeians and pious Catholics; but a philosopher might very legitimately have drawn the same conclusion.

THE REVEREND MR LARYNX

Nothing could be more logical.

MR ASTERIAS

Five years afterwards, some fishermen near Cadiz found in their nets a triton, or sea man; they spoke to him in several languages –

THE REVEREND MR LARYNX

They were very learned fishermen.

MR HILARY

They had the gift of tongues by especial favour of their brother fisherman, Saint Peter.

THE HONOURABLE MR LISTLESS

Is Saint Peter the tutelar saint of Cadiz?[6]

(*None of the company could answer this question, and* MR ASTERIAS *proceeded.*)

They spoke to him in several languages, but he was as mute as a fish. They handed him over to some holy friars, who exorcised him; but the devil was mute too. After some days he pronounced the name Lierganes. A monk took him to that village. His mother and brothers recognised and embraced him; but he was as insensible to their caresses as any other fish would have been. He had some scales on his body, which dropped off by degrees; but his skin was as hard and rough as shagreen. He stayed at home nine years, without recovering his speech or his reason: he then disappeared again; and one of his old acquaintance, some years after, saw him pop his head out of the water near the coast of the Asturias. These facts were certified by his brothers, and by Don Gaspardo de la Riba Aguero, Knight of Saint James, who lived near Lierganes, and often had the pleasure of our triton's company to dinner. – Pliny mentions [7] an embassy of the Olyssiponians to Tiberius, to give him intelligence of a triton which had been heard playing on its shell in a certain cave; with several other authenticated facts on the subject of tritons and nereids.

THE HONOURABLE MR LISTLESS

You astonish me. I have been much on the sea-shore, in the season, but I do not think I ever saw a mermaid. (*He rang, and summoned Fatout, who made his appearance half-seas-over.*) Fatout! did I ever see a mermaid?

FATOUT

Mermaid! mer-r-m-m-aid! Ah! merry maid! Oui, monsieur! Yes, sir, very many. I vish dere vas von or two here in de kitchen – ma foi! Dey be all as melancholic as so many tombstone.

THE HONOURABLE MR LISTLESS

I mean, Fatout, an odd kind of human fish.

FATOUT

De odd fish! Ah, oui! I understand de phrase: ve have seen nothing else since ve left town – ma foi!

THE HONOURABLE MR LISTLESS

You seem to have a cup too much, sir.

FATOUT

Nôn; monsieur: de cup too little. De fen be very unwhole-some, and I drink-a-de ponch vid Raven de butler, to keep out de bad air.

THE HONOURABLE MR LISTLESS

Fatout! I insist on your being sober.

FATOUT

Oui, monsieur; I vil be as sober as de révérendissime père Jean.[8] I should be ver glad of de merry maid; but de butler be de odd fish, and he swim in de bowl de ponch. Ah! ah! I do recollect de leetle-a song: – 'About fair maids, and about fair maids, and about my merry maids all.' (*Fatout reeled out, singing.*)

THE HONOURABLE MR LISTLESS

I am overwhelmed: I never saw the rascal in such a condi-tion before. But will you allow me, Mr Asterias, to inquire into the *cui bono* of all the pains and expense you have in-curred to discover a mermaid? The *cui bono*, sir, is the ques-tion I always take the liberty to ask when I see any one taking much trouble for any object. I am myself a sort of Signor Pococurante,[9] and should like to know if there be any thing better or pleasanter, than the state of existing and doing nothing?

MR ASTERIAS

I have made many voyages, Mr Listless, to remote and barren shores: I have travelled over desert and inhospitable lands: I have defied danger – I have endured fatigue – I have submitted to privation. In the midst of these I have experienced pleasures which I would not at any time have exchanged for that of existing and doing nothing. I have

known many evils, but I have never known the worst of all,
which, as it seems to me, are those which are comprehended
in the inexhaustible varieties of *ennui*: spleen, chagrin,
vapours, blue devils, time-killing, discontent, misanthropy,
and all their interminable train of fretfulness, querulous-
ness, suspicions, jealousies, and fears, which have alike
infected society, and the literature of society; and which
would make an arctic ocean of the human mind, if the more
humane pursuits of philosophy and science did not keep
alive the better feelings and more valuable energies of our
nature.

THE HONOURABLE MR LISTLESS

You are pleased to be severe upon our fashionable belles
lettres.

MR ASTERIAS

Surely not without reason, when pirates, highwaymen, and
other varieties of the extensive genus Marauder, are the
only *beau idéal* of the active, as splenetic and railing misanthropy is of the speculative energy. A gloomy brow and a
tragical voice seem to have been of late the characteristics
of fashionable manners: and a morbid, withering, deadly,
antisocial sirocco, loaded with moral and political despair,
breathes through all the groves and valleys of the modern
Parnassus; while science moves on in the calm dignity of its
course, affording to youth delights equally pure and vivid –
to maturity, calm and grateful occupation – to old age, the
most pleasing recollections and inexhaustible materials of
agreeable and salutary reflection; and, while its votary
enjoys the disinterested pleasure of enlarging the intellect
and increasing the comforts of society, he is himself independent of the caprices of human intercourse and the
accidents of human fortune. Nature is his great and inexhaustible treasure. His days are always too short for his
enjoyment: *ennui* is a stranger to his door. At peace with
the world and with his own mind, he suffices to himself,
makes all around him happy, and the close of his

pleasing and beneficial existence is the evening of a
beautiful day.[10]

THE HONOURABLE MR LISTLESS

Really I should like very well to lead such a life myself, but
the exertion would be too much for me. Besides, I have been
at college. I contrive to get through my day by sinking the
morning in bed, and killing the evening in company; dressing and dining in the intermediate space, and stopping the
chinks and crevices of the few vacant moments that remain
with a little easy reading. And that amiable discontent and
antisociality which you reprobate in our present drawing-
room-table literature, I find, I do assure you, a very fine
mental tonic, which reconciles me to my favourite pursuit of
doing nothing, by showing me that nobody is worth doing
any thing for.

MARIONETTA

But is there not in such compositions a kind of unconscious
self-detection, which seems to carry their own antidote
with them? For surely no one who cordially and truly either
hates or despises the world will publish a volume every three
months to say so.

MR FLOSKY

There is a secret in all this, which I will elucidate with a
dusky remark. According to Berkeley, the *esse* of things is
percipi. They exist as they are perceived. But, leaving for
the present, as far as relates to the material world, the
materialists, hyloists, and antihyloists, to settle this point
among them, which is indeed

> A subtle question, raised among
> Those out o' their wits, and those i' the wrong:[11]

for only we transcendentalists are in the right: we may very
safely assert that the *esse* of happiness is *percipi*. It exists
as it is perceived. 'It is the mind that maketh well or ill.'[12]
The elements of pleasure and pain are every where. The

degree of happiness that any circumstances or objects can confer on us depends on the mental disposition with which we approach them. If you consider what is meant by the common phrases, a happy disposition and a discontented temper, you will perceive that the truth for which I am contending is universally admitted.

(*Mr Flosky suddenly stopped: he found himself unintentionally trespassing within the limits of common sense.*)

MR HILARY

It is very true; a happy disposition finds materials of enjoyment every where. In the city, or the country – in society, or in solitude – in the theatre, or the forest – in the hum of the multitude, or in the silence of the mountains, are alike materials of reflection and elements of pleasure. It is one mode of pleasure to listen to the music of 'Don Giovanni,' in a theatre glittering with light, and crowded with elegance and beauty: it is another to glide at sunset over the bosom of a lonely lake, where no sound disturbs the silence but the motion of the boat through the waters. A happy disposition derives pleasure from both, a discontented temper from neither, but is always busy in detecting deficiencies, and feeding dissatisfaction with comparisons. The one gathers all the flowers, the other all the nettles, in its path. The one has the faculty of enjoying every thing, the other of enjoying nothing. The one realises all the pleasure of the present good; the other converts it into pain, by pining after something better, which is only better because it is not present, and which, if it were present, would not be enjoyed. These morbid spirits are in life what professed critics are in literature; they see nothing but faults, because they are predetermined to shut their eyes to beauties. The critic does his utmost to blight genius in its infancy; that which rises in spite of him he will not see; and then he complains of the decline of literature. In like manner, these cankers of society complain of human nature and society, when they have wilfully debarred themselves from all the good they contain, and done their utmost to blight their own happiness and that of all around them. Misanthropy is sometimes the product of disappointed benevolence; but it is more frequently the offspring of overweening and mortified vanity, quarrelling with the world for not being better treated than it deserves.

SCYTHROP (*to Marionetta*)

These remarks are rather uncharitable. There is great good in human nature, but it is at present ill-conditioned. Ardent spirits cannot but be dissatisfied with things as they are; and, according to their views of the probabilities of amelioration, they will rush into the extremes of either hope or despair – of which the first is enthusiasm, and the second misanthropy; but their sources in this case are the same, as the Severn and the Wye run in different directions, and both rise in Plinlimmon.

MARIONETTA

'And there is salmon in both;'[13] for the resemblance is about as close as that between Macedon and Monmouth.

*

CHAPTER VIII

MARIONETTA observed the next day a remarkable perturbation in Scythrop, for which she could not imagine any probable cause. She was willing to believe at first that it had some transient and trifling source, and would pass off in a day or two; but, contrary to this expectation, it daily increased. She was well aware that Scythrop had a strong tendency to the love of mystery, for its own sake; that is to say, he would employ mystery to serve a purpose, but would first choose his purpose by its capability of mystery. He seemed now to have more mystery on his hands than the laws of the system allowed, and to wear his coat of darkness with an air of great discomfort. All her little playful arts lost by degrees much of their power either to irritate or to soothe; and the first perception of her diminished influence produced in her an immediate depression of spirits, and a consequent sadness of demeanour, that rendered her very interesting to Mr Glowry; who, duly considering the improbability of accomplishing his wishes with respect to Miss Toobad (which improbability naturally increased in the diurnal ratio of that young lady's absence), began to reconcile himself by degrees to the idea of Marionetta being his daughter.

Marionetta made many ineffectual attempts to extract from Scythrop the secret of his mystery; and, in despair of drawing it from himself, began to form hopes that she might find a clue to it from Mr Flosky, who was Scythrop's dearest friend, and was more frequently than any other person admitted to his solitary tower. Mr Flosky, however, had ceased to be visible in a morning. He was engaged in the composition of a dismal ballad; and, Marionetta's uneasiness overcoming her scruples of decorum, she determined to seek him in the apartment which he had chosen for his study. She tapped at the door, and at the sound 'Come in,' entered the apartment. It was noon, and the sun was shining in full splendour, much to the annoyance of Mr Flosky, who had obviated the inconvenience by closing the shutters, and drawing the window-curtains. He was sitting at his table by the light of a solitary candle, with a pen in one hand, and a muffineer in the other, with which he occasionally sprinkled salt on the wick, to make it burn blue.[1] He sate with 'his eye in a fine frenzy rolling,'[2] and turned his inspired gaze on Marionetta as if she had been the ghastly ladie of a magical vision; then placed his hand before his eyes, with an appearance of manifest pain – shook his head – withdrew his hand – rubbed his eyes, like a waking man – and said, in a tone of ruefulness most jeremitaylorically pathetic, 'To what am I to attribute this very unexpected pleasure, my dear Miss O'Carroll?'

MARIONETTA

I must apologise for intruding on you, Mr Flosky; but the
interest which I – you – take in my cousin Scythrop –

MR FLOSKY

Pardon me, Miss O'Carroll; I do not take any interest in any
person or thing on the face of the earth; which sentiment, if
you analyse it, you will find to be the quintessence of the
most refined philanthropy.

MARIONETTA

I will take it for granted that it is so, Mr Flosky; I am not
conversant with metaphysical subtleties, but –

MR FLOSKY

Subtleties! my dear Miss O'Carroll. I am sorry to find you
participating in the vulgar error of the *reading public*, to
whom an unusual collocation of words, involving a juxta-
position of antiperistatical ideas,[3] immediately suggests the
notion of hyperoxysophistical paradoxology.[4]

MARIONETTA

Indeed, Mr Flosky, it suggests no such notion to me. I have
sought you for the purpose of obtaining information.

MR FLOSKY (*shaking his head*)

No one ever sought me for such a purpose before.

MARIONETTA

I think, Mr Flosky – that is, I believe – that is, I fancy –
that is, I imagine –

MR FLOSKY

The τουτεστι, the *id est*, the *cioè*, the *c'est à dire*, the *that
is*, my dear Miss O'Carroll, is not applicable in this case – if
you will permit me to take the liberty of saying so. Think is
not synonymous with believe – for belief, in many most im-

portant particulars, results from the total absence, the absolute negation of thought, and is thereby the sane and orthodox condition of mind; and thought and belief are both essentially different from fancy, and fancy, again, is distinct from imagination. This distinction between fancy and imagination is one of the most abstruse and important points of metaphysics. I have written seven hundred pages of promise [5] to elucidate it, which promise I shall keep as faithfully as the bank will its promise to pay.

MARIONETTA

I assure you, Mr Flosky, I care no more about metaphysics than I do about the bank; and, if you will condescend to talk to a simple girl in intelligible terms –

MR FLOSKY

Say not condescend! Know you not that you talk to the most humble of men, to one who has buckled on the armour of sanctity, and clothed himself with humility as with a garment?

MARIONETTA

My cousin Scythrop has of late had an air of mystery about him, which gives me great uneasiness.

MR FLOSKY

That is strange: nothing is so becoming to a man as an air of mystery. Mystery is the very key-stone of all that is beautiful in poetry, all that is sacred in faith, and all that is recondite in transcendental psychology. I am writing a ballad which is all mystery; it is 'such stuff as dreams are made of,' [6] and is, indeed, stuff made of a dream; for, last night I fell asleep as usual over my book, and had a vision of pure reason. [7] I composed five hundred lines in my sleep; [8] so that, having had a dream of a ballad, I am now officiating as my own Peter Quince, and making a ballad of my dream, and it shall be called Bottom's Dream, because it has no bottom. [9]

MARIONETTA

I see, Mr Flosky, you think my intrusion unseasonable, and are inclined to punish it, by talking nonsense to me. (*Mr Flosky gave a start at the word nonsense, which almost overturned the table.*) I assure you, I would not have intruded if I had not been very much interested in the question I wish to ask you. – (*Mr Flosky listened in sullen dignity.*) – My cousin Scythrop seems to have some secret preying on his mind. – (*Mr Flosky was silent.*) – He seems very unhappy – Mr Flosky. – Perhaps you are acquainted with the cause. – (*Mr Flosky was still silent.*) – I only wish to know – Mr Flosky – if it is any thing – that could be remedied by any thing – that any one – of whom I know any thing – could do.

MR FLOSKY (*after a pause*)

There are various ways of getting at secrets. The most approved methods, as recommended both theoretically and practically in philosophical novels, are eavesdropping at key-holes, picking the locks of chests and desks, peeping into letters, steaming wafers, and insinuating hot wire under sealing wax; none of which methods I hold it lawful to practise.

MARIONETTA

Surely, Mr Flosky, you cannot suspect me of wishing to adopt or encourage such base and contemptible arts.

MR FLOSKY

Yet are they recommended, and with well-strung reasons, by writers of gravity and note, as simple and easy methods of studying character, and gratifying that laudable curiosity which aims at the knowledge of man.

MARIONETTA

I am as ignorant of this morality which you do not approve, as of the metaphysics which you do: I should be glad to know by your means, what is the matter with my cousin; I do not like to see him unhappy, and I suppose there is some reason for it.

MR FLOSKY

Now I should rather suppose there is no reason for it: it is the fashion to be unhappy. To have a reason for being so would be exceedingly common-place: to be so without any is the province of genius: the art of being miserable for misery's sake, has been brought to great perfection in our days; and the ancient Odyssey, which held forth a shining example of the endurance of real misfortune, will give place to a modern one, setting out a more instructive picture of querulous impatience under imaginary evils.

MARIONETTA

Will you oblige me, Mr Flosky, by giving me a plain answer to a plain question?

MR FLOSKY

It is impossible, my dear Miss O'Carroll. I never gave a plain answer to a question in my life.

MARIONETTA

Do you, or do you not, know what is the matter with my cousin?

MR FLOSKY

To say that I do not know, would be to say that I am ignorant of something; and God forbid, that a trans-cendental metaphysician, who has pure anticipated cognitions of every thing, and carries the whole science of geometry in his head without ever having looked into Euclid,[10] should fall into so empirical an error as to declare himself ignorant of any thing: to say that I do know, would be to pretend to positive and circumstantial knowledge touching present matter of fact, which, when you consider the nature of evidence, and the various lights in which the same thing may be seen –

MARIONETTA

I see, Mr Flosky, that either you have no information, or are determined not to impart it; and I beg your pardon for having given you this unnecessary trouble.

MR FLOSKY

My dear Miss O'Carroll, it would have given me great pleasure to have said any thing that would have given you pleasure; but if any person living could make report of having obtained any information on any subject from Ferdinando Flosky, my transcendental reputation would be ruined for ever.

*

CHAPTER IX

SCYTHROP grew every day more reserved, mysterious, and *distrait*; and gradually lengthened the duration of his diurnal seclusions in his tower. Marionetta thought she perceived in all this very manifest symptoms of a warm love cooling.

It was seldom that she found herself alone with him in the morning, and, on these occasions, if she was silent in the hope of his speaking first, not a syllable would he utter; if she spoke to him indirectly, he assented monosyllabically; if she questioned him, his answers were brief, constrained, and evasive. Still, though her spirits were depressed, her playfulness had not so totally forsaken her, but that it illuminated at intervals the gloom of Nightmare Abbey; and if, on any occasion, she observed in Scythrop tokens of unextinguished or returning passion, her love of tormenting her lover immediately got the better both of her grief and her sympathy, though not of her curiosity, which Scythrop seemed determined not to satisfy. This playfulness, however, was in a great measure artificial, and usually vanished with the irritable Strephon, to whose annoyance it had been exerted. The Genius Loci, the *tutela* of Nightmare Abbey, the spirit of black melancholy, began to set his seal on her pallescent countenance. Scythrop perceived the change, found his tender sympathies awakened, and did his utmost to comfort the afflicted damsel, assuring her that his seeming inattention had only proceeded from his being involved in a profound meditation on a very hopeful scheme for the regeneration of human society. Marionetta called him ungrateful, cruel, cold-hearted, and accompanied her reproaches with many sobs and tears; poor Scythrop growing every moment more soft and submissive – till, at length, he threw himself at her feet, and declared that no competition of beauty, however dazzling, genius, however transcendent, talents, however cultivated, or philosophy, however enlightened, should ever make him renounce his divine Marionetta.

'Competition!' thought Marionetta, and suddenly, with an air of the most freezing indifference, she said, 'You are perfectly at liberty, sir, to do as you please; I beg you will follow your own plans, without any reference to me.'

Scythrop was confounded. What was become of all her passion and her tears? Still kneeling, he kissed her hand with rueful timidity, and said, in most pathetic accents, 'Do you not love me, Marionetta?'

'No,' said Marionetta, with a look of cold composure: 'No.' Scythrop still looked up incredulously. 'No, I tell you.'

'Oh! very well, madam,' said Scythrop, rising, 'if that is the case, there are those in the world –'

'To be sure there are, sir; – and do you suppose I do not see through your designs, you ungenerous monster?'

'My designs? Marionetta!'

'Yes, your designs, Scythrop. You have come here to cast me off, and artfully contrive that it should appear to be my doing, and not yours, thinking to quiet your tender conscience with this pitiful stratagem. But do not suppose that you are of so much consequence to me: do not suppose it:

you are of no consequence to me at all – none at all: there-fore, leave me: I renounce you: leave me; why do you not leave me?'

Scythrop endeavoured to remonstrate, but without success. She reiterated her injunctions to him to leave her, till, in the simplicity of his spirit, he was preparing to com-ply. When he had nearly reached the door, Marionetta said, 'Farewell.' Scythrop looked back. 'Farewell, Scythrop,' she repeated, 'you will never see me again.'

'Never see you again, Marionetta?'

'I shall go from hence to-morrow, perhaps to-day; and before we meet again, one of us will be married, and we might as well be dead, you know, Scythrop.'

The sudden change of her voice in the last few words, and the burst of tears that accompanied them, acted like electricity on the tender-hearted youth; and, in another instant, a complete reconciliation was accomplished without the intervention of words.

There are, indeed, some learned casuists, who maintain that love has no language, and that all the misunderstand-ings and dissensions of lovers arise from the fatal habit of employing words on a subject to which words are inapplic-able; that love, beginning with looks, that is to say, with the physiognomical expression of congenial mental dispositions, tends through a regular gradation of signs and symbols of affection, to that consummation which is most devoutly to be wished; and that it neither is necessary that there should be, nor probable that there would be, a single word spoken from first to last between two sympathetic spirits, were it not that the arbitrary institutions of society have raised, at every step of this very simple process, so many complicated impediments and barriers in the shape of settlements and ceremonies, parents and guardians, lawyers, Jew-brokers, and parsons, that many an adventurous knight (who, in order to obtain the conquest of the Hes-perian fruit, is obliged to fight his way through all these monsters), is either repulsed at the onset, or vanquished before the achievement of his enterprise: and such a

quantity of unnatural talking is rendered inevitably necessary through all the stages of the progression, that the
tender and volatile spirit of love often takes flight on the
pinions of some of the επεα πτεροεντα, or *winged words*
which are pressed into his service in despite of himself.

At this conjuncture, Mr Glowry entered, and sitting down
near them, said, 'I see how it is; and, as we are all sure to
be miserable do what we may, there is no need of taking
pains to make one another more so; therefore, with God's
blessing and mine, there' – joining their hands as he spoke.

Scythrop was not exactly prepared for this decisive step;
but he could only stammer out, 'Really, sir, you are too
good;' and Mr Glowry departed to bring Mr Hilary to ratify
the act.

Now, whatever truth there may be in the theory of love
and language, of which we have so recently spoken, certain
it is, that during Mr Glowry's absence, which lasted half an
hour, not a single word was said by either Scythrop or
Marionetta.

Mr Glowry returned with Mr Hilary, who was delighted at
the prospect of so advantageous an establishment for his
orphan niece, of whom he considered himself in some manner the guardian, and nothing remained, as Mr Glowry
observed, but to fix the day.

Marionetta blushed, and was silent. Scythrop was also
silent for a time, and at length hesitatingly said, 'My dear
sir, your goodness overpowers me; but really you are so
precipitate.'

Now, this remark, if the young lady had made it, would,
whether she thought it or not – for sincerity is a thing of no
account on these occasions, nor indeed on any other,
according to Mr Flosky – this remark, if the young lady had
made it, would have been perfectly *comme il faut*; but, being
made by the young gentleman, it was *toute autre chose*, and
was, indeed, in the eyes of his mistress, a most heinous and
irremissible offence. Marionetta was angry, very angry, but
she concealed her anger, and said, calmly and coldly,
'Certainly, you are much too precipitate, Mr Glowry. I

assure you, sir, I have by no means made up my mind; and, indeed, as far as I know it, it inclines the other way; but it will be quite time enough to think of these matters seven years hence. Before surprise permitted reply, the young lady had locked herself up in her own apartment.

'Why, Scythrop,' said Mr Glowry, elongating his face exceedingly, 'the devil is come among us sure enough, as Mr Toobad observes: I thought you and Marionetta were both of a mind.'

'So we are, I believe, sir,' said Scythrop, gloomily, and stalked away to his tower.

'Mr Glowry,' said Mr Hilary, 'I do not very well understand all this.'

'Whims, brother Hilary,' said Mr Glowry; 'some little foolish love quarrel, nothing more. Whims, freaks, April showers. They will be blown over by to-morrow.'

'If not,' said Mr Hilary, 'these April showers have made us April fools.'

'Ah!' said Mr Glowry, 'you are a happy man, and in all your afflictions you can console yourself with a joke, let it be ever so bad, provided you crack it yourself. I should be very happy to laugh with you, if it would give you any satisfaction; but, really, at present, my heart is so sad, that I find it impossible to levy a contribution on my muscles.'

*

CHAPTER X

ON the evening on which Mr Asterias had caught a glimpse of a female figure on the sea-shore, which he had translated into the visual sign of his interior cognition[1] of a mermaid, Scythrop, retiring to his tower, found his study preoccupied. A stranger, muffled in a cloak, was sitting at his table. Scythrop paused in surprise. The stranger rose at his entrance, and looked at him intently a few minutes, in silence. The eyes of the stranger alone were visible. All the rest of the figure was muffled and mantled in the folds of a black cloak, which was raised, by the right hand, to the level of the eyes. This scrutiny being completed, the stranger, dropping the cloak, said, 'I see, by your physiognomy, that you may be trusted;' and revealed to the astonished Scythrop a female form and countenance of dazzling grace and beauty, with long flowing hair of raven blackness, and large black eyes of almost oppressive brilliancy, which strikingly contrasted with a complexion of snowy whiteness. Her dress was extremely elegant, but had an appearance of foreign fashion, as if both the lady and her mantua-maker were of 'a far countree.'

> 'I guess 'twas frightful there to see
> A lady so richly clad as she,
> Beautiful exceedingly.'[2]

For, if it be terrible to one young lady to find another under a tree at midnight, it must, *à fortiori*, be much more terrible to a young gentleman to find a young lady in his study at that hour. If the logical consecutiveness of this conclusion be not manifest to my readers, I am sorry for their dulness, and must refer them, for more ample elucidation, to a treatise which Mr Flosky intends to write, on the Categories of Relation, which comprehend Substance and Accident, Cause and Effect, Action and Re-action.

Scythrop, therefore, either was or ought to have been frightened; at all events, he was astonished; and astonishment, though not in itself fear, is nevertheless a good stage towards it, and is, indeed, as it were, the half-way house between respect and terror, according to Mr Burke's graduated scale of the sublime.[3]

'You are surprised,' said the lady; 'yet why should you be surprised? If you had met me in a drawing-room, and I had been introduced to you by an old woman, it would have been a matter of course: can the division of two or three walls, and the absence of an unimportant personage, make the same object essentially different in the perception of a philosopher?'

'Certainly not,' said Scythrop; 'but when any class of objects has habitually presented itself to our perceptions in invariable conjunction with particular relations, then, on the sudden appearance of one object of the class divested of those accompaniments, the essential difference of the relation is, by an involuntary process, transferred to the object itself, which thus offers itself to our perceptions with all the strangeness of novelty.'

'You are a philosopher,' said the lady, 'and a lover of liberty. You are the author of a treatise, called "Philosophical Gas; or, a Project for a General Illumination of the Human Mind."'

'I am,' said Scythrop, delighted at this first blossom of his renown.

'I am a stranger in this country,' said the lady; 'I have been but a few days in it, yet I find myself immediately under the necessity of seeking refuge from an atrocious persecution. I had no friend to whom I could apply; and, in the midst of my difficulties, accident threw your pamphlet in my way. I saw that I had, at least, one kindred mind in this nation, and determined to apply to you.'

'And what would you have me do?' said Scythrop, more and more amazed, and not a little perplexed.

'I would have you,' said the young lady, 'assist me in finding some place of retreat, where I can remain concealed from the indefatigable search that is being made for me. I have been so nearly caught once or twice already, that I cannot confide any longer in my own ingenuity.'

Doubtless, thought Scythrop, this is one of my golden candlesticks. 'I have constructed,' said he, 'in this tower, an entrance to a small suite of unknown apartments in the main building, which I defy any creature living to detect. If you would like to remain there a day or two, till I can find you a more suitable concealment, you may rely on the honour of a transcendental eleutherarch.'

'I rely on myself,' said the lady. 'I act as I please, go where I please, and let the world say what it will. I am rich enough to set it at defiance. It is the tyrant of the poor and

the feeble, but the slave of those who are above the reach of
its injury.'

Scythrop ventured to inquire the name of his fair *protégée*.
'What is a name?' said the lady: 'any name will serve the
purpose of distinction. Call me Stella.⁴ I see by your looks,'
she added, 'that you think all this very strange. When you
know me better, your surprise will cease. I submit not to
be an accomplice in my sex's slavery. I am, like yourself, a
lover of freedom, and I carry my theory into practice.
*They alone are subject to blind authority who have no reliance
on their own strength.*' ⁵

Stella took possession of the recondite apartments. Scythrop intended to find her another asylum; but from day to
day he postponed his intention, and by degrees forgot it.
The young lady reminded him of it from day to day, till
she also forgot it. Scythrop was anxious to learn her
history; but she would add nothing to what she had
already communicated, that she was shunning an atrocious
persecution. Scythrop thought of Lord C. and the Alien
Act, and said, 'As you will not tell your name, I suppose it is
in the green bag.'⁶ Stella, not understanding what he
meant, was silent; and Scythrop, translating silence into
acquiescence, concluded that he was sheltering an *illuminée*⁷
whom Lord S.⁸ suspected of an intention to take the
Tower, and set fire to the Bank: exploits, at least, as likely
to be accomplished by the hands and eyes of a young
beauty, as by a drunken cobbler and doctor, armed with a
pamphlet and an old stocking.

Stella, in her conversations with Scythrop, displayed a
highly cultivated and energetic mind, full of impassioned
schemes of liberty, and impatience of masculine usurpation.
She had a lively sense of all the oppressions that are done
under the sun; and the vivid pictures which her imagination
presented to her of the numberless scenes of injustice and
misery which are being acted at every moment in every
part of the inhabited world, gave an habitual seriousness to
her physiognomy, that made it seem as if a smile had never
once hovered on her lips. She was intimately conversant

with the German language and literature; and Scythrop
listened with delight to her repetitions of her favourite
passages from Schiller and Goethe, and to her encomiums
on the sublime Spartacus Weishaupt,[9] the immortal founder
of the sect of the Illuminati. Scythrop found that his soul
had a greater capacity of love than the image of Marionetta
had filled. The form of Stella took possession of every
vacant corner of the cavity, and by degrees displaced that
of Marionetta from many of the outworks of the citadel;
though the latter still held possession of the *keep*. He
judged, from his new friend calling herself Stella, that, if it
were not her real name, she was an admirer of the principles
of the German play from which she had taken it, and took
an opportunity of leading the conversation to that subject;
but to his great surprise, the lady spoke very ardently of
the singleness and exclusiveness of love, and declared that
the reign of affection was one and indivisible; that it might
be transferred, but could not be participated. 'If I ever
love,' said she, 'I shall do so without limit or restriction. I
shall hold all difficulties light, all sacrifices cheap, all
obstacles gossamer. But for love so total, I shall claim a
return as absolute. I will have no rival: whether more or
less favoured will be of little moment. I will be neither first
nor second – I will be alone. The heart which I shall possess
I will possess entirely, or entirely renounce.'

Scythrop did not dare to mention the name of Marionetta;
he trembled lest some unlucky accident should reveal it to
Stella, though he scarcely knew what result to wish or
anticipate, and lived in the double fever of a perpetual
dilemma. He could not dissemble to himself that he was in
love, at the same time, with two damsels of minds and
habits as remote as the antipodes. The scale of predilection
always inclined to the fair one who happened to be present;
but the absent was never effectually outweighed, though
the degrees of exaltation and depression varied according
to accidental variations in the outward and visible signs of
the inward and spiritual graces of his respective charmers.
Passing and repassing several times a day from the company

of the one to that of the other, he was like a shuttlecock between two battledores, changing its direction as rapidly as the oscillations of a pendulum, receiving many a hard knock on the cork of a sensitive heart, and flying from point to point on the feathers of a super-sublimated head. This was an awful state of things. He had now as much mystery about him as any romantic transcendentalist or trans-cendental romancer could desire. He had his esoterical and his exoterical love. He could not endure the thought of losing either of them, but he trembled when he imagined the possibility that some fatal discovery might deprive him of both. The old proverb concerning two strings to a bow gave him some gleams of comfort; but that concerning two stools occurred to him more frequently, and covered his forehead with a cold perspiration. With Stella, he could indulge freely in all his romantic and philosophical visions. He could build castles in the air, and she would pile towers and turrets on the imaginary edifices. With Marionetta it was otherwise: she knew nothing of the world and society beyond the sphere of her own experience. Her life was all music and sunshine, and she wondered what any one could see to complain of in such a pleasant state of things. She loved Scythrop, she hardly knew why; indeed she was not always sure that she loved him at all: she felt her fondness increase or diminish in an inverse ratio to his. When she had manœuvred him into a fever of passionate love, she often felt and always assumed indifference: if she found that her coldness was contagious, and that Scythrop either was, or pretended to be, as indifferent as herself, she would be-come doubly kind, and raise him again to that elevation from which she had previously thrown him down. Thus, when his love was flowing, hers was ebbing: when his was ebbing, hers was flowing. Now and then there were mo-ments of level tide, when reciprocal affection seemed to promise imperturbable harmony; but Scythrop could scarcely resign his spirit to the pleasing illusion, before the pinnace of the lover's affections was caught in some eddy of the lady's caprice, and he was whirled away from the shore of his hopes, without rudder or compass, into an ocean of mists and storms. It resulted, from this system of conduct, that all that passed between Scythrop and Marionetta consisted in making and unmaking love. He had no opportunity to take measure of her understanding by conversations on general subjects, and on his favourite designs; and, being left in this respect to the exercise of indefinite conjecture, he took it for granted, as most lovers would do in similar circumstances, that she had great natural talents, which she wasted at present on trifles: but coquetry would end with marriage, and leave room for philosophy to exert its influence on her mind. Stella had no coquetry, no disguise: she was an enthusiast in subjects of general interest; and her conduct to Scythrop was always uniform, or rather showed a regular progression of partiality which seemed fast ripening into love.

*

CHAPTER XI

SCYTHROP, attending one day the summons to dinner, found in the drawing-room his friend Mr Cypress[1] the poet, whom he had known at college, and who was a great favourite of Mr Glowry. Mr Cypress said, he was on the point of leaving England, but could not think of doing so without a farewell-look at Nightmare Abbey and his respected friends, the moody Mr Glowry and the mysterious Mr Scythrop, the sublime Mr Flosky and the pathetic Mr Listless; to all of whom, and the morbid hospitality of the melancholy dwelling in which they were then assembled, he assured them he should always look back with as much affection as his lacerated spirit could feel for any thing. The sympathetic condolence of their respective replies was cut short by Raven's announcement of 'dinner on table.'

The conversation that took place when the wine was in circulation, and the ladies were withdrawn, we shall report with our usual scrupulous fidelity.

MR GLOWRY

You are leaving England, Mr Cypress. There is a delightful melancholy in saying farewell to an old acquaintance, when the chances are twenty to one against ever meeting again. A smiling bumper to a sad parting, and let us all be unhappy together.

MR CYPRESS (*filling a bumper*)

This is the only social habit that the disappointed spirit never unlearns.

THE REVEREND MR LARYNX (*filling*)

It is the only piece of academical learning that the finished educatee retains.

MR FLOSKY (*filling*)

It is the only objective fact which the sceptic can realise.

SCYTHROP (*filling*)

It is the only styptic for a bleeding heart.

THE HONOURABLE MR LISTLESS (*filling*)

It is the only trouble that is very well worth taking.

MR ASTERIAS (*filling*)

It is the only key of conversational truth.

MR TOOBAD (*filling*)

It is the only antidote to the great wrath of the devil.

MR HILARY (*filling*)

It is the only symbol of perfect life. The inscription 'HIC NON BIBITUR'[2] will suit nothing but a tombstone.

MR GLOWRY

You will see many fine old ruins, Mr Cypress; crumbling pillars, and mossy walls – many a one-legged Venus and headless Minerva – many a Neptune buried in sand – many a Jupiter turned topsy-turvy – many a perforated Bacchus doing duty as a water-pipe – many reminiscences of the ancient world, which I hope was better worth living in than the modern; though, for myself, I care not a straw more for one than the other, and would not go twenty miles to see any thing that either could show.

MR CYPRESS

It is something to seek, Mr Glowry. The mind is restless, and must persist in seeking, though to find is to be disappointed. Do you feel no aspirations towards the countries of Socrates and Cicero? No wish to wander among the venerable remains of the greatness that has passed for ever?

MR GLOWRY

Not a grain.

SCYTHROP

It is, indeed, much the same as if a lover should dig up the buried form of his mistress, and gaze upon relics which are any thing but herself, to wander among a few mouldy ruins, that are only imperfect indexes to lost volumes of glory, and meet at every step the more melancholy ruins of human nature – a degenerate race of stupid and shrivelled slaves,[3] grovelling in the lowest depths of servility and superstition.

THE HONOURABLE MR LISTLESS

It is the fashion to go abroad. I have thought of it myself, but am hardly equal to the exertion. To be sure, a little eccentricity and originality are allowable in some cases; and the most eccentric and original of all characters is an Englishman who stays at home.

SCYTHROP

I should have no pleasure in visiting countries that are past all hope of regeneration. There is great hope of our own;

and it seems to me that an Englishman, who, either by his station in society, or by his genius, or (as in your instance, Mr Cypress,) by both, has the power of essentially serving his country in its arduous struggle with its domestic enemies, yet forsakes his country,[4] which is still so rich in hope, to dwell in others which are only fertile in the ruins of memory, does what none of those ancients, whose fragmentary memorials you venerate, would have done in similar circumstances.

MR CYPRESS

Sir, I have quarrelled with my wife;[5] and a man who has quarrelled with his wife is absolved from all duty to his country. I have written an ode to tell the people as much, and they may take it as they list.

SCYTHROP

Do you suppose, if Brutus had quarrelled with his wife, he would have given it as a reason to Cassius for having nothing to do with his enterprise? Or would Cassius have been satisfied with such an excuse?

MR FLOSKY

Brutus was a senator; so is our dear friend:[6] but the cases are different. Brutus had some hope of political good: Mr Cypress has none. How should he, after what we have seen in France?

SCYTHROP

A Frenchman is born in harness, ready saddled, bitted, and bridled, for any tyrant to ride. He will fawn under his rider one moment, and throw him and kick him to death the next; but another adventurer springs on his back, and by dint of whip and spur on he goes as before. We may, without much vanity, hope better of ourselves.

MR CYPRESS

I have no hope for myself or for others. Our life is a false nature; it is not in the harmony of things; it is an all-

blasting upas, whose root is earth, and whose leaves are the
skies which rain their poison-dews upon mankind. We wither
from our youth; we gasp with unslaked thirst for unattainable good; lured from the first to the last by phantoms –
love, fame, ambition, avarice – all idle, and all ill – one
meteor of many names, that vanishes in the smoke of
death.[7]

MR FLOSKY

A most delightful speech, Mr Cypress. A most amiable and
instructive philosophy. You have only to impress its truth
on the minds of all living men, and life will then, indeed,
be the desert and the solitude; and I must do you, myself,
and our mutual friends, the justice to observe, that let
society only give fair play at one and the same time, as I
flatter myself it is inclined to do, to your system of morals,
and my system of metaphysics, and Scythrop's system of
politics, and Mr Listless's system of manners, and Mr Toobad's system of religion, and the result will be as fine a
mental chaos as even the immortal Kant himself could ever
have hoped to see; in the prospect of which I rejoice.

MR HILARY

'Certainly, ancient, it is not a thing to rejoice at:'[8] I am
one of those who cannot see the good that is to result from
all this mystifying and blue-devilling of society. The contrast
it presents to the cheerful and solid wisdom of antiquity is
too forcible not to strike any one who has the least knowledge of classical literature. To represent vice and misery
as the necessary accompaniments of genius, is as mischievous as it is false, and the feeling is as unclassical as
the language in which it is usually expressed.

MR TOOBAD

It is our calamity. The devil has come among us, and has
begun by taking possession of all the cleverest fellows. Yet,
forsooth, this is the enlightened age. Marry, how? Did our
ancestors go peeping about with dark lanterns, and do we

walk at our ease in broad sunshine? Where is the mani-
festation of our light? By what symptoms do you recognise
it? What are its signs, its tokens, its symptoms, its symbols,
its categories, its conditions? What is it, and why? How,
where, when is it to be seen, felt, and understood? What do
we see by it which our ancestors saw not, and which at the
same time is worth seeing? We see a hundred men hanged,
where they saw one. We see five hundred transported,
where they saw one. We see five thousand in the workhouse,
where they saw one. We see scores of Bible Societies, where
they saw none. We see paper, where they saw gold. We see
men in stays, where they saw men in armour. We see painted
faces, where they saw healthy ones. We see children perish-
ing in manufactories, where they saw them flourishing in
the fields. We see prisons, where they saw castles. We see
masters, where they saw representatives.[9] In short, they
saw true men, where we see false knaves. They saw Milton,
and we see Mr Sackbut.

MR FLOSKY

The false knave, sir, is my honest friend; therefore, I be-
seech you, let him be countenanced. God forbid but a knave
should have some countenance at his friend's request.[10]

MR TOOBAD

'Good men and true' was their common term, like the καλος
κἀγαθος[11] of the Athenians. It is so long since men have
been either good or true, that it is to be questioned which
is most obsolete, the fact or the phraseology.

MR CYPRESS

There is no worth nor beauty but in the mind's idea. Love
sows the wind and reaps the whirlwind.[12] Confusion, thrice
confounded, is the portion of him who rests even for an
instant on that most brittle of reeds – the affection of a
human being. The sum of our social destiny is to inflict or
to endure.[13]

MR HILARY

Rather to bear and forbear, Mr Cypress – a maxim which you perhaps despise. Ideal beauty is not the mind's creation: it is real beauty, refined and purified in the mind's alembic, from the alloy which always more or less accompanies it in our mixed and imperfect nature. But still the gold exists in a very ample degree. To expect too much is a disease in the expectant, for which human nature is not responsible; and, in the common name of humanity, I protest against these false and mischievous ravings. To rail against humanity for not being abstract perfection, and against human love for not realising all the splendid visions of the poets of chivalry, is to rail at the summer for not being all sunshine, and at the rose for not being always in bloom.

MR CYPRESS

Human love! Love is not an inhabitant of the earth. We worship him as the Athenians did their unknown God: but broken hearts are the martyrs of his faith, and the eye shall never see the form which phantasy paints, and which passion pursues through paths of delusive beauty, among flowers whose odours are agonies, and trees whose gums are poison.[14]

MR HILARY

You talk like a Rosicrucian,[15] who will love nothing but a sylph, who does not believe in the existence of a sylph, and who yet quarrels with the whole universe for not containing a sylph.

MR CYPRESS

The mind is diseased of its own beauty, and fevers into false creation. The forms which the sculptor's soul has seized exist only in himself.[16]

MR FLOSKY

Permit me to discept. They are the mediums of common forms combined and arranged into a common standard.

The ideal beauty of the Helen of Zeuxis was the combined medium of the real beauty of the virgins of Crotona.

MR HILARY

But to make ideal beauty the shadow in the water, and, like the dog in the fable, to throw away the substance in catching at the shadow, is scarcely the characteristic of wisdom, whatever it may be of genius. To reconcile man as he is to the world as it is, to preserve and improve all that is good, and destroy or alleviate all that is evil, in physical and moral nature – have been the hope and aim of the greatest teachers and ornaments of our species. I will say, too, that the highest wisdom and the highest genius have been invariably accompanied with cheerfulness. We have sufficient proofs on record that Shakspeare and Socrates were the most festive of companions. But now the little wisdom and genius we have seem to be entering into a conspiracy against cheerfulness.

MR TOOBAD

How can we be cheerful with the devil among us?

THE HONOURABLE MR LISTLESS

How can we be cheerful when our nerves are shattered?

MR FLOSKY

How can we be cheerful when we are surrounded by a *reading public*, that is growing too wise for its betters?

SCYTHROP

How can we be cheerful when our great general designs are crossed every moment by our little particular passions?

MR CYPRESS

How can we be cheerful in the midst of disappointment and despair?

MR GLOWRY

Let us all be unhappy together.

MR HILARY

Let us sing a catch.

MR GLOWRY

No: a nice tragical ballad. The Norfolk Tragedy[17] to the tune of the Hundredth Psalm.

MR HILARY

I say a catch.

MR GLOWRY

I say no. A song from Mr Cypress.

ALL

A song from Mr Cypress.

MR CYPRESS *sung* –

There is a fever of the spirit,
  The brand of Cain's unresting doom,[18]
Which in the lone dark souls that bear it
  Glows like the lamp in Tullia's tomb:[19]
Unlike that lamp, its subtle fire
  Burns, blasts, consumes its cell, the heart,
Till, one by one, hope, joy, desire,
  Like dreams of shadowy smoke depart.

When hope, love, life itself, are only
  Dust – spectral memories – dead and cold –
The unfed fire burns bright and lonely,
  Like that undying lamp of old:
And by that drear illumination,
  Till time its clay-built home has rent,
Thought broods on feeling's desolation –
  The soul is its own monument.

MR GLOWRY

Admirable. Let us all be unhappy together.

MR HILARY

Now, I say again, a catch.

THE REVEREND MR LARYNX

I am for you.

MR HILARY

'Seamen three.'

THE REVEREND MR LARYNX

Agreed. I'll be Harry Gill, with the voice of three.[20] Begin

MR HILARY AND THE REVEREND MR LARYNX

Seamen three! What men be ye?
Gotham's three wise men we be.
Whither in your bowl so free?
To rake the moon from out the sea.
The bowl goes trim. The moon doth shine.
And our ballast is old wine;
And your ballast is old wine.

Who art thou, so fast adrift?
I am he they call Old Care.
Here on board we will thee lift.
No: I may not enter there.
Wherefore so? 'Tis Jove's decree,
In a bowl Care may not be;
In a bowl Care may not be.

Fear ye not the waves that roll?
No: in charmed bowl we swim.
What the charm that floats the bowl?
Water may not pass the brim.
The bowl goes trim. The moon doth shine.
And our ballast is old wine;
And your ballast is old wine.

This catch was so well executed by the spirit and science of Mr Hilary, and the deep tri-une voice of the reverend gentleman, that the whole party, in spite of themselves, caught the contagion, and joined in chorus at the conclusion, each raising a bumper to his lips:

The bowl goes trim: the moon doth shine:
And our ballast is old wine.

Mr Cypress, having his ballast on board, stepped, the same evening, into his bowl, or travelling chariot, and departed to rake seas and rivers, lakes and canals,[21] for the moon of ideal beauty.

*

CHAPTER XII

IT was the custom of the Honourable Mr Listless, on adjourning from the bottle to the ladies, to retire for a few moments to make a second toilette, that he might present himself in becoming taste. Fatout, attending as usual, appeared with a countenance of great dismay, and informed his master that he had just ascertained that the abbey was haunted. Mrs Hilary's *gentlewoman*, for whom Fatout had lately conceived a *tendresse*, had been, as she expressed it, 'fritted out of her seventeen senses' the preceding night, as she was retiring to her bedchamber, by a ghastly figure which she had met stalking along one of the galleries, wrapped in a white shroud, with a bloody turban on its head. She had fainted away with fear; and, when she recovered, she found herself in the dark, and the figure was gone. '*Sacre – cochon – bleu!*' exclaimed Fatout, giving very deliberate emphasis to every portion of his terrible oath – 'I vould not meet de *revenant*, de ghost – *non* – not for all de *bowl-de-ponch* in de vorld.'

'Fatout,' said the Honourable Mr Listless, 'did I ever see a ghost?'

'*Jamais*, monsieur, never.'

'Then I hope I never shall, for, in the present shattered state of my nerves, I am afraid it would be too much for me. There – loosen the lace of my stays a little, for really this plebeian practice of eating – Not too loose – consider my shape. That will do. And I desire that you bring me no more stories of ghosts; for, though I do not believe in such things, yet, when one is awake in the night, one is apt, if one thinks of them, to have fancies that give one a kind of a chill, particularly if one opens one's eyes suddenly on one's dressing gown, hanging in the moonlight, between the bed and the window.'

The Honourable Mr Listless, though he had prohibited Fatout from bringing him any more stories of ghosts, could not help thinking of that which Fatout had already brought; and, as it was uppermost in his mind, when he descended to the tea and coffee cups, and the rest of the company in the library, he almost involuntarily asked Mr Flosky, whom he looked up to as a most oraculous personage, whether any story of any ghost that had ever appeared to any one, was entitled to any degree of belief?

MR FLOSKY

By far the greater number, to a very great degree.

THE HONOURABLE MR LISTLESS

Really, that is very alarming!

MR FLOSKY

Sunt geminæ somni portæ.[1] There are two gates through which ghosts find their way to the upper air: fraud and self-delusion. In the latter case, a ghost is a *deceptio visûs*, an ocular spectrum, an idea with the force of a sensation. I have seen many ghosts myself. I dare say there are few in this company who have not seen a ghost.

THE HONOURABLE MR LISTLESS

I am happy to say, I never have, for one.

THE REVEREND MR LARYNX

We have such high authority for ghosts, that it is rank scepticism to disbelieve them. Job saw a ghost, which came for the express purpose of asking a question, and did not wait for an answer.

THE HONOURABLE MR LISTLESS

Because Job was too frightened to give one.

THE REVEREND MR LARYNX

Spectres appeared to the Egyptians during the darkness
with which Moses covered Egypt. The witch of Endor raised
the ghost of Samuel. Moses and Elias appeared on Mount
Tabor. An evil spirit was sent into the army of Sennach-
erib, and exterminated it in a single night.

MR TOOBAD

Saying, The devil is come among you, having great wrath.

MR FLOSKY

Saint Macarius interrogated a skull, which was found in the
desert, and made it relate, in presence of several witnesses,
what was going forward in hell. Saint Martin of Tours,
being jealous of a pretended martyr, who was the rival saint
of his neighbourhood, called up his ghost, and made him
confess that he was damned. Saint Germain, being on his
travels, turned out of an inn a large party of ghosts, who
had every night taken possession of the *table d'hôte,* and
consumed a copious supper.

MR HILARY

Jolly ghosts, and no doubt all friars. A similar party took
possession of the cellar of M. Swebach,[2] the painter, in Paris,
drank his wine, and threw the empty bottles at his head.

THE REVEREND MR LARYNX

An atrocious act.

MR FLOSKY

Pausanias relates,[3] that the neighing of horses and the
tumult of combatants were heard every night on the field
of Marathon: that those who went purposely to hear these

sounds suffered severely for their curiosity; but those who heard them by accident passed with impunity.

THE REVEREND MR LARYNX

I once saw a ghost myself, in my study, which is the last place where any one but a ghost would look for me. I had not been into it for three months, and was going to consult Tillotson,[4] when, on opening the door, I saw a venerable figure in a flannel dressing gown, sitting in my armchair, and reading my Jeremy Taylor. It vanished in a moment, and so did I; and what it was or what it wanted I have never been able to ascertain.

MR FLOSKY

It was an idea with the force of a sensation.[5] It is seldom that ghosts appeal to two senses at once; but, when I was in Devonshire, the following story was well attested to me. A young woman, whose lover was at sea, returning one evening over some solitary fields, saw her lover sitting on a stile over which she was to pass. Her first emotions were surprise and joy, but there was a paleness and seriousness in his face that made them give place to alarm. She advanced towards him, and he said to her, in a solemn voice, 'The eye that hath seen me shall see me no more. Thine eye is upon me, but I am not.' And with these words he vanished; and on that very day and hour, as it afterwards appeared, he had perished by shipwreck.

The whole party now drew round in a circle, and each related some ghostly anecdote, heedless of the flight of time, till, in a pause of the conversation, they heard the hollow tongue of midnight sounding twelve.[6]

MR HILARY

All these anecdotes admit of solution on psychological principles. It is more easy for a soldier, a philosopher, or even a saint, to be frightened at his own shadow, than for a dead man to come out of his grave. Medical writers cite a thousand singular examples of the force of imagination. Persons of feeble, nervous, melancholy temperament, exhausted by fever, by labour, or by spare diet, will readily conjure up, in the magic ring of their own phantasy, spectres, gorgons, chimaeras, and all the objects of their hatred and their love. We are most of us like Don Quixote, to whom a windmill was a giant, and Dulcinea a magnificent princess: all more or less the dupes of our own imagination, though we do not all go so far as to see ghosts, or to fancy ourselves pipkins and teapots.[7]

MR FLOSKY

I can safely say I have seen too many ghosts myself to believe in their external existence.[8] I have seen all kinds of ghosts: black spirits and white, red spirits and grey. Some in the shapes of venerable old men, who have met me in my rambles at noon; some of beautiful young women,[9] who have peeped through my curtains at midnight.

THE HONOURABLE MR LISTLESS

And have proved, I doubt not, 'palpable to feeling as to sight.'[10]

MR FLOSKY

By no means, sir. You reflect upon my purity. Myself and my friends, particularly my friend Mr Sackbut,[11] are famous for our purity. No, sir, genuine untangible ghosts. I live in a world of ghosts. I see a ghost at this moment.

Mr Flosky fixed his eyes on a door at the farther end of the library. The company looked in the same direction. The door silently opened, and a ghastly figure, shrouded in white drapery, with the semblance of a bloody turban on its head, entered and stalked slowly up the apartment. Mr Flosky, familiar as he was with ghosts, was not prepared for this apparition, and made the best of his way out at the opposite door. Mrs Hilary and Marionetta followed, screaming. The Honourable Mr Listless, by two turns of his body,

rolled first off the sofa and then under it. The Reverend Mr
Larynx leaped up and fled with so much precipitation, that
he overturned the table on the foot of Mr Glowry. Mr
Glowry roared with pain in the ear of Mr Toobad. Mr Toobad's alarm so bewildered his senses, that, missing the
door, he threw up one of the windows, jumped out in his
panic, and plunged over head and ears in the moat. Mr
Asterias and his son, who were on the watch for their mermaid, were attracted by the splashing, threw a net over him,
and dragged him to land.

Scythrop and Mr Hilary meanwhile had hastened to his
assistance, and, on arriving at the edge of the moat, followed by several servants with ropes and torches, found
Mr Asterias and Aquarius busy in endeavouring to extri-
cate Mr Toobad from the net, who was entangled in the
meshes, and floundering with rage. Scythrop was lost in
amazement; but Mr Hilary saw, at one view, all the circumstances of the adventure, and burst into an immoderate
fit of laughter; on recovering from which, he said to Mr
Asterias, 'You have caught an odd fish, indeed.' Mr Toobad
was highly exasperated at this unseasonable pleasantry;
but Mr Hilary softened his anger, by producing a knife,
and cutting the Gordian knot of his reticular envelopment.
'You see,' said Mr Toobad, 'you see, gentlemen, in my unfortunate person proof upon proof of the present dominion
of the devil in the affairs of this world; and I have no doubt
but that the apparition of this night was Apollyon himself in disguise, sent for the express purpose of terrifying me
into this complication of misadventures. The devil is come
among you, having great wrath, because he knoweth that
he hath but a short time.'

*

CHAPTER XIII

Mr Glowry was much surprised, on occasionally visiting Scythrop's tower, to find the door always locked, and to be kept sometimes waiting many minutes for admission: during which he invariably heard a heavy rolling sound like that of a ponderous mangle, or of a waggon on a weighing-bridge, or of theatrical thunder.

He took little notice of this for some time; at length his curiosity was excited, and, one day, instead of knocking at the door, as usual, the instant he reached it, he applied his ear to the key-hole, and like Bottom, in the Midsummer Night's Dream, 'spied a voice,'[1] which he guessed to be of the feminine gender, and knew to be not Scythrop's, whose deeper tones he distinguished at intervals. Having attempted in vain to catch a syllable of the discourse, he knocked violently at the door, and roared for immediate admission. The voices ceased, the accustomed rolling sound was heard, the door opened, and Scythrop was discovered alone. Mr Glowry looked round to every corner of the apartment, and then said, 'Where is the lady?'

'The lady, sir?' said Scythrop.

'Yes, sir, the lady.'

'Sir, I do not understand you.'

'You don't, sir?'

'No, indeed, sir. There is no lady here.'

'But, sir, this is not the only apartment in the tower, and I make no doubt there is a lady up stairs.'

'You are welcome to search, sir.'

'Yes, and while I am searching, she will slip out from some lurking place, and make her escape.'

'You may lock this door, sir, and take the key with you.'

'But there is the terrace door: she has escaped by the terrace.'

'The terrace, sir, has no other outlet, and the walls are too high for a lady to jump down.'

'Well, sir, give me the key.'

Mr Glowry took the key, searched every nook of the tower, and returned.

'You are a fox, Scythrop; you are an exceedingly cunning fox, with that demure visage of yours. What was that lumbering sound I heard before you opened the door?'

'Sound, sir?'

'Yes, sir, sound.'

'My dear sir, I am not aware of any sound, except my great table, which I moved on rising to let you in.'

'The table! – let me see that. No, sir; not a tenth part heavy enough, not a tenth part.'

'But, sir, you do not consider the laws of acoustics: a whisper becomes a peal of thunder in the focus of reverberation. Allow me to explain this: sounds striking on concave surfaces are reflected from them, and, after reflection, converge to points which are the foci of these surfaces. It follows, therefore, that the ear may be so placed in one, as that it shall hear a sound better than when situated nearer to the point of the first impulse: again, in the case of two concave surfaces placed opposite to each other –'

'Nonsense, sir. Don't tell me of foci. Pray, sir, will concave surfaces produce two voices when nobody speaks? I heard two voices, and one was feminine; feminine, sir: what say you to that?'

'Oh, sir, I perceive your mistake: I am writing a tragedy, and was acting over a scene to myself. To convince you, I will give you a specimen; but you must first understand the plot. It is a tragedy on the German model. The Great Mogul is in exile, and has taken lodgings at Kensington, with his only daughter, the Princess Rantrorina, who takes in needlework, and keeps a day school. *The princess is discovered hemming a set of shirts for the parson of the parish: they are to be marked with a large R. Enter to her the Great Mogul. A pause, during which they look at each other expressively. The princess changes colour several times. The Mogul takes snuff in great agitation. Several grains are heard to fall on the stage. His heart is seen to beat through his upper benjamin.* – THE MOGUL (*with a mournful look at his left shoe*). 'My shoe-string is broken.' – THE PRINCESS (*after an interval of melancholy reflection*). 'I know it.' THE MOGUL. 'My second shoe-string! The first broke when I lost my empire: the second has broken to-day. When will my poor heart break?' – THE PRINCESS. 'Shoe-strings, hearts, and empires! Mysterious sympathy!'

'Nonsense, sir,' interrupted Mr Glowry. 'That is not at all like the voice I heard.'

'But, sir,' said Scythrop, 'a key-hole may be so constructed as to act like an acoustic tube, and an acoustic tube, sir, will modify sound in a very remarkable manner. Consider the construction of the ear, and the nature and causes of sound. The external part of the ear is a cartilaginous funnel.'[2]

'It wo'n't do, Scythrop. There is a girl concealed in this tower, and find her I will. There are such things as sliding panels and secret closets.' – He sounded round the room with his cane, but detected no hollowness. – 'I have heard, sir,' he continued, 'that during my absence, two years ago, you had a dumb carpenter closeted with you day after day. I did not dream that you were laying contrivances for carrying on secret intrigues. Young men will have their way: I had my way when I was a young man: but, sir, when your cousin Marionetta –'

Scythrop now saw that the affair was growing serious. To have clapped his hand upon his father's mouth, to have entreated him to be silent, would, in the first place, not have made him so; and, in the second, would have shown a dread of being overheard by somebody. His only resource, therefore, was to try to drown Mr Glowry's voice; and, having no other subject, he continued his description of the ear, raising his voice continually as Mr Glowry raised his.

'When your cousin Marionetta,' said Mr Glowry, 'whom you profess to love – whom you profess to love, sir –'

'The internal canal of the ear,' said Scythrop, 'is partly bony and partly cartilaginous. This internal canal is –'

'Is actually in the house, sir; and, when you are so shortly to be – as I expect –'

'Closed at the further end by the *membrana tympani* –'

'Joined together in holy matrimony –'

'Under which is carried a branch of the fifth pair of nerves –'

'I say, sir, when you are so shortly to be married to your cousin Marionetta –'

'The *cavitas tympani* –'

A loud noise was heard behind the book-case, which, to the astonishment of Mr Glowry, opened in the middle, and the massy compartments, with all their weight of books, receding from each other in the manner of a theatrical scene, with a heavy rolling sound (which Mr Glowry immediately recognised to be the same which had excited his curiosity,) disclosed an interior apartment, in the entrance of which stood the beautiful Stella, who, stepping forward, exclaimed, 'Married! Is he going to be married? The profligate!'

'Really, madam,' said Mr Glowry, 'I do not know what he is going to do, or what I am going to do, or what any one is going to do; for all this is incomprehensible.'

'I can explain it all,' said Scythrop, 'in a most satisfactory manner, if you will but have the goodness to leave us alone.'

'Pray, sir, to which act of the tragedy of the Great Mogul does this incident belong?'

'I entreat you, my dear sir, leave us alone.'

Stella threw herself into a chair, and burst into a tempest of tears. Scythrop sat down by her, and took her hand. She snatched her hand away, and turned her back upon him. He rose, sat down on the other side, and took her other hand. She snatched it away, and turned from him again. Scythrop continued entreating Mr Glowry to leave them alone; but the old gentleman was obstinate, and would not go.

'I suppose, after all,' said Mr Glowry maliciously, 'it is only a phænomenon in acoustics, and this young lady is a reflection of sound from concave surfaces.'

Some one tapped at the door: Mr Glowry opened it, and Mr Hilary entered. He had been seeking Mr Glowry, and had traced him to Scythrop's tower. He stood a few moments in silent surprise, and then addressed himself to Mr Glowry for an explanation.

'The explanation,' said Mr Glowry, 'is very satisfactory. The Great Mogul has taken lodgings at Kensington, and the external part of the ear is a cartilaginous funnel.'

'Mr Glowry, that is no explanation.'

'Mr Hilary, it is all I know about the matter.'

'Sir, this pleasantry is very unseasonable. I perceive that my niece is sported with in a most unjustifiable manner, and I shall see if she will be more successful in obtaining an intelligible answer.' And he departed in search of Marionetta.

Scythrop was now in a hopeless predicament. Mr Hilary made a hue and cry in the abbey, and summoned his wife and Marionetta to Scythrop's apartment. The ladies, not knowing what was the matter, hastened in great consternation. Mr Toobad saw them sweeping along the corridor, and judging from their manner that the devil had manifested his wrath in some new shape, followed from pure curiosity.

Scythrop meanwhile vainly endeavoured to get rid of Mr Glowry and to pacify Stella. The latter attempted to escape from the tower, declaring she would leave the abbey immediately, and he should never see her or hear of her more. Scythrop held her hand and detained her by force, till Mr Hilary reappeared with Mrs Hilary and Marionetta. Marionetta, seeing Scythrop grasping the hand of a strange beauty, fainted away in the arms of her aunt. Scythrop flew to her assistance; and Stella with redoubled anger sprang towards the door, but was intercepted in her intended flight by being caught in the arms of Mr Toobad, who exclaimed – 'Celinda!'

'Papa!' said the young lady disconsolately.

'The devil is come among you,' said Mr Toobad, 'how came my daughter here?'

'Your daughter!' exclaimed Mr Glowry.

'Your daughter!' exclaimed Scythrop, and Mr and Mrs Hilary.

'Yes,' said Mr Toobad, 'my daughter Celinda.'

Marionetta opened her eyes and fixed them on Celinda; Celinda in return fixed hers on Marionetta. They were at remote points of the apartment. Scythrop was equidistant from both of them, central and motionless, like Mahomet's coffin.

'Mr Glowry,' said Mr Toobad, 'can you tell by what means my daughter came here?'

'I know no more,' said Mr Glowry, 'than the Great Mogul.'

'Mr Scythrop,' said Mr Toobad, 'how came my daughter here?'

'I did not know, sir, that the lady was your daughter.'

'But how came she here?'

'By spontaneous locomotion,' said Scythrop, sullenly.

'Celinda,' said Mr Toobad, 'what does all this mean?'

'I really do not know, sir.'

'This is most unaccountable. When I told you in London that I had chosen a husband for you, you thought proper to run away from him; and now, to all appearance, you have run away to him.'

'How, sir! was that your choice?'

'Precisely; and if he is yours too we shall be both of a mind, for the first time in our lives.'

'He is not my choice, sir. This lady has a prior claim: I renounce him.'

'And I renounce him,' said Marionetta.

Scythrop knew not what to do. He could not attempt to conciliate the one without irreparably offending the other; and he was so fond of both, that the idea of depriving himself for ever of the society of either was intolerable to him: he therefore retreated into his stronghold, mystery; maintained an impenetrable silence; and contented himself with stealing occasionally a deprecating glance at each of the objects of his idolatry. Mr Toobad and Mr Hilary, in the mean time, were each insisting on an explanation from Mr Glowry, who they thought had been playing a double game on this occasion. Mr Glowry was vainly endeavouring to persuade them of his innocence in the whole transaction. Mrs Hilary was endeavouring to mediate between her

husband and brother. The Honourable Mr Listless, the Reverend Mr Larynx, Mr Flosky, Mr Asterias, and Aquarius, were
attracted by the tumult to the scene of action, and were
appealed to severally and conjointly by the respective dis-
putants. Multitudinous questions, and answers *en masse*,
composed a *charivari*, to which the genius of Rossini alone
could have given a suitable accompaniment, and which was
only terminated by Mrs Hilary and Mr Toobad retreating
with the captive damsels. The whole party followed, with
the exception of Scythrop, who threw himself into his
arm-chair, crossed his left foot over his right knee, placed
the hollow of his left hand on the interior ancle of his left
leg, rested his right elbow on the elbow of the chair, placed
the ball of his right thumb against his right temple, curved
the forefinger along the upper part of his forehead, rested
the point of the middle finger on the bridge of his nose, and
the points of the two others on the lower part of the palm,
fixed his eyes intently on the veins in the back of his left
hand, and sat in this position like the immoveable Theseus,
who, as is well known to many who have not been at college, and to some few who have, *sedet, æternumque sedebit.*[3]
We hope the admirers of the *minutiæ* in poetry and romance
will appreciate this accurate description of a pensive attitude.

*

CHAPTER XIV

SCYTHROP was still in this position when Raven entered
to announce that dinner was on table.

'I cannot come,' said Scythrop.

Raven sighed. 'Something is the matter,' said Raven:
'but man is born to trouble.'

'Leave me,' said Scythrop: 'go, and croak elsewhere.'

'Thus it is,' said Raven. 'Five-and-twenty years have I
lived in Nightmare Abbey, and now all the reward of my

affection is – Go, and croak elsewhere. I have danced you on my knee, and fed you with marrow.'

'Good Raven,' said Scythrop, 'I entreat you to leave me.'

'Shall I bring your dinner here?' said Raven. 'A boiled fowl and a glass of Madeira are prescribed by the faculty in cases of low spirits. But you had better join the party: it is very much reduced already.'

'Reduced! how?'

'The Honourable Mr Listless is gone. He declared that, what with family quarrels in the morning, and ghosts at night, he could get neither sleep nor peace; and that the agitation was too much for his nerves: though Mr Glowry assured him that the ghost was only poor Crow walking in his sleep, and that the shroud and bloody turban were a sheet and a red nightcap.'

'Well, sir?'

'The Reverend Mr Larynx has been called off on duty, to marry or bury (I don't know which) some unfortunate person or persons, at Claydyke: but man is born to trouble!'

'Is that all?'

'No. Mr Toobad is gone too, and a strange lady with him.'

'Gone!'

'Gone. And Mr and Mrs Hilary, and Miss O'Carroll: they are all gone. There is nobody left but Mr Asterias and his son, and they are going to-night.'

'Then I have lost them both.'

'Won't you come to dinner?'

'No.'

'Shall I bring your dinner here?'

'Yes.'

'What will you have?'

'A pint of port and a pistol.'[1]

'A pistol!'

'And a pint of port. I will make my exit like Werter. Go. Stay. Did Miss O'Carroll say any thing?'

'No.'

'Did Miss Toobad say any thing?'

'The strange lady? No.'

'Did either of them cry?'

'No.'

'What did they do?'

'Nothing.'

'What did Mr Toobad say?'

'He said, fifty times over, the devil was come among us.'

'And they are gone?'

'Yes; and the dinner is getting cold. There is a time for every thing under the sun. You may as well dine first, and be miserable afterwards.'

'True, Raven. There is something in that. I will take your advice: therefore, bring me –'

'The port and the pistol?'

'No; the boiled fowl and Madeira.'

Scythrop had dined, and was sipping his Madeira alone, immersed in melancholy musing, when Mr Glowry entered, followed by Raven, who, having placed an additional glass and set a chair for Mr Glowry, withdrew. Mr Glowry sat down opposite Scythrop. After a pause, during which each filled and drank in silence, Mr Glowry said, 'So, sir, you have played your cards well. I proposed Miss Toobad to you: you refused her. Mr Toobad proposed you to her: she refused you. You fell in love with Marionetta, and were going to poison yourself, because, from pure fatherly regard to your temporal interests, I withheld my consent. When, at length, I offered you my consent, you told me I was too precipitate. And, after all, I find you and Miss Toobad living together in the same tower, and behaving in every respect like two plighted lovers. Now, sir, if there be any rational solution of all this absurdity, I shall be very much obliged to you for a small glimmering of information.'

'The solution, sir, is of little moment; but I will leave it in writing for your satisfaction. The crisis of my fate is come: the world is a stage, and my direction is *exit*.'

'Do not talk so, sir; – do not talk so, Scythrop. What would you have?'

'I would have my love.'

'And pray, sir, who is your love?'

'Celinda – Marionetta – either – both.'

'Both! That may do very well in a German tragedy;[2] and the Great Mogul might have found it very feasible in his lodgings at Kensington; but it will not do in Lincolnshire. Will you have Miss Toobad?'

'Yes.'

'And renounce Marionetta?'

'No.'

'But you must renounce one.'

'I cannot.'

'And you cannot have both. What is to be done?'

'I must shoot myself.'

'Don't talk so, Scythrop. Be rational, my dear Scythrop. Consider, and make a cool, calm choice, and I will exert myself in your behalf.'

'Why should I choose, sir? Both have renounced *me*: I have no hope of either.'

'Tell me which you will have, and I will plead your cause irresistibly.'

'Well, sir, – I will have – no, sir, I cannot renounce either. I cannot choose either. I am doomed to be the victim of eternal disappointments; and I have no resource but a pistol.'

'Scythrop – Scythrop; – if one of them should come to you – what then?'

'That, sir, might alter the case: but that cannot be.'

'It can be, Scythrop; it will be: I promise you it will be. Have but a little patience – but a week's patience; and it shall be.'

'A week, sir, is an age: but, to oblige you, as a last act of filial duty, I will live another week. It is now Thursday evening, twenty-five minutes past seven. At this hour and minute, on Thursday next, love and fate shall smile on me, or I will drink my last pint of port in this world.'

Mr Glowry ordered his travelling chariot, and departed from the abbey.

*

CHAPTER XV

THE day after Mr Glowry's departure was one of incessant rain, and Scythrop repented of the promise he had given. The next day was one of bright sunshine: he sat on the terrace, read a tragedy of Sophocles, and was not sorry, when Raven announced dinner, to find himself alive. On the third evening, the wind blew, and the rain beat, and the owl flapped against his windows; and he put a new flint in his pistol. On the fourth day, the sun shone again; and he locked the pistol up in a drawer, where he left it undisturbed, till the morning of the eventful Thursday, when he ascended the turret with a telescope, and spied anxiously along the road that crossed the fens from Claydyke: but nothing appeared on it. He watched in this manner from ten A.M. till Raven summoned him to dinner at five; when he stationed Crow at the telescope, and descended to his own funeral-feast. He left open the communications between the tower and turret, and called aloud at intervals to Crow, – 'Crow, Crow, is any thing coming?' Crow answered, 'The wind blows, and the windmills turn, but I see nothing coming;' and, at every answer, Scythrop found the necessity of raising his spirits with a bumper. After dinner, he gave Raven his watch to set by the abbey clock. Raven brought it, Scythrop placed it on the table, and Raven departed. Scythrop called again to Crow; and Crow, who had fallen asleep, answered mechanically, 'I see nothing coming.' Scythrop laid his pistol between his watch and his bottle. The hour-hand passed the VII. – the minute-hand moved on; – it was within three minutes of the appointed time. Scythrop called again to Crow: Crow answered as before. Scythrop rang the bell: Raven appeared.

'Raven,' said Scythrop, 'the clock is too fast.'

'No, indeed,' said Raven, who knew nothing of Scythrop's intentions; 'if any thing, it is too slow.'

'Villain!' said Scythrop, pointing the pistol at him; 'it is too fast.'

'Yes – yes – too fast, I meant,' said Raven, in manifest fear.

'How much too fast?' said Scythrop.

'As much as you please,' said Raven.

'How much, I say?' said Scythrop, pointing the pistol again.

'An hour, a full hour, sir,' said the terrified butler.

'Put back my watch,' said Scythrop.

Raven, with trembling hand, was putting back the watch, when the rattle of wheels was heard in the court; and Scythrop, springing down the stairs by three steps together, was at the door in sufficient time to have handed either of the young ladies from the carriage, if she had happened to be in it; but Mr Glowry was alone.

'I rejoice to see you,' said Mr Glowry; 'I was fearful of being too late, for I waited till the last moment in the hope of accomplishing my promise; but all my endeavours have been vain, as these letters will show.'

Scythrop impatiently broke the seals. The contents were these:

Almost a stranger in England, I fled from parental tyranny, and the dread of an arbitrary marriage, to the protection of a stranger and a philosopher, whom I expected to find something better than, or at least something different from, the rest of his worthless species. Could I, after what has occurred, have expected nothing more from you than the common-place impertinence of sending your father to treat with me, and with mine, for me? I should be a little moved in your favour, if I could believe you capable of carrying into effect the resolutions which your father says you have taken, in the event of my proving inflexible; though I doubt not you will execute them, as far as relates to the pint of wine, twice over, at least. I wish you much happiness with Miss O'Carroll. I shall always cherish a grateful recollection of Nightmare Abbey, for having been the means of introducing me to a true transcendentalist; and, though he is a little older than myself, which is all one in Germany, I shall very soon have the pleasure of subscribing myself

CELINDA FLOSKY[1]

I hope, my dear cousin, that you will not be angry with me, but that you will always think of me as a sincere friend, who will always feel interested in your welfare; I am sure you love Miss Toobad much better than me, and I wish you much happiness with her. Mr Listless assures me that people do not kill themselves for love now-a-days, though it is still the fashion to talk about it. I shall, in a very short time, change my name and situation, and shall always be happy to see you in Berkeley Square, when, to the unalterable designation of your affectionate cousin, I shall subjoin the signature of

MARIONETTA LISTLESS

Scythrop tore both the letters to atoms, and railed in good set terms against the fickleness of women.

'Calm yourself, my dear Scythrop,' said Mr Glowry; 'there are yet maidens in England.'

'Very true, sir,' said Scythrop.

'And the next time,' said Mr Glowry, 'have but one string to your bow.'

'Very good advice, sir,' said Scythrop.

'And, besides,' said Mr Glowry, 'the fatal time is past, for it is now almost eight.'

'Then that villain, Raven,' said Scythrop, 'deceived me when he said that the clock was too fast; but, as you observe very justly, the time has gone by, and I have just reflected that these repeated crosses in love qualify me to take a very advanced degree in misanthropy; and there is, therefore, good hope that I may make a figure in the world. But I shall ring for the rascal Raven, and admonish him.'

Raven appeared. Scythrop looked at him very fiercely two or three minutes; and Raven, still remembering the pistol, stood quaking in mute apprehension, till Scythrop, pointing significantly towards the dining-room, said, 'Bring some Madeira.'

THE END

Facsimile title page of the first edition of
Crotchet Castle

CROTCHET CASTLE.

BY THE

AUTHOR OF HEADLONG HALL.

Le monde est plein de fous, et qui n'en veut pas voir,
Doit se tenir tout seul, et casser son miroir.

LONDON:

PUBLISHED BY T. HOOKHAM,

OLD BOND STREET.

1831.

Should once the world resolve to abolish
All that's ridiculous and foolish,
It would have nothing left to do,
To apply in jest or earnest to.

BUTLER

CROTCHET CASTLE

*

CHAPTER I

The Villa

Captain Jamy. I wad full fain hear some question
'tween you tway.

HENRY V[1]

IN one of those beautiful vallies, through which the Thames
(not yet polluted by the tide, the scouring of cities, or even
the minor defilement of the sandy streams of Surrey,) rolls
a clear flood through flowery meadows, under the shade of
old beech woods, and the smooth mossy greensward of the
chalk hills (which pour into it their tributary rivulets, as
pure and pellucid as the fountain of Bandusium, or the
wells of Scamander, by which the wives and daughters of
the Trojans washed their splendid garments in the days of
peace, before the coming of the Greeks); in one of those
beautiful vallies, on a bold round-surfaced lawn, spotted
with juniper, that opened itself in the bosom of an old
wood, which rose with a steep, but not precipitous ascent,
from the river to the summit of the hill, stood the castellated villa of a retired citizen. Ebenezer Mac Crotchet,
Esquire, was the London-born offspring of a worthy native
of the 'north countrie,' who had walked up to London on a
commercial adventure, with all his surplus capital, not very
neatly tied up in a not very clean handkerchief, suspended
over his shoulder from the end of a hooked stick, extracted
from the first hedge on his pilgrimage; and who, after having
worked himself a step or two up the ladder of life, had won
the virgin heart of the only daughter of a highly respectable merchant of Duke's Place,[2] with whom he inherited
the honest fruits of a long series of ingenuous dealings.

Mr Mac Crotchet had derived from his mother the instinct, and from his father the rational principle, of enriching himself at the expense of the rest of mankind, by all the recognised modes of accumulation on the windy side of the law. After passing many years in the alley,[3] watching the turn of the market, and playing many games almost as desperate as that of the soldier of Lucullus,[4] the fear of losing what he had so righteously gained predominated over the sacred thirst of paper-money; his caution got the better of his instinct, or rather transferred it from the department of acquisition to that of conservation. His friend, Mr Ramsbottom, the zodiacal mythologist,[5] told him that he had done well to withdraw from the region of Uranus or Brahma, the maker, to that of Saturn or Veeshnu, the preserver, before he fell under the eye of Jupiter or Seva, the destroyer, who might have struck him down at a blow.

It is said, that a Scotchman returning home, after some years' residence in England, being asked what he thought of the English, answered: 'They hanna ower muckle sense, but they are an unco braw people to live amang;' which would be a very good story, if it were not rendered apocryphal, by the incredible circumstance of the Scotchman going back.

Mr Mac Crotchet's experience had given him a just title to make, in his own person, the last-quoted observation, but he would have known better than to go back, even if himself, and not his father, had been the first comer of his line from the north. He had married an English Christian, and, having none of the Scotch accent, was ungracious enough to be ashamed of his blood. He was desirous to obliterate alike the Hebrew and Caledonian vestiges in his name, and signed himself E. M. Crotchet, which by degrees induced the majority of his neighbours to think that his name was Edward Matthew. The more effectually to sink the Mac, he christened his villa Crotchet Castle, and determined to hand down to posterity the honours of Crotchet of Crotchet. He found it essential to his dignity to furnish himself with a coat of arms, which, after the proper cere-

monies (payment being the principal), he obtained, videlicet: Crest, a crotchet rampant, in A sharp: Arms, three
empty bladders, turgescent, to show how opinions are
formed; three bags of gold, pendent, to show why they are
maintained; three naked swords, tranchant, to show how
they are administered; and three barbers' blocks, gaspant,
to show how they are swallowed.

Mr Crotchet was left a widower, with two children; and,
after the death of his wife, so strong was his sense of the
blessed comfort she had been to him, that he determined
never to give any other woman an opportunity of obliterat-
ing the happy recollection.

He was not without a plausible pretence for styling his
villa a castle, for, in its immediate vicinity, and within his
own enclosed domain, were the manifest traces, on the
brow of the hill, of a Roman station, or *castellum*, which
was still called the castle by the country people. The primitive mounds and trenches, merely overgrown with greensward, with a few patches of juniper and box on the vallum,
and a solitary ancient beech surmounting the place of the
prætorium, presented nearly the same depths, heights,
slopes, and forms, which the Roman soldiers had originally
given them. From this *castellum* Mr Crotchet christened his
villa. With his rustic neighbours he was of course immediately and necessarily a squire: Squire Crotchet of the
castle; and he seemed to himself to settle down as naturally
into an English country gentleman, as if his parentage had
been as innocent of both Scotland and Jerusalem, as his
education was of Rome and Athens.

But as, though you expel nature with a pitchfork, she will
yet always come back; [6] he could not become, like a true-
born English squire, part and parcel of the barley-giving
earth; he could not find in game-bagging, poacher-shooting,
trespasser-pounding, footpath-stopping, common-enclosing,
rack-renting, and all the other liberal pursuits and pastimes
which make a country gentleman an ornament to the world,
and a blessing to the poor; he could not find in these valuable and amiable occupations, and in a corresponding range

of ideas, nearly commensurate with that of the great King Nebuchadnezzar, when he was turned out to grass; he could not find in this great variety of useful action, and vast field of comprehensive thought, modes of filling up his time that accorded with his Caledonian instinct. The inborn love of disputation, which the excitements and engagements of a life of business had smothered, burst forth through the calmer surface of a rural life. He grew as fain as Captain Jamy, 'to hear some airgument betwixt ony tway;' and being very hospitable in his establishment, and liberal in his invitations, a numerous detachment from the advanced guard of the 'march of intellect,' often marched down to Crotchet Castle.

When the fashionable season filled London with exhibitors of all descriptions, lecturers and else, Mr Crotchet was in his glory; for, in addition to the perennial literati of the metropolis, he had the advantage of the visits of a number of hardy annuals, chiefly from the north, who, as the interval of their metropolitan flowering allowed, occasionally accompanied their London brethren in excursions to Crotchet Castle.

Amongst other things, he took very naturally to political economy, read all the books on the subject which were put forth by his own countrymen, attended all lectures thereon, and boxed the technology of the sublime science as expertly as an able seaman boxes the compass.

With this agreeable mania he had the satisfaction of biting his son, the hope of his name and race, who had borne off from Oxford the highest academical honours; and who, treading in his father's footsteps to honour and fortune, had, by means of a portion of the old gentleman's surplus capital, made himself a junior partner in the eminent loan-jobbing firm of Catchflat and Company. Here, in the days of paper prosperity, he applied his science-illumined genius to the blowing of bubbles, the bursting of which sent many a poor devil to the jail, the workhouse, or the bottom of the river, but left young Crotchet rolling in riches.

These riches he had been on the point of doubling, by a

marriage with the daughter of Mr Touchandgo, the great banker, when, one foggy morning, Mr Touchandgo and the contents of his till were suddenly reported absent; and as the fortune which the young gentleman had intended to marry was not forthcoming, this tender affair of the heart was nipped in the bud.

Miss Touchandgo did not meet the shock of separation quite so complacently as the young gentleman; for he lost only the lady, whereas she lost a fortune as well as a lover. Some jewels, which had glittered on her beautiful person as brilliantly as the bubble of her father's wealth had done in the eyes of his gudgeons, furnished her with a small portion of paper currency; and this, added to the contents of a fairy purse of gold, which she found in her shoe on the eventful morning when Mr Touchandgo melted into thin air, enabled her to retreat into North Wales, where she took up her lodging in a farm-house in Merionethshire, and boarded very comfortably for a trifling payment, and the additional consideration of teaching English, French, and music to the little Ap-Llymry's. In the course of this occupation, she acquired sufficient knowledge of Welsh to converse with the country people.

She climbed the mountains, and descended the dingles, with a foot which daily habit made by degrees almost as steady as a native's. She became the nymph of the scene; and if she sometimes pined in thought for her faithless Strephon, her melancholy was any thing but green and yellow;[7] it was as genuine white and red as occupation, mountain air, thyme-fed mutton, thick cream, and fat bacon, could make it: to say nothing of an occasional glass of double X, which Ap-Llymry,[8] who yielded to no man west of the Wrekin in brewage, never failed to press upon her at dinner and supper. He was also earnest, and sometimes successful, in the recommendation of his mead, and most pertinacious on winter nights in enforcing a trial of the virtues of his elder wine. The young lady's personal appearance, consequently, formed a very advantageous contrast to that of her quondam lover, whose physiognomy

the intense anxieties of his bubble-blowing days, notwithstanding their triumphant result, had left blighted, sal-
lowed, and crow's-footed, to a degree not far below that of
the fallen spirit who, in the expressive language of German
romance, is described as 'scathed by the ineradicable
traces of the thunderbolts of Heaven;' so that, contemplat-
ing their relative geological positions, the poor deserted
damsel was flourishing on slate, while her rich and false
young knight was pining on chalk.

Squire Crotchet had also one daughter, whom he had
christened Lemma,[9] and who, as likely to be endowed with
a very ample fortune, was, of course, an object very tempting to many young soldiers of fortune, who were marching
with the march of mind, in a good condition for taking
castles, as far as not having a groat is a qualification for
such exploits.[10] She was also a glittering bait to divers
young squires expectant (whose fathers were too well acquainted with the occult signification of mortgage), and
even to one or two sprigs of nobility, who thought that the
lining of a civic purse would superinduce a very passable
factitious nap upon a threadbare title. The young lady had
received an expensive and complicated education; complete in all the elements of superficial display. She was thus
eminently qualified to be the companion of any masculine
luminary who had kept due pace with the 'astounding progress' of intelligence. It must be confessed, that a man who
has not kept due pace with it is not very easily found; this
march being one of that 'astounding' character in which it
seems impossible that the rear can be behind the van. The
young lady was also tolerably good-looking: north of Tweed,
or in Palestine, she would probably have been a beauty;
but for the vallies of the Thames, she was perhaps a little
too much to the taste of Solomon, and had a nose which
rather too prominently suggested the idea of the tower of
Lebanon, which looked towards Damascus.[11]

In a village in the vicinity of the castle was the vicarage
of the Reverend Doctor Folliott, a gentleman endowed
with a tolerable stock of learning, an interminable swallow,

and an indefatigable pair of lungs. His pre-eminence in the latter faculty gave occasion to some etymologists to ring changes on his name, and to decide that it was derived from Follis Optimus, softened through an Italian medium into Folle Ottimo, contracted poetically into Folleotto, and elided Anglicé into Folliott, signifying a first-rate pair of bellows. He claimed to be descended lineally from the illustrious Gilbert Folliott,[12] the eminent theologian, who was a bishop of London in the twelfth century, whose studies were interrupted in the dead of night by the devil; when a couple of epigrams passed between them; and the devil, of course, proved the smaller wit of the two.[13]

This reverend gentleman, being both learned and jolly, became by degrees an indispensable ornament to the new squire's table. Mr Crotchet himself was eminently jolly, though by no means eminently learned. In the latter respect he took after the great majority of the sons of his father's land; had a smattering of many things, and a knowledge of none; but possessed the true northern art of making the most of his intellectual harlequin's jacket, by keeping the best patches always bright and prominent.

*

CHAPTER II

The March of Mind

Quoth Ralpho: nothing but the abuse
Of human learning you produce.
                                BUTLER[1]

'GOD bless my soul, sir!' exclaimed the Reverend Doctor Folliott, bursting, one fine May morning, into the break-fast-room at Crotchet Castle, 'I am out of all patience with this march of mind.[2] Here has my house been nearly burned down, by my cook taking it into her head to study hydro-statics, in a sixpenny tract, published by the Steam

Intellect Society,[3] and written by a learned friend who is for doing all the world's business as well as his own, and is equally well qualified to handle every branch of human knowledge. I have a great abomination of this learned friend; as author, lawyer, and politician, he is *triformis*, like Hecate: and in every one of his three forms he is *bifrons*, like Janus; the true Mr Facing-both-ways of Vanity Fair. My cook must read his rubbish in bed; and as might naturally be expected, she dropped suddenly fast asleep, overturned the candle, and set the curtains in a blaze. Luckily, the footman went into the room at the moment, in time to tear down the curtains and throw them into the chimney, and a pitcher of water on her night-cap extinguished her wick: she is a greasy subject, and would have burned like a short mould.'[4]

The reverend gentleman exhaled his grievance without looking to the right or to the left; at length, turning on his pivot, he perceived that the room was full of company, consisting of young Crotchet and some visitors whom he had brought from London. The Reverend Doctor Folliott was introduced to Mr Mac Quedy,[5] the economist; Mr Skionar,[6] the transcendental poet; Mr Firedamp, the meteorologist; and Lord Bossnowl,[7] son of the Earl of Foolincourt, and member for the borough of Rogueingrain.

The divine took his seat at the breakfast-table, and began to compose his spirits by the gentle sedative of a large cup of tea, the demulcent of a well-buttered muffin, and the tonic of a small lobster.

THE REV DR FOLLIOTT

You are a man of taste, Mr Crotchet. A man of taste is seen at once in the array of his breakfast-table. It is the foot of Hercules,[8] the far-shining face of the great work, according to Pindar's doctrine: ἀρχομένου ἔργου, πρόσωπον χρὴ θέμεν τηλαυγές.[9] The breakfast is the πρόσωπον of the great work of the day. Chocolate, coffee, tea, cream, eggs, ham, tongue, cold fowl, – all these are good, and bespeak good knowledge in him who sets them forth: but the touchstone is fish:

anchovy is the first step, prawns and shrimps the second; and I laud him who reaches even to these: potted char and lampreys are the third, and a fine stretch of progression; but lobster is, indeed, matter for a May morning,[10] and demands a rare combination of knowledge and virtue in him who sets it forth.

MR MAC QUEDY

Well, sir, and what say you to a fine fresh trout, hot and dry, in a napkin? or a herring out of the water into the frying pan, on the shore of Loch Fyne?

THE REV DR FOLLIOTT

Sir, I say every nation has some eximious virtue; and your country is pre-eminent in the glory of fish for breakfast. We have much to learn from you in that line at any rate.

MR MAC QUEDY

And in many others, sir, I believe. Morals and metaphysics, politics and political economy, the way to make the most of all the modifications of smoke; steam, gas, and paper currency; you have all these to learn from us; in short, all the arts and sciences. We are the modern Athenians.

THE REV DR FOLLIOTT

I, for one, sir, am content to learn nothing from you but the art and science of fish for breakfast. Be content, sir, to rival the Bœotians, whose redeeming virtue was in fish, touching which point you may consult Aristophanes and his scholiast, in the passage of Lysistrata, ἀλλ’ ἄφελε τὰς ἐγχέλεις,[11] and leave the name of Athenians to those who have a sense of the beautiful, and a perception of metrical quantity.

MR MAC QUEDY

Then, sir, I presume you set no value on the right principles of rent, profit, wages, and currency?

THE REV DR FOLLIOTT

My principles, sir, in these things are, to take as much as I can get, and to pay no more than I can help. These are every man's principles, whether they be the right principles or no. There, sir, is political economy in a nutshell.

MR MAC QUEDY

The principles, sir, which regulate production and consumption, are independent of the will of any individual as to giving or taking, and do not lie in a nutshell by any means.

THE REV DR FOLLIOTT

Sir, I will thank you for a leg of that capon.

LORD BOSSNOWL

But, sir, by the by, how came your footman to be going into your cook's room? It was very providential to be sure, but –

THE REV DR FOLLIOTT

Sir, as good came of it, I shut my eyes, and asked no questions. I suppose he was going to study hydrostatics, and he found himself under the necessity of practising hydraulics.

MR FIREDAMP

Sir, you seem to make very light of science.

THE REV DR FOLLIOTT

Yes, sir, such science as the learned friend deals in: every thing for every body, science for all, schools for all, rhetoric for all, law for all, physic for all, words for all, and sense for none. I say, sir, law for lawyers, and cookery for cooks: and I wish the learned friend, for all his life, a cook that will pass her time in studying his works; then every dinner he sits down to at home, he will sit on the stool of repentance.

LORD BOSSNOWL

Now really that would be too severe: my cook should read nothing but Ude.[12]

THE REV DR FOLLIOTT

No, sir! let Ude and the learned friend singe fowls together; let both avaunt from my kitchen. Θύρας δ' ἐπίθεσθε βεβήλοις.[13] Ude says an elegant supper may be given with sandwiches. *Horresco referens.*[14] An elegant supper! *Dî meliora piis.*[15] No Ude for me. Conviviality went out with punch and suppers. I cherish their memory. I sup when I can, but not upon sandwiches. To offer me a sandwich, when I am looking for a supper, is to add insult to injury. Let the learned friend, and the modern Athenians,[16] sup upon sandwiches.

MR MAC QUEDY

Nay, sir; the modern Athenians know better than that. A literary supper in sweet Edinbroo' would cure you of the prejudice you seem to cherish against us.

THE REV DR FOLLIOTT

Well, sir, well; there is cogency in a good supper; a good supper, in these degenerate days, bespeaks a good man; but much more is wanted to make up an Athenian. Athenians, indeed! where is your theatre? who among you has written a comedy? where is your attic salt? which of you can tell who was Jupiter's great grandfather? or what metres will successively remain, if you take off the three first syllables, one by one, from a pure antispastic acatalectic tetrameter? Now, sir, there are three questions for you; theatrical, mythological, and metrical; to every one of which an Athenian would give an answer that would lay me prostrate in my own nothingness.

MR MAC QUEDY

Well, sir, as to your metre and your mythology, they may e'en wait a wee. For your comedy, there is the Gentle Shepherd of the divine Allan Ramsay.

THE REV DR FOLLIOTT

The Gentle Shepherd! It is just as much a comedy as the book of Job.

MR MAC QUEDY

Well, sir, if none of us have written a comedy, I cannot see that it is any such great matter, any more than I can conjecture what business a man can have at this time of day with Jupiter's great grandfather.

THE REV DR FOLLIOTT

The great business is, sir, that you call yourselves Athenians, while you know nothing that the Athenians thought worth knowing, and dare not show your noses before the civilised world in the practice of any one art in which they were excellent. Modern Athens, sir! the assumption is a personal affront to every man who has a Sophocles in his library. I will thank you for an anchovy.

MR MAC QUEDY

Metaphysics, sir; metaphysics. Logic and moral ɪ̠qdlosophy There we are at home. The Athenians only sought the way, and we have found it; and to all this we have added political economy, the science of sciences.

THE REV DR FOLLIOTT

A hyperbarbarous technology, that no Athenian ear could have borne. Premises assumed without evidence, or in spite of it; and conclusions drawn from them so logically, that they must necessarily be erroneous.

MR SKIONAR

I cannot agree with you, Mr Mac Quedy, that you have found the true road of metaphysics, which the Athenians only sought. The Germans have found it, sir: the sublime Kant, and his disciples.

MR MAC QUEDY

I have read the sublime Kant, sir, with an anxious desire to understand him; and I confess I have not succeeded.

THE REV DR FOLLIOTT

He wants the two great requisites of head and tail.

MR SKIONAR

Transcendentalism is the philosophy of intuition, the development of universal convictions; truths which are inherent in the organisation of mind, which cannot be obliterated, though they may be obscured, by superstitious prejudice on the one hand, and by the Aristotelian logic on the other.

MR MAC QUEDY

Well, sir, I have no notion of logic obscuring a question.

MR SKIONAR

There is only one true logic, which is the transcendental; and this can prove only the one true philosophy, which is also the transcendental. The logic of your modern Athens can prove every thing equally; and that is, in my opinion, tantamount to proving nothing at all.

MR CROTCHET

The sentimental against the rational, the intuitive against the inductive, the ornamental against the useful, the intense against the tranquil, the romantic against the classical; these are great and interesting controversies, which I should like, before I die, to see satisfactorily settled.

MR FIREDAMP

There is another great question, greater than all these, seeing that it is necessary to be alive in order to settle any question; and this is the question of water against human woe. Wherever there is water, there is *malaria*, and wherever there is *malaria*, there are the elements of death. The great object of a wise man should be to live on a gravelly hill, without so much as a duck-pond within ten miles of him, eschewing cisterns and water-butts, and taking care that there be no gravel-pits for lodging the rain. The sun sucks up infection from water, wherever it exists on the face of the earth.

THE REV DR FOLLIOTT

Well, sir, you have for you the authority of the ancient mystagogue, who said, Ἔστιν ὕδωρ ψυχῇ θάνατος.[17] For my part I care not a rush (or any other aquatic and inesculent vegetable) who or what sucks up either the water or the infection. I think the proximity of wine a matter of much more importance than the longinquity of water. You are here within a quarter of a mile of the Thames; but in the cellar of my friend, Mr Crotchet, there is the talismanic antidote of a thousand dozen of old wine; a beautiful spectacle, I assure you, and a model of arrangement.

MR FIREDAMP

Sir, I feel the malignant influence of the river in every part of my system. Nothing but my great friendship for Mr Crotchet would have brought me so nearly within the jaws of the lion.

THE REV DR FOLLIOTT

After dinner, sir, after dinner, I will meet you on this question. I shall then be armed for the strife. You may fight like Hercules against Achelous, but I shall flourish the Bacchic thyrsus, which changed rivers into wine: as Nonnus sweetly sings, Οἴνῳ κυματόεντι μέλας κελάρυζεν Ὑδάσπης.[18]

MR CROTCHET, JUN

I hope, Mr Firedamp, you will let your friendship carry you a little closer into the jaws of the lion. I am fitting up a flotilla of pleasure boats, with spacious cabins, and a good cellar, to carry a choice philosophical party up the Thames and Severn, into the Ellesmere canal, where we shall be among the mountains of North Wales; which we may climb or not, as we think proper; but we will, at any rate, keep our floating hotel well provisioned and we will try to settle all the questions over which a shadow of doubt yet hangs in the world of philosophy.

MR FIREDAMP

Out of my great friendship for you, I will certainly go; but I do not expect to survive the experiment.

THE REV DR FOLLIOTT

Alter erit tum Tiphys, et altera quæ vehat Argo Delectos Heroas.[19] I will be of the party, though I must hire an officiating curate, and deprive poor Mrs Folliott, for several weeks, of the pleasure of combing my wig.

LORD BOSSNOWL

I hope if I am to be of the party, our ship is not to be the ship of fools: He! He!

THE REV DR FOLLIOTT

If you are one of the party, sir, it most assuredly will not: Ha! Ha!

LORD BOSSNOWL

Pray sir, what do you mean by Ha! Ha!?

THE REV DR FOLLIOTT

Precisely, sir, what you mean by He! He!

MR MAC QUEDY

You need not dispute about terms; they are two modes of expressing merriment, with or without reason; reason being in no way essential to mirth. No man should ask another why he laughs, or at what, seeing that he does not always know, and that, if he does, he is not a responsible agent. Laughter is an involuntary action of certain muscles, developed in the human species by the progress of civilisation. The savage never laughs.

THE REV DR FOLLIOTT

No, sir, he has nothing to laugh at. Give him Modern
Athens, the 'learned friend,' and the Steam Intellect
Society. They will develope his muscles.

*

CHAPTER III

The Roman Camp

> He loved her more than seven yere,
> Yet was he of her love never the nere;
> He was not ryche of golde and fe,
> A gentyll man forsoth was he.
> THE SQUYR OF LOW DEGRE[1]

THE Reverend Doctor Folliott having promised to return
to dinner, walked back to his vicarage, meditating whether
he should pass the morning in writing his next sermon, or
in angling for trout, and had nearly decided in favour of
the latter proposition, repeating to himself, with great
unction, the lines of Chaucer:

> And as for me, though that I can but lite,
> On bokis for to read I me delite,
> And to 'hem yeve I faithe and full credence,
> And in mine herte have 'hem in reverence,
> So hertily, that there is gamé none,
> That fro my bokis makith me to gone,
> But it be seldome, on the holie daie;
> Save certainly whan that the month of Maie
> Is comin, and I here the foulis sing,
> And that the flouris ginnin for to spring,
> Farewell my boke and my devocion:[2]

when his attention was attracted by a young gentleman who
was sitting on a camp stool with a portfolio on his knee,
taking a sketch of the Roman Camp, which, as has been

already said, was within the enclosed domain of Mr Crotchet. The young stranger, who had climbed over the fence, espying the portly divine, rose up, and hoped that he was not trespassing. 'By no means, sir,' said the divine; 'all the arts and sciences are welcome here: music, painting, and poetry; hydrostatics, and political economy; meteorology, transcendentalism, and fish for breakfast.'

THE STRANGER

A pleasant association, sir, and a liberal and discriminating hospitality. This is an old British camp, I believe, sir?

THE REV DR FOLLIOTT

Roman, sir; Roman: undeniably Roman. The vallum is past controversy. It was not a camp, sir, a *castrum*, but a *castellum*, a little camp, or watch-station, to which was attached, on the peak of the adjacent hill, a beacon for transmitting alarms. You will find such here and there, all along the range of chalk hills, which traverses the country from north-east to south-west, and along the base of which runs the ancient Ikenild road, whereof you may descry a portion in that long strait white line.

THE STRANGER

I beg your pardon, sir: do I understand this place to be your property?

THE REV DR FOLLIOTT

It is not mine, sir: the more is the pity; yet is it so far well, that the owner is my good friend, and a highly respectable gentleman.

THE STRANGER

Good and respectable, sir, I take it, mean rich?

THE REV DR FOLLIOTT

That is their meaning, sir.

143

THE STRANGER

I understand the owner to be a Mr Crotchet. He has a handsome daughter, I am told.

THE REV DR FOLLIOTT

He has, sir. Her eyes are like the fishpools of Heshbon,[3] by the gate of Bethrabbim; and she is to have a handsome fortune, to which divers disinterested gentlemen are paying their addresses. Perhaps you design to be one of them.

THE STRANGER

No, sir; I beg pardon if my questions seem impertinent; I have no such design. There is a son, too, I believe, sir, a great and successful blower of bubbles.

THE REV DR FOLLIOTT

A hero, sir, in his line. Never did angler in September hook more gudgeons.

THE STRANGER

To say the truth, two very amiable young people, with whom I have some little acquaintance, Lord Bossnowl, and his sister, Lady Clarinda, are reported to be on the point of concluding a double marriage with Miss Crotchet and her brother, by way of putting a new varnish on old nobility. Lord Foolincourt, their father, is terribly poor for a lord who owns a borough.

THE REV DR FOLLIOTT

Well, sir, the Crotchets have plenty of money, and the old gentleman's weak point is a hankering after high blood. I saw your acquaintance Lord Bossnowl this morning; but I did not see his sister. She may be there, nevertheless, and doing fashionable justice to this fine May morning, by lying in bed till noon.

THE STRANGER

Young Mr Crotchet, sir, has been, like his father, the architect of his own fortune, has he not? An illustrious example of the reward of honesty and industry?

THE REV DR FOLLIOTT

As to honesty, sir, he made his fortune in the city of London; and if that commodity be of any value there, you will find it in the price current. I believe it is below par, like the shares of young Crotchet's fifty companies. But his progress has not been exactly like his father's: it has been more rapid, and he started with more advantages. He began with a fine capital from his father. The old gentleman divided his fortune into three not exactly equal portions: one for himself, one for his daughter, and one for his son, which he handed over to him, saying, 'Take it once for all, and make the most of it; if you lose it where I won it, not another stiver do you get from me during my life.' But, sir, young Crotchet doubled, and trebled, and quadrupled it, and is, as you say, a striking example of the reward of industry; not that I think his labour has been so great as his luck.

THE STRANGER

But, sir, is all this solid? is there no danger of reaction? no day of reckoning, to cut down in an hour prosperity that has grown up like a mushroom?

THE REV DR FOLLIOTT

Nay, sir, I know not. I do not pry into these matters. I am, for my own part, very well satisfied with the young gentleman. Let those who are not so look to themselves. It is quite enough for me that he came down last night from London, and that he had the good sense to bring with him a basket of lobsters. Sir, I wish you a good morning.

The stranger, having returned the reverend gentleman's good morning, resumed his sketch, and was intently employed on it when Mr Crotchet made his appearance, with Mr Mac Quedy and Mr Skionar, whom he was escorting round his grounds, according to his custom with new visitors; the principal pleasure of possessing an extensive domain being that of showing it to other people. Mr Mac Quedy, according also to the laudable custom of his countrymen, had been appraising every thing that fell under his observation; but, on arriving at the Roman camp, of which the value was purely imaginary, he contented himself with exclaiming, 'Eh! this is just a curiosity, and very pleasant to sit in on a summer day.'

MR SKIONAR

And call up the days of old, when the Roman eagle spread its wings in the place of that beechen foliage. It gives a fine idea of duration, to think that that fine old tree must have sprung from the earth ages after this camp was formed.

MR MAC QUEDY

How old, think you, may the tree be?

MR CROTCHET

I have records which show it to be three hundred years old.

MR MAC QUEDY

That is a great age for a beech in good condition. But you see the camp is some fifteen hundred years, or so, older; and three times six being eighteen, I think you get a clearer idea of duration out of the simple arithmetic than out of your eagle and foliage.

MR SKIONAR

That is a very unpoetical, if not unphilosophical, mode of viewing antiquities. Your philosophy is too literal for our imperfect vision. We cannot look directly into the nature of things; we can only catch glimpses of the mighty shadow in the camera obscura of transcendental intelligence. These six and eighteen are only words to which we give conventional meanings. We can reason, but we cannot feel, by help of them. The tree and the eagle, contemplated in the ideality of space and time, become subjective realities, that rise up as landmarks in the mystery of the past.

MR MAC QUEDY

Well, sir, if you understand that, I wish you joy. But I must be excused for holding that my proposition, three times six are eighteen, is more intelligible than yours. A worthy friend of mine, who is a sort of amateur in philosophy, criticism, politics, and a wee bit of many things more, says, 'Men never begin to study antiquities till they are saturated with civilisation.'[4]

MR SKIONAR

What is civilisation?

MR MAC QUEDY

It is just respect for property: a state in which no man takes wrongfully what belongs to another, is a perfectly civilised state.

MR SKIONAR

Your friend's antiquaries must have lived in El Dorado, to have had an opportunity of being saturated with such a state.

MR MAC QUEDY

It is a question of degree. There is more respect for property here than in Angola.

MR SKIONAR

That depends on the light in which things are viewed.

Mr Crotchet was rubbing his hands, in hopes of a fine discussion, when they came round to the side of the camp where the picturesque gentleman was sketching. The stranger was rising up, when Mr Crotchet begged him not to disturb himself, and presently walked away with his two guests.

Shortly after Miss Crotchet and Lady Clarinda, who had breakfasted by themselves, made their appearance at the same spot, hanging each on an arm of Lord Bossnowl, who very much preferred their company to that of the philosophers, though he would have preferred the company of the latter, or any company, to his own. He thought it very singular that so agreeable a person as he held himself to be to others, should be so exceedingly tiresome to himself: he did not attempt to investigate the cause of this phenomenon, but was contented with acting on his knowledge of the fact, and giving himself as little of his own private society as possible.

The stranger rose as they approached, and was immediately recognised by the Bossnowls as an old acquaintance, and saluted with the exclamation of 'Captain Fitzchrome!' The interchange of salutation between Lady Clarinda and the Captain was accompanied with an amiable confusion on both sides, in which the observant eyes of Miss Crotchet seemed to read the recollection of an affair of the heart.

Lord Bossnowl was either unconscious of any such affair, or indifferent to its existence. He introduced the Captain very cordially to Miss Crotchet, and the young lady invited him, as the friend of their guests, to partake of her father's hospitality; an offer which was readily accepted.

The Captain took his portfolio under his right arm, his camp stool in his right hand, offered his left arm to Lady Clarinda, and followed at a reasonable distance behind Miss Crotchet and Lord Bossnowl, contriving, in the most natural manner possible, to drop more and more into the rear.

LADY CLARINDA

I am glad to see you can make yourself so happy with drawing old trees and mounds of grass.

CAPTAIN FITZCHROME

Happy, Lady Clarinda! oh, no! How can I be happy when
I see the idol of my heart about to be sacrificed on the shrine
of Mammon?

LADY CLARINDA

Do you know, though Mammon has a sort of ill name, I
really think he is a very popular character; there must be
at the bottom something amiable about him. He is certainly one of those pleasant creatures whom every body
abuses, but without whom no evening party is endurable. I
dare say, love in a cottage is very pleasant; but then it
positively must be a cottage ornée: but would not the same
love be a great deal safer in a castle, even if Mammon
furnished the fortification?

CAPTAIN FITZCHROME

Oh, Lady Clarinda! there is a heartlessness in that language
that chills me to the soul.

LADY CLARINDA

Heartlessness! No: my heart is on my lips. I speak just
what I think. You used to like it, and say it was as delightful as it was rare.

CAPTAIN FITZCHROME

True, but you did not then talk as you do now, of love in a
castle.

LADY CLARINDA

Well, but only consider: a dun is a horridly vulgar creature;
it is a creature I cannot endure the thought of: and a cottage
lets him in so easily. Now a castle keeps him at bay. You
are a half-pay officer, and are at leisure to command the
garrison: but where is the castle? and who is to furnish the
commissariat?

CAPTAIN FITZCHROME

Is it come to this, that you make a jest of my poverty? Yet is my poverty only comparative. Many decent families are maintained on smaller means.

LADY CLARINDA

Decent families: aye, decent is the distinction from respectable. Respectable means rich, and decent means poor. I should die if I heard my family called decent. And then your decent family always lives in a snug little place: I hate a little place; I like large rooms and large looking-glasses, and large parties, and a fine large butler, with a tinge of smooth red in his face; an outward and visible sign that the family he serves is respectable; if not noble, highly respectable.

CAPTAIN FITZCHROME

I cannot believe that you say all this in earnest. No man is less disposed than I am to deny the importance of the substantial comforts of life. I once flattered myself that in our estimate of these things we were nearly of a mind.

LADY CLARINDA

Do you know, I think an opera-box a very substantial comfort, and a carriage. You will tell me that many decent people walk arm in arm through the snow, and sit in clogs and bonnets in the pit at the English theatre. No doubt it is very pleasant to those who are used to it; but it is not to my taste.

CAPTAIN FITZCHROME

You always delighted in trying to provoke me; but I cannot believe that you have not a heart.

LADY CLARINDA

You do not like to believe that I have a heart, you mean. You wish to think I have lost it, and you know to whom;

and when I tell you that it is still safe in my own keeping, and that I do not mean to give it away, the unreasonable creature grows angry.

CAPTAIN FITZCHROME

Angry! far from it: I am perfectly cool.

LADY CLARINDA

Why, you are pursing your brows, biting your lips, and lifting up your foot as if you would stamp it into the earth. I must say anger becomes you; you would make a charming Hotspur. Your every-day-dining-out face is rather insipid: but I assure you my heart is in danger when you are in the heroics. It is so rare, too, in these days of smooth manners, to see any thing like natural expression in a man's face. There is one set form for every man's face in female society; a sort of serious comedy, walking gentleman's face: but the moment the creature falls in love, he begins to give himself airs, and plays off all the varieties of his physiognomy, from the Master Slender to the Petruchio; and then he is actually very amusing.

CAPTAIN FITZCHROME

Well, Lady Clarinda, I will not be angry, amusing as it may be to you: I listen more in sorrow than in anger. I half believe you in earnest, and mourn as over a fallen angel.

LADY CLARINDA

What, because I have made up my mind not to give away my heart when I can sell it? I will introduce you to my new acquaintance, Mr Mac Quedy: he will talk to you by the hour about exchangeable value, and show you that no rational being will part with any thing, except to the highest bidder.

CAPTAIN FITZCHROME

Now, I am sure you are not in earnest. You cannot adopt such sentiments in their naked deformity.

LADY CLARINDA

Naked deformity: why Mr Mac Quedy will prove to you that
they are the cream of the most refined philosophy. You live
a very pleasant life as a bachelor, roving about the country
with your portfolio under your arm. I am not fit to be a
poor man's wife. I cannot take any kind of trouble, or do
any one thing that is of any use. Many decent families roast
a bit of mutton on a string; but if I displease my father I
shall not have as much as will buy the string, to say nothing of the meat; and the bare idea of such cookery gives me
the horrors.

By this time they were near the castle, and met Miss
Crotchet and her companion, who had turned back to meet
them. Captain Fitzchrome was shortly after heartily wel-
comed by Mr Crotchet, and the party separated to dress for
dinner, the captain being by no means in an enviable state
of mind, and full of misgivings as to the extent of belief
that he was bound to accord to the words of the lady of his
heart.

*

CHAPTER IV

The Party

En quoi cognoissez-vous la folie anticque? En quoi
cognoissez-vous la sagesse présente?

RABELAIS[1]

'IF I were sketching a bandit who had just shot his last
pursuer, having outrun all the rest, that is the very face I
would give him,' soliloquised the captain, as he studied the
features of his rival in the drawing-room, during the miserable half-hour before dinner, when dulness reigns pre-
dominant over the expectant company, especially when

152

they are waiting for some one last comer, whom they all heartily curse in their hearts, and whom, nevertheless, or indeed therefore-the-more, they welcome as a sinner, more heartily than all the just persons who had been punctual to their engagement. Some new visitors had arrived in the morning, and, as the company dropped in one by one, the captain anxiously watched the unclosing door for the form of his beloved; but she was the last to make her appearance, and on her entry gave him a malicious glance, which he construed into a telegraphic communication that she had stayed away to torment him. Young Crotchet escorted her with marked attention to the upper end of the drawing-room, where a great portion of the company was congregated around Miss Crotchet. These being the only ladies in the company, it was evident that old Mr Crotchet would give his arm to Lady Clarinda, an arrangement with which the captain could not interfere. He therefore took his station near the door, studying his rival from a distance, and determined to take advantage of his present position, to secure the seat next to his charmer. He was meditating on the best mode of operation for securing this important post with due regard to *bienséance*, when he was twitched by the button by Mr Mac Quedy, who said to him: 'Lady Clarinda tells me, sir, that you are anxious to talk with me on the subject of exchangeable value, from which I infer that you have studied political economy; and as a great deal depends on the definition of value, I shall be glad to set you right on that point.' – 'I am much obliged to you, sir,' said the captain, and was about to express his utter disqualification for the proposed instruction, when Mr Skionar walked up, and said: 'Lady Clarinda informs me that you wish to talk over with me the question of subjective reality. I am delighted to fall in with a gentleman who duly appreciates the transcendental philosophy.' – 'Lady Clarinda is too good,' said the captain; and was about to protest that he had never heard the word transcendental before, when the butler announced dinner. Mr Crotchet led the way with Lady Clarinda: Lord Bossnowl followed with Miss Crotchet:

the economist and transcendentalist pinned in the captain, and held him, one by each arm, as he impatiently descended the stairs in the rear of several others of the company, whom they had forced him to let pass; but the moment he entered the dining-room he broke loose from them, and at the expense of a little *brusquerie*, secured his position.

'Well, captain,' said Lady Clarinda, 'I perceive you can still manœuvre.'

'What could possess you,' said the captain, 'to send two unendurable and inconceivable bores, to intercept me with rubbish about which I neither know nor care any more than the man in the moon?'

'Perhaps,' said Lady Clarinda, 'I saw your design, and wished to put your generalship to the test. But do not contradict any thing I have said about you, and see if the learned will find you out.'

'There is fine music, as Rabelais observes, in the *cliquetis d'assiettes*, a refreshing shade in the *ombre de salle à manger*, and an elegant fragrance in the *fumée de rôti*,' said a voice at the captain's elbow. The captain turning round, recognised his clerical friend of the morning, who knew him again immediately, and said he was extremely glad to meet him there; more especially as Lady Clarinda had assured him that he was an enthusiastic lover of Greek poetry.

'Lady Clarinda,' said the captain, 'is a very pleasant young lady.'

THE REV DR FOLLIOTT

So she is, sir: and I understand she has all the wit of the family to herself, whatever that *totum* may be. But a glass of wine after soup is, as the French say, the *verre de santé*. The current of opinion sets in favour of Hock: but I am for Madeira; I do not fancy Hock till I have laid a substratum of Madeira. Will you join me?

CAPTAIN FITZCHROME

With pleasure.

THE REV DR FOLLIOTT

Here is a very fine salmon before me: and May is the very
point nommé to have salmon in perfection. There is a fine
turbot close by, and there is much to be said in his behalf;
but salmon in May is the king of fish.

MR CROTCHET

That salmon before you, doctor, was caught in the Thames
this morning.

THE REV DR FOLLIOTT

Παπαπαῖ! Rarity of rarities! A Thames salmon caught this
morning. Now, Mr Mac Quedy, even in fish your Modern
Athens must yield. *Cedite Graii.*[2]

MR MAC QUEDY

Eh! sir, on its own ground, your Thames salmon has two
virtues over all others: first, that it is fresh; and, second,
that it is rare; for I understand you do not take half a
dozen in a year.

THE REV DR FOLLIOTT

In some years, sir, not one. Mud, filth, gas dregs, lock-weirs,
and the march of mind, developed in the form of poaching,
have ruined the fishery. But when we do catch a salmon,
happy the man to whom he falls.

MR MAC QUEDY

I confess, sir, this is excellent; but I cannot see why it
should be better than a Tweed salmon at Kelso.

THE REV DR FOLLIOTT

Sir, I will take a glass of Hock with you.

MR MAC QUEDY

With all my heart, sir. There are several varieties of the
salmon genus: but the common salmon, the *salmo salar*, is

only one species, one and the same every where, just like the human mind. Locality and education make all the difference.

THE REV DR FOLLIOTT

Education! Well, sir, I have no doubt schools for all[3] are just as fit for the species *salmo salar* as for the genus *homo*. But you must allow, that the specimen before us has finished his education in a manner that does honour to his college. However, I doubt that the *salmo salar* is only one species, that is to say, precisely alike in all localities. I hold that every river has its own breed, with essential differences; in flavour especially. And as for the human mind, I deny that it is the same in all men. I hold that there is every variety of natural capacity from the idiot to Newton and Shakspeare; the mass of mankind, midway between these extremes, being blockheads of different degrees; education leaving them pretty nearly as it found them, with this single difference, that it gives a fixed direction to their stupidity, a sort of incurable wry neck to the thing they call their understanding. So one nose points always east, and another always west, and each is ready to swear that it points due north.

MR CROTCHET

If that be the point of truth, very few intellectual noses point due north.

MR MAC QUEDY

Only those that point to the Modern Athens.

THE REV DR FOLLIOTT

Where all native noses point southward.

MR MAC QUEDY

Eh, sir, northward for wisdom, and southward for profit.

MR CROTCHET, JUN

Champagne, doctor?

THE REV DR FOLLIOTT

Most willingly. But you will permit my drinking it while it sparkles. I hold it a heresy to let it deaden in my hand, while the glass of my *compotator* is being filled on the opposite side of the table. By the bye, captain, you remember a passage in Athenæus,[4] where he cites Menander on the subject of fish-sauce: ὀψάριον ἐπὶ ἰχθύος. (*The captain was aghast for an answer that would satisfy both his neighbours, when he was relieved by the divine continuing.*) The science of fish sauce, Mr Mac Quedy, is by no means brought to perfection; a fine field of discovery still lies open in that line.

MR MAC QUEDY

Nay, sir, beyond lobster sauce, I take it, ye cannot go.

THE REV DR FOLLIOTT

In their line, I grant you, oyster and lobster sauce are the pillars of Hercules. But I speak of the cruet sauces, where the quintessence of the sapid is condensed in a phial. I can taste in my mind's palate a combination, which, if I could give it reality, I would christen with the name of my college, and hand it down to posterity as a seat of learning indeed.

MR MAC QUEDY

Well, sir, I wish you success, but I cannot let slip the question we started just now. I say, cutting off idiots, who have no minds at all, all minds are by nature alike. Education (which begins from their birth) makes them what they are.

THE REV DR FOLLIOTT

No, sir, it makes their tendencies, not their power. Cæsar would have been the first wrestler on the village common. Education might have made him a Nadir Shah;[5] it might also have made him a Washington; it could not have made him a merry-andrew, for our newspapers to extol as a model of eloquence.

MR MAC QUEDY

Now, sir, I think education would have made him just any thing, and fit for any station, from the throne to the stocks; saint or sinner, aristocrat or democrat, judge, counsel, or prisoner at the bar.

THE REV DR FOLLIOTT

I will thank you for a slice of lamb, with lemon and pepper. Before I proceed with this discussion, – Vin de Grave, Mr Skionar, – I must interpose one remark. There is a set of persons in your city, Mr Mac Quedy, who concoct every three or four months a thing which they call a review:[6] a sort of sugar-plum manufacturers to the Whig aristocracy.

MR MAC QUEDY

I cannot tell, sir, exactly, what you mean by that; but I hope you will speak of those gentlemen with respect, seeing that I am one of them.

THE REV DR FOLLIOTT

Sir, I must drown my inadvertence in a glass of Sauterne with you. There is a set of gentlemen in your city –

MR MAC QUEDY

Not in our city, exactly; neither are they a set. There is an editor, who forages for articles in all quarters, from John O'Groat's house to the Land's End. It is not a board, or a society: it is a mere intellectual bazaar, where A., B., and C. bring their wares to market.

THE REV DR FOLLIOTT

Well, sir, these gentlemen among them, the present company excepted, have practised as much dishonesty as, in any other department than literature, would have brought the practitioner under the cognisance of the police. In politics, they have run with the hare and hunted with the hound. In criticism they have, knowingly and unblushingly, given

false characters, both for good and for evil: sticking at no
art of misrepresentation, to clear out of the field of literature all who stood in the way of the interests of their own
clique. They have never allowed their own profound ignorance of any thing (Greek, for instance) to throw even an air
of hesitation into their oracular decision on the matter.
They set an example of profligate contempt for truth, of
which the success was in proportion to the effrontery; and
when their prosperity had filled the market with competi-
tors, they cried out against their own reflected sin, as if
they had never committed it, or were entitled to a mono-
poly of it. The latter, I rather think, was what they wanted.

MR CROTCHET

Hermitage, doctor?

THE REV DR FOLLIOTT

Nothing better, sir. The father who first chose the solitude
of that vineyard, knew well how to cultivate his spirit in
retirement. Now, Mr Mac Quedy, Achilles was distinguished
above all the Greeks for his inflexible love of truth: could
education have made Achilles one of your reviewers?

MR MAC QUEDY

No doubt of it, even if your character of them were true to
the letter.

THE REV DR FOLLIOTT

And I say, sir – chicken and asparagus – Titan had made
him of better clay.[7] I hold with Pindar: 'All that is most
excellent is so by nature.' Τὸ δὲ φυᾷ κράτιστον ἅπαν.[8] Education can give purposes, but not powers; and whatever
purposes had been given him, he would have gone straight
forward to them; straight forward, Mr Mac Quedy.

MR MAC QUEDY

No, sir, education makes the man, powers, purposes, and
all.

THE REV DR FOLLIOTT

There is the point, sir, on which we join issue.

Several others of the company now chimed in with their opinions, which gave the divine an opportunity to degustate one or two side dishes, and to take a glass of wine with each of the young ladies.

*

CHAPTER V

Characters

Ay imputé a honte plus que mediocre être vu spectateur ocieux de tant vaillans, disertz, et chevalereux person-naiges.

RABELAIS[1]

LADY CLARINDA (*to the Captain*)

I DECLARE the creature has been listening to all this rigmarole, instead of attending to me. Do you ever expect forgiveness? But now that they are all talking together, and you cannot make out a word they say, nor they hear a word that we say, I will describe the company to you. First, there is the old gentleman on my left hand, at the head of the table, who is now leaning the other way to talk to my brother. He is a good tempered, half-informed person, very unreasonably fond of reasoning, and of reasoning people; people that talk nonsense logically: he is fond of disputation himself, when there are only one or two, but seldom does more than listen in a large company of *illuminés*. He made a great fortune in the city, and has the comfort of a good conscience. He is very hospitable, and is generous in dinners; though nothing would induce him to give sixpence to the poor, because he holds that all misfortune is from imprudence, that none but the rich ought to marry, and that all ought to

thrive by honest industry, as he did. He is ambitious of
founding a family, and of allying himself with nobility; and
is thus as willing as other grown children, to throw away
thousands for a gew-gaw, though he would not part with a
penny for charity. Next to him is my brother, whom you
know as well as I do. He has finished his education with
credit, and as he never ventures to oppose me in any thing,
I have no doubt he is very sensible. He has good manners,
is a model of dress, and is reckoned ornamental in all
societies. Next to him is Miss Crotchet, my sister-in-law
that is to be. You see she is rather pretty, and very genteel.
She is tolerably accomplished, has her table always covered
with new novels, thinks Mr Mac Quedy an oracle, and is
extremely desirous to be called 'my lady.' Next to her is
Mr Firedamp, a very absurd person, who thinks that water
is the evil principle. Next to him is Mr Eavesdrop, a man
who, by dint of a certain something like smartness, has got
into good society. He is a sort of bookseller's tool, and coins
all his acquaintance in reminiscences and sketches of character. I am very shy of him, for fear he should print me.

CAPTAIN FITZCHROME

If he print you in your own likeness, which is that of an
angel, you need not fear him. If he print you in any other,
I will cut his throat. But proceed –

LADY CLARINDA

Next to him is Mr Henbane, the toxicologist, I think he calls
himself. He has passed half his life in studying poisons and
antidotes. The first thing he did on his arrival here, was to
kill the cat; and while Miss Crotchet was crying over her,
he brought her to life again. I am more shy of him than
the other.

CAPTAIN FITZCHROME

They are two very dangerous fellows, and I shall take care
to keep them both at a respectful distance. Let us hope that

Eavesdrop will sketch off Henbane, and that Henbane will poison him for his trouble.

LADY CLARINDA

Well, next to him sits Mr Mac Quedy, the Modern Athenian, who lays down the law about every thing, and therefore may be taken to understand every thing. He turns all the affairs of this world into questions of buying and selling. He is the Spirit of the Frozen Ocean to every thing like romance and sentiment. He condenses their volume of steam into a drop of cold water in a moment. He has satisfied me that I am a commodity in the market, and that I ought to set myself at a high price. So you see he who would have me must bid for me.

CAPTAIN FITZCHROME

I shall discuss that point with Mr Mac Quedy.

LADY CLARINDA

Not a word for your life. Our flirtation is our own secret. Let it remain so.

CAPTAIN FITZCHROME

Flirtation, Clarinda! Is that all that the most ardent –

LADY CLARINDA

Now, don't be rhapsodical here. Next to Mr Mac Quedy is Mr Skionar, a sort of poetical philosopher, a curious compound of the intense and the mystical. He abominates all the ideas of Mr Mac Quedy, and settles every thing by sentiment and intuition.

CAPTAIN FITZCHROME

Then, I say, he is the wiser man.

LADY CLARINDA

They are two oddities; but a little of them is amusing, and I like to hear them dispute. So you see I am in training for a philosopher myself.

CAPTAIN FITZCHROME

Any philosophy, for heaven's sake, but the pound-shilling-and-pence philosophy of Mr Mac Quedy.

LADY CLARINDA

Why, they say that even Mr Skionar, though he is a great dreamer, always dreams with his eyes open, or with one eye at any rate, which is an eye to his gain: but I believe that in this respect the poor man has got an ill name by keeping bad company. He has two dear friends, Mr Wilful Wontsee, and Mr Rumblesack Shantsee,[2] poets of some note, who used to see visions of Utopia, and pure republics beyond the Western deep: but finding that these El Dorados brought them no revenue, they turned their vision-seeing faculty into the more profitable channel of espying all sorts of virtues in the high and mighty, who were able and willing to pay for the discovery.

CAPTAIN FITZCHROME

I do not fancy these virtue-spyers.

LADY CLARINDA

Next to Mr Skionar, sits Mr Chainmail, a good-looking young gentleman, as you see, with very antiquated tastes. He is fond of old poetry, and is something of a poet himself. He is deep in monkish literature, and holds that the best state of society was that of the twelfth century, when nothing was going forward but fighting, feasting, and praying, which he says are the three great purposes for which man was made. He laments bitterly over the inventions of gunpowder, steam, and gas, which he says have ruined the world. He lives within two or three miles, and has a large hall, adorned with rusty pikes, shields, helmets, swords, and tattered banners, and furnished with yew-tree chairs, and two long, old, worm-eaten oak tables, where he dines with all his household, after the fashion of his favourite age. He wants us all to dine with him, and I believe we shall go.

CAPTAIN FITZCHROME

That will be something new at any rate.

LADY CLARINDA

Next to him is Mr Toogood,[3] the co-operationist, who will have neither fighting nor praying; but wants to parcel out the world into squares like a chess-board, with a community on each, raising every thing for one another, with a great steam-engine to serve them in common for tailor and hosier, kitchen and cook.

CAPTAIN FITZCHROME

He is the strangest of the set, so far.

LADY CLARINDA

This brings us to the bottom of the table, where sits my humble servant, Mr Crotchet the younger. I ought not to describe him.

CAPTAIN FITZCHROME

I entreat you do.

LADY CLARINDA

Well, I really have very little to say in his favour.

CAPTAIN FITZCHROME

I do not wish to hear any thing in his favour; and I rejoice to hear you say so, because –

LADY CLARINDA

Do not flatter yourself. If I take him, it will be to please my father, and to have a town and country-house, and plenty of servants, and a carriage and an opera-box, and make some of my acquaintance who have married for love, or for rank, or for any thing but money, die for envy of my jewels. You do not think I would take him for himself. Why he is very smooth and spruce, as far as his dress goes; but as to his face, he looks as if he had tumbled headlong into a volcano, and been thrown up again among the cinders.

CAPTAIN FITZCHROME

I cannot believe, that, speaking thus of him, you mean to take him at all.

LADY CLARINDA

Oh! I am out of my teens. I have been very much in love; but now I am come to years of discretion, and must think, like other people, of settling myself advantageously. He was in love with a banker's daughter, and cast her off on her father's bankruptcy, and the poor girl has gone to hide herself in some wild place.

CAPTAIN FITZCHROME

She must have a strange taste, if she pines for the loss of him.

LADY CLARINDA

They say he was good-looking, till his bubble-schemes, as they call them, stamped him with the physiognomy of a desperate gambler. I suspect he has still a *penchant* towards his first flame. If he takes me, it will be for my rank and connection, and the second seat of the borough of Rogueingrain. So we shall meet on equal terms, and shall enjoy all the blessedness of expecting nothing from each other.

CAPTAIN FITZCHROME

You can expect no security with such an adventurer.

LADY CLARINDA

I shall have the security of a good settlement, and then if *andare al diavolo* be his destiny, he may go, you know, by himself. He is almost always dreaming and *distrait*. It is very likely that some great reverse is in store for him: but that will not concern me, you perceive.

CAPTAIN FITZCHROME

You torture me, Clarinda, with the bare possibility.

LADY CLARINDA

Hush! Here is music to soothe your troubled spirit. Next to him, on this side, sits the dilettante composer, Mr Trillo; [4] they say his name was O'Trill, and he has taken the O from the beginning, and put it at the end. I do not know how this may be. He plays well on the violoncello, and better on the piano: sings agreeably; has a talent at verse-making, and improvises a song with some felicity. He is very agreeable company in the evening, with his instruments and music-books. He maintains that the sole end of all enlightened society is to get up a good opera, and laments that wealth, genius, and energy, are squandered upon other pursuits, to the neglect of this one great matter.

CAPTAIN FITZCHROME

That is a very pleasant fancy at any rate.

LADY CLARINDA

I assure you he has a great deal to say for it. Well, next to him again, is Dr Morbific, who has been all over the world to prove that there is no such thing as contagion; and has inoculated himself with plague, yellow fever, and every variety of pestilence, and is still alive to tell the story. I am very shy of him, too; for I look on him as a walking phial of wrath, corked full of all infections, and not to be touched without extreme hazard.

CAPTAIN FITZCHROME

This is the strangest fellow of all.

LADY CLARINDA

Next to him sits Mr Philpot, [5] the geographer, who thinks of nothing but the heads and tails of rivers, and lays down the streams of Terra Incognita as accurately as if he had been

there. He is a person of pleasant fancy, and makes a sort of
fairy land of every country he touches, from the Frozen
Ocean to the Deserts of Zahara.

CAPTAIN FITZCHROME

How does he settle matters with Mr Firedamp?

LADY CLARINDA

You see Mr Firedamp has got as far as possible out of his
way. Next to him is Sir Simon Steeltrap, of Steeltrap
Lodge, Member for Crouching-Curtown, Justice of Peace
for the county, and Lord of the United Manors of Spring-
gun and Treadmill; a great preserver of game and public
morals. By administering the laws which he assists in
making, he disposes, at his pleasure, of the land and its live
stock, including all the two-legged varieties, with and without feathers, in a circumference of several miles round
Steeltrap Lodge. He has enclosed commons and woodlands;
abolished cottage-gardens; taken the village cricket-ground
into his own park, out of pure regard to the sanctity of
Sunday; shut up footpaths and alehouses, (all but those
which belong to his electioneering friend, Mr Quassia, the
brewer;) [6] put down fairs and fiddlers; committed many
poachers; shot a few; convicted one third of the peasantry;
suspected the rest; and passed nearly the whole of them
through a wholesome course of prison discipline, which has
finished their education at the expense of the county.

CAPTAIN FITZCHROME

He is somewhat out of his element here: among such a diversity of opinions he will hear some he will not like.

LADY CLARINDA

It was rather ill-judged in Mr Crotchet to invite him to-day.
But the art of assorting company is above these *parvenus*.
They invite a certain number of persons without considering how they harmonise with each other. Between Sir Simon
and you is the Reverend Doctor Folliott. He is said to be

an excellent scholar, and is fonder of books than the majority of his cloth; he is very fond, also, of the good things of this world. He is of an admirable temper, and says rude things in a pleasant half-earnest manner, that nobody can take offence with. And next to him, again, is one Captain Fitzchrome, who is very much in love with a certain person that does not mean to have any thing to say to him, because she can better her fortune by taking somebody else.

CAPTAIN FITZCHROME

And next to him, again, is the beautiful, the accomplished, the witty, the fascinating, the tormenting Lady Clarinda, who traduces herself to the said captain by assertions which it would drive him crazy to believe.

LADY CLARINDA

Time will show, sir. And now we have gone the round of the table.

CAPTAIN FITZCHROME

But I must say, though I know you had always a turn for sketching characters, you surprise me by your observation, and especially by your attention to opinions.

LADY CLARINDA

Well, I will tell you a secret: I am writing a novel.

CAPTAIN FITZCHROME

A novel!

LADY CLARINDA

Yes, a novel. And I shall get a little finery by it: trinkets and fal-lals, which I cannot get from papa. You must know I have been reading several fashionable novels, the fashionable this, and the fashionable that; and I thought to myself, why I can do better than any of these myself. So I wrote a chapter or two, and sent them as a specimen to Mr Puffall, the bookseller, telling him they were to be a part of the fashionable something or other, and he offered me, I will not say how much, to finish it in three volumes, and let him pay all the newspapers for recommending it as the work of a lady of quality, who had made very free with the characters of her acquaintance.

CAPTAIN FITZCHROME

Surely you have not done so?

LADY CLARINDA

Oh, no; I leave that to Mr Eavesdrop. But Mr Puffall made it a condition that I should let him say so.

CAPTAIN FITZCHROME

A strange recommendation.

LADY CLARINDA

Oh, nothing else will do. And it seems you may give yourself any character you like, and the newspapers will print it as if it came from themselves. I have commended you to three of our friends here, as an economist, a transcendentalist, and a classical scholar; and if you wish to be renowned through the world for these, or any other accomplishments, the newspapers will confirm you in their possession for half-a-guinea a piece.

CAPTAIN FITZCHROME

Truly, the praise of such gentry must be a feather in any one's cap.

LADY CLARINDA

So you will see, some morning, that my novel is 'the most popular production of the day.' This is Mr Puffall's favourite phrase. He makes the newspapers say it of every thing he publishes. But 'the day,' you know, is a very convenient phrase; it allows of three hundred and sixty-five 'most popular productions' in a year. And in leap-year one more.

*

CHAPTER VI

Theories

But when they came to shape the model,
Not one could fit the other's noddle.
                                   BUTLER[1]

MEANWHILE, the last course, and the dessert, passed by.
When the ladies had withdrawn, young Crotchet addressed
the company.

MR CROTCHET, JUN

There is one point in which philosophers of all classes seem
to be agreed; that they only want money to regenerate the
world.

MR MAC QUEDY

No doubt of it. Nothing is so easy as to lay down the out-
lines of perfect society. There wants nothing but money to
set it going. I will explain myself clearly and fully by reading a paper. (*Producing a large scroll.*) 'In the infancy of
society –'

THE REV DR FOLLIOTT

Pray, Mr Mac Quedy, how is it that all gentlemen of your
nation begin every thing they write with the 'infancy of
society'?

MR MAC QUEDY

Eh, sir, it is the simplest way to begin at the beginning. 'In
the infancy of society, when government was invented to
save a percentage;[2] say two and a half per cent. –'

THE REV DR FOLLIOTT

I will not say any such thing.

MR MAC QUEDY

Well, say any percentage you please.

THE REV DR FOLLIOTT

I will not say any percentage at all.

MR MAC QUEDY

'On the principle of the division of labour –'

THE REV DR FOLLIOTT

Government was invented to spend a percentage.

MR MAC QUEDY

To save a percentage.

THE REV DR FOLLIOTT

No, sir, to spend a percentage; and a good deal more than two and a half per cent. Two hundred and fifty per cent.; that is intelligible.

MR MAC QUEDY

'In the infancy of society –'

MR TOOGOOD

Never mind the infancy of society. The question is of society in its maturity. Here is what it should be. (*Producing a paper*.) I have laid it down in a diagram.[3]

MR SKIONAR

Before we proceed to the question of government, we must nicely discriminate the boundaries of sense, understanding, and reason. Sense is a receptivity –

MR CROTCHET, JUN

We are proceeding too fast. Money being all that is wanted to regenerate society, I will put into the hands of this company a large sum for the purpose. Now let us see how to dispose of it.

MR MAC QUEDY

We will begin by taking a committee-room in London, where we will dine together once a week, to deliberate.

THE REV DR FOLLIOTT

If the money is to go in deliberative dinners, you may set me down for a committee man and honorary caterer.

MR MAC QUEDY

Next, you must all learn political economy, which I will teach you, very compendiously, in lectures over the bottle.

THE REV DR FOLLIOTT

I hate lectures over the bottle. But pray, sir, what is political economy?

MR MAC QUEDY

Political economy is to the state what domestic economy is to the family.[4]

THE REV DR FOLLIOTT

No such thing, sir. In the family there is a *paterfamilias*, who regulates the distribution, and takes care that there shall be no such thing in the household as one dying of hunger, while another dies of surfeit. In the state it is all hunger at one end, and all surfeit at the other. Matchless claret, Mr Crotchet.

MR CROTCHET

Vintage of fifteen, doctor.

MR MAC QUEDY

The family consumes, and so does the state.

THE REV DR FOLLIOTT

Consumes, sir! Yes: but the mode, the proportions; there is the essential difference between the state and the family. Sir, I hate false analogies.

MR MAC QUEDY

Well, sir, the analogy is not essential. Distribution will come under its proper head.

THE REV DR FOLLIOTT

Come where it will, the distribution of the state is in no respect analogous to the distribution of the family. The *paterfamilias*, sir: the *paterfamilias*.

MR MAC QUEDY

Well, sir, let that pass. The family consumes, and in order to consume, it must have supply.[5]

THE REV DR FOLLIOTT

Well, sir, Adam and Eve knew that, when they delved and span.

MR MAC QUEDY

Very true, sir (*reproducing his scroll*). 'In the infancy of society –'

MR TOOGOOD

The reverend gentleman has hit the nail on the head. It is the distribution that must be looked to: it is the *pater-familias* that is wanting in the state. Now here I have provided him. (*Reproducing his diagram.*)

MR TRILLO

Apply the money, sir, to building and endowing an opera house, where the ancient altar of Bacchus may flourish, and justice may be done to sublime compositions. (*Producing a part of a manuscript opera.*)

MR SKIONAR

No, sir, build *sacella* for transcendental oracles to teach the world how to see through a glass darkly. (*Producing a scroll.*)

MR TRILLO

See through an opera-glass brightly.

THE REV DR FOLLIOTT

See through a wine-glass, full of claret: then you see both darkly and brightly. But, gentlemen, if you are all in the humour for reading papers, I will read you the first half of my next Sunday's sermon. (*Producing a paper.*)

OMNES

No sermon! No sermon!

THE REV DR FOLLIOTT

Then I move that our respective papers be committed to our respective pockets.

MR MAC QUEDY

Political economy is divided into two great branches, production and consumption.

THE REV DR FOLLIOTT

Yes, sir; there are two great classes of men: those who produce much and consume little; and those who consume much and produce nothing. The *fruges consumere nati* [6] have the best of it. Eh, captain! you remember the characteristics of a great man according to Aristophanes: ὅστις γε πίνειν οἶδε καὶ βίνειν μόνον.[7] Ha! ha! ha! Well, captain, even in these tight-laced days, the obscurity of a learned language allows a little pleasantry.

CAPTAIN FITZCHROME

Very true, sir: the pleasantry and the obscurity go together: they are all one, as it were; – to me at any rate. (*aside.*)

MR MAC QUEDY

Now, sir –

THE REV DR FOLLIOTT

Pray, sir, let your science alone, or you will put me under the painful necessity of demolishing it bit by bit, as I have done your exordium. I will undertake it any morning; but it is too hard exercise after dinner.

MR MAC QUEDY

Well, sir, in the meantime I hold my science established.

THE REV DR FOLLIOTT

And I hold it demolished.

MR CROTCHET, JUN

Pray, gentlemen, pocket your manuscripts; fill your glasses; and consider what we shall do with our money.

MR MAC QUEDY

Build lecture rooms and schools for all.

MR TRILLO

Revive the Athenian theatre: regenerate the lyrical drama.

MR TOOGOOD

Build a grand co-operative parallelogram, with a steam-engine in the middle for a maid of all work.

MR FIREDAMP

Drain the country, and get rid of *malaria*, by abolishing duck-ponds.

DR MORBIFIC

Found a philanthropic college of anti-contagionists, where all the members shall be inoculated with the virus of all known diseases. Try the experiment on a grand scale.

MR CHAINMAIL

Build a great dining-hall: endow it with beef and ale, and hang the hall round with arms to defend the provisions.

MR HENBANE

Found a toxicological institution for trying all poisons and antidotes. I myself have killed a frog twelve times, and brought him to life eleven; but the twelfth time he died. I have a phial of the drug which killed him in my pocket, and shall not rest till I have discovered its antidote.

THE REV DR FOLLIOTT

I move that the last speaker be dispossessed of his phial, and that it be forthwith thrown into the Thames.

MR HENBANE

How, sir? my invaluable, and in the present state of human knowledge, infallible poison?

THE REV DR FOLLIOTT

Let the frogs have all the advantage of it.

MR CROTCHET

Consider, doctor, the fish might participate. Think of the salmon.

THE REV DR FOLLIOTT

Then let the owner's right-hand neighbour swallow it.

MR EAVESDROP

Me, sir! What have I done, sir, that I am to be poisoned, sir?

THE REV DR FOLLIOTT

Sir, you have published a character of your facetious friend, the Reverend Doctor F., wherein you have sketched off me; me, sir, even to my nose and wig. What business have the public with my nose and wig?

MR EAVESDROP

Sir, it is all good humoured: all in *bonhommie*: all friendly and complimentary.

THE REV DR FOLLIOTT

Sir, the bottle, *la Dive Bouteille*,[8] is a recondite oracle, which makes an Eleusinian temple of the circle in which it moves. He who reveals its mysteries must die. Therefore, let the dose be administered. *Fiat experimentum in animâ vili.*[9]

MR EAVESDROP

Sir, you are very facetious at my expense.

THE REV DR FOLLIOTT

Sir, you have been very unfacetious, very inficete at mine. You have dished me up, like a savory omelette, to gratify the appetite of the reading rabble for gossip. The next time, sir, I will respond with the *argumentum baculinum*. Print that, sir, put it on record as a promise of the Reverend Doctor F., which shall be most faithfully kept, with an exemplary bamboo.

MR EAVESDROP

Your cloth protects you, sir.

THE REV DR FOLLIOTT

My bamboo shall protect me, sir.

MR CROTCHET

Doctor, doctor, you are growing too polemical.

THE REV DR FOLLIOTT

Sir, my blood boils. What business have the public with my nose and wig?

MR CROTCHET

Doctor! Doctor!

MR CROTCHET, JUN

Pray, gentlemen, return to the point. How shall we employ our fund?

MR PHILPOT

Surely in no way so beneficially as in exploring rivers. Send a fleet of steamboats down the Niger, and another up the Nile. So shall you civilise Africa, and establish stocking factories in Abyssinia and Bambo.[10]

THE REV DR FOLLIOTT

With all submission, breeches and petticoats must precede stockings. Send out a crew of tailors. Try if the king of Bambo will invest inexpressibles.

MR CROTCHET, JUN

Gentlemen, it is not for partial, but for general benefit, that this fund is proposed: a grand and universally applicable scheme for the amelioration of the condition of man.

SEVERAL VOICES

That is my scheme. I have not heard a scheme but my own that has a grain of common sense.

MR TRILLO

Gentlemen, you inspire me. Your last exclamation runs itself into a chorus, and sets itself to music. Allow me to lead, and to hope for your voices in harmony.

> After careful meditation,
> And profound deliberation,
> On the various pretty projects which have just been shown,
> Not a scheme in agitation,
> For the world's amelioration,
> Has a grain of common sense in it, except my own.

SEVERAL VOICES

We are not disposed to join in any such chorus.

THE REV DR FOLLIOTT

Well, of all these schemes, I am for Mr Trillo's. Regenerate the Athenian theatre. My classical friend here, the captain, will vote with me.

CAPTAIN FITZCHROME

I, sir? oh! of course, sir.

MR MAC QUEDY

Surely, captain, I rely on you to uphold political economy.

CAPTAIN FITZCHROME

Me, sir? oh! to be sure, sir.

THE REV DR FOLLIOTT

Pray, sir, will political economy uphold the Athenian theatre?

MR MAC QUEDY

Surely not. It would be a very unproductive investment.

THE REV DR FOLLIOTT

Then the captain votes against you. What, sir, did not the Athenians, the wisest of nations, appropriate to their theatre their most sacred and intangible fund? Did not they give to melopœia, choregraphy, and the sundry forms of didascalics, the precedence of all other matters, civil and military? Was it not their law, that even the proposal to divert this fund to any other purpose should be punished with death? But, sir, I further propose that the Athenian theatre being resuscitated, the admission shall be free to all who can expound the Greek choruses, constructively, mythologically, and metrically, and to none others. So shall all the world learn Greek: Greek, the Alpha and Omega of all knowledge. At him who sits not in the theatre, shall be pointed the finger of scorn: he shall be called in the highway of the city, 'a fellow without Greek.'

MR TRILLO

But the ladies, sir, the ladies.

THE REV DR FOLLIOTT

Every man may take in a lady: and she who can construe and metricise a chorus, shall, if she so please, pass in by herself.

MR TRILLO

But, sir, you will shut me out of my own theatre. Let there at least be a double passport, Greek and Italian.

THE REV DR FOLLIOTT

No, sir; I am inexorable. No Greek, no theatre.

MR TRILLO

Sir, I cannot consent to be shut out from my own theatre.

THE REV DR FOLLIOTT

You see how it is, Squire Crotchet the younger; you can scarcely find two to agree on a scheme, and no two of those can agree on the details. Keep your money in your pocket. And so ends the fund for regenerating the world.

MR MAC QUEDY

Nay, by no means. We are all agreed on deliberative dinners.

THE REV DR FOLLIOTT

Very true; we will dine and discuss. We will sing with Robin Hood,[11] 'If I drink water while this doth last;' and while it lasts we will have no adjournment, if not to the Athenian theatre.

MR TRILLO

Well, gentlemen, I hope this chorus at least will please you:

> If I drink water while this doth last,
> May I never again drink wine:
> For how can a man, in his life of a span,
> Do any thing better than dine?

We'll dine and drink, and say if we think
That any thing better can be;
And when we have dined, wish all mankind
May dine as well as we.

And though a good wish will fill no dish,
And brim no cup with sack,
Yet thoughts will spring, as the glasses ring,
To illume our studious track.
On the brilliant dreams of our hopeful schemes
The light of the flask shall shine;
And we'll sit till day, but we'll find the way
To drench the world with wine.

The schemes for the world's regeneration evaporated in a tumult of voices.

*

CHAPTER VII

The Sleeping Venus

Quoth he: In all my life till now,
I ne'er saw so profane a show.
BUTLER[1]

THE library of Crotchet Castle was a large and well furnished apartment, opening on one side into an anteroom, on the other into a music-room. It had several tables stationed at convenient distances; one consecrated to the novelties of literature, another to the novelties of embellishment; others unoccupied, and at the disposal of the company. The walls were covered with a copious collection of ancient and modern books; the ancient having been selected and arranged by the Reverend Doctor Folliott. In the anteroom were card-tables; in the music-room were various instruments, all popular operas, and all fashionable music. In this suite of apartments, and not in the drawing-room, were the evenings of Crotchet Castle usually passed.

The young ladies were in the music-room; Miss Crotchet at the piano, Lady Clarinda, at the harp, playing and occasionally singing, at the suggestion of Mr Trillo, portions of *Matilde di Shabran*.² Lord Bossnowl was turning over the leaves for Miss Crotchet; the captain was performing the same office for Lady Clarinda, but with so much more attention to the lady than the book, that he often made sad work with the harmony, by turning over two leaves together. On these occasions Miss Crotchet paused, Lady Clarinda laughed, Mr Trillo scolded, Lord Bossnowl yawned, the captain apologised, and the performance proceeded.

In the library, Mr Mac Quedy was expounding political economy to the Reverend Doctor Folliott, who was *pro more* demolishing its doctrines *seriatim*.

Mr Chainmail was in hot dispute with Mr Skionar, touching the physical and moral well-being of man. Mr Skionar was enforcing his friend Mr Shantsee's views of moral discipline; maintaining that the sole thing needful for man in this world, was loyal and pious education; the giving men good books to read, and enough of the hornbook to read them; with a judicious interspersion of the lessons of Old Restraint, which was his poetic name for the parish stocks. Mr Chainmail, on the other hand, stood up for the exclusive necessity of beef and ale, lodging and raiment, wife and children, courage to fight for them all, and armour wherewith to do so.

Mr Henbane had got his face scratched, and his finger bitten, by the cat, in trying to catch her for a second experiment in killing and bringing to life; and Doctor Morbific was comforting him with a disquisition, to prove that there were only four animals having the power to communicate hydrophobia, of which the cat was one; and that it was not necessary that the animal should be in a rabid state, the nature of the wound being every thing, and the idea of contagion a delusion. Mr Henbane was listening very lugubriously to this dissertation.

Mr Philpot had seized on Mr Firedamp, and pinned him down to a map of Africa, on which he was tracing imaginary courses of mighty inland rivers, terminating in lakes and marshes, where they were finally evaporated by the heat of the sun; and Mr Firedamp's hair was standing on end at the bare imagination of the mass of *malaria* that must be engendered by the operation. Mr Toogood had begun explaining his diagrams to Sir Simon Steeltrap; but Sir Simon grew testy, and told Mr Toogood that the promulgators of such doctrines ought to be consigned to the treadmill. The philanthropist walked off from the country gentleman, and proceeded to hold forth to young Crotchet, who stood silent, as one who listens, but in reality without hearing a syllable. Mr Crotchet senior, as the master of the house, was left to entertain himself with his own meditations, till the Reverend Doctor Folliott tore himself from Mr Mac Quedy, and proceeded to expostulate with Mr Crotchet on a delicate topic.

There was an Italian painter, who obtained the name of *Il Bragatore*,[3] by the superinduction of inexpressibles on the naked Apollos and Bacchuses of his betters. The fame of this worthy remained one and indivisible, till a set of heads, which had been, by a too common mistake of nature's journeymen, stuck upon magisterial shoulders, as the Corinthian capitals of 'fair round bellies with fat capon lined,'[4] but which nature herself had intended for the noddles of porcelain mandarins, promulgated simultaneously from the east and the west of London, an order that no plaster-of-Paris Venus should appear in the streets without petticoats. Mr Crotchet, on reading this order in the evening paper, which, by the postman's early arrival, was always laid on his breakfast-table, determined to fill his house with Venuses of all sizes and kinds. In pursuance of this resolution, came packages by water-carriage, containing an infinite variety of Venuses. There were the Medicean Venus, and the Bathing Venus; the Uranian Venus, and the Pandemian Venus; the Crouching Venus, and the Sleeping Venus; the Venus rising from the sea, the Venus with the apple of Paris, and the Venus with the armour of Mars.

The Reverend Doctor Folliott had been very much

astonished at this unexpected display. Disposed, as he was, to hold, that whatever had been in Greece, was right; he was more than doubtful of the propriety of throwing open the classical *adytum* to the illiterate profane. Whether, in his interior mind, he was at all influenced, either by the consideration that it would be for the credit of his cloth, with some of his vice-suppressing neighbours, to be able to say that he had expostulated; or by curiosity, to try what sort of defence his city-bred friend, who knew the classics only by translations, and whose reason was always a little a-head of his knowledge, would make for his somewhat ostentatious display of liberality in matters of taste; is a question, on which the learned may differ: but, after having duly deliberated on two full-sized casts of the Uranian and Pandemian Venus, in niches on each side of the chimney, and on three alabaster figures, in glass cases, on the mantelpiece, he proceeded, peirastically, to open his fire.

THE REV DR FOLLIOTT

These little alabaster figures on the mantelpiece, Mr Crotchet, and those large figures in the niches – may I take the liberty to ask you what they are intended to represent?

MR CROTCHET

Venus, sir; nothing more, sir; just Venus.

THE REV DR FOLLIOTT

May I ask you, sir, why they are there?

MR CROTCHET

To be looked at, sir; just to be looked at: the reason for most things in a gentleman's house being in it at all; from the paper on the walls, and the drapery of the curtains, even to the books in the library, of which the most essential part is the appearance of the back.

THE REV DR FOLLIOTT

Very true, sir. As great philosophers hold that the *esse* of things is *percipi*, so a gentleman's furniture exists to be

looked at. Nevertheless, sir, there are some things more
fit to be looked at than others; for instance, there is nothing
more fit to be looked at than the outside of a book. It is, as
I may say, from repeated experience, a pure and unmixed
pleasure to have a goodly volume lying before you, and to
know that you may open it if you please, and need not open
it unless you please. It is a resource against *ennui*, if *ennui*
should come upon you. To have the resource and not to feel
the *ennui*, to enjoy your bottle in the present, and your
book in the indefinite future, is a delightful condition of
human existence. There is no place, in which a man can
move or sit, in which the outside of a book can be otherwise than an innocent and becoming spectacle. Touching
this matter, there cannot, I think, be two opinions. But
with respect to your Venuses there can be, and indeed there
are, two very distinct opinions. Now, sir, that little figure
in the centre of the mantelpiece, – as a grave *paterfamilias*,
Mr Crotchet, with a fair nubile daughter, whose eyes are
like the fish-pools of Heshbon, – I would ask you if you
hold that figure to be altogether delicate?

MR CROTCHET

The Sleeping Venus, sir? Nothing can be more delicate than
the entire contour of the figure, the flow of the hair on the
shoulders and neck, the form of the feet and fingers. It is
altogether a most delicate morsel.

THE REV DR FOLLIOTT

Why, in that sense, perhaps, it is as delicate as whitebait in
July. But the attitude, sir, the attitude.

MR CROTCHET

Nothing can be more natural, sir.

THE REV DR FOLLIOTT

That is the very thing, sir. It is too natural: too natural,
sir: it lies for all the world like – I make no doubt, the pious

cheesemonger, who recently broke its plaster fac-simile over the head of the itinerant vendor, was struck by a certain similitude to the position of his own sleeping beauty, and felt his noble wrath thereby justly aroused.

MR CROTCHET

Very likely, sir. In my opinion, the cheesemonger was a fool, and the justice who sided with him was a greater.

THE REV DR FOLLIOTT

Fool, sir, is a harsh term: call not thy brother a fool.

MR CROTCHET

Sir, neither the cheesemonger nor the justice is a brother of mine.

THE REV DR FOLLIOTT

Sir, we are all brethren.

MR CROTCHET

Yes, sir, as the hangman is of the thief; the 'squire of the poacher; the judge of the libeller; the lawyer of his client; the statesman of his colleague; the bubble-blower of the bubble-buyer; the slave-driver of the negro: as these are brethren, so am I and the worthies in question.

THE REV DR FOLLIOTT

To be sure, sir, in these instances, and in many others, the term brother must be taken in its utmost latitude of inter-pretation: we are all brothers, nevertheless. But to return to the point. Now these two large figures, one with drapery on the lower half of the body, and the other with no drapery at all; upon my word, sir, it matters not what godfathers and godmothers may have promised and vowed for the children of this world, touching the devil and other things to be re-nounced, if such figures as those are to be put before their eyes.

MR CROTCHET

Sir, the naked figure is the Pandemian Venus, and the half-draped figure is the Uranian Venus; and I say, sir, that figure realises the finest imaginings of Plato, and is the personification of the most refined and exalted feeling of which the human mind is susceptible; the love of pure, ideal, intellectual beauty.

THE REV DR FOLLIOTT

I am aware, sir, that Plato, in his Symposium, discourseth very eloquently touching the Uranian and Pandemian Venus: but you must remember that, in our Universities, Plato is held to be little better than a misleader of youth; and they have shown their contempt for him, not only by never reading him (a mode of contempt in which they deal very largely), but even by never printing a complete edition of him; although they have printed many ancient books, which nobody suspects to have been ever read on the spot, except by a person attached to the press, who is therefore emphatically called 'the reader.'

MR CROTCHET

Well, sir?

THE REV DR FOLLIOTT

Why, sir, to 'the reader' aforesaid (supposing either of our Universities to have printed an edition of Plato), or to any one else who can be supposed to have read Plato, or indeed to be ever likely to do so, I would very willingly show these figures; because to such they would, I grant you, be the outward and visible signs of poetical and philosophical ideas: but, to the multitude, the gross carnal multitude, they are but two beautiful women, one half undressed, and the other quite so.

MR CROTCHET

Then, sir, let the multitude look upon them and learn modesty.

THE REV DR FOLLIOTT

I must say that, if I wished my footman to learn modesty, I should not dream of sending him to school to a naked Venus.

MR CROTCHET

Sir, ancient sculpture is the true school of modesty. But where the Greeks had modesty, we have cant; where they had poetry, we have cant; where they had patriotism, we have cant; where they had any thing that exalts, delights, or adorns humanity, we have nothing but cant, cant, cant. And, sir, to show my contempt for cant in all its shapes, I have adorned my house with the Greek Venus, in all her shapes, and am ready to fight her battle against all the societies that ever were instituted for the suppression of truth and beauty.

THE REV DR FOLLIOTT

My dear sir, I am afraid you are growing warm. Pray be cool. Nothing contributes so much to good digestion as to be perfectly cool after dinner.

MR CROTCHET

Sir, the Lacedæmonian virgins wrestled naked with young men: and they grew up, as the wise Lycurgus had foreseen, into the most modest of women, and the most exemplary of wives and mothers.

THE REV DR FOLLIOTT

Very likely, sir; but the Athenian virgins did no such thing, and they grew up into wives who stayed at home, – stayed at home, sir; and looked after the husband's dinner, – his dinner, sir, you will please to observe.

MR CROTCHET

And what was the consequence of that, sir? that they were such very insipid persons that the husband would not go home to eat his dinner, but preferred the company of some Aspasia, or Lais.

THE REV DR FOLLIOTT

Two very different persons, sir, give me leave to remark.

MR CROTCHET

Very likely, sir; but both too good to be married in Athens.

THE REV DR FOLLIOTT

Sir, Lais was a Corinthian.

MR CROTCHET

'Od's vengeance, sir, some Aspasia and any other Athenian name of the same sort of person you like –

THE REV DR FOLLIOTT

I do not like the sort of person at all: the sort of person I like, as I have already implied, is a modest woman, who stays at home and looks after her husband's dinner.

MR CROTCHET

Well, sir, that was not the taste of the Athenians. They preferred the society of women who would not have made any scruple about sitting as models to Praxiteles; as you know, sir, very modest women in Italy did to Canova: one of whom, an Italian countess,[5] being asked by an English lady, 'how she could bear it?' answered, 'Very well; there was a good fire in the room.'

THE REV DR FOLLIOTT

Sir, the English lady should have asked how the Italian lady's husband could bear it. The phials of my wrath would overflow if poor dear Mrs Folliott –: sir, in return for your story, I will tell you a story of my ancestor, Gilbert Folliott. The devil haunted him, as he did Saint Francis, in the likeness of a beautiful damsel; but all he could get from the exemplary Gilbert was an admonition to wear a stomacher and longer petticoats.

MR CROTCHET

Sir, your story makes for my side of the question. It proves that the devil, in the likeness of a fair damsel, with short petticoats and no stomacher, was almost too much for Gilbert Folliott. The force of the spell was in the drapery.

THE REV DR FOLLIOTT

Bless my soul, sir!

MR CROTCHET

Give me leave, sir. Diderot –

THE REV DR FOLLIOTT

Who was he, sir?

MR CROTCHET

Who was he, sir? the sublime philosopher, the father of the encyclopædia, of all the encyclopædias that have ever been printed.

THE REV DR FOLLIOTT

Bless me, sir, a terrible progeny! they belong to the tribe of *Incubi*.

MR CROTCHET

The great philosopher, Diderot –

THE REV DR FOLLIOTT

Sir, Diderot is not a man after my heart. Keep to the Greeks, if you please; albeit this Sleeping Venus is not an antique.

MR CROTCHET

Well, sir, the Greeks: why do we call the Elgin marbles inestimable? Simply because they are true to nature. And why are they so superior in that point to all modern works, with all our greater knowledge of anatomy? Why, sir, but because the Greeks, having no cant, had better opportunities of studying models?

THE REV DR FOLLIOTT

Sir, I deny our greater knowledge of anatomy. But I shall take the liberty to employ, on this occasion, the *argumentum ad hominem*. Would you have allowed Miss Crotchet to sit for a model to Canova?

MR CROTCHET

Yes, sir.

'God bless my soul, sir!' exclaimed the Reverend Doctor Folliott, throwing himself back into a chair, and flinging up his heels, with the premeditated design of giving emphasis to his exclamation: but by miscalculating his *impetus*, he overbalanced his chair, and laid himself on the carpet in a right angle, of which his back was the base.

*

CHAPTER VIII

Science and Charity

Chi sta nel mondo un par d'ore contento,
Nè gli vien tolta, ovver contaminata,
Quella sua pace in veruno momento,
Può dir che Giove drittamente il guata.
FORTEGUERRI[1]

THE Reverend Doctor Folliott took his departure about ten o'clock, to walk home to his vicarage. There was no moon; but the night was bright and clear, and afforded him as much light as he needed. He paused a moment by the Roman camp, to listen to the nightingale; repeated to himself a passage of Sophocles;[2] proceeded through the park gate, and entered the narrow lane that led to the village. He walked on in a very pleasant mood of the state called *reverie*; in which fish and wine, Greek and political economy, the Sleeping Venus he had left behind and poor dear Mrs Folliott, to whose fond arms he was returning, passed as in a *camera obscura* over the tablets of his imagination. Presently the image of Mr Eavesdrop, with a printed sketch of the Reverend Doctor F., presented itself before him, and he began mechanically to flourish his bamboo. The movement was prompted by his good genius, for the uplifted bamboo received the blow of a ponderous cudgel, which was intended for his head. The reverend gentleman recoiled two or three paces, and saw before him a couple of ruffians, who were preparing to renew the attack, but whom, with two swings of his bamboo, he laid with cracked sconces on the earth, where he proceeded to deal with them like corn beneath the flail of the thresher. One of them drew a pistol, which went off in the very act of being struck aside by the bamboo, and lodged a bullet in the brain of the other. There was then only one enemy, who vainly struggled to rise, every effort being attended with a new and more signal prostration. The fellow roared for mercy. 'Mercy, rascal!' cried the divine; 'what mercy were you going to show me, villain? What! I warrant me, you thought it would be an easy matter, and no sin, to rob and murder a parson on his way home from dinner. You said to yourselves, doubtless, "We'll waylay the fat parson (you irreverent knave) as he waddles home (you disparaging ruffian), half-seas-over (you calumnious vagabond)."' And with every dyslogistic term, which he supposed had been applied to himself, he inflicted a new bruise on his rolling and roaring antagonist. 'Ah, rogue!' he proceeded; 'you can roar now, marauder; you were silent enough when you devoted my brains to dispersion under your cudgel. But seeing that I cannot bind you, and that I intend you not to escape, and that it would be dangerous to let you rise, I will disable you in all your members; I will contund you as Thestylis did strong-smelling herbs,[3] in the quality whereof you do most gravely partake, as my nose beareth testimony, ill weed that you are. I will beat you to a jelly, and I will then roll you into the ditch, to lie till the constable comes for you, thief.'

'Hold! hold! reverend sir,' exclaimed the penitent culprit, 'I am disabled already in every finger, and in every joint. I will roll myself into the ditch, reverend sir.'

'Stir not, rascal,' returned the divine, 'stir not so much as the quietest leaf above you, or my bamboo rebounds on your body like hail in a thunder storm. Confess speedily, villain; are you simple thief, or would you have manufactured me into a subject, for the benefit of science? Ay, miscreant caitiff, you would have made me a subject for science,[4] would you? You are a schoolmaster abroad,[5] are you? You are marching with a detachment of the march of mind, are you? You are a member of the Steam Intellect Society, are you? You swear by the learned friend, do you?'

'Oh, no! reverend sir,' answered the criminal, 'I am innocent of all these offences, whatever they are, reverend sir. The only friend I had in the world is lying dead beside me, reverend sir.'

The reverend gentleman paused a moment, and leaned on his bamboo. The culprit, bruised as he was, sprang on his legs, and went off in double quick time. The doctor gave him chase, and had nearly brought him within arm's length, when the fellow turned at right angles, and sprang clean over a deep dry ditch. The divine, following with equal ardour, and less dexterity, went down over head and ears into a thicket of nettles. Emerging with much discomposure, he proceeded to the village, and roused the constable; but the constable found, on reaching the scene of action, that the dead man was gone, as well as his living accomplice.

'Oh, the monster!' exclaimed the Reverend Doctor Folliott, 'he has made a subject for science of the only friend he had in the world.' 'Ay, my dear,' he resumed, the next morning at breakfast, 'if my old reading, and my early gymnastics (for as the great Hermann says, before I was demulced by the Muses, I was *ferocis ingenii puer, et ad arma quam ad literas paratior*),[6] had not imbued me indelibly with some of the holy rage of *Frère Jean des Entommeures*,[7] I should be, at this moment, lying on the table of some flinty-hearted anatomist, who would have sliced and disjointed me as unscrupulously as I do these remnants of the capon and chine, wherewith you consoled yourself yesterday for my absence at dinner. Phew! I have a noble thirst upon me, which I will quench with floods of tea.'

The reverend gentleman was interrupted by a messenger, who informed him that the Charity Commissioners[8] requested his presence at the inn, where they were holding a sitting.

'The Charity Commissioners!' exclaimed the reverend gentleman, 'who on earth are they?'

The messenger could not inform him, and the reverend gentleman took his hat and stick, and proceeded to the inn.

On entering the best parlour, he saw three well-dressed and bulky gentlemen sitting at a table, and a fourth officiating as clerk, with an open book before him, and a pen in his hand. The churchwardens, who had been also summoned, were already in attendance.

The chief commissioner politely requested the Reverend Doctor Folliott to be seated; and after the usual meteorological preliminaries had been settled by a resolution, *nem. con.*, that it was a fine day but very hot, the chief commissioner stated, that in virtue of the commission of Parliament, which they had the honour to hold, they were now to inquire into the state of the public charities of this village.

THE REV DR FOLLIOTT

The state of the public charities, sir, is exceedingly simple. There are none. The charities here are all private, and so private, that I for one know nothing of them.

FIRST COMMISSIONER

We have been informed, sir, that there is an annual rent charged on the land of Hautbois, for the endowment and repair of an almshouse.

THE REV DR FOLLIOTT

Hautbois! Hautbois!

FIRST COMMISSIONER

The manorial farm of Hautbois, now occupied by Farmer Seedling, is charged with the endowment and maintenance of an almshouse.

THE REV DR FOLLIOTT (*to the Churchwarden*)

How is this, Mr Bluenose?

FIRST CHURCHWARDEN

I really do not know, sir. What say you, Mr Appletwig?

MR APPLETWIG (*parish-clerk and schoolmaster; an old man*)

I do remember, gentlemen, to have been informed, that there did stand at the end of the village a ruined cottage, which had once been an almshouse, which was endowed and maintained, by an annual revenue of a mark and a half, or one pound sterling, charged some centuries ago on the farm of Hautbois; but the means, by the progress of time, having become inadequate to the end, the almshouse tumbled to pieces.

FIRST COMMISSIONER

But this is a right which cannot be abrogated by desuetude, and the sum of one pound per annum is still chargeable for charitable purposes on the manorial farm of Hautbois.

THE REV DR FOLLIOTT

Very well, sir.

MR APPLETWIG

But sir, the one pound per annum is still received by the parish, but was long ago, by an unanimous vote in open vestry, given to the minister.

THE THREE COMMISSIONERS (*unâ voce*)

The   inister!

FIRST COMMISSIONER

This is an unjustifiable proceeding.

SECOND COMMISSIONER

A misappropriation of a public fund.

THIRD COMMISSIONER

A flagrant perversion of a charitable donation.

THE REV DR FOLLIOTT

God bless my soul, gentlemen! I know nothing of this matter. How is this, Mr Bluenose? Do I receive this one pound per annum?

FIRST CHURCHWARDEN

Really, sir, I know no more about it than you do.

MR APPLETWIG

You certainly receive it, sir. It was voted to one of your predecessors. Farmer Seedling lumps it in with his tithes.

FIRST COMMISSIONER

Lumps it in, sir! Lump in a charitable donation!

SECOND AND THIRD COMMISSIONER

Oh-oh-oh-h-h!

FIRST COMMISSIONER

Reverend sir, and gentlemen, officers of this parish, we are under the necessity of admonishing you that this is a most improper proceeding; and you are hereby duly admonished accordingly. Make a record, Mr Milky.

MR MILKY (*writing*)

The clergyman and churchwardens of the village of Hm-m-m-m gravely admonished. Hm-m-m-m.

THE REV DR FOLLIOTT

Is that all, gentlemen?

THE COMMISSIONERS

That is all, sir; and we wish you a good morning.

THE REV DR FOLLIOTT

A very good morning to you, gentlemen.

'What in the name of all that is wonderful, Mr Bluenose,' said the Reverend Doctor Folliott, as he walked out of the inn, 'what in the name of all that is wonderful, can those fellows mean? They have come here in a chaise and four, to make a fuss about a pound per annum, which, after all, they leave as it was. I wonder who pays them for their trouble, and how much.'

MR APPLETWIG

The public pay for it, sir. It is a job of the learned friend whom you admire so much. It makes away with public money in salaries, and private money in lawsuits, and does no particle of good to any living soul.

THE REV DR FOLLIOTT

Ay, ay, Mr Appletwig; that is just the sort of public service to be looked for from the learned friend. Oh, the learned friend! the learned friend! He is the evil genius of every thing that falls in his way.

The reverend doctor walked off to Crotchet Castle, to narrate his misadventures, and exhale his budget of grievances on Mr Mac Quedy, whom he considered a ringleader of the march of mind.

*

CHAPTER IX

The Voyage

Οἱ μὲν ἔπειτ' ἀναβάντες ἐπέπλεον ὑγρὰ κέλευθα.

Mounting the bark, they cleft the watery ways.

HOMER[1]

FOUR beautiful cabined pinnaces, one for the ladies, one for the gentlemen, one for kitchen and servants, one for a dining-room and band of music, weighed anchor, on a fine July morning, from below Crotchet Castle, and were towed merrily, by strong trotting horses, against the stream of the Thames. They passed from the district of chalk, successively into the districts of clay, of sand-rock, of oolite, and so forth. Sometimes they dined in their floating dining-room, sometimes in tents, which they pitched on the dry smooth-shaven green of a newly mown meadow; sometimes they left their vessels to see sights in the vicinity; sometimes they passed a day or two in a comfortable inn.

At Oxford, they walked about to see the curiosities of architecture, painted windows, and undisturbed libraries. The Reverend Doctor Folliott laid a wager with Mr Crotchet 'that in all their perlustrations they would not find a man reading,' and won it. 'Ay, sir,' said the reverend gentleman, 'this is still a seat of learning, on the principle of – once a captain always a captain. We may well ask, in these great reservoirs of books whereof no man ever draws a sluice, *Quorsum pertinuit stipare Platona Menandro?* [2] What is done here for the classics? Reprinting German editions on better paper. A great boast, verily! What for mathematics? What for metaphysics? What for history? What for any thing worth knowing? This was a seat of learning in the days of Friar Bacon. But the friar is gone, and his learning with him. Nothing of him is left but the immortal nose,[3] which when his brazen head had tumbled to pieces, crying 'Time's past,' was the only palpable fragment among its minutely pulverised atoms, and which is still resplendent over the portals of its cognominal college. That nose, sir, is the only thing to which I shall take off my hat, in all this Babylon of buried literature.

MR CROTCHET

But, doctor, it is something to have a great reservoir of learning, at which some may draw if they please.

THE REV DR FOLLIOTT

But, here, good care is taken that nobody shall please. If even a small drop from the sacred fountain, πίδακος ἐξ ἱερῆς ὀλίγη λιβάς,[4] as Callimachus has it, were carried off by any one, it would be evidence of something to hope for. But the system of dissuasion from all good learning is brought here to a pitch of perfection that baffles the keenest aspirant. I run over to myself the names of the scholars of Germany, a glorious catalogue! but ask for those of Oxford – Where are they? The echoes of their courts, as vacant as their heads, will answer, Where are they? The tree shall be known by its fruit; and seeing that this great tree, with all its specious seeming, brings forth no fruit, I do denounce it as a barren fig.

MR MAC QUEDY

I shall set you right on this point. We do nothing without motives. If learning get nothing but honour, and very little of that; and if the good things of this world, which ought to be the rewards of learning, become the mere gifts of self-interested patronage; you must not wonder if, in the finishing of education, the science which takes precedence of all others, should be the science of currying favour.

THE REV DR FOLLIOTT

Very true, sir. Education is well finished, for all worldly purposes, when the head is brought into the state whereinto I am accustomed to bring a marrow-bone, when it has been set before me on a toast, with a white napkin wrapped round it. Nothing trundles along the high road of preferment so trimly as a well-biased sconce, picked clean within, and polished without; *totus teres atque rotundus*.[5] The perfection of the finishing lies in the bias, which keeps it trundling in the given direction. There is good and sufficient reason for the fig being barren, but it is not therefore the less a barren fig.

At Godstow, they gathered hazel on the grave of Rosamond;[6] and, proceeding on their voyage, fell into a discussion on legendary histories.

LADY CLARINDA

History is but a tiresome thing in itself; it becomes more agreeable the more romance is mixed up with it. The great enchanter has made me learn many things which I should never have dreamed of studying, if they had not come to me in the form of amusement.

THE REV DR FOLLIOTT

What enchanter is that? There are two enchanters: he of the North,[7] and he of the South.

MR TRILLO

Rossini?

THE REV DR FOLLIOTT

Ay, there is another enchanter. But I mean the great enchanter of Covent Garden:[8] he who, for more than a quarter of a century, has produced two pantomimes a year, to the delight of children of all ages, including myself at all ages. That is the enchanter for me. I am for the pantomimes. All the northern enchanter's romances put together would not furnish materials for half the southern enchanter's pantomimes.

LADY CLARINDA

Surely you do not class literature with pantomime?

THE REV DR FOLLIOTT

In these cases I do. They are both one, with a slight difference. The one is the literature of pantomime, the other is the pantomime of literature. There is the same variety of character, the same diversity of story, the same copiousness of incident, the same research into costume, the same display of heraldry, falconry, minstrelsy, scenery, monkery, witchery, devilry, robbery, poachery, piracy, fishery, gipsy-astrology, demonology, architecture, fortification, castra-metation, navigation; the same running base of love and battle. The main difference is, that the one set of amusing fictions is told in music and action; the other in all the worst dialects of the English language. As to any sentence worth remembering, any moral or political truth, any thing having a tendency, however remote, to make men wiser or better, to make them think, to make them even think of thinking; they are both precisely alike: *nuspiam, nequaquam, nullibi, nullimodis.*[9]

LADY CLARINDA

Very amusing, however.

THE REV DR FOLLIOTT

Very   using, very amusing.

MR CHAINMAIL

My quarrel with the northern enchanter is, that he has grossly misrepresented the twelfth century.

THE REV DR FOLLIOTT

He has misrepresented every thing, or he would not have been very amusing. Sober truth is but dull matter to the reading rabble. The angler, who puts not on his hook the bait that best pleases the fish, may sit all day on the bank without catching a gudgeon.[10]

MR MAC QUEDY

But how do you mean that he has misrepresented the twelfth century? By exhibiting some of its knights and ladies in the colours of refinement and virtue, seeing that they were all no better than ruffians, and something else that shall be nameless?

MR CHAINMAIL

By no means. By depicting them as much worse than they were, not, as you suppose, much better. No one would infer from his pictures that theirs was a much better state of society than this which we live in.

MR MAC QUEDY

No, nor was it. It was a period of brutality, ignorance, fanaticism, and tyranny; when the land was covered with castles, and every castle contained a gang of banditti, headed by a titled robber, who levied contributions with fire and sword; plundering, torturing, ravishing, burying his captives in loathsome dungeons, and broiling them on gridirons, to force from them the surrender of every particle of treasure which he suspected them of possessing; and fighting every now and then with the neighbouring lords, his conterminal bandits, for the right of marauding on the boundaries. This was the twelfth century, as depicted by all contemporary historians and poets.

MR CHAINMAIL

No, sir. Weigh the evidence of specific facts; you will find more good than evil. Who was England's greatest hero; the mirror of chivalry, the pattern of honour, the fountain of generosity, the model to all succeeding ages of military glory? Richard the First. There is a king of the twelfth century. What was the first step of liberty? Magna Charta. That was the best thing ever done by lords. There are lords of the twelfth century. You must remember, too, that these lords were petty princes, and made war on each other as legitimately as the heads of larger communities did or do. For their system of revenue, it was, to be sure, more rough and summary than that which has succeeded it, but it was certainly less searching and less productive. And as to the people, I content myself with these great points: that every man was armed, every man was a good archer, every man could and would fight effectively with sword or pike, or even with oaken cudgel: no man would live quietly without beef and ale; if he had them not, he fought till he either got them, or was put out of condition to want them. They were not, and could not be, subjected to that powerful pressure of all the other classes of society, combined by gunpowder, steam, and *fiscality*, which has brought them to that dismal degradation in which we see them now. And there are the people of the twelfth century.

MR MAC QUEDY

As to your king, the enchanter has done him ample justice, even in your own view. As to your lords and their ladies, he has drawn them too favourably, given them too many of the false colours of chivalry, thrown too attractive a light on their abominable doings. As to the people, he keeps them so much in the back-ground, that he can hardly be said to have represented them at all, much less misrepresented them, which indeed he could scarcely do, seeing that, by your own showing, they were all thieves, ready to knock down any man for what they could not come by honestly.

MR CHAINMAIL

No, sir. They could come honestly by beef and ale, while they were left to their simple industry. When oppression interfered with them in that, then they stood on the defensive, and fought for what they were not permitted to come by quietly.

MR MAC QUEDY

If A, being aggrieved by B, knocks down C, do you call that standing on the defensive?

MR CHAINMAIL

That depends on who or what C is.

THE REV DR FOLLIOTT

Gentlemen, you will never settle this controversy, till you have first settled what is good for man in this world; the great question, *de finibus*, which has puzzled all philosophers. If the enchanter has represented the twelfth century too brightly for one, and too darkly for the other of you, I should say, as an impartial man, he has represented it fairly. My quarrel with him is, that his works contain nothing worth quoting; and a book that furnishes no quotations, is, *me judice*, no book – it is a plaything. There is no question about the amusement – amusement of multitudes; but if he who amuses us most, is to be our enchanter κατ᾽ ἐξοχὴν,[11] then my enchanter is the enchanter of Covent Garden.

*

CHAPTER X

The Voyage, Continued

Continuant nostre routte, navigasmes par trois jours
sans rien descouvrir.

RABELAIS[1]

'THERE is a beautiful structure,' said Mr Chainmail, as they
glided by Lechlade church; 'a subject for the pencil, Captain. It is a question worth asking, Mr Mac Quedy, whether
the religious spirit which reared these edifices, and connected with them everywhere an asylum for misfortune and
a provision for poverty, was not better than the commercial
spirit, which has turned all the business of modern life into
schemes of profit, and processes of fraud and extortion. I do
not see, in all your boasted improvements, any compensation for the religious charity of the twelfth century. I do
not see any compensation for that kindly feeling which,
within their own little communities, bound the several
classes of society together, while full scope was left for the
development of natural character, wherein individuals
differed as conspicuously as in costume. Now, we all wear
one conventional dress, one conventional face; we have no
bond of union, but pecuniary interest; we talk any thing
that comes uppermost, for talking's sake, and without
expecting to be believed; we have no nature, no simplicity,
no picturesqueness: every thing about us is as artificial and
as complicated as our steam-machinery: our poetry is a
kaleidoscope of false imagery, expressing no real feeling,
portraying no real existence. I do not see any compensation
for the poetry of the twelfth century.'

MR MAC QUEDY

I wonder to hear you, Mr Chainmail, talking of the religious
charity of a set of lazy monks and beggarly friars, who were
much more occupied with taking than giving; of whom,

those who were in earnest did nothing but make themselves, and every body about them, miserable, with fastings, and penances, and other such trash; and those who were not, did nothing but guzzle and royster, and, having no wives of their own, took very unbecoming liberties with those of honester men. And as to your poetry of the twelfth century, it is not good for much.

MR CHAINMAIL

It has, at any rate, what ours wants, truth to nature, and simplicity of diction. The poetry, which was addressed to the people of the dark ages, pleased in proportion to the truth with which it depicted familiar images, and to their natural connection with the time and place to which they were assigned. In the poetry of our enlightened times, the characteristics of all seasons, soils, and climates, may be blended together, with much benefit to the author's fame as an original genius. The cowslip of a civic poet is always in blossom, his fern is always in full feather; he gathers the celandine, the primrose, the heath-flower, the jasmine, and the chrysanthemum, all on the same day, and from the same spot: his nightingale sings all the year round, his moon is always full, his cygnet is as white as his swan, his cedar is as tremulous as his aspen, and his poplar as embowering as his beech. Thus all nature marches with the march of mind; but, among barbarians, instead of mead and wine, and the best seat by the fire, the reward of such a genius would have been, to be summarily turned out of doors in the snow, to meditate on the difference between day and night, and between December and July. It is an age of liberality, indeed, when not to know an oak from a burdock is no disqualification for sylvan minstrelsy. I am for truth and simplicity.

THE REV DR FOLLIOTT

Let him who loves them read Greek: Greek, Greek, Greek.

MR MAC QUEDY

If he can, sir.

THE REV DR FOLLIOTT

Very true, sir; if he can. Here is the captain, who can. But
I think he must have finished his education at some very
rigid college, where a quotation, or any other overt act
showing acquaintance with classical literature, was visited
with a severe penalty. For my part, I make it my boast
that I was not to be so subdued. I could not be abated
of a single quotation by all the bumpers in which I was
fined.

In this manner they glided over the face of the waters,
discussing every thing and settling nothing. Mr Mac Quedy
and the Reverend Doctor Folliott had many digladiations
on political economy: wherein, each in his own view, Doctor
Folliott demolished Mr Mac Quedy's science, and Mr Mac
Quedy demolished Doctor Folliott's objections.

We would print these dialogues if we thought any one
would read them: but the world is not yet ripe for this *haute
sagesse Pantagrueline*. We must, therefore, content ourselves with an *échantillon* of one of the Reverend Doctor's
perorations.

'You have given the name of a science to what is yet an
imperfect inquiry; and the upshot of your so-called science
is this, that you increase the wealth of a nation by increasing in it the quantity of things which are produced by
labour: no matter what they are, no matter how produced,
no matter how distributed. The greater the quantity of
labour that has gone to the production of the quantity of
things in a community, the richer is the community. That is
your doctrine. Now, I say, if this be so, riches are not the
object for a community to aim at. I say, the nation is best
off, in relation to other nations, which has the greatest
quantity of the common necessaries of life distributed
among the greatest number of persons; which has the

greatest number of honest hearts and stout arms united in a common interest, willing to offend no one, but ready to fight in defence of their own community against all the rest of the world, because they have something in it worth fighting for. The moment you admit that one class of things, without any reference to what they respectively cost, is better worth having than another; that a smaller commercial value, with one mode of distribution, is better than a greater commercial value, with another mode of distribution; the whole of that curious fabric of postulates and dogmas, which you call the science of political economy, and which I call *politicæ œconomiæ inscientia*, tumbles to pieces.'

Mr Toogood agreed with Mr Chainmail against Mr Mac Quedy, that the existing state of society was worse than that of the twelfth century; but he agreed with Mr Mac Quedy against Mr Chainmail, that it was in progress to something much better than either, – to which 'something much better' Mr Toogood and Mr Mac Quedy attached two very different meanings.

Mr Chainmail fought with Doctor Folliott, the battle of the romantic against the classical in poetry; and Mr Skionar contended with Mr Mac Quedy for intuition and synthesis, against analysis and induction in philosophy.

Mr Philpot would lie along for hours, listening to the gurgling of the water round the prow, and would occasionally edify the company with speculations on the great changes that would be effected in the world by the steam-navigation of rivers: sketching the course of a steam-boat up and down some mighty stream which civilisation had either never visited, or long since deserted; the Missouri and the Columbia, the Oroonoko and the Amazon, the Nile and the Niger, the Euphrates and the Tigris, the Oxus and the Indus, the Ganges and the Hoangho; under the overcanopying forests of the new, or by the long-silent ruins of the ancient, world; through the shapeless mounds of Babylon, or the gigantic temples of Thebes.

Mr Trillo went on with the composition of his opera, and

took the opinions of the young ladies on every step in its progress; occasionally regaling the company with specimens, and wondering at the blindness of Mr Mac Quedy, who could not, or would not, see that an opera in perfection, being the union of all the beautiful arts, – music, painting, dancing, poetry, – exhibiting female beauty in its most attractive aspects, and in its most becoming costume, – was, according to the well-known precept, *Ingenuas didicisse*, &c.,[2] the most efficient instrument of civilisation, and ought to take precedence of all other pursuits in the minds of true philanthropists. The Reverend Doctor Folliott, on these occasions, never failed to say a word or two on Mr Trillo's side, derived from the practice of the Athenians, and from the combination, in their theatre, of all the beautiful arts, in a degree of perfection unknown to the modern world.

Leaving Lechlade, they entered the canal that connects the Thames with the Severn; ascended by many locks; passed by a tunnel three miles long, through the bowels of Sapperton Hill; agreed unanimously that the greatest pleasure derivable from visiting a cavern of any sort was that of getting out of it; descended by many locks again, through the valley of Stroud into the Severn; continued their navigation into the Ellesmere canal; moored their pinnaces in the Vale of Llangollen by the aqueduct of Pontycysyllty; and determined to pass some days in inspecting the scenery, before commencing their homeward voyage.

The captain omitted no opportunity of pressing his suit on Lady Clarinda, but could never draw from her any reply but the same doctrines of worldly wisdom, delivered in a tone of *badinage*, mixed with a certain kindness of manner that induced him to hope she was not in earnest.

But the morning after they had anchored under the hills of the Dee, – whether the lady had reflected more seriously than usual, or was somewhat less in good humour than usual, or the Captain was more pressing than usual, – she said to him, 'It must not be, Captain Fitzchrome; ''the course of true love never did run smooth:"[3] my father must keep his borough, and I must have a town house and a country house, and an opera box, and a carriage. It is not well for either of us that we should flirt any longer: "I must be cruel only to be kind."[4] Be satisfied with the assurance that you alone, of all men, have ever broken my rest. To be sure, it was only for about three nights in all; but that is too much.'

The captain had *le cœur navré*. He took his portfolio under his arm, made up the little *valise* of a pedestrian, and, without saying a word to any one, wandered off at random among the mountains.

After the lapse of a day or two, the captain was missed, and every one marvelled what was become of him. Mr Philpot thought he must have been exploring a river, and fallen in and got drowned in the process. Mr Firedamp had no doubt he had been crossing a mountain bog, and had been suddenly deprived of life by the exhalations of marsh miasmata. Mr Henbane deemed it probable that he had been tempted in some wood by the large black brilliant berries of the *Atropa Belladonna*, or Deadly Nightshade; and lamented that he had not been by, to administer an infallible antidote. Mr Eavesdrop hoped the particulars of his fate would be ascertained; and asked if any one present could help him to any authentic anecdotes of their departed friend. The Reverend Doctor Folliott proposed that an inquiry should be instituted as to whether the march of intellect had reached that neighbourhood; as, if so, the captain had probably been made a subject for science. Mr Mac Quedy said it was no such great matter to ascertain the precise mode in which the surplus population was diminished by one. Mr Toogood asseverated that there was no such thing as surplus population, and that the land, properly managed, would maintain twenty times its present inhabitants: and hereupon they fell into a disputation.

Lady Clarinda did not doubt that the captain had gone away designedly: she missed him more than she could have anticipated; and wished she had at least postponed her last piece of cruelty till the completion of their homeward voyage.

*

CHAPTER XI

Correspondence

'Base is the slave that pays.'
ANCIENT PISTOL[1]

THE captain was neither drowned nor poisoned, neither miasmatised nor anatomised. But, before we proceed to account for him, we must look back to a young lady, of whom some little notice was taken in the first chapter; and who, though she has since been out of sight, has never with us been out of mind; Miss Susannah Touchandgo, the forsaken of the junior Crotchet, whom we left an inmate of a solitary farm, in one of the deep valleys under the cloudcapt summits of Meirion, comforting her wounded spirit with air and exercise, rustic cheer, music, painting, and poetry, and the prattle of the little Ap Llymrys.

One evening, after an interval of anxious expectation, the farmer, returning from market, brought for her two letters, of which the contents were these:

> *Dotandcarryonetown,*
> *State of Apodidraskiana:* [2]
> *April 1. 18..*

MY DEAR CHILD,

I am anxious to learn what are your present position, intention, and prospects. The fairies who dropped gold in your shoe, on the morning when I ceased to be a respectable man in London, will soon find a talismanic channel for transmitting you a stocking full of dollars, which will fit the shoe, as well as the foot of Cinderella fitted her slipper. I am happy to say, I am again become a respectable man. It was always my ambition to be a respectable man; and I am a very respectable man here, in this new township of a new state, where I have purchased five thousand acres of land, at two dollars an acre, hard cash, and established a very flourishing bank. The notes of Touchandgo and Company, soft cash, are now the exclusive currency of all this vicinity. This is the land in which all men flourish; but there are three classes of men who flourish especially, – Methodist preachers, slave-drivers, and paper-money manufacturers; and as one of the latter, I have just painted the word BANK on a fine slab of maple, which was green and growing when I arrived, and have discounted for the settlers, in my own currency, sundry bills, which are to be paid when the proceeds of the crop they have just sown shall return from New Orleans; so that my notes are the representatives of vegetation that is to be, and I am accordingly a capitalist of the first magnitude. The people here know very well that I ran away from London, but the most of them have run away from some place or other; and they have a great respect for me, because they think I ran away with something worth taking, which few of them had the luck or the wit to do. This gives them confidence in my resources, at the same time that, as there is nothing portable in the settlement except my own notes, they have no fear that I shall run away with them. They know I am thoroughly conversant with the principles of banking; and as they have plenty of industry, no lack of sharpness, and abundance of land, they wanted nothing but capital to organise a flourishing settlement; and this capital I have manufactured to the extent required, at the expense of a small importation of pens, ink, and paper, and two or three inimitable copper plates. I have abundance here of all good things, a good conscience included; for I really cannot see that I have done any wrong. This was my position: I owed half a million of money; and I had a trifle in my pocket. It was clear that this trifle could never find its way to the right owner. The question was, whether I should keep it, and live like a gentleman; or hand it over to lawyers and commissioners of bankruptcy, and die like a dog on a dunghill. If I could have thought that the said lawyers, &c., had a better title to it than myself, I might have hesitated; but, as such title was not apparent to my satisfaction, I decided the question in my own favour; the right owners, as I have already said, being out of the question altogether. I have always taken scientific views of morals and politics, a habit from which I derive much comfort under existing circumstances.

I hope you adhere to your music, though I cannot hope again to accompany your harp with my flute. My last *andante* movement was too *forte* for those whom it took by surprise. Let not your *allegro vivace* be damped by young Crotchet's desertion, which, though I have not heard it, I take for granted. He is, like myself, a scientific politician, and has an eye as keen as a needle, to his own interest. He has had good luck so far, and is gorgeous in the spoils of many gulls; but I think the Polar Basin and Walrus Company will be too much for him yet. There has been a splendid outlay on credit; and he is the only man, of the original parties concerned, of whom his majesty's sheriffs could give any account.

I will not ask you to come here. There is no husband for you. The men smoke, drink, and fight, and break more of their own heads than of girls' hearts. Those among them who are musical sing nothing but psalms. They are excellent fellows in their way, but you would not like them.

Au reste, here are no rents, no taxes, no poor-rates, no tithes, no church-establishment, no routs, no clubs, no rotten boroughs, no operas, no concerts, no theatres, no beggars, no thieves, no king, no lords, no ladies, and only one gentleman, videlicet, your loving father,

TIMOTHY TOUCHANDGO.[3]

P.S. – I send you one of my notes; I can afford to part with it. If you are accused of receiving money from me, you may pay it over to my assignees. Robthetill continues to be my factotum; I say no more of him in this place: he will give you an account of himself.

Dotandcarryonetown, &c.

DEAR MISS,

Mr Touchandgo will have told you of our arrival here, of our setting up a bank, and so forth. We came here in a tilted waggon, which served us for parlour, kitchen, and all. We soon got up a log-house; and, unluckily, we as soon got it down again, for the first fire we made in it burned down house and all. However, our second experiment was more fortunate; and we are pretty well lodged in a house of three rooms on a floor; I should say the floor, for there is but one.

This new state is free to hold slaves;[4] all the new states have not this privilege: Mr Touchandgo has bought some, and they are building him a villa. Mr Touchandgo is in a thriving way, but he is not happy here: he longs for parties and concerts, and a seat in congress. He thinks it very hard that he cannot buy one with his own coinage, as he used to do in England. Besides, he is afraid of the regulators,[5] who, if they do not like a man's character, wait upon him and flog him, doubling the dose at stated intervals, till he takes himself off. He does not like this system of administering justice: though I think he has nothing to fear from it. He has the character of having money, which is the best of all characters here, as at home. He lets his old English prejudices influence his opinions of his new neighbours; but I assure you they have many virtues. Though they do keep slaves, they are all ready to fight for their own liberty; and I should not like to be an enemy within reach of one of their rifles. When I say enemy, I include bailiff in the term. One was shot not long ago. There was a trial; the jury gave two dollars damages; the judge said they must find guilty or not guilty; but the counsel for the defendant (they would not call him prisoner), offered to fight the judge upon the point: and as this was said literally, not metaphorically, and the counsel was a stout fellow, the judge gave in. The two dollars damages were not paid after all; for the defendant challenged the foreman to box for double or quits, and the foreman was beaten. The folks in New York made a great outcry about it, but here it was considered all as it should be. So you see, Miss, justice, liberty, and every thing else of that kind, are different in different places, just as suits the convenience of those who have the sword in their own hands. Hoping to hear of your health and happiness, I remain,

Dear Miss, your dutiful servant,
RODERICK ROBTHETILL.

Miss Touchandgo replied as follows, to the first of these letters:

MY DEAR FATHER,

I am sure you have the best of hearts, and I have no doubt you have acted with the best intentions. My lover, or I should rather say, my fortune's lover, has indeed forsaken me. I cannot say I did not feel it; indeed, I cried very much; and the altered looks of people who used to be so delighted to see me, really annoyed me, so that I determined to change the scene altogether. I have come into Wales, and am boarding with a farmer and his wife. Their stock of English is very small, but I managed to agree with them; and they have four of the sweetest children I ever saw, to whom I teach all I know, and I manage to pick up some Welsh. I have puzzled out a little song, which I think very pretty; I have translated it into English, and I send it you, with the original air. You shall play it on your flute at eight o'clock every Saturday evening, and I will play and sing it at the same time, and I will fancy that I hear my dear papa accompanying me.

The people in London said very unkind things of you: they hurt me very much at the time; but now I am out of their way, I do not seem to think their opinion of much consequence. I am sure, when I recollect, at leisure, every thing I have seen and heard among them, I cannot make out what they do that is so virtuous as to set them up for judges of morals. And I am sure they never speak the truth about any thing, and there is no sincerity in either their love or their friendship. An old Welsh bard here, who wears a waistcoat embroidered with leeks, and is called the Green Bard of Cadair Idris, says the Scotch would be the best people in the world if there was nobody but themselves to give them a character; and so, I think, would the Londoners. I hate the very thought of them, for I do believe they would have broken my heart if I had not got out of their way. Now I shall write you another letter very soon, and describe to you the country, and the people, and the children, and how I amuse myself, and every thing that I think you will like to hear about: and when I seal this letter, I shall drop a kiss on the cover.

> Your loving daughter,
> SUSANNAH TOUCHANDGO.

P.S. – Tell Mr Robthetill I will write to him in a day or two. This is the little song I spoke of:

> Beyond the sea, beyond the sea,
> My heart is gone, far, far from me;
> And ever on its track will flee
> My thoughts, my dreams, beyond the sea.

Beyond the sea, beyond the sea,
The swallow wanders fast and free:
Oh, happy bird! were I like thee,
I, too, would fly beyond the sea.

Beyond the sea, beyond the sea,
Are kindly hearts and social glee:
But here for me they may not be;
My heart is gone beyond the sea.[6]

*

CHAPTER XII

The Mountain Inn

'Ὡς ἡδὺ τῷ μισοῦντι τοὺς φαύλους τρόπους
'Ερημία.

How sweet to minds that love not sordid ways
Is solitude!

MENANDER

THE captain wandered despondingly up and down hill for
several days, passing many hours of each in sitting on rocks;
making, almost mechanically, sketches of waterfalls, and
mountain pools; taking care, nevertheless, to be always
before nightfall in a comfortable inn, where, being a
temperate man, he wiled away the evening with making a
bottle of sherry into negus. His rambles brought him at
length into the interior of Merionethshire, the land of all
that is beautiful in nature, and all that is lovely in woman.

Here, in a secluded village, he found a little inn, of small
pretension and much comfort. He felt so satisfied with his
quarters, and discovered every day so much variety in the
scenes of the surrounding mountains, that his inclination to
proceed farther diminished progressively.

It is one thing to follow the high road through a country,
with every principally remarkable object carefully noted

down in a book, taking, as therein directed, a guide, at particular points, to the more recondite sights: it is another to sit down on one chosen spot, especially when the choice is unpremeditated, and from thence, by a series of explorations, to come day by day on unanticipated scenes. The latter process has many advantages over the former; it is free from the disappointment which attends excited expectation, when imagination has outstripped reality, and from the accidents that mar the scheme of the tourist's single day, when the valleys may be drenched with rain, or the mountains shrouded with mist.

The captain was one morning preparing to sally forth on his usual exploration, when he heard a voice without, inquiring for a guide to the ruined castle. The voice seemed familiar to him, and going forth into the gateway, he recognised Mr Chainmail. After greetings and inquiries for the absent, 'You vanished very abruptly, captain,' said Mr Chainmail, 'from our party on the canal.'

CAPTAIN FITZCHROME

To tell you the truth, I had a particular reason for trying the effect of absence from a part of that party.

MR CHAINMAIL

I surmised as much: at the same time, the unusual melancholy of an in general most vivacious young lady made me wonder at your having acted so precipitately. The lady's heart is yours, if there be truth in signs.

CAPTAIN FITZCHROME

Hearts are not now what they were in the days of the old song, 'Will love be controlled by advice?'[1]

MR CHAINMAIL

Very true; hearts, heads, and arms have all degenerated, most sadly. We can no more feel the high impassioned love of the ages, which some people have the impudence to call dark, than we can wield King Richard's battleaxe, bend

Robin Hood's bow, or flourish the oaken graff of the Pinder of Wakefield. Still we have our tastes and feelings, though they deserve not the name of passions; and some of us may pluck up spirit to try to carry a point, when we reflect that we have to contend with men no better than ourselves.

CAPTAIN FITZCHROME

We do not now break lances for ladies.

MR CHAINMAIL

No, nor even bulrushes. We jingle purses for them, flourish paper-money banners, and tilt with scrolls of parchment.

CAPTAIN FITZCHROME

In which sort of tilting I have been thrown from the saddle. I presume it was not love that led you from the flotilla.

MR CHAINMAIL

By no means. I was tempted by the sight of an old tower, not to leave this land of ruined castles, without having collected a few hints for the adornment of my baronial hall.

CAPTAIN FITZCHROME

I understand you live *en famille* with your domestics. You will have more difficulty in finding a lady who would adopt your fashion of living, than one who would prefer you to a richer man.

MR CHAINMAIL

Very true. I have tried the experiment on several as guests; but once was enough for them: so, I suppose, I shall die a bachelor.

CAPTAIN FITZCHROME

I see, like some others of my friends, you will give up any thing except your hobby.

MR CHAINMAIL

I will give up any thing but my baronial hall.

CAPTAIN FITZCHROME

You will never find a wife for your purpose, unless in the daughter of some old-fashioned farmer.

MR CHAINMAIL

No, I thank you. I must have a lady of gentle blood; I shall not marry below my own condition: I am too much of a herald; I have too much of the twelfth century in me for that.

CAPTAIN FITZCHROME

Why then your chance is not much better than mine. A well-born beauty would scarcely be better pleased with your baronial hall, than with my more humble offer of love in a cottage. She must have a town-house, and an opera-box, and roll about the streets in a carriage; especially if her father has a rotten borough, for the sake of which he sells his daughter, that he may continue to sell his country. But you were inquiring for a guide to the ruined castle in this vicinity; I know the way, and will conduct you.

The proposal pleased Mr Chainmail, and they set forth on their expedition.

*

CHAPTER XIII

The Lake – The Ruin

Or vieni, Amore, e quà meco t'assetta.
ORLANDO INNAMORATO[1]

MR CHAINMAIL

WOULD it not be a fine thing, captain, – you being pictur-esque, and I poetical; you being for the lights and shadows of the present, and I for those of the past, – if we were to go

together over the ground which was travelled in the twelfth
century by Giraldus de Barri, when he accompanied
Archbishop Baldwin to preach the crusade?

CAPTAIN FITZCHROME

Nothing, in my present frame of mind, could be more
agreeable to me.

MR CHAINMAIL

We would provide ourselves with his *Itinerarium*; compare
what has been with what is; contemplate in their decay the
castles and abbeys which he saw in their strength and
splendour; and, while you were sketching their remains, I
would dispassionately inquire what has been gained by the
change.

CAPTAIN FITZCHROME

Be it so.

But the scheme was no sooner arranged than the captain
was summoned to London by a letter on business, which he
did not expect to detain him long. Mr Chainmail, who, like
the captain, was fascinated with the inn and the scenery,
determined to await his companion's return; and, having
furnished him with a list of books, which he was to bring
with him from London, took leave of him, and began to pass
his days like the heroes of Ariosto, who

— tutto il giorno, al bel oprar intenti,
Saliron balze, e traversar torrenti.[2]

One day Mr Chainmail traced upwards the course of a
mountain-stream, to a spot where a small waterfall threw
itself over a slab of perpendicular rock, which seemed to
bar his farther progress. On a nearer view, he discovered a
flight of steps, roughly hewn in the rock, on one side of the
fall. Ascending these steps, he entered a narrow winding
pass, between high and naked rocks, that afforded only
space for a rough footpath carved on one side, at some
height above the torrent.

The pass opened on a lake, from which the stream issued, and which lay like a dark mirror, set in a gigantic frame of mountain precipices. Fragments of rock lay scattered on the edge of the lake, some half-buried in the water: Mr Chainmail scrambled some way over these fragments, till the base of a rock, sinking abruptly in the water, effectually barred his progress. He sat down on a large smooth stone; the faint murmur of the stream he had quitted, the occasional flapping of the wings of the heron, and at long intervals the solitary springing of a trout, were the only sounds that came to his ear. The sun shone brightly half-way down the opposite rocks, presenting, on their irregular faces, strong masses of light and shade. Suddenly he heard the dash of a paddle, and, turning his eyes, saw a solitary and beautiful girl gliding over the lake in a coracle; she was proceeding from the vicinity of the point he had quitted towards the upper end of the lake. Her apparel was rustic, but there was in its style something more *recherché*, in its arrangement something more of elegance and precision, than was common to the mountain peasant girl. It had more of the *contadina* of the opera than of the genuine mountaineer; so at least thought Mr Chainmail; but she passed so rapidly, and took him so much by surprise, that he had little opportunity for accurate observation. He saw her land, at the farther extremity, and disappear among the rocks: he rose from his seat, returned to the mouth of the pass, stepped from stone to stone across the stream, and attempted to pass round by the other side of the lake; but there again the abruptly sinking precipice closed his way.

Day after day he haunted the spot, but never saw again either the damsel or the coracle. At length, marvelling at himself for being so solicitous about the apparition of a peasant girl in a coracle, who could not, by any possibility, be any thing to him, he resumed his explorations in another direction.

One day he wandered to the ruined castle, on the seashore, which was not very distant from his inn; and sitting on the rock, near the base of the ruin, was calling up the forms of past ages on the wall of an ivied tower, when on its summit appeared a female figure, whom he recognised in an instant for his nymph of the coracle. The folds of the blue gown pressed by the sea breeze against one of the most symmetrical of figures, the black feather of the black hat, and the ringleted hair beneath it fluttering in the wind; the apparent peril of her position, on the edge of the mouldering wall, from whose immediate base the rock went down perpendicularly to the sea, presented a singularly interesting combination to the eye of the young antiquary.

Mr Chainmail had to pass half round the castle, on the land side, before he could reach the entrance: he coasted the dry and bramble-grown moat, crossed the unguarded bridge, passed the unportcullised arch of the gateway, entered the castle court, ascertained the tower, ascended the broken stairs, and stood on the ivied wall. But the nymph of the place was gone. He searched the ruins within and without, but he found not what he sought: he haunted the castle day after day, as he had done the lake, but the damsel appeared no more.

*

CHAPTER XIV

The Dingle

> The stars of midnight shall be dear
> To her, and she shall lean her ear
> In many a secret place
> Where rivulets dance their wayward round,
> And beauty, born of murmuring sound,
> Shall pass into her face.
> WORDSWORTH[1]

Miss Susannah Touchandgo had read the four great poets of Italy, and many of the best writers of France. About the time of her father's downfall, accident threw into

her way *Les Rêveries du Promeneur Solitaire*; and from the
impression which these made on her, she carried with her
into retirement all the works of Rousseau. In the midst of
that startling light which the conduct of old friends on a
sudden reverse of fortune throws on a young and inex-
perienced mind, the doctrines of the philosopher of Geneva
struck with double force upon her sympathies: she imbibed
the sweet poison, as somebody calls it, of his writings, even
to a love of truth; which, every wise man knows, ought to
be left to those who can get any thing by it. The society
of children, the beauties of nature, the solitude of the
mountains, became her consolation, and, by degrees, her
delight. The gay society from which she had been excluded
remained on her memory only as a disagreeable dream.
She imbibed her new monitor's ideas of simplicity of dress,
assimilating her own with that of the peasant girls in the
neighbourhood; the black hat, the blue gown, the black
stockings, the shoes tied on the instep.

Pride was, perhaps, at the bottom of the change; she was
willing to impose in some measure on herself, by marking a
contemptuous indifference to the characteristics of the
class of society from which she had fallen,

> And with the food of pride sustained her soul
> In solitude.[2]

It is true that she somewhat modified the forms of her
rustic dress: to the black hat she added a black feather, to
the blue gown she added a tippet, and a waistband fastened
in front with a silver buckle; she wore her black stockings
very smooth and tight on her ancles, and tied her shoes in
tasteful bows, with the nicest possible ribbon. In this
apparel, to which, in winter, she added a scarlet cloak, she
made dreadful havoc among the rustic mountaineers, many
of whom proposed to 'keep company' with her in the
Cambrian fashion, an honour which, to their great surprise,
she always declined. Among these, Harry Ap-Heather,
whose father rented an extensive sheepwalk, and had a
thousand she-lambs wandering in the mountains, was the

most strenuous in his suit, and the most pathetic in his lamentations for her cruelty.

Miss Susannah often wandered among the mountains alone, even to some distance from the farm-house. Sometimes she descended into the bottom of the dingles, to the black rocky beds of the torrents, and dreamed away hours at the feet of the cataracts. One spot in particular, from which she had at first shrunk with terror, became by degrees her favourite haunt. A path turning and returning at acute angles, led down a steep wood-covered slope to the edge of a chasm,[3] where a pool, or resting-place of a torrent, lay far below. A cataract fell in a single sheet into the pool; the pool boiled and bubbled at the base of the fall, but through the greater part of its extent lay calm, deep, and black, as if the cataract had plunged through it to an unimaginable depth without disturbing its eternal repose. At the opposite extremity of the pool, the rocks almost met at their summits, the trees of the opposite banks intermingled their leaves, and another cataract plunged from the pool into a chasm on which the sunbeams never gleamed. High above, on both sides, the steep woody slopes of the dingle soared into the sky; and from a fissure in the rock, on which the little path terminated, a single gnarled and twisted oak stretched itself over the pool, forming a fork with its boughs at a short distance from the rock. Miss Susannah often sat on the rock, with her feet resting on this tree: in time, she made her seat on the tree itself, with her feet hanging over the abyss; and at length she accustomed herself to lie along upon its trunk, with her side on the mossy boll of the fork, and an arm round one of the branches. From this position a portion of the sky and the woods was reflected in the pool, which, from its bank, was but a mass of darkness. The first time she reclined in this manner, her heart beat audibly; in time, she lay down as calmly as on the mountain heather: the perception of the sublime was probably heightened by an intermingled sense of danger; and perhaps that indifference to life, which early disappointment forces upon sensitive minds, was necessary to the first

experiment. There was, in the novelty and strangeness of
the position, an excitement which never wholly passed
away, but which became gradually subordinate to the influence, at once tranquillising and elevating, of the mingled
eternity of motion, sound, and solitude.

One sultry noon, she descended into this retreat with a
mind more than usually disturbed by reflections on the
past. She lay in her favourite position, sometimes gazing
on the cataract; looking sometimes up the steep sylvan
acclivities into the narrow space of the cloudless ether;
sometimes down into the abyss of the pool, and the deep
bright-blue reflections that opened another immensity below
her. The distressing recollections of the morning, the world,
and all its littlenesses, faded from her thoughts like a dream;
but her wounded and wearied spirit drank in too deeply
the tranquillising power of the place, and she dropped
asleep upon the tree like a ship-boy on the mast.

At this moment Mr Chainmail emerged into daylight, on a
projection of the opposite rock, having struck down
through the woods in search of unsophisticated scenery.
The scene he discovered filled him with delight: he seated
himself on the rock, and fell into one of his romantic
reveries; when suddenly the semblance of a black hat and
feather caught his eye among the foliage of the projecting
oak. He started up, shifted his position, and got a glimpse
of a blue gown. It was his lady of the lake, his enchantress
of the ruined castle, divided from him by a barrier, which,
at a few yards below, he could almost overleap, yet un-
approachable but by a circuit perhaps of many hours. He
watched with intense anxiety. To listen if she breathed was
out of the question: the noses of a dean and chapter would
have been soundless in the roar of the torrent. From her
extreme stillness, she appeared to sleep: yet what creature,
not desperate, would go wilfully to sleep in such a place?
Was she asleep then? Nay, was she alive? She was as
motionless as death. Had she been murdered, thrown from
above, and caught in the tree? She lay too regularly and too
composedly for such a supposition. She was asleep then, and

in all probability her waking would be fatal. He shifted his position. Below the pool two beetle-browed rocks nearly overarched the chasm, leaving just such a space at the summit as was within the possibility of a leap; the torrent roared below in a fearful gulf. He paused some time on the brink, measuring the practicability and the danger, and casting every now and then an anxious glance to his sleeping beauty. In one of these glances he saw a slight movement of the blue gown, and, in a moment after, the black hat and feather dropped into the pool. Reflection was lost for a moment, and, by a sudden impulse, he bounded over the chasm.

He stood above the projecting oak; the unknown beauty lay like the nymph of the scene; her long black hair, which the fall of her hat had disengaged from its fastenings, drooping through the boughs: he saw that the first thing to be done was to prevent her throwing her feet off the trunk, in the first movements of waking. He sat down on the rock, and placed his feet on the stem, securing her ancles between his own: one of her arms was round a branch of the fork, the other lay loosely on her side. The hand of this arm he endeavoured to reach, by leaning forward from his seat; he approximated, but could not touch it: after several tantalising efforts, he gave up the point in despair. He did not attempt to wake her, because he feared it might have bad consequences, and he resigned himself to expect the moment of her natural waking, determined not to stir from his post, if she should sleep till midnight.

In this period of forced inaction, he could contemplate at leisure the features and form of his charmer. She was not one of the slender beauties of romance; she was as plump as a partridge; her cheeks were two roses, not absolutely damask, yet verging thereupon; her lips twin-cherries, of equal size; her nose regular, and almost Grecian; her forehead high, and delicately fair; her eyebrows symmetrically arched; her eyelashes long, black, and silky, fitly corresponding with the beautiful tresses that hung among the leaves of the oak, like clusters of wandering grapes.[4] Her eyes were yet to be seen; but how could he doubt that their opening would be the rising of the sun, when all that surrounded their fringy portals was radiant as 'the forehead of the morning sky'? [5]

*

CHAPTER XV

The Farm

> Da ydyw'r gwaith, rhaid d'we'yd y gwir,
> Ar fryniau Sîr Meirionydd;
> Golwg oer o'r gwaela gawn
> Mae hi etto yn llawn llawenydd.[1]

> Though Meirion's rocks, and hills of heath
>   Repel the distant sight;
> Yet where, than those bleak hills beneath,
>   Is found more true delight?

AT length the young lady awoke. She was startled at the sudden sight of the stranger, and somewhat terrified at the first perception of her position. But she soon recovered her self-possession, and, extending her hand to the offered hand of Mr Chainmail, she raised herself up on the tree, and stepped on the rocky bank.

Mr Chainmail solicited permission to attend her to her home, which the young lady graciously conceded. They emerged from the woody dingle, traversed an open heath, wound along a mountain road by the shore of a lake, descended to the deep bed of another stream, crossed it by a series of stepping stones, ascended to some height on the opposite side, and followed upwards the line of the stream, till the banks opened into a spacious amphitheatre, where stood, in its fields and meadows, the farm-house of Ap-Llymry.

During this walk, they had kept up a pretty animated conversation. The lady had lost her hat; and, as she turned towards Mr Chainmail, in speaking to him, there was no envious projection of brim to intercept the beams of those radiant eyes he had been so anxious to see unclosed. There was in them a mixture of softness and brilliancy, the perfection of the beauty of female eyes, such as some men have passed through life without seeing, and such as no man ever saw, in any pair of eyes, but once; such as can never be seen and forgotten. Young Crotchet had seen it; he had not forgotten it; but he had trampled on its memory, as the renegade tramples on the emblems of a faith which his interest only, and not his heart or his reason, has rejected.

Her hair streamed over her shoulders; the loss of the black feather had left nothing but the rustic costume, the blue gown, the black stockings, and the ribbon-tied shoes. Her voice had that full soft volume of melody which gives to common speech the fascination of music. Mr Chainmail could not reconcile the dress of the damsel with her conversation and manners. He threw out a remote question or two, with the hope of solving the riddle; but, receiving no reply, he became satisfied that she was not disposed to be communicative respecting herself, and, fearing to offend her, fell upon other topics. They talked of the scenes of the mountains, of the dingle, the ruined castle, the solitary lake. She told him that lake lay under the mountains behind her home, and the coracle and the pass at the extremity saved a long circuit to the nearest village, whither she sometimes went to inquire for letters.

Mr Chainmail felt curious to know from whom these letters might be; and he again threw out two or three fishing questions, to which, as before, he obtained no answer.

The only living biped they met in their walk was the unfortunate Harry Ap-Heather, with whom they fell in by the stepping-stones, who, seeing the girl of his heart hanging on another man's arm, and concluding at once that they were 'keeping company,' fixed on her a mingled look of surprise, reproach, and tribulation; and, unable to control his feelings under the sudden shock, burst into a flood of tears, and blubbered till the rocks re-echoed.

They left him mingling his tears with the stream, and his lamentations with its murmurs. Mr Chainmail inquired who that strange creature might be, and what was the matter with him. The young lady answered, that he was a very worthy young man, to whom she had been the innocent cause of much unhappiness.

'I pity him sincerely,' said Mr Chainmail; and, nevertheless, he could scarcely restrain his laughter at the exceedingly original figure which the unfortunate rustic lover had presented by the stepping-stones.

The children ran out to meet their dear Miss Susan, jumped all round her, and asked what was become of her hat. Ap-Llymry came out in great haste, and invited Mr Chainmail to walk in and dine: Mr Chainmail did not wait to be asked twice. In a few minutes the whole party, Miss Susan and Mr Chainmail, Mr and Mrs Ap-Llymry, and progeny, were seated over a clean homespun tablecloth, ornamented with fowls and bacon, a pyramid of potatoes, another of cabbage, which Ap-Llymry said 'was poiled with the pacon, and as coot as marrow,' a bowl of milk for the children, and an immense brown jug of foaming ale, with which Ap-Llymry seemed to delight in filling the horn of his new guest.

Shall we describe the spacious apartment, which was at once kitchen, hall, and dining-room, – the large dark rafters, the pendent bacon and onions, the strong old oaken furniture, the bright and trimly arranged utensils? Shall we describe the cut of Ap-Llymry's coat, the colour and tie of his neckcloth, the number of buttons at his knees, – the structure of Mrs Ap-Llymry's cap, having lappets over the ears, which were united under the chin, setting forth especially whether the bond of union were a pin or a ribbon? We shall leave this tempting field of interesting expatiation to those whose brains are high-pressure steam engines for spinning prose by the furlong, to be trumpeted in paid-for paragraphs in the quack's corner of newspapers: modern literature having attained the honourable distinction of sharing with blacking and macassar oil, the space which used to be monopolized by razor-strops and the lottery, whereby that very enlightened community, the reading public, is tricked into the perusal of much exemplary nonsense; though the few who see through the trickery have no reason to complain, since as 'good wine needs no bush,' so, *ex vi oppositi*, these bushes of venal panegyric point out very clearly that the things they celebrate are not worth reading.

The party dined very comfortably in a corner most remote from the fire; and Mr Chainmail very soon found his head swimming with two or three horns of ale, of a potency to which even he was unaccustomed. After dinner, Ap-Llymry made him finish a bottle of mead, which he willingly accepted, both as an excuse to remain, and as a drink of the dark ages, which he had no doubt was a genuine brewage, from uncorrupted tradition.

In the meantime, as soon as the cloth was removed, the children had brought out Miss Susannah's harp. She began, without affectation, to play and sing to the children, as was her custom of an afternoon, first in their own language, and their national melodies, then in English; but she was soon interrupted by a general call of little voices for 'Ouf! di giorno.' She complied with the request, and sang the ballad from Paër's Camilla: *Un dì carco il mulinaro.*[2] The children were very familiar with every syllable of this ballad, which had been often fully explained to them. They danced in a circle with the burden of every verse, shouting out the chorus with good articulation and joyous energy; and at the end of the second stanza, where the traveller has his nose pinched by his grandmother's ghost, every nose in the party was nipped by a pair of little fingers. Mr Chainmail, who was not prepared for the process, came in for a very energetic tweak, from a chubby girl that sprang suddenly on his knees for the purpose, and made the roof ring with her laughter.

So passed the time till evening, when Mr Chainmail moved to depart. But it turned out on inquiry that he was some miles from his inn, that the way was intricate, and that

he must not make any difficulty about accepting the
farmer's hospitality till morning. The evening set in with
rain: the fire was found agreeable; they drew around it.
The young lady made tea; and afterwards, from time to
time, at Mr Chainmail's special request, delighted his ear
with passages of ancient music. Then came a supper of lake
trout, fried on the spot, and thrown, smoking hot, from
the pan to the plate. Then came a brewage, which the
farmer called his nightcap, of which he insisted on Mr
Chainmail's taking his full share. After which the gentleman remembered nothing, till he awoke, the next morning,
to the pleasant consciousness that he was under the same
roof with one of the most fascinating creatures under the
canopy of heaven.

*

CHAPTER XVI

The Newspaper

Ποίας δ' ἀποσπασθεῖσα φύτλας
'Ορέων κευθμῶνας ἔχει σκιοέντων;

Sprung from what line, adorns the maid
These valleys deep in mountain shade?
PIND. *Pyth*. IX

MR CHAINMAIL forgot the captain and the route of
Giraldus de Barri. He became suddenly satisfied that the
ruined castle in his present neighbourhood was the best
possible specimen of its class, and that it was needless to
carry his researches further.

He visited the farm daily: found himself always welcome;
flattered himself that the young lady saw him with pleasure,
and dragged a heavier chain at every new parting from Miss
Susan, as the children called his nymph of the mountains.
What might be her second name, he had vainly endeavoured
to discover.

231

Mr Chainmail was in love; but the determination he had long before formed and fixed in his mind, to marry only a lady of gentle blood, without a blot on her escutcheon, repressed the declarations of passion which were often rising to his lips. In the meantime, he left no means untried, to pluck out the heart of her mystery.[1]

The young lady soon divined his passion, and penetrated his prejudices. She began to look on him with favourable eyes; but she feared her name and parentage would present an insuperable barrier to his feudal pride.

Things were in this state when the captain returned, and unpacked his maps and books in the parlour of the inn.

MR CHAINMAIL

Really, captain, I find so many objects of attraction in this neighbourhood, that I would gladly postpone our purpose.

CAPTAIN FITZCHROME

Undoubtedly, this neighbourhood has many attractions; but there is something very inviting in the scheme you laid down.

MR CHAINMAIL

No doubt, there is something very tempting in the route of Giraldus de Barri. But there are better things in this vicinity even than that. To tell you the truth, captain, I have fallen in love.

CAPTAIN FITZCHROME

What! while I have been away?

MR CHAINMAIL

Even so.

CAPTAIN FITZCHROME

The plunge must have been very sudden, if you are already over head and ears.

MR CHAINMAIL

As deep as Llyn-y-dreiddiad-vrawd.

CAPTAIN FITZCHROME

And what may that be?

MR CHAINMAIL

A pool not far off: a resting-place of a mountain stream, which is said to have no bottom. There is a tradition connected with it; and here is a ballad on it, at your service:

LLYN-Y-DREIDDIAD-VRAWD
THE POOL OF THE DIVING FRIAR

Gwenwynwyn withdrew from the feasts of his hall;
He slept very little, he prayed not at all;
He pondered, and wandered, and studied alone;
And sought, night and day, the philosopher's stone.

He found it at length, and he made its first proof
By turning to gold all the lead of his roof:
Then he bought some magnanimous heroes, all fire,
Who lived but to smite and be smitten for hire.

With these, on the plains like a torrent he broke;
He filled the whole country with flame and with smoke;
He killed all the swine, and he broached all the wine;
He drove off the sheep, and the beeves, and the kine;

He took castles and towns; he cut short limbs and lives;
He made orphans and widows of children and wives:
This course many years he triumphantly ran,
And did mischief enough to be called a great man.[2]

When, at last, he had gained all for which he had striven,
He bethought him of buying a passport to heaven;
Good and great as he was, yet he did not well know
How soon, or which way, his great spirit might go.

He sought the grey friars, who, beside a wild stream,
Refected their frames on a primitive scheme;
The gravest and wisest Gwenwynwyn found out,
All lonely and ghostly, and angling for trout.

Below the white dash of a mighty cascade,
Where a pool of the stream a deep resting-place made,
And rock-rooted oaks stretched their branches on high,
The friar stood musing, and throwing his fly.

To him said Gwenwynwyn, 'Hold, father, here's store,
For the good of the church, and the good of the poor;'
Then he gave him the stone; but, ere more he could speak,
Wrath came on the friar, so holy and meek:

He had stretched forth his hand to receive the red gold,
And he thought himself mocked by Gwenwynwyn the Bold;
And in scorn of the gift, and in rage at the giver,
He jerked it immediately into the river.

Gwenwynwyn, aghast, not a syllable spake;
The philosopher's stone made a duck and a drake:
Two systems of circles a moment were seen,
And the stream smoothed them off, as they never had been.

Gwenwynwyn regained, and uplifted, his voice:
'Oh friar, grey friar, full rash was thy choice;
The stone, the good stone, which away thou hast thrown,
Was the stone of all stones, the philosopher's stone!'

The friar looked pale, when his error he knew;
The friar looked red, and the friar looked blue;
And heels over head, from the point of a rock,
He plunged, without stopping to pull off his frock.

He dived very deep, but he dived all in vain,
The prize he had slighted he found not again:
Many times did the friar his diving renew,
And deeper and deeper the river still grew.

Gwenwynwyn gazed long, of his senses in doubt,
To see the grey friar a diver so stout:
Then sadly and slowly his castle he sought,
And left the friar diving, like dabchick distraught.

Gwenwynwyn fell sick with alarm and despite,
Died, and went to the devil, the very same night:
The magnanimous heroes he held in his pay
Sacked his castle, and marched with the plunder away.

No knell on the silence of midnight was rolled,
For the flight of the soul of Gwenwynwyn the Bold:
The brethren, unfeed, let the mighty ghost pass,
Without praying a prayer, or intoning a mass.

The friar haunted ever beside the dark stream;
The philosopher's stone was his thought and his dream:
And day after day, ever head under heels,
He dived all the time he could spare from his meals.

He dived, and he dived, to the end of his days,
As the peasants oft witnessed with fear and amaze:
The mad friar's diving-place long was their theme,
And no plummet can fathom that pool of the stream.

And still, when light clouds on the midnight winds ride,
If by moonlight you stray on the lone river-side,
The ghost of the friar may be seen diving there,
With head in the water, and heels in the air.

CAPTAIN FITZCHROME

Well, your ballad is very pleasant: you shall show me the
scene, and I will sketch it; but just now I am more interested
about your love. What heroine of the twelfth century has
risen from the ruins of the old castle, and looked down on
you from the ivied battlements?

MR CHAINMAIL

You are nearer the mark than you suppose. Even from those
battlements a heroine of the twelfth century has looked
down on me.

CAPTAIN FITZCHROME

Oh! some vision of an ideal beauty. I suppose the whole
will end in another tradition and a ballad.

MR CHAINMAIL

Genuine flesh and blood; as genuine as Lady Clarinda. I will
tell you the story.

Mr Chainmail narrated his adventures.

CAPTAIN FITZCHROME

Then you seem to have found what you wished. Chance has thrown in your way what none of the gods would have ventured to promise you.

MR CHAINMAIL

Yes, but I know nothing of her birth and parentage. She tells me nothing of herself, and I have no right to question her directly.

CAPTAIN FITZCHROME

She appears to be expressly destined for the light of your baronial hall. Introduce me: in this case, two heads are better than one.

MR CHAINMAIL

No, I thank you. Leave me to manage my chance of a prize, and keep you to your own chance of a –

CAPTAIN FITZCHROME

Blank. As you please. Well, I will pitch my tent here, till I have filled my portfolio, and shall be glad of as much of your company as you can spare from more attractive society.

Matters went on pretty smoothly for several days, when an unlucky newspaper threw all into confusion. Mr Chainmail received newspapers by the post, which came in three times a week. One morning, over their half-finished breakfast, the captain had read half a newspaper very complacently, when suddenly he started up in a frenzy, hurled over the breakfast table, and, bouncing from the apartment, knocked down Harry Ap-Heather, who was coming in at the door to challenge his supposed rival to a boxing-match.

Harry sprang up, in a double rage, and intercepted Mr Chainmail's pursuit of the captain, placing himself in the doorway, in a pugilistic attitude. Mr Chainmail, not being disposed for this mode of combat, stepped back into the parlour, took the poker in his right hand, and displacing the loose bottom of a large elbow chair, threw it over his left arm, as a shield. Harry, not liking the aspect of the enemy in this imposing attitude, retreated with backward steps into the kitchen, and tumbled over a cur, which immediately fastened on his rear.

Mr Chainmail, half-laughing, half-vexed, anxious to over-take the captain, and curious to know what was the matter with him, pocketed the newspaper, and sallied forth, leaving Harry roaring for a doctor and a tailor, to repair the lacerations of his outward man.

Mr Chainmail could find no trace of the captain. Indeed, he sought him but in one direction, which was that leading to the farm; where he arrived in due time, and found Miss Susan alone. He laid the newspaper on the table, as was his custom, and proceeded to converse with the young lady: a conversation of many pauses, as much of signs as of words. The young lady took up the paper, and turned it over and over, while she listened to Mr Chainmail, whom she found every day more and more agreeable, when, suddenly, her eye glanced on something which made her change colour, and dropping the paper on the ground, she rose from her seat, exclaiming, 'Miserable must she be who trusts any of your faithless sex! Never, never, never, will I endure such misery twice.' And she vanished up the stairs. Mr Chain-mail was petrified. At length, he cried aloud, 'Cornelius Agrippa[3] must have laid a spell on this accursed news-paper;' and was turning it over, to look for the source of the mischief, when Mrs Ap-Llymry made her appearance.

MRS AP-LLYMRY

What have you done to poor dear Miss Susan? She is crying, ready to break her heart.

MR CHAINMAIL

So help me the memory of Richard Cœur-de-Lion, I have not the most distant notion of what is the matter!

MRS AP-LLYMRY

Oh, don't tell me, sir; you must have ill-used her. I know
how it is. You have been keeping company with her, as if
you wanted to marry her; and now, all at once, you have
been trying to make her your mistress. I have seen such
tricks more than once, and you ought to be ashamed of
yourself.

MR CHAINMAIL

My dear madam, you wrong me utterly. I have none but
the kindest feelings and the most honourable purposes towards her. She has been disturbed by something she has seen
in this rascally paper.

MRS AP-LLYMRY

Why, then, the best thing you can do is to go away, and
come again tomorrow.

MR CHAINMAIL

Not I, indeed, madam. Out of this house I stir not, till I
have seen the young lady, and obtained a full explanation.

MRS AP-LLYMRY

I will tell Miss Susan what you say. Perhaps she will come
down.

Mr Chainmail sate with as much patience as he could
command, running over the paper, from column to column.
At length, he lighted on an announcement of the approaching marriage of Lady Clarinda Bossnowl with Mr Crotchet
the younger. This explained the captain's discomposure, but
the cause of Miss Susan's was still to be sought; he could
not know that it was one and the same.

Presently the sound of the longed-for step was heard on
the stairs; the young lady reappeared, and resumed her
seat: her eyes showed that she had been weeping. The gentleman was now exceedingly puzzled how to begin, but the

young lady relieved him by asking, with great simplicity,
'What do you wish to have explained, sir?'

MR CHAINMAIL

I wish, if I may be permitted, to explain myself to you. Yet
could I first wish to know what it was that disturbed you in
this unlucky paper. Happy should I be if I could remove the
cause of your inquietude!

MISS SUSANNAH

The cause is already removed. I saw something that excited
painful recollections; nothing that I could now wish otherwise than as it is.

MR CHAINMAIL

Yet, may I ask why it is that I find one so accomplished
living in this obscurity, and passing only by the name of
Miss Susan?

MISS SUSANNAH

The world and my name are not friends. I have left the
world, and wish to remain for ever a stranger to all whom I
once knew in it.

MR CHAINMAIL

You can have done nothing to dishonour your name.

MISS SUSANNAH

No, sir. My father has done that of which the world dis-
approves, in matters of which I pretend not to judge. I have
suffered for it as I will never suffer again. My name is my
own secret; I have no other, and that is one not worth knowing. You see what I am, and all I am. I live according to the
condition of my present fortune; and here, so living, I
have found tranquillity.

MR CHAINMAIL

Yet, I entreat you, tell me your name.

MISS SUSANNAH

Why, sir?

MR CHAINMAIL

Why, but to throw my hand, my heart, my fortune, at your feet, if –

MISS SUSANNAH

If my name be worthy of them.

MR CHAINMAIL

Nay, nay, not so; if your hand and heart are free.

MISS SUSANNAH

My hand and heart are free; but they must be sought from myself, and not from my name.

She fixed her eyes on him, with a mingled expression of mistrust, of kindness, and of fixed resolution, which the far-gone *innamorato* found irresistible.

MR CHAINMAIL

Then from yourself alone I seek them.

MISS SUSANNAH

Reflect. You have prejudices on the score of parentage. I have not conversed with you so often, without knowing what they are. Choose between them and me. I too have my own prejudices on the score of personal pride.

MR CHAINMAIL

I would choose you from all the world, were you even the daughter of the *exécuteur des hautes œuvres*,[4] as the heroine of a romantic story I once read turned out to be.

MISS SUSANNAH

I am satisfied. You have now a right to know my history; and, if you repent, I absolve you from all obligations.

She told him her history; but he was out of the reach of repentance. 'It is true,' as at a subsequent period he said to the captain, 'she is the daughter of a moneychanger; one who, in the days of Richard the First, would have been plucked by the beard in the streets; but she is, according to modern notions, a lady of gentle blood. As to her father's running away, that is a minor consideration: I have always understood, from Mr Mac Quedy, who is a great oracle in this way, that promises to pay ought not to be kept; the essence of a safe and economical currency being an interminable series of broken promises. There seems to be a difference among the learned as to the way in which the promises ought to be broken; but I am not deep enough in their casuistry to enter into such nice distinctions.'

In a few days there was a wedding, a pathetic leave-taking of the farmer's family, a hundred kisses from the bride to the children, and promises twenty times reclaimed and renewed, to visit them in the ensuing year.

*

CHAPTER XVII

The Invitation

A cup of wine, that's brisk and fine,
And drink unto the leman mine.
MASTER SILENCE[1]

THIS veridicous history began in May, and the occurrences already narrated have carried it on to the middle of autumn. Stepping over the interval to Christmas, we find ourselves in our first locality, among the chalk hills of the Thames; and we discover our old friend, Mr Crotchet, in the act of accepting an invitation, for himself, and any friends who might be with him, to pass their Christmas-day at Chainmail Hall, after the fashion of the twelfth century. Mr Crotchet had assembled about him, for his own Christmasfestivities, nearly the same party which was introduced to the reader in the spring. Three of that party were wanting. Dr Morbific, by inoculating himself once too often with non-contagious matter, had explained himself out of the world. Mr Henbane had also departed, on the wings of an infallible antidote. Mr Eavesdrop, having printed in a magazine some of the after-dinner conversations of the castle, had had sentence of exclusion passed upon him, on the motion of the Reverend Doctor Folliott, as a flagitious violator of the confidences of private life.

Miss Crotchet had become Lady Bossnowl, but Lady Clarinda had not yet changed her name to Crotchet. She had, on one pretence and another, procrastinated the happy event, and the gentleman had not been very pressing; she had, however, accompanied her brother and sister-in-law, to pass Christmas at Crotchet Castle. With these, Mr Mac Quedy, Mr Philpot, Mr Trillo, Mr Skionar, Mr Toogood, and Mr Firedamp, were sitting at breakfast, when the Reverend Doctor Folliott entered and took his seat at the table.

THE REV DR FOLLIOTT

Well, Mr Mac Quedy, it is now some weeks since we have met: how goes on the march of mind?

MR MAC QUEDY

Nay, sir; I think you may see that with your own eyes.

THE REV DR FOLLIOTT

Sir, I have seen it, much to my discomfiture. It has marched into my rick-yard,[2] and set my stacks on fire, with chemical materials, most scientifically compounded. It has marched up to the door of my vicarage, a hundred and fifty strong; ordered me to surrender half my tithes; consumed all the provisions I had provided for my audit feast, and drunk up my old October. It has marched in through my back-parlour shutters, and out again with my silver spoons, in the dead of the night. The policeman, who was sent down to examine, says my house has been broken open on the most scientific principles. All this comes of education.

MR MAC QUEDY

I rather think it comes of poverty.

THE REV DR FOLLIOTT

No, sir. Robbery perhaps comes of poverty, but scientific principles of robbery come of education. I suppose the learned friend has written a sixpenny treatise on mechanics, and the rascals who robbed me have been reading it.

MR CROTCHET

Your house would have been very safe, doctor, if they had had no better science than the learned friend's to work with.

THE REV DR FOLLIOTT

Well, sir, that may be. Excellent potted char. The Lord deliver me from the learned friend.

MR CROTCHET

Well, doctor, for your comfort, here is a declaration of the learned friend's that he will never take office.

THE REV DR FOLLIOTT

Then, sir, he will be in office next week. Peace be with him! Sugar and cream.

MR CROTCHET

But, doctor, are you for Chainmail Hall on Christmas-day?

THE REV DR FOLLIOTT

That am I, for there will be an excellent dinner, though, peradventure, grotesquely served.

MR CROTCHET

I have not seen my neighbour since he left us on the canal.

THE REV DR FOLLIOTT

He has married a wife, and brought her home.

LADY CLARINDA

Indeed! If she suits him, she must be an oddity: it will be amusing to see them together.

LORD BOSSNOWL

Very amusing. He! he!

MR FIREDAMP

Is there any water about Chainmail Hall?

THE REV DR FOLLIOTT

An old moat.

MR FIREDAMP

I shall die of *malaria*.

MR TRILLO

Shall we have any music?

THE REV DR FOLLIOTT

An old harper.

MR TRILLO

Those fellows are always horridly out of tune. What will he play?

THE REV DR FOLLIOTT

Old songs and marches.

MR SKIONAR

Amongst so many old things, I hope we shall find Old Philosophy.

THE REV DR FOLLIOTT

An old woman.

MR PHILPOT

Perhaps an old map of the river in the twelfth century.

THE REV DR FOLLIOTT

No doubt.

MR MAC QUEDY

How many more old things?

THE REV DR FOLLIOTT

Old hospitality, old wine, old ale – all the images of old England; an old butler.

MR TOOGOOD

Shall we all be welcome?

THE REV DR FOLLIOTT

Heartily; you will be slapped on the shoulder, and called old boy.

LORD BOSSNOWL

I think we should all go in our old clothes. He! he!

THE REV DR FOLLIOTT

You will sit on old chairs, round an old table, by the light of old lamps, suspended from pointed arches, which, Mr Chainmail says, first came into use in the twelfth century; with old armour on the pillars, and old banners in the roof.

LADY CLARINDA

And what curious piece of antiquity is the lady of the mansion?

THE REV DR FOLLIOTT

No antiquity there; none.

LADY CLARINDA

Who was she?

THE REV DR FOLLIOTT

That I know not.

LADY CLARINDA

Have you seen her?

THE REV DR FOLLIOTT

I have.

LADY CLARINDA

Is she pretty?

THE REV DR FOLLIOTT

More – beautiful. A subject for the pen of Nonnus, or the pencil of Zeuxis. Features of all loveliness, radiant with all virtue and intelligence. A face for Antigone. A form at once plump and symmetrical, that, if it be decorous to divine it by externals, would have been a model for the Venus of Cnidos. Never was any thing so goodly to look on, the present company excepted, and poor dear Mrs Folliott. She reads moral philosophy, Mr Mac Quedy, which indeed she might as well let alone; she reads Italian poetry, Mr Skionar; she sings Italian music, Mr Trillo; but, with all this, she has the greatest of female virtues, for she superintends the household, and looks after her husband's dinner. I believe she was a mountaineer: παρθένος οὐρεσίφοιτος, ἐρήμαδι σύντροφος ὕλη,[3] as Nonnus sweetly sings.

*

CHAPTER XVIII

Chainmail Hall

Vous autres dictes que ignorance est mere de tous
maulx, at dictes vray: mais toutesfoys vous ne la ban-
nissez mye de vos entendemens, et vivez en elle, avec-
ques elle, et par elle. C'est pourquoy tant de maulx vous
meshaignent de jour en jour.

RABELAIS, 1. 5. c. 7[1]

THE party which was assembled on Christmas-day in
Chainmail Hall, comprised all the guests of Crotchet Castle,
some of Mr Chainmail's other neighbours, all his tenants
and domestics, and Captain Fitzchrome. The hall was
spacious and lofty; and with its tall fluted pillars and
pointed arches, its windows of stained glass, its display of
arms and banners intermingled with holly and mistletoe,
its blazing cressets and torches, and a stupendous fire in
the centre, on which blocks of pine were flaming and
crackling, had a striking effect on eyes unaccustomed to
such a dining-room. The fire was open on all sides, and the
smoke was caught and carried back, under a funnel-formed
canopy, into a hollow central pillar. This fire was the line
of demarcation between gentle and simple, on days of high
festival. Tables extended from it on two sides, to nearly the
end of the hall.

Mrs Chainmail was introduced to the company. Young
Crotchet felt some revulsion of feeling at the unexpected
sight of one whom he had forsaken, but not forgotten, in a
condition apparently so much happier than his own. The
lady held out her hand to him with a cordial look of more
than forgiveness; it seemed to say that she had much to
thank him for. She was the picture of a happy bride,
rayonnante de joie et d'amour.[2]

Mr Crotchet told the Reverend Doctor Folliott the news
of the morning. 'As you predicted,' he said, 'your friend,

247

the learned friend, is in office; he has also a title; he is now
Sir Guy de Vaux.'[3]

THE REV DR FOLLIOTT

Thank heaven for that! he is disarmed from further mischief. It is something, at any rate, to have that hollow and
wind-shaken reed rooted up for ever from the field of public
delusion.[4]

MR CROTCHET

I suppose, doctor, you do not like to see a great reformer in
office; you are afraid for your vested interests.

THE REV DR FOLLIOTT

Not I, indeed, sir; my vested interests are very safe from all
such reformers as the learned friend. I vaticinate what will
be the upshot of all his schemes of reform. He will make a
speech of seven hours' duration, and this will be its quintessence: that, seeing the exceeding difficulty of putting salt
on the bird's tail, it will be expedient to consider the best
method of throwing dust in the bird's eyes. All the rest will
be

> Τιτιτιτιτιμπρό.
> Ποποποί, ποποποί.
> Τιοτιοτιοτιοτιοτιοτίγξ.
> Κικκαβαῦ, κικκαβαῦ.
> Τοροτοροτοροτορολιλιλίγξ.[5]

as Aristophanes has it; and so I leave him, in Nephelococcygia.[6]

Mr Mac Quedy came up to the divine as Mr Crotchet left
him, and said: 'There is one piece of news which the old
gentleman has not told you. The great firm of Catchflat and
Company, in which young Crotchet is a partner, has stopped
payment.'

THE REV DR FOLLIOTT

Bless me! that accounts for the young gentleman's melancholy. I thought they would over-reach themselves with

their own tricks. The day of reckoning, Mr Mac Quedy, is the point which your paper-money science always leaves out of view.

MR MAC QUEDY

I do not see, sir, that the failure of Catchflat and Company has any thing to do with my science.

THE REV DR FOLLIOTT

It has this to do with it, sir, that you would turn the whole nation into a great paper-money shop, and take no thought of the day of reckoning. But the dinner is coming. I think you, who are so fond of paper promises, should dine on the bill of fare.

The harper at the head of the hall struck up an ancient march, and the dishes were brought in, in grand procession.

The boar's head, garnished with rosemary, with a citron in its mouth, led the van. Then came tureens of plum-porridge; then a series of turkeys, and, in the midst of them, an enormous sausage, which it required two men to carry. Then came geese and capons, tongues and hams, the ancient glory of the Christmas pie, a gigantic plum-pudding, a pyramid of minced pies, and a baron of beef bringing up the rear.

'It is something new under the sun,' said the divine, as he sat down, 'to see a great dinner without fish.'

MR CHAINMAIL

Fish was for fasts, in the twelfth century.

THE REV DR FOLLIOTT

Well, sir, I prefer our reformed system of putting fasts and feasts together. Not but here is ample indemnity.

Ale and wine flowed in abundance. The dinner passed off merrily; the old harper playing all the while the oldest music in his repertory. The tables being cleared, he indemnified himself for lost time at the lower end of the hall, in company with the old butler and the other domestics, whose attendance on the banquet had been indispensable.

The scheme of Christmas gambols, which Mr Chainmail had laid for the evening, was interrupted by a tremendous clamour without.

THE REV DR FOLLIOTT

What have we here? Mummers?

MR CHAINMAIL

Nay, I know not. I expect none.

'Who is there?' he added, approaching the door of the hall.

'Who is there?' vociferated the divine, with the voice of Stentor.

'Captain Swing,'[7] replied a chorus of discordant voices.

THE REV DR FOLLIOTT

Ho, ho! here is a piece of the dark ages we did not bargain for. Here is the Jacquerie. Here is the march of mind with a witness.

MR MAC QUEDY

Do you not see that you have brought disparates together? the Jacquerie and the march of mind.

THE REV DR FOLLIOTT

Not at all, sir. They are the same thing, under different names. Πολλῶν ὀνομάτων μορφὴ μία.[8] What was Jacquerie in the dark ages, is the march of mind in this very enlightened one – very enlightened one.

MR CHAINMAIL

The cause is the same in both; poverty in despair.

MR MAC QUEDY

Very likely; but the effect is extremely disagreeable.

THE REV DR FOLLIOTT

It is the natural result, Mr Mac Quedy, of that system of state seamanship which your science upholds. Putting the crew on short allowance, and doubling the rations of the officers, is the sure way to make a mutiny on board a ship in distress, Mr Mac Quedy.

MR MAC QUEDY

Eh! sir, I uphold no such system as that. I shall set you right as to cause and effect. Discontent increases with the increase of information.[9] That is all.

THE REV DR FOLLIOTT

I said it was the march of mind. But we have not time for discussing cause and effect now. Let us get rid of the enemy.

And he vociferated at the top of his voice, 'What do you want here?'

'Arms, arms,' replied a hundred voices, 'Give us the arms.'

THE REV DR FOLLIOTT

You see, Mr Chainmail, this is the inconvenience of keeping an armoury, not fortified with sand bags, green bags,[10] and old bags of all kinds.

MR MAC QUEDY

Just give them the old spits and toasting irons, and they will go away quietly.

MR CHAINMAIL

My spears and swords! not without my life. These assailants are all aliens to my land and house. My men will fight for me, one and all. This is the fortress of beef and ale.

MR MAC QUEDY

Eh! sir, when the rabble is up, it is very indiscriminating. You are e'en suffering for the sins of Sir Simon Steeltrap, and the like, who have pushed the principle of accumulation a little too far.

MR CHAINMAIL

The way to keep the people down is kind and liberal usage.

MR MAC QUEDY

That is very well (where it can be afforded), in the way of prevention; but in the way of cure, the operation must be more drastic. (*Taking down a battle-axe.*) I would fain have a good blunderbuss charged with slugs.

MR CHAINMAIL

When I suspended these arms for ornament, I never dreamed of their being called into use.

MR SKIONAR

Let me address them. I never failed to convince an audience that the best thing they could do was to go away.

MR MAC QUEDY

Eh! sir, I can bring them to that conclusion in less time than you.

MR CROTCHET

I have no fancy for fighting. It is a very hard case upon a guest, when the latter end of a feast is the beginning of a fray.[11]

MR MAC QUEDY

Give them the old iron.

THE REV DR FOLLIOTT

Give them the weapons! *Pessimo, medius fidius, exemplo.*[12] Forbid it the spirit of *Frère Jean des Entommeures!* No! let us see what the church militant, in the armour of the twelfth century, will do against the march of mind. Follow me who will, and stay who list. Here goes: *Pro aris et focis!*[13] that is, for tithe pigs and fires to roast them!

He clapped a helmet on his head, seized a long lance, threw open the gates, and tilted out on the rabble, side by side with Mr Chainmail, followed by the greater portion of the male inmates of the hall, who had armed themselves at random.

The rabble-rout, being unprepared for such a sortie, fled in all directions, over hedge and ditch.

Mr Trillo stayed in the hall, playing a march on the harp, to inspirit the rest to sally out. The water-loving Mr Philpot had diluted himself with so much wine, as to be quite *hors de combat*. Mr Toogood, intending to equip himself in purely defensive armour, contrived to slip a ponderous coat of mail over his shoulders, which pinioned his arms to his sides; and in this condition, like a chicken trussed for roasting, he was thrown down behind a pillar, in the first rush of the sortie. Mr Crotchet seized the occurrence as a pretext for staying with him, and passed the whole time of the action in picking him out of his shell.

'Phew!' said the divine, returning; 'an inglorious victory: but it deserves a devil and a bowl of punch.'

MR CHAINMAIL

A wassail-bowl.

THE REV DR FOLLIOTT

No, sir. No more of the twelfth century for me.

MR CHAINMAIL

Nay, doctor. The twelfth century has backed you well. Its manners and habits, its community of kind feelings between master and man, are the true remedy for these ebullitions.

MR TOOGOOD

Something like it: improved by my diagram: arts for arms.[14]

THE REV DR FOLLIOTT

No wassail-bowl for me. Give me an unsophisticated bowl of punch, which belongs to that blissful middle period, after the Jacquerie was down, and before the march of mind was up. But, see, who is floundering in the water?

Proceeding to the edge of the moat, they fished up Mr Firedamp, who had missed his way back, and tumbled in. He was drawn out, exclaiming, 'that he had taken his last dose of *malaria* in this world.'

THE REV DR FOLLIOTT

Tut, man; dry clothes, a turkey's leg and rump, well devilled, and a quart of strong punch, will set all to rights.

'Wood embers,' said Mr Firedamp, when he had been accommodated with a change of clothes, 'there is no antidote to *malaria* like the smoke of wood embers; pine embers.' And he placed himself, with his mouth open, close by the fire.

THE REV DR FOLLIOTT

Punch, sir, punch: there is no antidote like punch.

MR CHAINMAIL

Well, doctor, you shall be indulged. But I shall have my wassail-bowl nevertheless.

An immense bowl of spiced wine, with roasted apples hissing on its surface, was borne into the hall by four men, followed by an empty bowl of the same dimensions, with all the materials of arrack punch, for the divine's especial brewage. He accinged himself to the task, with his usual heroism; and having finished it to his entire satisfaction, reminded his host to order in the devil.

THE REV DR FOLLIOTT

I think, Mr Chainmail, we can amuse ourselves very well here all night. The enemy may be still excubant: and we had better not disperse till daylight. I am perfectly satisfied with my quarters. Let the young folks go on with their gambols; let them dance to your old harper's minstrelsy; and if they please to kiss under the mistletoe, whereof I espy a goodly bunch suspended at the end of the hall, let those who like it not, leave it to those who do. Moreover, if among the more sedate portion of the assembly, which, I foresee, will keep me company, there were any to revive the good old custom of singing after supper, so to fill up the intervals of the dances, the steps of night would move more lightly.

MR CHAINMAIL

My Susan will set the example, after she has set that of joining in the rustic dance, according to good customs long departed.

After the first dance, in which all classes of the company mingled, the young lady of the mansion took her harp, and following the reverend gentleman's suggestion, sang a song of the twelfth century.

FLORENCE AND BLANCHFLOR[15]

Florence and Blanchflor, loveliest maids,
    Within a summer grove,
Amid the flower-enamelled shades
    Together talked of love.

A clerk sweet Blanchflor's heart had gained;
    Fair Florence loved a knight:
And each with ardent voice maintained,
    She loved the worthiest wight.

Sweet Blanchflor praised her scholar dear,
    As courteous, kind, and true;
Fair Florence said her chevalier
    Could every foe subdue.

And Florence scorned the bookworm vain,
    Who sword nor spear could raise;
And Blanchflor scorned the unlettered brain
    Could sing no lady's praise.

From dearest love, the maidens bright
  To deadly hatred fell;
Each turned to shun the other's sight,
  And neither said farewell.

The king of birds, who held his court
  Within that flowery grove,
Sang loudly: ''Twill be rare disport
  To judge this suit of love.'

Before him came the maidens bright,
  With all his birds around,
To judge the cause, if clerk or knight
  In love be worthiest found.

The falcon and the sparrow-hawk
  Stood forward for the fight:
Ready to do, and not to talk,
  They voted for the knight.

And Blanchflor's heart began to fail,
  Till rose the strong-voiced lark,
And, after him, the nightingale,
  And pleaded for the clerk.

The nightingale prevailed at length,
  Her pleading had such charms;
So eloquence can conquer strength,
  And arts can conquer arms.

The lovely Florence tore her hair,
  And died upon the place;
And all the birds assembled there,
  Bewailed the mournful case.

They piled up leaves and flowerets rare,
  Above the maiden bright,
And sang: 'Farewell to Florence fair,
  Who too well loved her knight.'

Several others of the party sang in the intervals of the dances. Mr Chainmail handed to Mr Trillo another ballad of the twelfth century, of a merrier character than the former. Mr Trillo readily accommodated it with an air, and sang,

THE PRIEST AND THE MULBERRY TREE[16]

Did you hear of the curate who mounted his mare,
And merrily trotted along to the fair?
Of creature more tractable none ever heard,
In the height of her speed she would stop at a word;
And again with a word, when the curate said Hey,
She put forth her mettle, and galloped away.

As near to the gates of the city he rode,
While the sun of September all brilliantly glowed,
The good priest discovered, with eyes of desire,
A mulberry tree in a hedge of wild briar;
On boughs long and lofty, in many a green shoot,
Hung large, black, and glossy, the beautiful fruit.

The curate was hungry and thirsty to boot;
He shrunk from the thorns, though he longed for the fruit;
With a word he arrested his courser's keen speed,
And he stood up erect on the back of his steed;
On the saddle he stood, while the creature stood still,
And he gathered the fruit, till he took his good fill.

'Sure never,' he thought, 'was a creature so rare,
So docile, so true, as my excellent mare.
Lo, here, how I stand' (and he gazed all around),
'As safe and as steady as if on the ground,
Yet how had it been, if some traveller this way,
Had, dreaming no mischief, but chanced to cry Hey?'

He stood with his head in the mulberry tree,
And he spoke out aloud in his fond reverie:
At the sound of the word, the good mare made a push,
And down went the priest in the wild-briar bush.
He remembered too late, on his thorny green bed,
Much that well may be thought, cannot wisely be said.

Lady Clarinda, being prevailed on to take the harp in her turn, sang the following stanzas:

> In the days of old,
> Lovers felt true passion,
> Deeming years of sorrow
> By a smile repaid.

Now the charms of gold,
Spells of pride and fashion,
Bid them say good morrow
To the best-loved maid.

Through the forests wild,
O'er the mountains lonely,
They were never weary
Honour to pursue.
If the damsel smiled
Once in seven years only,
All their wanderings dreary
Ample guerdon knew.

Now one day's caprice
Weighs down years of smiling,
Youthful hearts are rovers,
Love is bought and sold:
Fortune's gifts may cease,
Love is less beguiling;
Wiser were the lovers,
In the days of old.

The glance which she threw at the Captain, as she sang the last verse, awakened his dormant hopes. Looking round for his rival, he saw that he was not in the hall; and, approaching the lady of his heart, he received one of the sweetest smiles of their earlier days.

After a time, the ladies, and all the females of the party, retired. The males remained on duty with punch and wassail, and dropped off one by one into sweet forgetfulness; so that when the rising sun of December looked through the painted windows on mouldering embers and flickering lamps, the vaulted roof was echoing to a mellifluous concert of noses, from the clarionet of the waiting-boy at one end of the hall, to the double bass of the Reverend Doctor, ringing over the empty punch-bowl, at the other.

CONCLUSION

FROM this eventful night, young Crotchet was seen no more on English mould. Whither he had vanished, was a question that could no more be answered in his case than in that of King Arthur, after the battle of Camlan. The great firm of Catchflat and Company figured in the Gazette and paid sixpence in the pound; and it was clear that he had shrunk from exhibiting himself on the scene of his former greatness, shorn of the beams of his paper prosperity. Some supposed him to be sleeping among the undiscoverable secrets of some barbel-pool in the Thames; but those who knew him best were more inclined to the opinion that he had gone across the Atlantic, with his pockets full of surplus capital, to join his old acquaintance, Mr Touchandgo, in the bank of Dotandcarryonetown.

Lady Clarinda was more sorry for her father's disappointment than her own; but she had too much pride to allow herself to be put up a second time in the money-market; and when the Captain renewed his assiduities, her old partiality for him, combining with a sense of gratitude for a degree of constancy which she knew she scarcely deserved, induced her, with Lord Foolincourt's hard-wrung consent, to share with him a more humble, but less precarious fortune, than that to which she had been destined as the price of a rotten borough.

THE END

NOTES

NIGHTMARE ABBEY

Peacock's own notes are marked (P.)

The verse on the 1818 title-page is a composite quotation, with some lines modified, from Butler's *Hudibras* (Part I, Canto 1, 505–6; Part III, Canto 3, 19–20) and his satire *Upon the Weakness and Misery of Man* (71–2 and 229–31). The second motto of the novel, the Jonson quotation on page 38, was provided by Shelley in a letter to Peacock of 25 July 1818.

CHAPTER I

1 (p. 39) *Rabelais:* 'I have elected to chirrup, and cackle as a Goose among Swans, as the Proverb hath it, rather than be esteemed dumb among so many gentle Poets and eloquent Orators.' (W. F. Smith's translation.)

2 (p. 39) *blue devils:* depression of spirits.

3 (p. 40) *'he woke and found his lady dead':* Sir Leoline, in Coleridge's 'Christabel', 'rose and found his lady dead'.

4 (p. 40) *Scythrop:* from σκυθρωπος – 'of sad or gloomy countenance'. A character based on Shelley.

5 (p. 41) *tandem and random:* Peacock's own variant of 'random-tandem', i.e. with three horses harnessed in tandem.

6 (p. 41) *to drink deep ere he departed: Hamlet*, Act I, Sc. ii.

7 (p. 41) *Miss Emily Girouette:* Scythrop's attachment to Emily is usually taken to be modelled on Shelley's to his cousin, Harriet Grove. In giving her the name Girouette ('Weathercock') Peacock was perhaps glancing at the apparent ease with which Harriet transferred her affections elsewhere.

8 (p. 41) *locked up in his seraglio:* cf. Shelley, notes to *Queen Mab*, Canto VIII: 'Solomon kept a thousand concubines, and owned in despair that all was vanity'.

9 (p. 44) *Mr Flosky:* A corruption of Filosky, quasi Φιλοσκιος, a lover, or sectator, of shadows. (P.) A character based on Coleridge.

10 (p. 44) *a raw-head and bloody-bones:* a bugbear to terrify children, a bogey.

11 (p. 44) *nothing is but what is not: Macbeth*, Act I, Sc. iii.

12 (p. 44) *as many as called 'God save King Richard':* a mere handful. See *Richard III*, Act III, Sc. vii.

13 (p. 45) *the drum ecclesiastic:* the pulpit, or perhaps the cushion on the pulpit. See Butler, *Hudibras*, Pt I, Canto 1, 11.

14 (p. 45) *Mr Toobad, the Manichæan Millenarian:* a Manichæan in his belief that the world is ruled by good and evil powers, but a Millenarian in so far as he believes that the evil power now in the ascendant will eventually be succeeded by the good, though 'not in our time'. A character based on J. F. Newton, a member of the Shelley circle.

15 (p. 45) *all-fours:* a card game for two players.

CHAPTER II

1 (p. 46) '. . . *in cogibundity of cogitation':* from the opening scene of Henry Carey's burlesque *Tragedy of Chrononhotonthologos* (1734).

2 (p. 47) *the passion for reforming the world:* See Forsyth's *Principles of Moral Science*. (P.)

3 (p. 47) *illuminati:* a term used originally for members of certain heretical sects, later applied to members of Adam ('Spartacus') Weishaupt's secret society, the *Illumenaten*. See note 7 to Chapter X.

4 (p. 47) *Horrid Mysteries:* a translation by P. Will, published 1796, of 'Marquis' C. F. A. Grosse's novel, *Der Genius*.

5 (p. 47) *eleutherarchs:* rulers of secret societies. *O.E.D.* quotes T. J. Hogg's novel, *Alexy Haimatoff* (1813): 'The Eleutherarch . . . asked if they had any objection to my being initiated in the mysteries of the Eleutheri'.

6 (p. 47) *Action . . . is the result of opinion:* the theme of Chapter V of William Godwin's *Political Justice*, entitled 'The Voluntary Actions of Men originate in their Opinions'.

7 (p. 48) *published a treatise:* probably an allusion to Shelley's *Proposals for an Association of those Philanthropists who convinced of the inadequacy of the moral & political state of Ireland to produce benefits which are nevertheless attainable*

are willing to unite to accomplish its regeneration. The pamphlet ended with an invitation to favourably disposed readers
to communicate with the author at an address in Dublin,
where it was published in 1812.

CHAPTER III

1 (p. 49) *graves, worms, and epitaphs: Richard II*, Act III,
Sc. ii.

2 (p. 49) *the Honourable Mr Listless:* a character based on Sir
Lumley Skeffington, a friend of Shelley's.

3 (p. 49) *'stretched on the rack of a too easy chair':* Pope, *The
Dunciad*, Bk IV, 342.

4 (p. 50) *Miss Marionetta Celestina O'Carroll:* a character
partly based on Harriet Shelley.

5 (p. 50) *anticipated cognitions:* a phrase from Sir William
Drummond's unsympathetic account in his *Academical
Questions* (1805), Bk II, Chapter 9, of the Kantian transcendentalists. He refers to the 'anticipated cognitions' and
'visions of pure reason' of philosophers who 'teach the
science of metaphysics upon infallible principles which they
have obtained from intuition'.

6 (p. 52) *'. . . like a man of this world': Henry IV, Pt II*,
Act V, Sc. iii.

7 (p. 52) *Rosalia . . . Carlos:* characters in *Horrid Mysteries*
(see note 4 to Chapter II above).

8 (p. 53) *vanity, and vexation of spirit: Ecclesiastes*, I, 14.

CHAPTER IV

1 (p. 55) *decorum, and dignity, &c. &c. &c.:* We are not
masters of the whole vocabulary. See any novel by any
literary lady. (P.)

2 (p. 56) *his Ahrimanic philosophy:* Ahrimanes, in the Persian
mythology, is the evil power, the prince of the kingdom of
darkness. He is the rival of Oromazes, the prince of the
kingdom of light. These two powers have divided and equal
dominion. Sometimes one of the two has a temporary
supremacy. – According to Mr Toobad, the present period
would be the reign of Ahrimanes. Lord Byron seems to be
of the same opinion, by the use he has made of Ahrimanes

NOTES

in 'Manfred'; where the great Alastor, or Κακος Δαιμων, of
Persia, is hailed king of the world by the Nemesis of Greece,
in concert with three of the Scandinavian Valkyrae, under
the name of the Destinies; the astrological spirits of the
alchemists of the middle ages; an elemental witch, trans-
planted from Denmark to the Alps; and a chorus of Dr
Faustus's devils, who come in the last act for a soul. It is
difficult to conceive where this heterogeneous mythological
company could have originally met, except at a *table d'hôte*,
like the six kings in 'Candide'. (P.) See Peacock's un-
finished poem, *Ahrimanes*, and note 14 to Chapter I above.

3 (p. 56) *antithalian*: opposed to festivity.

CHAPTER V

1 (p. 57) '*Zitti, zitti* . . .': 'Hush, hush! Softly, softly! Let's
make no disturbance.' Rossini, *The Barber of Seville*, Act II.

2 (p. 58) *Nina pazza per amore*: an opera by Paisiello (1741–
1816).

3 (p. 60) *pensions*: 'PENSION. Pay given to a slave of state
for treason to his country.' – JOHNSON's *Dictionary*. (P.)
'Slave of state' is a misquotation for 'state hireling'.

4 (p. 60) '*Devilman, a novel*': William Godwin's *Mandeville*
(1817).

5 (p. 60) *morbid anatomy*: the anatomy of diseased organs or
structures.

6 (p. 60) *Paul Jones*: Scottish-born American privateer
(1747–92) who raided the British coast during the American
War of Independence, regarded as a pirate in Britain.

7 (p. 60) *the Red Book*: popular name for the *Royal Kalen-
dar*. In a more general sense, any book listing the names
of state officials and pensioners.

8 (p. 60) *Roderick Sackbut*: Robert Southey. 'Roderick'
alludes to his poem *Roderick, the last of the Goths* and 'Sackbut' to his annual emolument, as Poet Laureate, of a butt
of sack. As Laureate, his name was listed among the members of the royal household in the Red Book.

9 (p. 62) *written or suggested by myself*: an allusion to
Coleridge's collaboration with Wordsworth and Southey in
Lyrical Ballads and *Omniana*, respectively.

NOTES

CHAPTER VI

1 (p. 64) *the finale of Don Giovanni:* where the Don is carried off to hell by demons.

2 (p. 64) *he is growing fashionable:* H. F. Cary completed what was to become a popular translation of *The Divine Comedy* in 1814.

3 (p. 66) *late dinners:* during Peacock's lifetime the fashionable hour for dinner gradually moved from early afternoon to mid evening.

4 (p. 67) *Emanuel Kant Flosky:* cf. Coleridge, *Biographia Literaria,* Chapter X: 'So profound was my admiration at this time of Hartley's ESSAY ON MAN, that I gave his name to my first-born.'

5 (p. 68) *the reading public:* a phrase often used by Coleridge and thought to have been coined by him.

6 (p. 68) *base, common, and popular: Henry V,* Act IV, Sc. i.

7 (p. 68) *purple shred:* purple patch. The phrase is from Horace's *purpureus pannus* (*Ars Poetica,* 15–16).

8 (p. 70) *may:* maiden.

CHAPTER VII

1 (p. 71) *Asterias:* a genus including the common starfish.

2 (p. 71) *the Sepia Octopus . . . the colossal polypus:* Peacock appears to have taken his details about these creatures from Denys Montfort, *Histoire Naturelle . . . des Mollusques* (Paris, 1801) to which he refers in note 10 below.

3 (p. 72) *'sleeking her soft alluring locks':* Milton, *Comus,* 882.

4 (p. 74) *a mermaid . . . in a Dutch lake:* the mermaid of Edam, who was found stranded on mud after the dikes had broken during a storm. See G. Benwell and A. Waugh, *Sea Enchantress* (1961) for a recent version of this tale.

5 (p. 74) *the illustrious Don Feijoo:* Benito Jerónimo Feijóo y Montenegro (1676–1764), a Benedictine whose scepticism earned him the title of 'the Spanish Voltaire'. His examination of the story of Francis de la Vega ('El Anfibio de Liérganes') is in his *Teatro Critico.*

6 (p. 74) *the tutelar saint of Cadiz:* SS. Servando and Germán.

7 (p. 75) *Pliny mentions: Historia Naturalis,* Bk IX, iv (Loeb edn, 1938).

8 (p. 76) *de révérendissime père Jean:* Père Jean de Domfront, a character in *Le Compère Matthieu,* by Du Laurens. See Peacock's essay, 'French Comic Romances', for an interesting appraisal of the novel.

9 (p. 76) *Signor Pococurante:* a character in Voltaire's *Candide.*

10 (p. 78) *... of a beautiful day:* See Denys Montfort: *Histoire Naturelle des Mollusques; Vues Générales,* pp. 37, 38. (P.) The second half of this speech by Mr Asterias and the opening sentence of his previous speech are a paraphrase from Montfort, pp. 37-9.

11 (p. 78) *... and those i' the wrong:* Butler, *Hudibras,* Pt I, Canto 2, 703-4.

12 (p. 78) *'... that maketh well or ill':* Faerie Queene, Bk VI, Canto IX, 30.

13 (p. 80) *'And there is salmon in both':* Henry V, Act IV, Sc. vii.

CHAPTER VIII

1 (p. 81) *to make it burn blue:* for a flame to burn blue was at one time taken to indicate the presence of a ghost. See e.g. *Richard III*, Act V, Sc. iii.

2 (p. 81) *'his eye in a fine frenzy rolling':* A Midsummer Night's Dream, Act V, Sc. i.

3 (p. 82) *antiperistatical:* heightened by contrast.

4 (p. 82) *hyperoxysophistical paradoxology:* paradoxes advanced with the extremest sophistry. Coleridge himself said 'there was nothing which he bore with less patience' than hearing his opinions described as paradoxical (*The Friend,* 1837, Vol. III, p. 336).

5 (p. 83) *seven hundred pages of promise:* see e.g. Chapter XIII of Coleridge's *Biographia Literaria* for one such promise.

6 (p. 83) *'such stuff as dreams are made of':* The Tempest, Act IV, Sc. i.

7 (p. 83) *a vision of pure reason:* see note 5 to Chapter III above.

8 (p. 83) *I composed ... in my sleep:* an allusion to Coleridge's account, in his preface to 'Kubla Khan', of how the poem was composed.

9 (p. 83) *because it has no bottom: A Midsummer Night's Dream*, Act IV, Sc. i.

10 (p. 85) *without ever having looked into Euclid:* a quip borrowed from Drummond, *Academical Questions*, p. 358. (See note 5 to Chapter III above.) He refers to the Kantians 'who know metaphysics *à priori* ... and who carried the whole science of geometry in their heads, before they ever looked into Euclid'.

CHAPTER X

1 (p. 90) *his interior cognition:* see note 5 to Chapter III above.

2 (p. 91) '*I guess 'twas frightful ...*': Coleridge, 'Christabel', Part I.

3 (p. 91) *Mr Burke's graduated scale of the sublime:* There must be some mistake in this, for the whole honourable band of gentlemen-pensioners has resolved unanimously, that Mr Burke was a very sublime person, particularly after he had prostituted his own soul, and betrayed his country and mankind, for 1200*l.* a year: yet he does not appear to have been a very terrible personage, and certainly went off with a very small portion of human respect, though he contrived to excite, in a great degree, the astonishment of all honest men. Our immaculate laureate (who gives us to understand that, if he had not been purified by holy matrimony into a mystical type, he would have died a virgin,) is another sublime gentleman of the same genus: he very much astonished some persons when he sold his birthright for a pot of sack; but not even his *Sosia* has a grain of respect for him, though, doubtless, he thinks his name very terrible to the enemy, when he flourishes his criticopoeticopolitical tomahawk, and sets up his Indian yell for the blood of his old friends: but, at best, he is a mere political scarecrow, a man of straw, ridiculous to all who know of what materials he is made; and to none more so, than to those who have stuffed him, and set him up, as the Priapus of the garden of the golden apples of corruption. (P.) For Burke's 'graduated scale of the sublime', see his *Philosophical Inquiry into the Origin of our Ideas of the Sublime and Beautiful* (1757).
Our immaculate laureate: Southey.
Sosia: a name given to a person who closely resembles

another, after a character in Plautus' *Amphitryon*. By 'his
Sosia', Peacock probably intends Coleridge, whom he
usually pillories with Southey, though Wordsworth is also
a possibility, especially as he and Southey were active together in the Tory interest in the Westmorland election of
1818, just before *Nightmare Abbey* was finished.

4 (p. 93) *Stella:* a character based on Mary Godwin, Shelley's
second wife. Goethe's Stella, in his play of the same name,
is the heroine in a three-cornered situation similar to that of
Scythrop, Marionetta, and 'Stella'.

5 (p. 93) *They alone are subject . . . :* Mary Wollstonecraft,
A Vindication of the Rights of Woman, Chapter V, Section 4.

6 (p. 93) *green bag:* a bag used for carrying a lawyer's docu-
ments. The implication of Scythrop's remark is that Stella
is concealing her real name because she is being sought on
a charge under Lord Castlereagh's Alien Act of 1816, which
gave the Government new powers over aliens and especially
over political refugees.

7 (p. 93) *an illuminée:* one of the Illuminati. See note 3 to
Chapter II above.

8 (p. 93) *Lord S.:* Lord Sidmouth, Home Secretary in 1816
when 'a drunken cobbler and doctor' (Thomas Preston
and Dr James Watson, Snr) were arrested, with others, for
their part in a riot in the City on 2 December. One of the
charges against Watson at his trial for high treason was that
of planning to attack the Bank and the Tower. The supply
of ammunition for this wild scheme was carried in the old
stocking to which Peacock refers.

9 (p. 94) *Spartacus Weishaupt:* see note 3 to Chapter II
above.

CHAPTER XI

1 (p. 96) *Mr Cypress:* Byron. The name suggests funereal
gloom.

2 (p. 97) 'HIC NON BIBITUR': 'Here there is no drinking.' Rabelais, Bk I, Chapter I.

3 (p. 98) *stupid and shrivelled slaves:* cf. Shelley's letter to
Peacock, 20 April 1818, from Milan: 'The men are hardly
men, they look like a tribe of stupid and shrivelled slaves.'

4 (p. 99) *forsakes his country:* cf. Shelley's letter quoted immediately above: 'The number of English who pass through

this town is very great. They ought to be in their own country at the present crisis. Their conduct is wholly inexcusable.' Shelley presumably excluded himself from his own strictures on the grounds of ill health.

5 (p. 99) *I have quarrelled with my wife:* Byron's quarrel with his wife was notorious. The two poems that he wrote on the subject were published without his consent.

6 (p. 99) *so is our dear friend:* an allusion to Byron's being a member of the House of Lords.

7 (p. 100) *... vanishes in the smoke of death: Childe Harold,* canto 4. cxxiv. cxxvi. (P.) This speech by Mr Cypress is largely made up of phrases from the two stanzas.

8 (p. 100) '*... not a thing to rejoice at*': *Henry V,* Act III, Sc. vi.

9 (p. 101) *representatives:* individuals representing the various classes, especially the governing class.

10 (p. 101) *... at his friend's request: Henry IV, Pt II,* Act V, Sc. i.

11 (p. 101) καλος κἀγαθος: 'beautiful and good'.

12 (p. 101) *... and reaps the whirlwind: Childe Harold,* canto 4. cxxiii. (P.)

13 (p. 101) *... or to endure: Ibid.* canto 3. lxxi. (P.)

14 (p. 102) *... whose gums are poison: Ibid.* canto 4. cxxi. cxxxvi. (P.) See also cxx.

15 (p. 102) *a Rosicrucian:* a member of a society or order, said to have been founded by Christian Rosenkreuz in 1484, which claimed to have secret and magic knowledge. A tenet of Rosicrucian belief which became generally known was that sylphs might have human lovers. See Pope, *The Rape of the Lock, passim.*

16 (p. 102) *... exist only in himself: Childe Harold,* canto 4. cxxii. (P.)

17 (p. 104) *The Norfolk Tragedy:* the ballad on the story of the Babes in the Wood.

18 (p. 104) *Cain's unresting doom: Childe Harold,* Canto I, lxxxiii.

19 (p. 104) *the lamp in Tullia's tomb:* a sepulchral lamp was said to have been found still burning when the supposed tomb of Cicero's daughter Tullia was opened in the sixteenth century.

20 (p. 105) *Harry Gill, with the voice of three:* Wordsworth, 'Goody Blake and Harry Gill'.

21 (p. 106) *... and canals:* perhaps an allusion to Byron's living in Venice at the time of writing.

CHAPTER XII

1 (p. 107) *Sunt geminæ somni portæ:* 'There are twin gates of sleep.' Virgil, *Aeneid*, VI, 893.

2 (p. 108) *M. Swebach:* James Swebach-Desfontaines (1769–1823). Best known as a painter of military scenes.

3 (p. 108) *Pausanias relates: Itinerary of Greece*, I, 32, §4.

4 (p. 109) *Tillotson:* John Tillotson (1630–94), Archbishop of Canterbury, reputedly the best preacher of his time. His sermons were often reprinted.

5 (p. 109) *an idea with the force of a sensation:* cf. Peacock, *Memoirs of Shelley:* 'Coleridge has written much and learnedly on this subject of ideas with the force of sensations, of which he found many examples in himself.'

6 (p. 109) *the hollow tongue of midnight ...:* cf. *A Midsummer Night's Dream*, Act V, Sc. i: 'The iron tongue of midnight hath told twelve.'

7 (p. 110) *fancy ourselves pipkins and teapots:* delusions of the splenetic. See Pope, *The Rape of the Lock*, Canto IV, 49–51.

8 (p. 110) *... to believe in their external existence:* cf. Coleridge, *The Friend:* 'A lady once asked me if I believed in ghosts and apparitions. I answered with truth and simplicity: No, madam! I have seen far too many myself.' (Vol. I, p. 195, 3rd edn.)

9 (p. 110) *venerable old men ... beautiful young women:* allusions to 'The Ancient Mariner' and 'Christabel'.

10 (p. 110) *'palpable to feeling as to sight':* Macbeth, Act II, Sc. i ('palpable' is a misquotation for 'sensible').

11 (p. 110) *particularly my friend Mr Sackbut:* see *Biographia Literaria*, Chapter III, for Coleridge's eulogy of Southey's 'strict purity of disposition and conduct'.

CHAPTER XIII

1 (p. 112) *'spied a voice':* cf. Bottom as Pyramus:

> I see a voice: now will I to the chink,
> To spy an I can hear my Thisby's face.
> Act V, Sc. i.

2 (p. 114) ... *is a cartilaginous funnel:* this sentence and Scythrop's subsequent remarks on the structure of the ear are from Drummond, *Academical Questions*, pp. 112–13.

3 (p. 118) *sedet, æternumque sedebit:* Sits, and will sit for ever. (P.) Virgil, *Aeneid*, VI, 617.

CHAPTER XIV

1 (p. 119) *a pint of port and a pistol:* See *The Sorrows of Werter*, Letter 93. (P.) Goethe's hero, having decided on suicide, sends his servant to borrow pistols and then orders him to bring in a bottle of wine.

2 (p. 121) *a German tragedy:* perhaps another allusion to Goethe's *Stella*, where the hero, just before the tragic ending, believes he may be able to have both his loves.

CHAPTER XV

1 (p. 123) *Celinda Flosky:* In his edition of *Nightmare Abbey* (1891), Richard Garnett remarked that it was to be hoped that Celinda knew of the existence of the Emanuel Kant Flosky mentioned in Chapter VI.

*

CROTCHET CASTLE

Peacock's own notes are marked (P.)

The couplet quoted on the 1831 title-page (which may be translated 'The world is full of fools and whoever wishes not to see any of them must live alone and break his mirror') has been attributed to the Marquis de Sade but derives from the fourth satire in le Petit's *Discours Satiriques* (1686). The lines by Butler on the verso of the title-page are from his *Miscellaneous Thoughts*.

CHAPTER I

1 (p. 127) *Captain Jamy: Henry V*, Act III, Sc. ii.

2 (p. 127) *Duke's Place:* in Aldgate. The implication is that his bride was Jewish.

3 (p. 128) *the alley:* 'Change Alley, in the City.

4 (p. 128) *the soldier of Lucullus:* Luculli miles, &c. HOR. *Ep.* II. 2. 26. 'In Anna's wars, a soldier poor and bold,' &c. – POPE'S *Imitation.* (P.)

5 (p. 128) *Mr Ramsbottom, the zodiacal mythologist:* J. F. Newton, the friend of Shelley on whom Mr Toobad of *Nightmare Abbey* was based. In his *Memoirs of Shelley* Peacock gives an amusing instance of Newton's obsession with the zodiac and an outline of his mythological system.

6 (p. 129) *nature . . . will yet always come back:* Naturam expellas furcâ, tamen usque recurret. – HOR. *Ep.* I. 10. 24. (P.)

7 (p. 131) *her melancholy was any thing but green and yellow: Twelfth Night*, Act II, Sc. iv.

8 (p. 131) *Llymry: Anglicé* flummery. (P.)

9 (p. 132) *Lemma:* (Gr.) gain, profit.

10 (p. 132) *a groat . . . for such exploits:* 'Let him take castles who has ne'er a groat.' – POPE, *ubi suprà.* (P.)

11 (p. 132) *the tower . . . which looked towards Damascus: The Song of Solomon*, VII, 4.

12 (p. 133) *Gilbert Folliott:* usually Foliot. Bishop of London from 1163; died 1187.

13 (p. 133) *the smaller wit of the two:* The devil began: (he had caught the bishop musing on politics)

> Oh Gilberte Folliott!
> Dum revolvis tot et tot,
> Deus tuus est Astarot.

> Oh Gilbert Folliott!
> While thus you muse and plot,
> Your god is Astarot.

The bishop answered:

> Tace, dæmon: qui est deus
> Sabbaot, est ille meus.

> Peace, fiend; the power I own
> Is Sabbaoth's Lord alone.

It must be confessed, the devil was easily posed in the twelfth century. He was a sturdier disputant in the sixteenth.

> Did not the devil appear to Martin
> Luther in Germany for certain?

when 'the heroic student,' as Mr Coleridge calls him, was forced to proceed to '*voies de fait*.' The curious may see at this day, on the wall of Luther's study, the traces of the inkbottle which he threw at the devil's head. (P.)

The couplet, 'Did not the devil . . .', is from Butler, *Hudibras*, Pt II, Canto 3, 103–4.

CHAPTER II

1 (p. 133) *Quoth Ralpho . . .*: Butler, *Hudibras*, Pt I, Canto 3, 1271–2.

2 (p. 133) (*The march of mind*: a catchphrase of the time. An ode by Mary Mitford under that title was recited at the first anniversary celebrations of the British and Foreign Schools Society in 1807.

3 (p. 134) *the Steam Intellect Society*: the Society for the Diffusion of Useful Knowledge, founded in 1827, the prime mover being Henry Brougham ('the learned friend'). The sixpenny booklet on hydrostatics in the Society's 'Library of Useful Knowledge' was written by Brougham.

4 (p. 134) *mould*: a candle made in a mould, as distinct from one made by dipping.

5 (p. 134) *Mr Mac Quedy*: Quasi Mac Q.E.D., son of a demonstration. (P.) See Introduction for identification of Mac Quedy with J. R. McCulloch.

6 (p. 134) *Mr Skionar*: ΣΚΙᾶς ΟΝΑΡ. *Umbræ somnium*. (P.) 'A dream of a shade.' See Introduction for identification of Skionar with Coleridge.

7 (p. 134) *Lord Bossnowl*: perhaps from *boss* and *noll* and meaning 'knob-head'.

8 (p. 134) *the foot of Hercules*: to judge of Hercules by his foot is to judge the whole by the part.

9 (p. 134) ἀρχομένου ἔργου, πρόσωπον χρὴ θέμεν τηλαυγές :

> Far-shining be the face
> Of a great work begun.
> PIND. *Ol.* vi. (P.)

10 (p. 135) *matter for a May morning: Twelfth Night*, Act III, Sc. iv.

11 (p. 135) ἀλλ' ἄφελε τὰς ἐγχέλεις: Calonice wishes destruction to all Bœotians. Lysistrata answers, '*Except the eels.*' *Lysistrata*, 36. (P.)

12 (p. 136) *Ude:* Louis Eustache Ude, celebrated chef, author of *The French Cook* (1813).

13 (p. 137) Θύρας δ' ἐπίθεσθε βεβήλοις: 'Shut the doors against the profane.' *Orphica, passim.* (P.)

14 (p. 137) *Horresco referens:* 'I shudder to tell the tale.' Virgil, *Aeneid*, II, 204.

15 (p. 137) *Di meliora piis:* 'May the gods grant to the good a better fate.' Virgil, *Georgics*, III, 513.

16 (p. 137) *the modern Athenians:* the intelligentsia of Edinburgh. James Stuart (1713–88), joint author of *The Antiquities of Athens*, is said to have been the first to remark on the similarities between Athens and Edinburgh.

17 (p. 140) Ἔστιν ὕδωρ ψυχῇ θάνατος: Literally, which is sufficient for the present purpose, 'Water is death to the soul.' *Orphica: Fr.* XIX. (P.)

18 (p. 140) Οἴνῳ κυματόεντι μέλας κελάρυζεν Ὑδάσπης: Hydaspes gurgled, dark with billowy wine. *Dionysiaca*, XXV. 280. (P.)

19 (p. 141) *Alter erit . . . :*

> Another Tiphys on the waves shall float,
> And chosen heroes freight his glorious boat.
> VIRG. *Ecl.* IV. (P.)

CHAPTER III

1 (p. 142) *The Squyr of Low Degre:* a metrical romance dating, in this version, from the mid fifteenth century.

2 (p. 142) *And as for me . . . :* Chaucer, *The Legend of Good Women*, Prologue, 29–39.

3 (p. 144) *the fishpools of Heshbon: The Song of Solomon*, VII, 4.

4 (p. 147) '*. . . saturated with civilisation*': *Edinburgh Review*, somewhere. (P.)

CHAPTER IV

1 (p. 152) *Rabelais:* 'Pray, how came you to know that men were formerly fools? How did you find that they are now

wise?' Bk V, Author's Prologue (Urquhart and Motteux translation).

2 (p. 155) *Cedite Graii:* 'Give place, Greeks.' Propertius, *Elegies*, II, xxxiv, 65.

3 (p. 156) *schools for all:* the title of a pamphlet written by James Mill in 1812 which was taken up as a slogan.

4 (p. 157) *a passage in Athenœus: Deipnosophistœ*, IX, 385e. The Greek phrase means 'relish on fish'.

5 (p. 157) *Nadir Shah:* 'the Conqueror' (1688–1747). After freeing Persia from Afghan rule and usurping the throne, he conquered Afghanistan and ravaged north-west India.

6 (p. 158) *a thing which they call a review:* the *Edinburgh Review.*

7 (p. 159) *Titan had made him of better clay:* ᴊᴜᴠ. xiv.35. (P.)

8 (p. 159) Τὸ δὲ φυᾷ κράτιστον ἅπαν: *Ol.* ix. 152. (P.)

CHAPTER V

1 (p. 160) *Rabelais:* 'I held it not a little disgraceful to be only an idle spectator of so many valorous, eloquent, and warlike persons.' Bk III, Author's Prologue (Urquhart and Motteux translation).

2 (p. 163) *Wontsee ... Shantsee:* Wordsworth and Southey. Both were republicans in youth but it was with Coleridge that Southey planned a utopian community in America.

3 (p. 164) *Mr Toogood:* a character based on Robert Owen. He first put forward in 1817 the plan for self-sufficient communities living round large quadrangles which is referred to here. For a further reference to 'Mr Owen's parallelograms' or 'quadrangular paradises', as they were called at the time, see note 3 to Chapter VI below.

4 (p. 166) *Mr Trillo:* a character based on Tom Moore.

5 (p. 166) *Mr Philpot:* ΦΙΛοΠΟΤαμος. *Fluviorum amans.* (P.) 'The lover of rivers.' The identification of the source of the Nile and the mouth of the Niger ('the heads and tails of rivers') were current geographical problems. The latter was solved by the Lander brothers while *Crotchet Castle* was in the press.

6 (p. 167) *Mr Quassia, the brewer:* quassia was sometimes used in brewing as a substitute for hops.

CHAPTER VI

1 (p. 170) *Butler: Hudibras*, Pt III, Canto 2, 201–2.
2 (p. 170) *to save a percentage:* cf. Sir Edward Strachey's anecdote in his 'Recollections of Thomas Love Peacock', included in *Calidore and Miscellanea,* ed. R. Garnett (1891):
'One day [Peacock] came to my father's room and said, with
mock indignation, " I will never dine with Mill again, for he
asks me to meet only political economists. I dined with him
last night, when he had Mushet and MacCulloch, and after
dinner Mushet took a paper out of his pocket and began to
read: 'In the infancy of society, when Government was invented to save a percentage – say, of 3½ per cent.' – on
which he was stopped by MacCulloch with, 'I will say no
such thing,' meaning that this was not the proper percentage."'
3 (p. 171) *a diagram:* Robert Owen's plan for a 'quadrangular
village'. See note 3 to Chapter V above.
4 (p. 172) *Political economy . . . is to the family:* W. F. Kennedy
(*Nineteenth Century Fiction,* September 1966) noticed that
this was the opening sentence of James Mill's *Elements of
Political Economy* (1821).
5 (p. 173) *The family consumes, and . . . must have supply:* cf.
James Mill, *ibid.,* p. 1: 'The family consumes; and in order
to consume, it must be supplied by production.'
6 (p. 174) *fruges consumere nati:* those born to consume the
fruits of the earth. Horace, *Epistles,* I, ii, 27.
7 (p. 174) ὅστις γε πίνειν οἶδε καὶ βίνειν μόνον: *The Frogs,* 740.
'He's all for wine and women.'
8 (p. 177) *la Dive Bouteille:* the oracular Holy Bottle con-
sulted by Panurge. Rabelais, Bk V, Chapter XLIV.
9 (p. 177) *Fiat experimentum . . . :* Let the experiment be
tried on a worthless life.
10 (p. 178) *Bambo:* on the Niger.
11 (p. 180) *sing with Robin Hood:* an allusion to the ballad
'Robin Hood and the Four Beggars', which ends with Robin
and Little John rejoicing over the large sum taken from the
four beggars, who are in fact impostors:

> Then Robin Hood took Little John by the hand,
> And danced about the oak tree;
> 'If we drink water while this doth last,
> Then an ill death may we die.'

CHAPTER VII

1 (p. 181) *Butler: Hudibras*, Pt II, Canto 2, 665–6.

2 (p. 182) *Matilde di Shabran:* an opera by Rossini, first performed 1821.

3 (p. 183) *Il Bragatore:* Daniele da Volterra (1509–66), employed by Pius IV to paint draperies on nude figures in Michelangelo's 'Last Judgment' and earning thereby the nickname 'Il Braghettone', 'the breeches maker'.

4 (p. 183) '. . . *with fat capon lined':* As You Like It, Act II, Sc. vii.

5 (p. 189) *an Italian countess:* Napoleon's sister Pauline, the model for Canova's 'Venus Victrix' and 'Galatea'.

CHAPTER VIII

1 (p. 191) *Forteguerri:* or Fortiguerra, Niccolò. The lines are from *Il Ricciardetto* (1738), Canto XIV, i. 'Whoever in this world is content for a while and whose peace is neither taken away from him nor spoilt can say that Jove is watching over him directly.'

2 (p. 192) *a passage of Sophocles:* Peacock perhaps had in mind the opening of the first choral ode in *Oedipus at Colonus*, with its reference to leafy valleys thronged with nightingales.

3 (p. 193) *as Thestylis did strong-smelling herbs:*

> Thestylis . . .
> . . . herbas contundit olentes.
> VIRG. *Ecl.* ii. 10, 11. (P.)

4 (p. 193) *a subject for science:* an allusion to the contemporary case of Burke and Hare, who committed several murders to provide an Edinburgh surgeon with subjects for dissection.

5 (p. 193) *a schoolmaster abroad:* an allusion to Henry Brougham's celebrated phrase 'The schoolmaster is abroad', said to have been first used in a speech of his to the London Mechanics' Institute in 1825.

6 (p. 194) *ferocis ingenii puer* . . . : 'A boy of fierce disposition, more inclined to arms than to letters.' – HERMANN'S *Dedication of Homer's Hymns to his Preceptor Ilgen.* (P.)

7 (p. 194) *Frère Jean des Entommeures:* See Rabelais, Bk I,

Chapter XXVII. Frère Jean routed single-handed an army that was pillaging his monastery's vineyard.

8 (p. 194) *the Charity Commissioners:* Brougham, the leader of the movement for investigating abuses of charities, introduced legislation setting up a Charity Commission in 1818. It was superseded by a further Act in 1819.

CHAPTER IX

1 (p. 198) *Homer: Iliad,* I, 312.

2 (p. 199) *Quorsum pertinuit...:* Wherefore is Plato on Menander piled? HOR. *Sat.* ii. 3. 11. (P.)

3 (p. 199) *the immortal nose:* Roger Bacon was reputed to have made a brazen head which, except for the nose, collapsed in fragments after pronouncing the words 'Time's past'. There are conflicting accounts of how Brasenose, 'its cognominal college', got its name.

4 (p. 199) *Callimachus: Hymn to Apollo,* 112. 'The trickling stream that springs from a holy fountain.'

5 (p. 200) *totus teres atque rotundus:* All smooth and round. (P.) Horace, *Satires,* II, vii, 86.

6 (p. 200) *Rosamond:* daughter of Walter Lord Clifford and mistress of Henry II, died 1177 and buried in Godstow nunnery. See Peacock's note to *The Genius of the Thames,* Part II, 203–60, for the legends that gathered about her name and for the hazel, 'the fruit of which is always apparently perfect, but is invariably found to be hollow'.

7 (p. 200) *he of the North:* Sir Walter Scott.

8 (p. 200) *the great enchanter of Covent Garden:* Charles Farley, the producer to whom Covent Garden pantomimes owed much of their success in the years 1806–34.

9 (p. 201) *nuspiam...:* nowhere, by no means, never, no how.

10 (p. 202) *without catching a gudgeon:* Eloquentiæ magister, nisi, tamquam piscator, eam imposuerit hamis escam, quam scierit appetituros esse pisciculos, sine spe prædæ moratur in scopulo. PETRONIUS ARBITER. (P.) *Satyricon,* Cap. III. 'The teacher of eloquence, unless he baits his hooks like a fisherman with what he knows the fish will bite at, waits on the rock without hope of catching anything.'

11 (p. 204) κατ' ἐξοχὴν: *par excellence.*

NOTES

CHAPTER X

1 (p. 205) *Rabelais:* 'Pursuing our voyage, we sailed three days, without discovering any thing.' Bk V, Chapter I (Urquhart and Motteux translation).
2 (p. 209) *Ingenuas didicisse, &c.:*

> Ingenuas didicisse fideliter artes
> Emollit mores, nec sinit esse feros.
> OVID, *Epistulae ex Ponto*, II, ix, 47–8.

'Faithful study of the liberal arts humanizes the character and does not permit it to be cruel.'
3 (p. 210) '... *never did run smooth*': *A Midsummer Night's Dream*, Act I, Sc. i.
4 (p. 210) '... *only to be kind*': *Hamlet*, Act III, Sc. iv.

CHAPTER XI

1 (p. 211) *Ancient Pistol: Henry V*, Act II, Sc. i.
2 (p. 211) *Apodidraskiana:* formed from a Greek verb meaning 'to run away'.
3 (p. 213) *Touchandgo:* Timothy Touchandgo and Roderick Robthetill were modelled on Rowland Stephenson, a Lombard Street banker, and his clerk James Lloyd who absconded from London in December 1828 and sailed for Savannah.
4 (p. 214) *free to hold slaves:* In the early years of the nineteenth century the political balance between North and South was maintained by admitting alternately slave and free states to the Union.
5 (p. 214) *regulators:* volunteer committees formed to preserve order and prevent crime.
6 (p. 216) '*Beyond the sea*': a poem in the style of the 'pennillion' which was given the Welsh title 'Tros y Mor' in an early draft.

CHAPTER XII

1 (p. 217) '*Will love be controlled by advice?*': *The Beggar's Opera*, Act I, Sc. viii.

CHAPTER XIII

1 (p. 219) *Or vieni, Amore . . .:* 'Come now, Love, and settle here with me.' Boiardo, *Orlando Innamorato*.

2 (p. 220) *tutto il giorno . . .:* 'All day long, intent on noble deeds, they scaled heights and crossed torrents.'

CHAPTER XIV

1 (p. 222) *Wordsworth:* 'Three years she grew in sun and shower'.

2 (p. 223) *'And with the food of pride . . .':* Wordsworth, 'Lines left upon a seat in a yew-tree'.

3 (p. 224) *a chasm:* 'The "dingle", in *Crotchet Castle*, is a real scene, on the river Velenrhyd, in Merionethshire. There is no chasm on that river which it is possible to leap over; but there is more than one on the river Cynfael, which flows into the same valley. I took the poetical licence of approximating the scenes. That on the Velenrhyd is called Llyn-y-Gygfraen, the Ravens' Pool.' Peacock, in a letter to Thomas L'Estrange, 11 July 1861.

4 (p. 226) *like clusters of wandering grapes:* 'Αλήμονα βότρυν ἐθείρας. — NONNUS. (P.)

5 (p. 227) *'the forehead of the morning sky':* Milton, *Lycidas*, 171.

CHAPTER XV

1 (p. 227) *Da ydyw'r gwaith . . .:* ll. 1–4 of 'pennill' XXXIX, from *The Cambro-Briton*, Vol. I (February 1820). D. Garnett noted that Peacock's translation differed from that given in *The Cambro-Briton* and was presumably his own.

2 (p. 230) *Un dì carco il mulinaro:* In this ballad, the terrors of the Black Forest are narrated to an assemblage of domestics and peasants, who, at the end of every stanza, dance in a circle round the narrator. The second stanza is as follows:

> Una notte in un stradotto
> Un incauto s'inoltrò;
> E uno strillo udì di botto
> Che l'orecchio gl'intronò:
> Era l'ombra di sua nonna,
> Che pel naso lo pigliò.

Ouf! di giorno nè di sera,
Non passiam la selva nera.
(*Ballano in Giro*.) (P.)

'One night a reckless man went far down a lane and suddenly heard a shriek that stunned his ear. It was his grandmother's ghost, which seized him by the nose. Ouf! let's not
pass through the Black Forest either by day or night. (They
dance in a ring.)'

CHAPTER XVI

1 (p. 232) *to pluck out the heart of her mystery: Hamlet*, Act III,
Sc. ii.

2 (p. 233) *And did mischief enough to be called a great man:* cf.
Fielding, *Jonathan Wild*, Bk I, Chapter I: 'Greatness consists in bringing all manner of mischief on mankind.'

3 (p. 237) *Cornelius Agrippa:* diplomat, doctor, occult philosopher, and reputed magician. Born Cologne 1486, died
Grenoble 1535.

4 (p. 240) *exécuteur des hautes œuvres:* executioner. The
'romantic story' was probably 'The Headsman' (*Black-
wood's*, February 1830, Pt I). It was set in France and
turned upon a legal requirement that an executioner's son-
in-law had to take up the office if there were no sons to
succeed to it.

CHAPTER XVII

1 (p. 241) *A cup of wine . . .: Henry IV, Pt II*, Act V, Sc. iii.

2 (p. 242) *marched into my rick-yard:* Late in 1830, while the
novel was being written, there was widespread agitation for
an increase in agricultural wages marked by riots, rick
burning, and the destruction of threshing machines.

3 (p. 246) παρθένος οὐρεσίφοιτος, ἐρήμαδι σύντροφος ὕλη:

A mountain-wandering maid,
Twin-nourished with the solitary wood.
(P.)

CHAPTER XVIII

1 (p. 247) *Rabelais:* 'You men of the other world say that
ignorance is the mother of all evil, and so far you are right;

yet for all that, you do not take the least care to get rid of
it, but still plod on, and live in it, with it, and by it; for
which a plaguey deal of mischief lights on you every day.'
(Urquhart and Motteux translation.)

2 (p. 247) *rayonnante de joie et d'amour:* a favourite phrase of
Pigault le Brun, one of the minor French novelists considered in Peacock's essay, 'French Comic Romances'.

3 (p. 248) *he is now Sir Guy de Vaux:* Henry Brougham became Lord Brougham and Vaux in November 1830, on
taking office as Lord Chancellor.

4 (p. 248) *rooted up . . . from the field of public delusion:* I may
here insert, as somewhat germane to the matter, some lines
which were written by me, in March, 1831, and printed in
the *Examiner* of August 14, 1831. They were then called 'An
Anticipation:' they may now (1837), be fairly entitled 'A
Prophecy fulfilled.'

The Fate of a Broom: An Anticipation

Lo! in Corruption's lumber-room,
The remnants of a wondrous broom;
That walking, talking, oft was seen,
Making stout promise to sweep clean;
But evermore, at every push,
Proved but a stump without a brush.
Upon its handle-top, a sconce,
Like Brahma's, looked four ways at once,
Pouring on king, lords, church, and rabble,
Long floods of favour-currying gabble;
From four-fold mouth-piece always spinning
Projects of plausible beginning,
Whereof said sconce did ne'er intend
That any one should have an end;
Yet still, by shifts and quaint inventions,
Got credit for its good intentions,
Adding no trifle to the store,
Wherewith the devil paves his floor.
Worn out at last, found bare and scrubbish,
And thrown aside with other rubbish,
We'll e'en hand o'er the enchanted stick,
As a choice present for Old Nick,
To sweep, beyond the Stygian lake,
The pavement it has helped to make.

(P.)

5 (p. 248)... τοροτοροτοροτοροτορολιλιλίγξ: sounds without meaning; imitative of the voices of birds. From the Ὄρνιθες of Aristophanes. (P.) A composite quotation from *The Birds*, *passim*.

6 (p. 248) *Nephelococcygia:* 'Cuckoo-city-in-the-clouds.' From the same comedy. (P.) l. 819.

7 (p. 250) *'Captain Swing' :* the pseudonymous signature on threatening letters sent to farmers and landowners during the rural disturbances in the autumn of 1830.

8 (p. 250) Πολλῶν ὀνομάτων μορφὴ μία: 'One shape of many names.' Aeschylus, *Prometheus*. (P.) l. 212.

9 (p. 251) *Discontent increases ...:* This looks so like caricature (a thing abhorrent to our candour), that we must give authority for it. 'We ought to look the evil manfully in the face, and not amuse ourselves with the dreams of fancy. The discontent of the labourers in our times is rather a proof of their superior information than of their deterioration.' *Morning Chronicle: December 20*, 1830. (P.)

10 (p. 251) *green bags:* bags made of green material used formerly by lawyers for papers. See note 6 to Chapter X of *Nightmare Abbey*.

11 (p. 252) *the beginning of a fray: Henry IV, Pt I*, Act IV, Sc. ii.

12 (p. 252) *Pessimo, medius fidius, exemplo:* A most pernicious example, by Hercules! – Petronius Arbiter. (P.) *Satiricon*, 104.

13 (p. 252) *Pro aris et focis:* For hearths and homes.

14 (p. 253) *improved by my diagram: arts for arms:* the sense here is that while Toogood agrees on the need for 'kind feelings between master and man', he believes that a mediaeval community could be improved by his 'diagram', i.e. by the adoption of his plan for a 'quadrangular paradise' (see note 3 to Chapter V) and by the substitution of useful arts for the art of war.

15 (p. 255) *Florence and Blanchflor:* Imitated from the Fabliau, *De Florance et de Blanche Flor, alias Jugement d'Amour*. (P.)

16 (p. 257) *The Priest and the Mulberry Tree:* Imitated from the Fabliau, *Du Provoire qui mengea des Môres*. (P.)

*

Romantic novels in the Penguin English Library

EMILY BRONTË
WUTHERING HEIGHTS

Edited by David Daiches

'Stronger than a man, simpler than a child, her nature stood alone.' So Emily Brontë appeared in the eyes of her sister, Charlotte. Her one novel, *Wuthering Heights*, published a year before her death in 1848 at the age of thirty, similarly stands alone as perhaps the most passionately original work in the English language. This dark, unforgettable story of Catherine Earnshaw and the swarthy Heathcliff 'is moorish, and wild, and knotty as a root of heath', and Emily Brontë records the progress of their love with such truth, imagination, and emotional intensity that a plain tale of the Yorkshire moors acquires the depth and simplicity of ancient tragedy.

THREE GOTHIC NOVELS

WALPOLE/THE CASTLE OF OTRANTO
BECKFORD/VATHEK
MARY SHELLEY/FRANKENSTEIN

With an introduction by Mario Praz

The Gothic novel, that curious literary genre which flourished from about 1765 until 1825, revels in the horrible and the supernatural, in suspense and exotic settings. This volume, with its erudite introduction by Mario Praz, presents three of the most celebrated Gothic novels: *The Castle of Otranto*, published pseudonymously in 1765, is one of the first of the genre and the most truly Gothic of the three; in its blending of two kinds of romanticism, ancient and modern, it is a precursor of Romanticism. *Vathek* (1786), an oriental tale by an eccentric millionaire, exotically combines Gothic romanticism with the vivacity of *The Arabian Nights*, and is a narrative *tour de force*. The story of *Frankenstein* (1818) and the monster he created is as spine-chilling today as it ever was; as in all Gothic novels, horror is the keynote.

THE PENGUIN ENGLISH LIBRARY

'It seems certain that the P.E.L. will continue to offer the best supply of well-edited literary texts for academic and general use in paperback form, and that the series will survive and grow' – John Sutherland, author of *Fiction and the Fiction Industry*

A selection:

ADAM BEDE
GEORGE ELIOT
Edited by Stephen Gill

ROMOLA
GEORGE ELIOT
Edited by Andrew Sanders

THE WOODLANDERS
THOMAS HARDY
Introduction by Ian Gregor and edited by James Gibson

SELECTED POEMS AND PROSE
EDWARD THOMAS
Edited by David Wright

PAMELA
SAMUEL RICHARDSON
Introduction by Margaret A. Doody and edited by Peter Sabor

IVANHOE
SIR WALTER SCOTT
Edited by A. N. Wilson

SELECTIONS FROM THE *TATLER* AND *SPECTATOR*
Edited by Angus Ross